The Transformation

CATHERINE CHIDGEY

The Transformation

PICADOR

First published 2003 by Victoria University Press, Wellington, New Zealand

This edition published 2005 by Picador
an imprint of Pan Macmillan Ltd
Pan Macmillan, 20 New Wharf Road, London N1 9RR
Basingstoke and Oxford
Associated companies throughout the world
www.panmacmillan.com

ISBN 0 330 43322 9

1 3 5 7 9 8 6 4 2

A CIP catalogue record for this book is available from
the British Library.

Printed and bound in Great Britain by
Mackays of Chatham plc, Chatham, Kent

To Kate Camp

The Transformation

I begin by weaving a net. It must be light yet strong, and the tension exactly judged: too tight is as dangerous as too loose. This is a trick which takes many years to master—it consumed my childhood, as well as those years when a man should be selecting a bride—but once it is learned, all society is at one's command, and any price may be asked. My tiny nets, my little foundations of holes, are as fine as gossamer; neither pins nor messy adhesives are required to keep them in place. A simple adjustment of springs is all that is necessary to maintain the tension, but this is a painless procedure, and the devices are quite invisible.

In my trade, the net is known as a caul. Perhaps you associate this word with the piece of skin which is sometimes found clinging to the skulls of newborn children, and which is kept as a charm against drowning? I like to think my hand-woven cauls similarly lucky; I like to consider myself a maker of charms. You will see no sign above my door save my name, for many of my customers value their privacy, but my trade card is more illuminating:

Monsieur Lucien Goulet III
Manufacturer of Ladies' Imperceptible Hair Pieces
& Gentlemen's Invisible Coverings

Some in my profession sneer at these terms, dismissing them as old-fashioned. People need to know what one is selling, they say. Call the thing by its true name. Wig. Toupee. It's a matter of honesty. I, however, am an old-fashioned man, and prefer to maintain a certain mystique. Besides, my customers are more comfortable in my coy hands than in those of a common tradesman. Imperceptibility, invisibility: these are my areas of expertise. If you can afford the price, I can work miracles. I can take years off your life.

PART I

This Side of Heaven

February 1898

With its tangle of Moorish minarets, cupolas, and arches, its Byzantine domes and its thirteen crescent moons, the Tampa Bay Hotel was a fairy-tale castle anchored at the water's edge. It was open only a few months a year, and during the immense summers it stood empty, its glittering roofs blinding even the crows. From December through April, however, it was full of the best sorts of people: bankers and industrialists, stockbrokers and shipping merchants, attorneys and architects, and a number of celebrities. They came from the big northern cities and from Europe, these guests, each man accompanied by a sleek wife. Any children they brought with them were, like the Hotel maids, silent until asked to speak. Wealthy invalids came, too: women of delicate constitution and sensitive nerves, feeble second sons, consumptives, rheumatics, all ordered south by physicians weary of the illnesses of the rich, whether phantom or genuine. Florida was a place where wonders could happen, where there was no winter worth mentioning, and where the soil was so fertile that dry sticks took root and flowered like Aaron's staff. Heart cases did well there.

Once inside the gates of the Tampa Bay Hotel there was no need to leave, no reason to venture into the dirty, dangerous parts of town, where the Negroes and Latins lived. It was a city unto itself, with a drugstore, a schoolhouse, a barbershop, a newsstand, a beauty salon, and a telegraph office. There were spa facilities, an exposition hall, a casino, a bowling alley, tennis and croquet courts, kennels and stables. Every room had a telephone, hot and cold running water, and electric lighting designed by Edison himself. The grounds contained one hundred and fifty varieties of tropical plants and were so vast that porters were available to squeeze the lazier guests into rickshaws, transporting them like luggage along the ornamental walkways so that they could admire the peacocks and the mirror pool. To the north and the west lay the wilderness, which an army of gardeners kept at bay, and which shook with easy quarry: trout, alligators, tarpon, egrets, plover, deer, and snakes. Upon one's return to the Hotel these could be cooked by the chef, fashioned into a handbag, secured to a hat, or stuffed by the resident taxidermist.

Marion Unger stood at her window on Fortune Street brushing her hair. Across the river she could see the Tampa Bay Hotel gleaming like quicksilver under the February sun, and if she lowered her gaze to the water's surface she could watch the entire structure rippling and dissolving, then reassembling itself. She had come to Tampa because of the Hotel, not as a guest but as a bricklayer's bride, and she had watched the resort grow to one-quarter of a mile from its foundation stone. She had married Jack at the age of nineteen, almost ten years before, and at their wedding in Detroit she had worn a crown of orange blossoms, as if Florida had claimed her already. She had wanted to put the flowers in water before she went to bed, but she could not untangle them from her hair without tearing the petals, catching them in the white-blond strands.

"Don't worry," said Jack. "You can have as many orange blossoms as you like once we're in Tampa. Come here." And he opened the starchy sheets to her, and she climbed into the cool, high bed.

The next weeks were spent preparing for their departure. As Marion filled her trunk with her new clothes, the clothes of a wife, she tried to imagine what her life would be like so far south, on the edge of that low-lying peninsula. At breakfast each morning, she thought, when she would wear her new silk kimono, she and Jack would drink juice the color of the sun, and she would make him orange marmalade and her mother's orange cake—the secret was the zest, rubbed as fine as sand—and if it were ever cold enough to light a fire she would sprinkle the kindling with curls of peel and their house would be warm and spicy. She folded the burial robe she had sewn as part of her trousseau, admiring the tiny tucks in the bodice, the handmade lace at the wrists and throat. It seemed a shame she could not wear it as a nightgown; the satin felt so luxurious to the touch. On top of the neat pile of clothes she placed the woollen stockings her mother had knitted, although Jack said she would never need them, and that she was foolish to take such things along.

They arrived in the summer of 1888, when there was no grand resort and no bridge, just acres of swamp and underbrush to be cleared, and alligators prowling the sandy streets, and serpents stirring in the palmetto scrub. Marion had never known such heat. The wild orange trees were bright with ripening fruit, and the air clung to her skin.

"We'll get used to it—everyone does," said Jack, his brow glossy, his cheeks too flushed. "And come hurricane season, you'll long for this calm."

He meant it as a joke, but Marion was too hot to laugh. As he led her into their house she thought of her hometown, where the hottest weather was smoothed by its passage across the Great Lakes.

Jack stroked the humid strands of hair at her temples. She could feel the grain of his skin, the whorls and ridges rough to the touch, like the rind of citrus fruits. He had confident hands; she had watched him build a wall not a fraction out of true, the liver-colored bricks rising from the ground and obscuring his legs, his chest, his face, until he disappeared. He was confident in society, too, able to transform himself into a gentleman whenever he wished, always wearing the right trousers with the right coat, the correct shade of gloves, the appropriate hat. He felt as comfortable at a grand ball or a ceremonious dinner as he did at home, and indeed, he sought out such events, always delighted to make the acquaintance of members of the fashionable set. He became known by a number of society hostesses as a desirable guest; he could be relied upon to invite the plainest wallflower to dance, and was never at a loss for conversation, entertaining many a table with snippets gleaned from the latest periodicals and presented in such a way that one might think them his personal observations. To mark their engagement Marion had given him a spirit level made of brass and engraved with his initials, but she suspected he seldom needed such devices; he trusted his eye. On their wedding night his broad hands had moved over her, expertly arranging and nudging and tap-tap-tapping, placing her in line. And afterward he had looked at her so—there was no other word for it—so *proudly*, drawing back to see her in perspective, then smiling and saying, "Perfect," as if she were his own creation.

They would be in Florida two years, he told her. Quite apart from the generous wage, it was an honor for him to be chosen for the job; the railroad magnate Henry B. Plant had handpicked twenty-five bricklayers, and they would build the most luxurious hotel in the world.

"I'm so proud of you," she said when he returned from his first day on the site. And then, fanning herself with his straw hat, "How long will the summer last?"

Day by day she willed the building to take shape as she watched the barges moving up the Hillsborough and depositing their cargo. Bricks and cedar came, and a great coil of steel cable, and fifteen hundred barrels of oyster shells from an old Indian mound. They would be added to the concrete, Jack said, and would bind together the walls of Mr. Plant's palace. He liked that about the project: it was innovative. Mr. Plant saw any problem as a riddle to which he could find a shrewd solution, and that was why he was so wealthy. Take the coil of steel, for example. Tampa had a reputation for catching alight, but the lengths of cable winding through the Hotel's concrete floors would protect the building, he assured her.

"The only fireproof resort in the country," said Jack.

"But what do you mean, a reputation?" said Marion. She did not think she had room for another danger; there were too many in this primitive place. She was to stay inside when the sun was fierce; she was to be on her guard against alligators and snakes, especially at night, when anyone venturing out of doors should carry a gun; if she heard an alligator hissing she should move away as quickly as possible. Then there were the regular outbreaks of disease: only six months before she and Jack had arrived, yellow fever had been epidemic. Many families had fled to the woods for fear of infection, and there were tar barrels burning on every corner in the hope that the smoke would kill the germs. Even now, any railcars bringing building materials from Jacksonville, where the disease was still spreading, had to be fumigated before they were unloaded. One of the first things Marion had done was to buy lengths of mosquito netting and hang it about their bed, and in the early morning, when she first awoke and tried to make sense of her veiled surroundings, it was as if clouds of smoke had risen up and hidden the whole world, and Jack was the only thing real to her. And she did not want to leave their misty sanctuary for a place so full of danger, but as soon as she moved her feet or rubbed her eyes, Jack awoke and dressed and was gone. Now, it seemed, there were fires to be taken into account. She would not like to raise a child here, and hoped she would not fall pregnant until they were safely back in Detroit.

"It was an old submarine telegraph line that took messages to the Florida Keys and the West Indies," Jack was saying. "The copper wire salvaged from the core covered the cost of bringing it to the site. Innovative, do you see?" He tapped his knife against his plate for emphasis. The bridge across the Hillsborough was another example—rather than build a new one at great cost, Mr. Plant had simply cannibalized an old one. And the Hotel walls and ceilings—they were reinforced with outmoded tracks from his South Florida Railroad.

"No wonder he's a wealthy man," said Marion.

"Mrs. Plant is playing her part too," said Jack. "She's making a Grand Tour of Europe and the Orient, buying furnishings for the place. Onyx chairs from the Far East, antique tapestries from France—Mr. Plant is joining her for some of it." He laughed. "I like the way people operate down here. There are lots of possibilities."

There it was again: an emphatic tap of the knife against their wedding china. Marion thought of the Indians who had dropped their oyster shells as they ate, every generation doing the same so that the mound grew and grew until it changed the landscape, making a hill where before there was none.

She could feel the bristles of the brush pushing through each strand of hair, scratching her other palm like stubble, and if she closed her eyes she could imagine that Jack was home again, rubbing his face against her hand. And she could imagine, too, that from her window she saw not the shining Hotel but the wild orange trees, pretty and sour, that had surrounded their house in the beginning.

It faced south, turning its back on the wilderness where the wild animals prowled and where men could go, so Marion had understood, to buy the company of a woman. She had never seen any of these creatures, these scrubland females who displayed their colors and whistled and cawed and brushed their pulse points with scent, but Jack assured her they were there, and that it was a place best ignored. The house looked toward the center of town, where the roads were being paved: toward the future, Marion had told herself, and she thought of Jack piecing Mr. Plant's palace together, sending its shadow across the water to her, brick by brick.

During those first few weeks in Tampa, when she had felt she might evaporate in the heat, she made her way through the orange trees to the river and bathed, her body as light as a leaf, her toes now and then tracing the stony bed. Once, when she found Jack already home upon her return, he said, "We seem to have a mermaid living in the river. She must have lost her way."

"What does she look like?" said Marion, smiling, her hair trickling down her back.

Jack took her by the shoulders and turned her to the left and to the right, lifting her wet hair over her breasts, examining her face for features he might recognize. "A little like you. But I couldn't be sure," he said. Then he told her that in Tampa men outnumbered women by seven to one, and that she should be careful about displaying herself. If the heat was unbearable he would do something about it, and for a moment Marion believed he could change the weather to please her. "I'll look after you," he said. "You're a rarity here. An endangered species."

The next day he bought her an ostrich-feather fan. He placed it on the sideboard in the parlor as if it were a bouquet of flowers, and when she opened it and used it during the hot afternoons it made a murmuring sound: the sound of a marriage beginning to breathe. And she knew that she must be at home in this close place, with this man who had brought the wind inside, and it was only for two years, and the heat could not last.

Then, in November of 1888, Jack told her that Mr. Plant had decided to make the Hotel even bigger, adding fifty more rooms, sixteen private parlor suites, and a domed dining hall that would seat six hundred and fifty. It would take an extra year to complete.

"But he can't just add rooms. He can't just change the plans halfway through," said Marion, her voice shrinking.

As she watched from her side of the river, however, the Moorish palace grew and grew, rising from the wilderness and expanding all through the mild winter months and again in the heat of summer, the sky shining through its bones, the scaffolding spreading like vines. It was too big to hate, this castle conjured from the swamp, from oyster shells and railroad tracks and telegraph cables. Marion imagined the long-gone feasts set into its cement, and the journeys by train, and the ghosts of messages that had once shivered along the undersea cables. There were wishes in its walls, she thought, and in spite of herself she admired it, just as she admired Jack for his part in its creation.

As the Hotel neared completion, bonfires were lit so that Mr. Plant's rail passengers could admire it at night. Jack's days became longer and longer, until just before the grand opening he and several hundred others were working until well after dark. Even with her curtains and shades drawn, even with her eyes shut, Marion could see the glow from the site, and she never slept until Jack was in bed beside her, his arm resting about her waist, the smell of brick dust in his hair. He told her of the treasures from Mrs. Plant's Grand Tour that were filling the Hotel. Every day they were arriving on the trains, forty-one carloads in all. There were one hundred and ten carved mirrors from Venice and Florence; there was a life-size bronze of Victor Hugo's Esmeralda and her goat; there were pieces once belonging to Napoleon, Queen Victoria, Marie Antoinette, Louis XIV, and Mary, Queen of Scots. Placed throughout the grounds would be a range of jardinières—pretty porcelain stands shaped like mushrooms and elephants, monkeys and frogs, to be used as seats by weary strollers. Inside the building stretched thirty thousand yards of red carpeting woven with lions—it was made for the English Royal Family, but they refused to walk on their emblem—and in the basement a Parisian music box operated by steam sent melodies drifting through the rooms.

"When I have made my fortune, we'll stay in one of Mr. Plant's parlor suites," he told her. "We'll dine on the finest food prepared by the finest chefs—the pastry cook comes from Delmonico's in New York, the baker from the Manhattan Club—and if you don't care to attend the concerts in the Ballroom or on the verandas, you can simply telephone the front desk and arrange for a piano to be sent up, complete with pianist." If she took a short stroll down to

Franklin Street, he said, she could shop for trinkets to remind her of their stay, such as whimsically carved alligators' teeth, or coquina vases embedded with ancient shells and corals, or the vivid wings of curlews and flamingos, with which she could decorate a new hat. For a prank, she could even purchase a foot-long hatchling alligator, have him packed in Spanish moss and delivered by one of Mr. Plant's express trains to her mother in Detroit.

The Tampa Bay Hotel is the palace of a prince, read the brochure, *a museum of costly and pleasing paintings, statuary, cabinets, and bric-à-brac from many lands. It typifies all that the refined, cultured, and luxurious tastes of our modern civilization term elegance, and to be once a guest within its portals is to remain always under the subtle fascination of its alluring charms. The Grand Salon is a dream of magnificence indescribable; a Jewel Casket into which have been gathered Rare and Exquisite Gems; the great Hotel and its surroundings are a world within themselves, where the days pass as hours, and the hours as minutes.*

Marion remembered how she had looked forward to the grand ball that marked the Hotel's opening. She had decided to wear her green costume, which was Jack's favorite: a sleeveless, crossover bodice of satin, a swishing bustle, and a train that spread and rippled like seaweed. She had waited in her underthings and Jack came to her with his cut-throat razor. Lifting first one arm and then the other, she stood very still—a dancer who has forgotten the next step—and he shaved her. "Now don't move," Jack said when he came to the little hollow level with her breast. "Don't blink. Don't breathe."

As they were crossing the river and approaching the finished building it seemed like a dream to her, this glittering structure rising up before them with its keyhole-shaped windows, its gingerbread latticework, its silver crowns. And everywhere there were women wrapped in silk and velvet and brocade, with aigrettes and stars in their hair, or diamond crescent moons as sharp as those poised on the minarets. Bows and feathers sprouted from their shoulders, and fringes of jet shimmered as they moved, and their trains whispered to each other of wealth and style and rank. The men wore full dress too, and as they led their partners up the steps their swallow-tail coats flicked in the warm breeze like snakes' tongues. Carriages lined the cobblestone paths, and car upon car of guests arrived in Plant System trains that hissed right up to the Solarium. Many more rail-cars were backed up for miles as the thousands of guests flowed into Tampa. There were fairy candles all along the crushed-shell walk-ways, and the live oaks and the palmettos, now clipped and shaped, were strung with Chinese lanterns. After an orchestra brought from New York gave a concert in the Music Room, there was dancing in the domed Dining Room. The guests whirled beneath the carved mahogany galleries and the friezes of palms and tropical flowers, their feet picking out the patterns of waltzes, lancers, schottische, and the new Tampa Bay Hotel Galop. Now and then Marion caught sight of Mr. and Mrs. Plant, he with his waxed mustaches and his contented smile, she moving like one of his large and luxurious rail-cars through the throng.

When Marion grew breathless from dancing, Jack took her out-side to where the minarets shone under the moonlight, as bright as the rustling river. He showed her the wine cellar he had made, with its bottles set into the curving walls. "Above ground, you see, because the land is so low," he said, and Marion agreed that it was indeed innovative. She did not ask whether Tampa flooded often; tonight she had no wish to think of danger. She allowed herself to be led along the shell-strewn paths that glimmered before them like a trail of breadcrumbs, happy to listen to Jack identifying the guava trees, the fruit and palm trees imported from Jamaica and the West Indies, the roses and oleanders, the mangoes, papayas, pineapples, and bamboos.

All too soon it was time to leave, and Jack was farewelling his col-leagues who would be returning to their homes in the north—the plumbers and electricians, the stonemasons, the carvers.

Over the next few weeks, when she went into the town center, Marion saw the wives of these men buying valises for the trip home, or souvenirs to remind them of their stay in such an odd little place: stuffed birds, snakeskin coin purses, alligator handbags held shut with wizened claws. Many purchased commemorative items from the Hotel itself, and she imagined the tea parties back in Chicago or Seattle or Los Angeles. "If you examine the bowl of your spoon," they would instruct their guests, "you can see the Hotel built by my husband."

Marion decided to buy one or two small things for her family, although they were not the sort of people who gave gifts without good reason. She went to Lafayette Street, where Mr. Stuart sold his Florida Curiosities, and as she was browsing the coral rings and brooches for something for her mother, and regarding a wood-stork positioned just so in its crown-of-thorns nest, she heard a woman saying, "Don't you have any bigger ones?" The woman was standing back and frowning at a stuffed panther that Mr. Stuart had lifted onto the counter.

"The Florida ones don't grow any bigger than this, ma'am," he said, dusting the cat's bared teeth with his finger. "There are some others in the window, if you want to take a look."

The woman went out to the street and peered in through the glass for a moment, then began pointing to the panther she wanted to inspect. "No," she said through the window, her mouth exaggerating the shape of the word. "That one, with the longer whiskers— no, to the right, the right, no, *that* one, to the *right*." Mr. Stuart stood behind his window, picking up four different panthers until his hand alighted on the correct one. "Yes!" mouthed the woman, and clapped her hands together, as gleeful as a child at a puppet show.

Marion could not wait to leave Tampa. "My mother wants us to bring her a box of navel oranges," she said to Jack that evening. "And look what I bought for her. It's coral, to ward off the evil eye." She held the little brooch up to him, and he put his book aside and looked at it and nodded, then gazed at her hands as she began to wrap it in a sheet of tissue. "Put your finger here," she said, circling the tiny package with ribbon, and Jack pressed down on the knot.

When she pulled the ends tight, however, she caught his finger, and they had to start all over again.

"I've been thinking," he said. "Maybe we shouldn't be in such a rush to get back to Detroit. There's little work to be had there."

Marion paused and the ribbon loosened again, the gift opening itself. "There's none here, though, now that the Hotel is finished."

"Not for bricklayers, no," said Jack. "But there are other possibilities." Some of the men he had worked with were staying on to grow oranges, he said, and they made it sound so promising that he had started to research the subject. He held up his book: *Treatise and Hand-Book of Orange Culture in Florida*, by the Reverend T.W. Moore. " 'Florida certainly has a bright future before her if her sons are wise enough to labor for that future,' " he read aloud. " 'In her broad acres there is ample room, not only for her natural and adopted sons, but for the hundreds of thousands of their fellow-citizens to whom they extend a hearty invitation to come and occupy with them these generous expanses, this genial climate, and this vast wealth, enough for all, and quite as good as can be found this side of Heaven.' "

Marion looked at her husband. He was smiling at her, wanting her to be as delighted with his scheme as he was. "You'd better tell me all the details," she said.

They would purchase the old grapefruit grove neighboring their property and would clear the land between their house and the water's edge. Citrus fruits rather than brick and stone would make their fortune: there were acres of wild oranges just waiting to be transplanted into orderly rows. The Indians had spread them right across Florida hundreds of years before, when they had eaten the fruit and dropped the pips, and if Marion saw a cluster of trees she could be certain it had grown from the seeds of a single orange consumed on that spot, so fertile was the soil. And the Port of Tampa was just at the end of the peninsula, not ten miles away. Before the end of winter Jack would graft the sour wild oranges with their sweeter cousins, and within two or three years each acre would yield thousands of fruits, and eventually each of their seven hundred trees would be bearing between one thousand and three thousand oranges, perhaps more. In the meantime, they would earn a little from the older grapefruit trees. There was no end to the possibilities for profit. They could make orange-blossom honey if they bought some hives, and in Europe the extracts from the citrus were as valuable as the fruit itself. No part was wasted: essential oil was distilled from the rinds, the leaves, and the tender shoots, and the most exquisite perfumes were manufactured from the flowers. The orange was a beautiful plant, he said, and could seduce the sternest heart; he had heard of an officer who, during the war, was ordered to destroy all the orange trees in a Florida town, but one grove in particular was so lovely that instead of razing it he picketed his men there.

Jack was looking at her. Marion thought of the soldiers camped beneath the dark, fragrant leaves, and she imagined them reaching up and plucking the sweet fruit and opening it with their swords. She did not wrap the coral brooch for her mother, but kept it for herself.

Soon citrus groves filled all the land between the house and the river. Jack set them out with his bricklayer's precision, measuring the grid with his brass set square, calculating the distance between trees as if he were building a house, where the misplacing of a single stone could set the whole structure out of true. Marion even saw him placing his spirit level on the soil and watching for the bubble of air to settle in the middle like a tiny eye. He planted a tree below their bedroom window as a present for her, so she would have something pretty to look at. He had budded it himself, he said, but that was true of every tree in the grove. Marion could not understand why he paid it such special attention, why he examined the blossoms every day once they appeared, comparing one with another, closing his eyes and sniffing the flowers in turn. It made her think of a game she and her sister had played as children: one blindfolded the other, then, wordlessly, presented her companion with a number of familiar substances to be identified—nutmeg, apple, raw potato. It was curious how foreign the most ordinary things could seem, and how wrong one could be.

"Wait and see" was all Jack would say when asked about the tree.

And then, when the fruits appeared, Marion had to look twice to convince herself of what she saw: glinting through the leaves, speckling the branches in equal abundance, were both oranges and lemons. And she thought perhaps it would be successful, their sandy grove, for Jack, it appeared, could work miracles.

She liked to watch him from the house. Through the rows of trees she caught glimpses of him irrigating the dry ground, pruning, checking the humming hives for honey, spraying the fruit with a brass pump that was green with poison. The blades of his plow left patterns between the trunks, great thumbprints on the soil.

On the day of the 1893 hurricane, when much of Florida was suffering while Tampa remained untouched, her baby arrived. It was born white and cold, and she learned she would have no others, and that was a second death. Over the following weeks she tried not to dwell on it, tried to think of another outlet for her energies, as the doctor advised—many women found charity work very rewarding, he said, and there were plenty of people all over the Southeast without a roof over their heads, their possessions and loved ones lost to the storm. Marion could not feel sorry for those souls, nor even for the nineteen thousand dead. She wished the hurricane had struck Tampa, torn the entire town from its brackish roots. Then her child might have lived; it might have had the air blown into its lungs, the color shaken into its cheeks.

Jack nursed her with soft rice puddings and mild broths—things she had not known he could make—and he dug a little grave beneath the two-fruit tree so that the child would be close to them at night. Although there was no marker—for there had been no baptism, no name bestowed—Marion noticed that he never walked on that small piece of earth. And she loved him.

Once, when a moderate frost fell, he and all the other local growers fired their groves, burning logs between the trees throughout the chilly night. The dark trunks and crowns were silhouetted against the flames, and now and then Marion caught sight of Jack's face, alight with purpose, as proud as Mr. Plant when he had opened his Hotel. Jack looked up to her lit window and waved. There was no reason to fear the drop in temperature; it would make the oranges sweeter. The fragrant smoke rose above the river.

However, at the end of 1894 a severe frost came, and no amount of firing could stop the fruit from freezing on the trees. The temperature fell to eighteen degrees in Tampa, and Jack's first real orange crop was rendered useless. Every young grove in the area was ruined, with only the older trees surviving.

"We still have the grapefruits," said Jack. "We'll just start over with the oranges."

By the end of a mild and wet January the more mature trees were beginning to grow again, putting out new shoots, and by early February they were showing their first spring flush. The sap was up and the bloom had begun to form, and Jack no longer stood and stared at the empty grove, which now afforded a clear view across the river to the Tampa Bay Hotel.

Then, in the second week of February 1895, an Arctic blizzard surged into Tampa, whipping the sandy streets into a haze and making the wires wail. The temperature fell fifty-five degrees in less than twenty-four hours, and the rising sap froze in the trees. All through the night Marion and Jack listened to bark splitting open, branches cracking, and in the morning, on top of their bedroom water pitcher, there lay a disk as thick as window glass. All the earth was white, and all the trees were webbed with frost, and when Marion went to the kitchen she found the eggs frozen and burst from their shells as if they were hatching birds of ice.

Jack was twenty-seven when he died. It was the day after the freeze, and they had worked until nightfall to try to pick the frozen grapefruits. Marion did not have the heart to tell him that it would be impossible to juice them; with so many growers in the same situation, the market was flooded already. When he failed to return to the house for dinner she took a lantern and went to look for him, her feet crunching across the fallen bark as if she were walking on shells.

Even the bees were dead in their hives, caught on the cold bricks of honeycomb. The only thing to survive the freeze was the two-tone tree; perhaps, Marion thought, it was sheltered by the closeness of their house. Jack would know.

She found him in the packing house, slumped over a pile of ruined fruits as if trying to gather them to himself, to throw his arms around the icy globes. The doctor said it was a massive hemorrhage in the brain, but Marion could not help thinking that his blood had simply frozen, expanding until something cracked.

Some ruined growers abandoned their properties, leaving equipment in their barns and plates on their tables. Marion's mother urged her to come home to Detroit, but when Marion looked across the stripped grove and saw the Hillsborough flowing past the house and down to the heart-shaped bay, she remembered how she used to swim in it when she first came to Tampa, and how, once, Jack had leaned into the water and caught her ankles in his hands. He held them for a moment until she slipped away again, and that night he told her that her feet were as soft and cool as the belly of a trout. And on the other side of the river, clearer now, was the Hotel. Marion had half-expected it to vanish in the freeze, had imagined Jack's careful brickwork crumbling, the icy towers shattering and falling. She had never quite believed in it, had always suspected it could be swallowed by the water, the land reverting to swamp and scrubby palmetto and undergrowth. Despite the loss of many of his finest tropical specimens, however, Mr. Plant's guests still strolled his garden paths and the rickshaws still carried them around the grounds and the pleasure boats still ferried them up and down the river. She heard Jack saying, "We'll take a parlor suite there. You will walk on carpet fit for royalty, and admire yourself in the Louis the Fourteenth mirror, and sit on the throne chair of Marie Antoinette and on the sofa of Queen Victoria."

She would stay, she told her mother.

Now, in February of 1898, she stood at her window, brushing her hair and occasionally catching the scent of orange blossom. It mingled with the smell of the tobacco rolled in West Tampa and in Ybor City. The Hotel and the cigar factories had transformed the town, and Marion's house was now very well situated. The land where Jack's groves had stood had provided her with a handsome sum when she sold it, and a number of fine homes had been built there. After the freeze all growers were offered free seeds from the railroad company, and many had sown crops of potatoes, tomatoes, and celery. Marion had never considered this option. The reason for Henry Plant's altruism was obvious: he needed fruit and vegetables to freight north so his railroad would make money. Once in a lifetime the great freeze may have been, but Marion would take no more risks. She invested the proceeds from the sale of the land—most shrewdly, her bank manager said as he eyed her fine silk costume and plumed hat—keeping just enough garden for a small vegetable patch, some rosebushes, and the two-fruit tree, now fifteen feet tall. It afforded some shade at the hottest times of the day, although the branches sagged with the weight of the fruit in winter, and she had to prop them with boards to prevent them from breaking. She could never use all the oranges and lemons. Some she made into marmalade and some into juice, and some she used in cakes or simply peeled and ate, but most she gave away or left to rot on the ground, the skins turning chalky, sending up little puffs of dust if touched. From her bed the glossy leaves filled the window and rattled when the wind blew, and sometimes she could believe that the groves were still there, their lines converging to triangles when seen from above, arrowheads pointing at the house.

She had no wish to take another husband. The neighbors greeted her when she passed them on the street or saw them at the store, and for the last three years Miss Harrow, a lady's companion from New

York who had lost her intended to the seminary, had lived with her. One was rarely isolated in Tampa.

In her hands the silver-backed brush glittered and flashed in the setting sun as if sending a coded message. Fortune Street was still, quiet; even the river was soundless. There were cherubs on the beaten back of the brush, plump babies with clouds of hair, wings like stubby fingers. Now and then Marion paused and ran her hands over their cool little faces, then plucked the pale strands from the bristles and fed them into the mouth of the crystal hair-receiver on her dressing table. When it was full she would smooth them into a single length and add them to the skein she kept wrapped in silk in her top drawer. And when the skein was fat and fine, she would take it to Monsieur Goulet, the wig-maker, and have it woven into a hair-piece indistinguishable from the hair on her head.

She settled down with a book. It was easier to fall asleep if she read until her eyes began to close of their own accord; if she put out the lamp before she was tired, all manner of thoughts crowded into her. She always left the window open a crack at night, and the woody scent of the cigars crept inside her room, as if Jack were there. She heard the whistle of a train as it crossed the river. They carried news of the weather now: another of Mr. Plant's innovations. When the gleaming carriages reached Tampa ahead of a frost, four long blasts sounded, and all the growers scrambled to cover their trees or fire their groves. Although no one welcomed those icy warnings, all agreed that they were a blessing, and that Mr. Plant was a fine man.

The next morning Miss Harrow brought her some tea and a boiled egg, handed her the *Tampa Tribune*, and settled herself on the edge of a low chair. The two women started each day like this, away from the sun on the east side of the house. They discussed news stories, and what they would make for dinner, and how many eggs the hens had laid. Marion would choose an article she thought might interest her companion, and read it aloud. Usually she skipped the advertisements, having no interest in revitalizing elixirs or vanishing creams or miracle stays, but today a small notice caught her eye.

*Do you have loved ones who have passed over? Would
you like to revive your contact with them? Come join*
The Harmonious Companions,
*meeting every Wednesday at two o'clock P.M. at the home of
Mrs. Adelina Flood, No. 145, Hyde Park Avenue, Tampa. All welcome.*

"Do you know these people?" she asked.

Miss Harrow peered at the notice. "Adelina Flood—she was one of the López girls. Very wealthy cigar-factory owners, Cuban. She married an American man—their wedding was featured in *Ladies' Home Journal*, don't you remember? Ivory peau de soie, with a thousand seed pearls on the bodice alone, and tobacco leaves embroidered around the hem?" Miss Harrow could always be relied upon to remember such details; weddings were her speciality.

When Marion was alone again she clipped the notice from the newspaper, then washed and dressed, hanging a fine chain about her neck. From it swung a small silver locket, and within the locket was a scrap of something like leather. It resembled a little ear, and she whispered secrets to it. Today she said, "Adelina Flood, Mrs. Adelina Flood. Perhaps we shall call on her soon."

⌒

There is a legend that Ponce de León, discoverer of Florida, came to this part of the world in search of the Fountain of Youth. As with most pretty stories, this one is untrue, but it helps to attract the crowds. Like squawking birds they flock south each winter on the trail of beauty, vitality, life. One can tell the tubercular cases at a glance; those with heart troubles are less conspicuous. Whether here on doctor's orders or simply on vacation, however, all wish to leave looking somehow improved—and this is where I can assist. My products are a remedy for a multitude of ills: who does not appear more vital beneath a lustrous coiffure? And, unlike the rigorous treatments administered at some of Tampa's most exclusive hostelries and spas, my remedies are quick and painless. Dr. Hampton's Sanitarium, for instance, for the Cure of Cancer, Rupture, Scrofula, and Kindred Diseases, with Tapeworm Positively Removed, is no match for a Goulet hair-piece; Friskin's Magnetic Life Tonic might as well be gin and water—and possibly is. Do not waste your time on them. Many a wealthy convalescent, a vain businessman, an unwed woman past her prime has returned home with a new head of hair, loudly applauding the miracle of Florida sunshine, fresh air, and citrus fruits. I need not advertise; the word *wig* need never offend the sensibilities of readers of the *Tampa Tribune*. Via a network of whispered recommendations and furtively scribbled notes—as if a love affair were being conducted—my reputation reaches the ears of those unfavored by Nature. Indeed, I suspect that more than a few thin-haired wives persuade their husbands to winter in Tampa precisely because they have heard of my expertise. From time to time a newspaper article or a sermon accuses the Perruquier of encouraging duplicity between spouses; of engaging in the devil's work. Such accusations are nothing new; why, two hundred years ago the Bishop of Lincoln condemned the wearing of periwigs in his book *Spiritual Armour to Defend the Head from the Superfluity of Naughtiness*. The missionary John Eliot declared that the sufferings of the colonists at the hands of the Indians were *a divine punishment for wearing false hair*, and just thirty years ago Bishop Odenheimer of New Jersey refused to lay his hands in confirmation *upon any woman, young or old, whose hair is adorned with borrowed tresses*. However, the large numbers of clergymen on my books appear to feel otherwise, and I see no harm in making a vacuous wife pretty, or a boring husband handsome. Every marriage requires a little deception, does it not?

Do not misunderstand me: I am no philanthropist. I give nothing away. I have a business to consider, and charity will not buy a good reputation. From humble beginnings five years ago, I have prospered in Tampa; for like Ponce de León I am a sensible man. He did not come to Florida in search of a magic potion. He came in search of gold.

I do not believe in the notion of Home as today's woman understands it. Let me quote *The Splendor of Eve*, a text popular amongst my female clientèle, which covers matters of fashion, etiquette, and grooming as well as more delicate topics:

The furniture of a lady of refinement, the appearance of her reception rooms, her pictures and statuary, her own costume and adornments, should give pleasure and edification to her every visitor. Why should not her drawing room be as pretty a work of art as any painting? Is she not herself, in her air and manner, in pose and gesture, in dress and ornament, a work of art? Her sphere is to refine, to cheer, to bless.

Unfortunately, in most cases this amounts to a clutter of doilies and dust-trap ornaments, and dark little parlors with hard little chairs, and on the wall the hostess's watercolors, which must be admired, although it is seldom clear whether one is admiring a country church or the rear view of a bullock. No, I do not believe in Home, but rather in good taste. Harmoniously decorated apartments are a balm for even the most distressed soul, and no rooms outside of Paris are more harmonious than those of the Tampa Bay Hotel. It is a freedom to live there, in my roomy minaret, where I own none of the trappings, not even the bed in which I sleep. If I desire feminine company, I simply visit a pair of actresses who understand me as well as any woman could. I watch the guests arrive here and depart, and I know that I, too, can pack my bags and leave whenever I please. For although it is true that I have been five years in Tampa, I will not settle.

It so happens that I met the Henry B. Plants in 1889, when they were on a buying trip in Paris—Mrs. Plant wanted a waterfall chignon of the best quality, and quite naturally was referred to me. Mr. Plant, railroad magnate, must have been satisfied with the change I wrought in his sturdy Irish wife—although, to be honest, to me she still recalled an overstuffed chesterfield, and would have benefited from a strict regimen of raw fruits and sassafras tea—for he gave me his card and insisted I stay at their Hotel the next time I found myself in Florida. I thanked him and said I should do so with pleasure, having, of course, no intention of setting foot in that vulgar part of the globe. And yet, in a time of great necessity, that is where I went. Strange, is it not, how man often does the very thing against which he has sworn?

But perhaps I shall tell you of my arrival in Tampa at some other point; it is a complex story, and I suspect you do not know me well enough to judge my actions fairly. Suffice it to say, for the moment, that after I had endured my first months in America in a dire boarding-house, I was able to take apartments at the Hotel and spend a mild winter there. Only when the season was drawing to a close did I realize I had no choice but to contact Plant and make an unusual request of him.

As I expected, when I stepped into his office—a luxuriously appointed railcar—his face showed no sign of recognition.

"Would it surprise you, Monsieur Plant, to know that we have met before?" I said after we had exchanged pleasantries on the mildness of the weather, the magnificence of the Hotel, and the convenience of an office on wheels. "Perhaps you will recall—I made a hair-piece, a waterfall chignon, for your beautiful wife when you were in Paris."

He scrutinized me, his waxed mustaches twitching, trying to pick up an old scent.

"It was four years ago, in 1889. You were undertaking a Grand Tour in order to purchase furnishings for your Hotel, I believe."

"Yes," he said eventually. "Your face is familiar. But you must forgive me, Mr., Mr.—"

"Goulet," I repeated. "Lucien Goulet the Third."

He paused. "Are you quite sure?" he said. "I could have sworn you were Boudoir, Borgia—something like that—I meet so many people—"

"I have discarded that old moniker," I said, although I did not utter my former name. "It was never mine in the first place, but was given me when I became an apprentice. It was like a stage name, Monsieur, a name taken by an actor. Here in America I have decided to be true to my roots."

Plant approved of this intention, and I chose that moment to make my request.

When the words were out of my mouth there was a short delay before Plant said, "But the Hotel is a winter resort, Mr. Goulet. It closes at the end of April, and won't reopen until December."

I was aware of that, I said, smiling, but I wondered whether he might not make an exception, whether we might not come to some arrangement. Since I would be taking apartments again the following winter, it seemed sensible to establish a semipermanent base at the Hotel. I only wished I had been present at the opening of his glorious haven, and seen the ravishing Madame Plant in her waterfall chignon.

He gave a brief, lovestruck smile, then resumed his businesslike face, its folds as stiff as those on a rich man's purse. "There's only a skeleton staff over the summer. A few gardeners and groundsmen— elaborate meals would not be available, nor would the telegraph office, the newsstand, the taxidermist—"

"All the same," I said, "there is nowhere else I would feel so at home. I should hate to leave town just when I had decided to situate my business here. You will pardon me for speaking so frankly, Monsieur Plant, but a Perruquier of my skill attracts a stream of wealthy visitors wherever he is based—and they all, of course, require accommodation."

He nodded slowly. "You do know how hot the summers are?"

"I don't mind the heat. And naturally I would pay the full rate all year round."

And so our special arrangement was reached, and each year, when the guests leave, I stay on, prince of the palace. I happen to know that Mrs. Plant recommends me to her acquaintances, and whenever

I meet her she remarks that it is an honor to have such a gifted artiste resident in the Hotel (I paraphrase a little).

In summer, when I am left to my own devices, I like to visit the subterranean mineral baths. Sometimes as I wallow underground I think: perhaps it is true that there is healing to be had in Florida, for no matter how hot it is outside, they are as cool as the moon's heart. As I climb from the water I feel heavy, and I imagine the salts and minerals and trace elements that have penetrated the outer layer of my skin, as if I have been buried for a time.

⟞⟞

Rafael Méndez had come to Ybor City, a suburb of Tampa, in August of 1897 and now, six months later, was about to turn fifteen. He was growing more accustomed to the town, with its sandy streets and its absence of hills, and some days he could believe he was still in Cuba, or at least in the Cuba he preferred to recall. English was rarely heard in Ybor City, and in the mornings the baker's boy delivered Cuban bread, fixing the warm, fragrant sticks to the nails on each front porch. The climate also reminded him of home: it had been hot and humid and full of rain when he'd arrived at the height of summer, in hurricane season, and now the days were dry and mild, the nights cool. Living at sea level, he found it easy to convince himself that Florida was an island, and sometimes, when the waves were very rough, he thought of the tides that broke over the Malecón Promenade in Havana, and he had to remind himself that he was in America now, and that an entire continent stretched above him.

During his first few days in Tampa he had stayed at a boardinghouse where every room smelled of old smoke, where the bed sagged and the walls were dark with flyspecks. The landlady said that an excellent restaurant supplied the food, but every night she served the same watery soup with potatoes. *I am well situated*, he wrote to his father. *I am comfortable and happy and expect to find work soon. Don't worry about me.* And the magical thing about telling lies in this new country, Rafael found, was that they came true: within a week he had taken a room with a Cuban family, and he was employed at the Ybor-Manrara Company cigar factory. The more he told himself that he had been right to leave home, the truer it became.

The Estradas' casita was one of dozens of such houses built for the cigar-makers who had families; they could rent one for a few dollars a week, or buy one for a few hundred. The shotgun houses, as they were called, were rather plain seen from the street: narrow white boxes with no latticework on the porches, no bow windows or stained glass or beveled panes, no finials, no towers. The walls and floors were of Florida pine, and the roofs, tiled with cedar, were steeply pitched so the heat could rise and gather there in the summer. There were no attics in the casitas; no places for secrets. In the yards stood the water pumps and the outhouses, and behind them ran a narrow lane of sand, then the yards of other casitas. Most families grew vegetables—yams, okra, corn—and the Estradas had a fragrant patch of herbs, tended by their daughter, Serafina. They had hens too, and one cockerel, and a large cage that housed the children's pet spider monkey, a gift from a boarder who had visited Brazil.

"It wasn't a gift," said Señora Estrada. "If we hadn't agreed to keep it, he would have left it in the street, or fed it to an alligator." Still, she gave it little scraps of fruit and meat.

If the casitas looked bare from the outside, inside they were gracious and pleasing to the eye, filled with tapestry-covered chairs, sideboards carved from Cuban mahogany, lampshades of scalloped and colored glass, and curtains of brocade or of printed cotton. The Estradas even had an icebox, and beside it hung a thin wooden dial. Rafael had thought it was a clock, but Señora Estrada explained that it showed different weights, so the ice man would know how much to leave when he made his deliveries.

The casitas stood on brick pilings as a defense against the warm earth and wild animals, but were so close to one another that children, or perhaps nimble lovers, could lay an ironing board between the windows and climb in and out of their neighbors' rooms. Any conversation louder than a whisper could be heard in the next casita, Rafael found, and secrets had to be told with all doors and windows shut. In the evenings or on Sundays, if he wanted to be alone, he went to the beach, where he could watch the storms rolling across Tampa Bay, sweeping inland. He enjoyed the suddenness with which they struck, the way they shook the slender palms and turned the sea to spray and then, just as suddenly, stopped. These storms had already passed over the Vuelta Abajo, he imagined; they were the same squalls, making their way north.

He thought then of his mother, who had been frightened of bad weather, foreseeing doom in thunderheads and hearing death in high winds. She had never forgotten the hurricane she had witnessed as a child, which had killed hundreds in Cuba; many times she had told Rafael and his sisters how she had stepped into her parents' garden afterward and found a child hanging in their almond tree, his throat pierced by a branch. Hurricanes upset the natural order of things, she said. They left the roof on the floor and the floor on the roof; they made leaves fall in summer; they let the tide take over the land. When the weather was unsettled, she refused to leave their house at the sloping foot of the mountains. She sheltered in her bedroom, praying for deliverance from the storm, wishing it away, and when lightning made the white walls flare as bright as magnesium she made offerings to her holy statues. As if they too sought shelter, they were crowded into an alcove by the fireplace, the edges of the recess hung with lace, the little ceiling sooty from the nervous flames of candles. She made many offerings to Oyá, goddess of twisting storms, anxious to pacify her with star apples, pepper cress, and rainwater. Beside her bed was a special altar to Ochún, the sensual and beneficent Virgin, which she draped with rosary beads of jet and garnet and colored glass. In the town of El Cobre, where she was born, a figure of Ochún was found floating on the stormy bay in the 1600s, a mulatto baby Jesus in one arm and a jeweled cross in the other. Ever since then, she told Rafael, the waters had possessed healing properties, and the proof of Ochún's power was Rafael's own great-grandfather, whose gout had been cured by bathing there. She used to pray to the goddess during bad weather, selecting one of her rosaries and passing the glassy decades through her fingers, placing before the statue little dishes of anise flowers and honey, and saucers of chamomile tea made from river water, as if she expected the wooden Virgin to lap it up with a cat's deft tongue.

Already nine months had passed since his mother's death, but when storms struck Tampa, Rafael could not help thinking she had succeeded in making them pass from her doorstep, and had sent them on to him, her youngest child and only son, as a reminder of home.

Rafael's parents had worked on a tobacco plantation in the Vuelta Abajo region of Pinar del Río, where the finest wrapper leaves and the richest filler were grown. From the time he was small Rafael had helped his father sow the seeds every September, dropping them into the pulverized soil and smoothing it over so it seemed nothing was there. A month later, when the six-inch seedlings were ready to be transplanted, Rafael always felt a little anxious as his father lifted them from the ground, their white roots hanging through his fingers like broken webs. They never failed to thrive in their new beds, however, the filler leaves growing dark green and heavy under the direct sun, the lighter wrapper leaves sheltered beneath canopies of white cloth. Seen from the windows of their house, which perched above the plantation with all the other workers' homes, the sheeting moved in the breeze like a drowsy surf, and when it was hot Rafael liked to wander beneath it, or to lie between the rows of plants and watch the pinpoints of sky shining through the weave.

The seedlings were fully grown by the new year, standing three and a half feet high, and Rafael and his sisters helped with the harvest as soon as they were old enough to use a knife. Their mother stitched the cut leaves together, passing a needle and thread through the head of the stems and hanging them to dry—for two weeks if the weather was fine, up to six if it was wet. Then they were placed in the *casa de tabaco* to sweat. It was a place best avoided during the day, when the vertical sun drummed on the thatched palm roof and nothing cast a shadow. "A hellhole," said Rafael's mother, and for a time, until he decided he did not believe in hell, nor heaven either, Rafael thought that wicked spirits could inhabit such a place, with its fumes streaming from the sweaty leaves and its hot, oxblood walls.

After several more weeks the tobacco was sorted according to length and texture, then bundled into groups and baled, the tips of the leaves facing inward for protection. Around fifty leaves made one hand, four hands made a carat, and eighty carats made a bale, so that each burlap-wrapped bundle contained sixteen thousand leaves of tobacco. In mid-June the cigar manufacturers or their agents arrived from Tampa and Key West, Chicago and New York. Some were American, but many were Cuban, and Rafael would stand at the door of the *casa de tabaco* and watch them haggle in their brocade vests and their swallow-tail coats, sleek birds picking through the leaves. His mother could not relax until the harvest had been sold, and she made extravagant offerings to her statue of Orisha Oko, god of crops, in order to influence the outcome. She made many visits to the *bruja*, too, asking her to consult the cowrie shells to discover whether the tobacco buyers would pay a good price. She was relieved when the bales were finally taken away, always worrying that an early hurricane might strike to destroy her family's hard work, or that some kind of disease might set in. And in the end, thought Rafael, a blight of sorts had struck, driving them from their home and into the filthy, infected city and the reconcentration zones of the Spanish.

I have bought myself a pocket watch so that I am always at the factory by seven, Rafael wrote to his father. *We have two breaks a day, and most of us finish at five, although we are allowed to keep our own hours. I wear a white shirt, a collar, and studs, and a panama hat. You would not know me.* He also bought an English dictionary, which he studied at night, its pages as fine and as closely printed as a Bible's. He did not allow himself to feel homesick. This was his home now, this continent that felt like an island, and whenever he woke thinking, Perhaps a letter will come today, he stopped the thought before it could take root, banished it as one banishes a half dream, so that by the time he had walked to his washstand in his room at the Estradas' house, splashed his face with water, and observed himself in the speckled mirror, the thought had wilted and disappeared. He knew the tyranny of waiting for news, had seen how it could swallow a person. At the cigar factory, there was always somebody who rushed home during a break and checked for mail, just as there was always somebody who had a fresh letter and held it aloft like a trophy. They would be passed from hand to hand, these clutches of worn pages, as soft and light as wrapper leaves, to be consumed by those who had no letters of their own. Rafael always declined to read news of other men's families, other people's weather. Whenever his father wrote to him he read the letter once, then shut it away in a drawer and did not look at it again. He did the same with letters from his four sisters, all of whom were living with their husbands in the camps. He did not like to think about where his family was, what their surroundings were like, and every letter told him the same thing: that Cuba was not Cuba anymore.

The situation had been worsening before he left. Inflation was out of control, with the Spanish government printing money as if it were propaganda. They were forcing people from areas like the Vuelta Abajo out of their homes and into reconcentration zones in the cities; those who resisted were killed. Thousands were crammed into the camps in Havana, including Rafael and his family. They were among the fortunate: they were able to find employment at a cigar factory, and while Rafael and his father learned the art of rolling, his mother worked in the boxing room, wrapping a pretty label around the throat of each cigar and pasting the medallions and lithographs to the cedar boxes. The illustrations showed smiling young women with roses in their hair, clear-eyed heroes on horseback, fields of tobacco lush and unravaged. When his mother fell ill, Rafael's eldest sister took over her job.

In the reconcentration zones, smallpox and yellow fever were epidemic. Rags used to tend the sick were thrown into the streets, where the wind and the stray dogs found them and spread the infections like pollen. Trenches were dug in the cemeteries, and the dead thrown in at night and covered with quicklime. His mother was wrong, Rafael thought: the *casa de tabaco* was no hellhole. He longed for their life on the plantation and tried not to picture what it would be like now: in some parts of the countryside, it was said, the only movement came from the wings of buzzards and vultures.

When his mother died of yellow fever, they disposed of her body so quickly that there was no time for grief, no time for prayers and offerings to the saints. It was then that his father told him to leave Cuba. Many young tobacco workers were making a good life for themselves as cigar-makers in Florida, he said, and Rafael had shown a talent for rolling.

"It takes four years to learn," said Rafael. "I've had six months."

"Rodrigo Aguado has gone," said his father. "The Suárez boys have gone." And he recited the names of those who had left for America, a litany of missing men. Rafael imagined them bundled together into hands and carats, packed into bales, wrapped in burlap to sweat and age. He thought, too, of the tobacco smokers Columbus had witnessed in America: frightening, distorted creatures. When the great explorer had reported back to the King and Queen of Spain, he had told them that the New World was a strange place, with sirens in its waters and men with heads on their chests, and others who used their feet as parasols, and trees whose shade made one sleep, and chimney men, who from their mouths and noses breathed smoke that drowsed the flesh and made one drunk in such a way that tiredness never came. Rafael would wait for another three months in the camp, he told his father. In that time, surely, something would happen—the Cuban rebels would rise up victorious against the Spanish, or the Americans would come.

The only change, however, was that the number of people forced into the camps increased, and the number dying. In August of 1897, Rafael boarded the S.S. *Mascotte* and, like countless crops of leaves and men before him, sailed to Tampa.

Six days a week now, he rolled cigars at the Eighth Avenue factory founded by Vicente Martínez Ybor himself.

"A great man," said Señor Estrada. "He was Spanish by birth, but a Cuban at heart—the whole town went into mourning when he died."

He and Rafael were making their way to the factory, starched collars scuffing their throats. All the *torcedores* wore suits to work; early in the morning they could be seen emerging from the casitas and the boarding-houses in the hundreds, as well groomed as bankers. Rafael felt older than fourteen when he was dressed for work, and when he caught sight of himself in the window of a store he thought he saw his father.

"He built the casitas for us. And one Christmas, for no reason at all, he gave away six thousand dollars to his employees. You came too late, Rafael," said Señor Estrada. On he talked about the virtuous Ybor, who had taken a carved statue of the Virgin with him when he went on business trips. "Life-size. She advertized the cigars for him, and people knew he was a good man." Rafael thought of his mother, who had said that the Catholic Virgin was not Mary at all, but a disguise for Ochún, the sensual goddess of rivers. Señor Estrada told Rafael about picnics at the Ybor home where the wine never ran dry, where whole hogs were roasted in the oak grove and the beautiful Ybor daughters danced until their satin slippers were worn through. All Rafael could think was that it was too late; he had come too late, and everything was different now.

The factory was a light and airy place, with high windows open to the sea breezes and to the sun, so that the different grades of leaf could be distinguished. Wooden beams rose like masts to the ceiling, and the workbenches were arranged in rows, giving the appearance of a church or a schoolhouse. The more accomplished *torcedores* took their places at the front of the factory, and they could produce one hundred cigars each per day: the record was one hundred and twenty-one. Their hands moved so quickly they seemed grafted to the binders and wrappers, as if the fragrant leaves were sprouting from their very fingers. Rafael sat toward the back, with the others who were still learning, and with every cigar he completed he thought of the money he would make. Like everyone else, he contributed one day's wages per week to the Liga Patriótica Cubana so that military supplies could be purchased. He lined up and collected his pay, then lined up again and gave a sixth of it back. He did not object to this Día de la Patria, this Day for the Motherland; nobody did, for money would win the war, and in America there was plenty of money to be earned. When Rafael was in bed and almost asleep he could picture it packed into tight bales, as fine and rich and full of promise as the best tobacco leaves.

There was no excuse for feeling lonely at the factory; it was too busy a place for such indulgence. One of Rafael's favorite times was when the Galician knife-sharpener called, stopping his wheel outside and sounding a thin six-note arpeggio. The cigar-makers brought Señor Rivera their *chavetas*, and he brought news from the towns he had visited, telling them of men who had returned to Cuba to fight, and of rumors of American involvement in the war, and of the latest casualties.

"Does the wheel wear away the knife or does the knife wear away the wheel?" Rafael asked him one day.

"Both," said the *afilador*. "Each takes a little from the other."

He slept in a barn or a hayloft or sometimes in a house, now and then accepting a meal in place of payment. His wheel was painted with mimosa and olives, and the colors shone against his black coat. Up and down his foot moved, working the pedal as if keeping time to music, the walnut frame creaking, the emery stone turning and turning. He talked to the rhythm of it.

A few of the cigar-makers did not trust him; *afiladores* were sly men, they said, from misty mountain country full of wolves. They used a private language, *el barallete*, so that the secrets of their trade would not be revealed. Rafael should be careful what he chose to believe: the *afilador* was Spanish, after all, and could invent any story he liked.

"Teach me some words," said Rafael, but Señor Rivera smiled and said if he wanted to learn *el barallete* he would have to become an *afilador* himself. And Rafael did not want that: although he did not say so, he knew he could not travel from place to place, welcome enough as a guest but without a real home. When the last *chaveta* was sharp, Señor Rivera moved his wheel to the butchers, the barbers, the houses—wherever there were knives. He took his new information with him, and the *torcedores* returned to their benches.

As the cool of early morning evaporated, the factory filled with the sweet scent of tobacco resin and pomade, and the musky basenotes of warm skin. The sound of the leaves rolling against the apple-wood tablets was as regular as a tide: hush, hush, all day long. Sometimes the men talked as they worked, but when the lector was reading no one said a word.

The man the Ybor-Manrara factory workers had chosen for the position was considered one of the best, and a far more reliable source of information than the *afilador*. He had been a professional actor in Cuba, and his voice carried to every corner of the room. He was fluent in seven languages, and when he could not obtain books in Spanish he read from the original French or Italian, English or German, Russian or Polish, translating without pause. English was rare in the factory, and as the lector spoke, the outside world dissolved, and the cigar-makers could pretend that they were still in Havana and that in the evening they would return home to their families. Often the lector read the speeches of José Martí, and Rafael pictured the great revolutionary riding his white horse into battle in Cuba. Martí had visited Tampa many times before his death in 1895; in Ybor City he had survived an attempt to poison him, and it was from Ybor City that he had issued his message to begin the war—a small note for such an orator, rolled as tightly as a furled leaf and hidden in the belly of a cigar. It was Martí who had proposed teaching *torcedores* by reading to them, and his *lectores*—the very first of their kind—had read to prisoners in the galleys of the Havana Arsenal. As Rafael listened and worked he pictured the thieves and arsonists and traitors and murderers all concentrating on stories as they rolled tobacco, imagining themselves elsewhere.

The cigar-makers themselves paid the lector, their small contributions amounting to a fine weekly wage. The workers also selected the texts: when it was time for a new book, the lector moved from bench to bench, taking note of the titles suggested. He then read his list aloud, paring it down to the two most popular choices, and votes were cast to determine the winner. Rafael was always impatient for this procedure to be over and for the lector to continue with his reading, but as the weeks passed he began to understand why the cigar workers were so painstaking: if they could not vote in Cuba, they would vote here, and if not for a government, then for a book.

Dressed in white from head to toe, the lector perched on a tribune in the middle of the factory, the workers surrounding him in rows like a congregation. He began in the morning with articles from the Spanish-language newspapers, moving in the early afternoon to extracts on economics or philosophy. The final period of the day was reserved for the classics: Cervantes's *Don Quixote*, or the novels of Zola, Hugo, Tolstoy, and Dickens, or sometimes the libretto of an opera to be performed at the Liceo Cubano. These were the texts Rafael enjoyed most. At the back of the factory, he could hear the lector but could not see him without looking up, and it was as if the characters were right there in the room, as if they were hovering somewhere above the scored benches in the warm and pungent haze. Sometimes, if the sun was in the right place and Rafael lifted his eyes, he glimpsed the white-clad figure in the distance, glowing like a benevolent spirit.

Rafael wondered whether he would make a good reader himself. He practiced when he was alone in the casita, sitting before Señora Estrada's cheval mirror and trying out different voices, different identities, catching himself in the eye now and then and wondering: Who is that?

The false head of Mrs. Rim, which I have completed but for the coating of beeswax, suggests a most unattractive woman: it is heavy and broad, the largest of all my wig-blocks. My regular customers have their own, made to measure; they are lined up on shelves in my studio, and in the murk of evening they loom like the impaled heads of traitors. During the day, of course, one sees that these forms are eyeless, noseless, as featureless indeed as the real persons. Each is labeled with its name, as if it were the bust of someone famous—but there are no famous people in Tampa. There are wealthy people, certainly, people who have inherited property and people who have made fortunes in the cigar industry or in agriculture or, like Mr. Henry B. Plant, in shipping, railroads, and resort hotels. There are those, too, who consider themselves leaders in the social throng, who make known to members of the fashionable set their regular day for receiving, and who give matinées, soirées, and private the-atricals as well as the most ceremonious of dinners, complete with menu cards, bonbonnières, and costly favors—but there is no one truly celebrated here. No one of note. Even my actresses, talented girls the pair of them, can pass through the streets unrecognized. I am grateful to be able to take dinner at the Hotel each night, for the regular fare of the citizens of Tampa is as flavorless as their charac-ters: potatoes, bread, suet puddings, overcooked meats. It comes as no surprise to me that many have embraced the flaked cereal of Dr. Kellogg, who believes that a bland diet reduces unhealthful carnal desire in general, and self-abuse in particular. And here is something else I have observed: the faces of Tampa's wealthy are singularly dull and flat, as if they have been sanded and waxed as smooth as my false heads. When one makes the acquaintance of Mrs. Rim, for example, the unattractiveness suggested by the Mrs. Rim block is borne out: she is all chins and bosom, all bulbous brow and large, low ears, and never an engaging thought in her brain.

Allow me to relate our conversation of some weeks ago, when

first she called at my premises. We had been discussing the specifications of her new frisette when all of a sudden she paused.

"Have you seen my Pomeranian?" she said.

"I beg your pardon?"

"My Pomeranian. My little Raisin."

And it was only then that I noticed the foxy-faced insect crawling about my floor and showing particular interest in the turned mahogany leg of one of my cabinets.

"Raisin," she said, "this is Mr. Gauntlet," presenting *me* to the *dog*, instead of vice versa. I wondered whether she owned a copy of *The Splendor of Eve*, and whether she had read the section on the etiquette of introductions, but I did not have long to muse on this, for the dog was extending its paw, and I was obliged to bend down and greet it like a gentleman. I could feel the soft bones as pliant as rose stems beneath the hair.

"How do you do, Monsieur Raisin," I said.

"Good boy!" said Mrs. Rim, beaming at each of us in turn and rewarding the animal with a lump of sugar. "I think we like you."

I was unsure to whom these remarks were addressed, and so I proceeded with my measuring.

Now, as I applied the wax to Mrs. Rim's custom-made block, I recalled a wig-block owned by my master in Paris, who taught me my trade. It was he who had plucked me from the Home for Foundlings after a number of women—first my mother, then a childless wife, then the Sisters at the Home—had discarded me. I was permitted to play with the block as a boy, as it was an outmoded piece of equipment, and gradually, as is the way with cherished objects, I cherished it so much that it came to be mine. It was constructed of leather and resembled a close-fitting hood, like that of a hangman, and there was a little door at the base of the skull that allowed tools to be kept within the head. It was empty when my master first gave it to me, but I filled it with things of my own, little keepsakes and mementos—a buckle from my outgrown shoes, one of my master's collar studs, some empty shells—until one day the head was so full it could accommodate nothing more, and when I shook it, it made no sound, and when I opened the door I found my treasures were jammed tight inside. I tried to prize them out with a knotting hook, but found I could not do so without damaging the contents. And so, to preserve them, I secured the little door with steel block-points, and it must have been around this time that my master, observing my interest in the leather head, and the way I kept it near me at all times, and my neat handiwork on the door, started to teach me his tricks and secrets.

As his apprentice I was to regard him as my parent, and during the seven years of my servitude I was to consider my time no longer my own property but my master's, and to employ it all in his service, except that part of it dedicated by law to public worship. He gave me a document recording these rules, and they seemed to me, at the age of nine (or thereabouts; I cannot tell how old I am exactly), an efficient means of simplifying the act of living. I can recall them by heart: *You are always to consult your master's credit and advantage, to be sober, careful, and diligent in his business, and neither to wrong him yourself, nor suffer him to be wronged by others; always remembering that you hope in time to become a master yourself, and that you must in reason expect to be treated by your apprentices and servants as you shall behave to your master during the course of your apprenticeship. Lastly, to enable you to continue in the performance of your duty, let me advise you to avoid the company of the idle, the vicious, and the profane, whose conversation and example cannot fail, sooner or later, to debauch your principles and drive you into unjustifiable and destructive practices, such as must end in your inevitable ruin. By pursuing the advice now given to you, you will, among other advantages, secure to yourself the favor of your master, the good opinion of the world, and what is above all—the blessing of Almighty God.* I never called him anything but Master, even after my apprenticeship was served; some habits cannot be discarded.

It is curious what we remember. For instance, although I can still recite the above rules, I do not remember the fate of my old wig-block with the tacked-shut door. Sometimes I recall the neat row of headless nails and I think, What dexterous work I performed when I was just nine years old, and how clever of my master to see that I had the talent to become a master myself. And sometimes I think, What treasures did I seal inside that head? And would they still be treasures, were I to force it open now? And I think it best that it is no longer in my possession.

Discarded at birth, I must have been an ugly child, and I know I am an ugly man, but unsightliness can work to one's advantage, because one is obliged to develop certain skills, certain aspects of the personality that remain stunted in more attractive fellows. I have my charm, and I have my hands. Women often comment on them. "You have a very gentle touch," they say. "Your hands are so agile, so soft." And in my mirrors they watch me dressing their false hair, and who knows what indecent thoughts are dancing beneath my work? I have a gift, the complexity of which can surprise me even after more than forty years in the trade. When I begin a new piece and I see my fingers weaving the caul, flickering behind the holes like white fish in a net, I wonder from whom I inherited this ability—and then I catch myself, for it does not pay to wonder about things we can never know. That which can be seen with the eye, felt with the hands, is far more trustworthy.

Would it surprise you to learn that we each of us carry a map of our own nature? Lift your hand to your head and you will find it: the private landscape of the skull. Is it not fascinating to consider that all the manifestations of the mind—the feelings, the passions, the very spirit of a man—are dependent upon the shape of the brain? I speak, of course, of the science of Phrenology. Over the years I have familiarized myself with the meanings of these various contours, and I find it useful to imagine the human head apportioned like cuts of meat. I like to read the personalities of my customers for my own amusement— I have no intention of establishing myself as a soothsayer—but it is also an effective means of detaching myself from the person whose scalp I must handle. If necessary, I am able to consider a customer simply as a map, as a head removed from a body, a voice, a banal conversation.

Ask me about any of my clients and I shall tell you their true nature. The porcine Mrs. Rim, mistress of the Pomeranian, for instance, has massively inflated organs of Alimentativeness, Marvelousness, and Self-Esteem, combined with stunted Perceptive faculties. The first explains her attachment to all things buttery and sweet, and hence her stoutness—a quality she seems determined to reproduce in the sugar-fed Raisin. (Whether she will succeed I cannot tell, for I have had no opportunity to examine the skull of the dog.) The overdeveloped Marvelousness, coupled with small Perceptives, manifests itself in her regular attendance at the meetings of a group of spirit-rappers. I never encourage her to relate their ridiculous goings on, but this does not prevent her from doing so, and she revels in telling me of her latest encounters with the Invisible Companions. As for Self-Esteem, where do I begin? It is difficult to draw her away from my mirrors, and never a fitting goes by that she is not wearing a new dress. She is at pains to endow the Tampa Rims with a whiff of nobility, making a great deal of the fact that she can trace her ancestors to one particular English village. "Hartlepool," she says—the word never failing to remind me of a magpie's throaty nonsense—"Hartlepool, England."

She seems unaware that the residents of this northern mess are known for their stupidity—a fact that corresponds nicely with her tiny Causality, the organ that measures the intellect. During the Napoleonic Wars a monkey was found washed up on a Hartlepool beach, the only creature to survive a ship-wreck. Being as unfamiliar with Frenchmen as they were with monkeys, the townsfolk took its screeches and grunts to be the language of the enemy, and they declared it a French spy, tried it, found it guilty of espionage, and hanged it.

"Oh yes," she says, "the Rims are of English extraction, like Queen Victoria."

As Sister Marie-Bernadette said when she found me toying with one of the more co-operative girl foundlings, the apple does not fall far from the tree.

The secrets I could tell about the good people of Tampa! On my books I have gentlemen who wish to look like ladies, ladies who wish to look like maidens, and ladies who wish to look like gentlemen. I have a range of entirely bald women, and several grandfathers who on business trips like to pass themselves off as bachelors. The heiress to the Perfection Pudding Blancher fortune is as mangy as a cur. A chanteuse at the Cherokee Club, admired for her raven tresses as much as for her husky contralto, has been gray for ten years. A certain swashbuckling thespian, able to make women swoon with a curl of his rouged lip, has been fitted for a chest-wig. A young lady bicyclist, who created a stir when she donned a skirt that could be buttoned around each leg, owns one of my Patent Fringes for Cycling, with Automatic Fastening. Such is the intelligence a man in my position amasses. I do not ask questions and I do not pass on information, and that, as much as my exquisite handiwork, is why I am the best in the trade.

"You would like a chignon identical to your pretty sister's, only bigger?" I say. "You wish to order for your husband a peruke that replicates the President's coiffure?" "When you look at your wife, you long to see the hair-style of your dear mother, God rest her soul? But of course. Leave the matter in my hands."

I never express surprise or shock at a request, but I find it best to avoid the eyes when matters are delicate. I examine the work in progress, or I toy with my price lists, as if the information is of no consequence. I can tell that my customers are grateful for this discretion, yet I can also tell that they know they have surrendered to me, given up a little of their power. I show them the skein of hair I will use for them, running my hands down its length, still avoiding their eyes.

"This is my vision for you," I say. "This will satisfy your needs."

It is as if I am addressing the hair itself. I invite them to touch it, to feel its quality, to compare it with their natural shade if it is their wish to appear natural. And this is the point at which I know I have snared them. They smile at the silky skein. They say, *Yes, this will do very well. Yes, this is just what I need. This will make me happy.* Their hands fly when they describe their fantastical notions to me. *Like this*, they say, drawing airy pictures of themselves, jerking like marionettes caught on their own strings. It is all I can do not to giggle.

The women are particularly stupid. They take great pains to apparel themselves in the latest fashions, devoting many hours to the adornment of the head's exterior, with no regard for its contents. Indeed, some of my gentleman customers feel at liberty to remark on the foolishness of the fairer sex. The physical proximity demanded by peruke fittings seems to provoke such comments, the gentleman imagining some sort of camaraderie between us. Given any encouragement, his observations are bound to lead to those of a more intimate nature, as if I am a common barber and might be interested in his conjugal deficiencies. I always quash this possibility with a simple and scientific explanation: after years of measuring the skulls of the weaker sex, I say, it is obvious why a woman is less agile intellectually than a man. Her brain is smaller.

With my lady customers, of course, I am charm itself, and occasionally I do business with true beauties. These women I do not flatter. With them I am quick, professional. They do not need me, you see; they do not require my services to turn heads. I do not flatter those who do not need me.

I know other secrets too, beyond those revealed in the privacy of my studio; things my customers would not tell a priest. These I glean during my after-hours work, when I supplement my stock of raw material. It is necessary for the expert Perruquier to have quantities of hair of every shade at his disposal, and I endeavor to see that the shelves in my storage room are always filled. This narrow space consists of many cedar-lined pigeon-holes, each pinned with a switch of hair for reference, and I call the room Bluebeard's Chamber to amuse my customers. I am often asked about my sources, but am coy with anyone wishing to know the provenance of her Imperceptible Hair-Piece, his Invisible Covering. I lower my head, I raise my eyes.

"Where do you think it comes from?" I ask, smiling a little. "Do you think I secrete it myself, like a silkworm, like a spider perhaps?"

And they laugh, and I laugh, and that is that.

From the cool of the parlor Marion heard a simple tune: the knife-sharpener's six-note whistle. Miss Harrow jumped, dropping her book. Marion could never decide whether her companion was afraid of the *afilador* or whether she simply disliked him. It was true, his clothes were sometimes less than clean, and Miss Harrow was wary of dirt of any kind—she had heard too much about the yellow fever epidemics, Marion suspected, ever to feel at ease here. Sometimes she wondered why Miss Harrow stayed in the dusty frontier town at all, why she did not move back to New York, where the sand did not creep into every crack like ants into a larder—and then Marion remembered that she was the reason Miss Harrow remained, and she was grateful to her for it.

She collected the kitchen knives, Miss Harrow's dress-making scissors, and some gardening tools and went outside. Señor Rivera lifted his grimy hat and smiled, and soon the whetstone was spinning and sparks were jumping from the blades. Marion studied his sun-darkened face. She had no idea how old he was or what his Christian name was, although he had been visiting Tampa all the time she had lived there. When the orange groves had covered the land around the house he had kept Jack's axes sharp, and Marion wished she could offer him work like that now, rather than her small domestic jumble. She liked the regularity of his visits, the way he appeared just when he was needed, his whistle calling the women from their houses. His cart was painted with curling flowers, and attached to one side was an umbrella that he raised in wet weather. He clenched a cigar between his teeth, and the sweet smoke rose as his wheel spun, and the blades made a sound like the sea in a shell. With his

long black coat and his black cap and his umbrella, he reminded
Marion of a figure on a German weather house: the little man who
comes outside to warn of rain.

He handed the knives back to her one by one, handle first. Would
there ever come a time, Marion wondered, when there would be no
more blade left, when it had been honed into nothing? But it was
important to keep a sharp edge, Jack used to tell her; blunt knives
caused the most accidents.

Jack had been full of such pieces of knowledge. He owned hundreds of books and subscribed to half a dozen journals and newspapers. That was how he had taught himself the basic skills of
horticulture: by reading about it. And, unlike Marion, he had never
felt obliged to begin at the start and read until he reached the end.
Rather, he flicked and browsed until he found the information he
sought, moistening his thumb and leafing through the pages like a
tycoon counting his fortune. Sometimes Marion envied him his ability to filter superfluous detail. It was as if, she thought now, he knew
he had to live life in a hurry. Often she had found him reading the
last pages of a novel, to see if it was the kind of book he would enjoy.

He had a similar way of eliciting information from people: leafing
through until he came to what he wanted. To a third party, this may
have seemed rather one-sided, even intrusive, but few took exception to Jack's conversational style. On the contrary, they seemed to
bask in the attention, and to offer all manner of personal facts. That
was how he had charmed Marion: by his interest in her, his tireless
questions. What was her earliest memory? Did she believe in God?
If she were a man, what would seem strange to her about women?
Sometimes she still heard his voice, as clearly as if he were standing
behind her. She would stare into his glass-fronted bookcases, which
lined the parlor walls, and convince herself that she could see his
reflection in them, close enough to touch.

When she was convalescing after the still-birth, Jack brought her
books and journal articles as if to cheer her with facts, as if to put
information in place of the little life that would not be known.

"Here's something that might interest you," he said, sitting on the edge of her bed, his weight pulling the covers so tight she could scarcely move. He opened an issue of the *Century Magazine* and showed her a photograph. "Rameses the Second," he said. "He lived three thousand years ago." She studied the face of the Egyptian king while Jack told her about the tomb's discovery, plucking snippets for her from the article, reading aloud the words of the Englishman who had unwrapped the mummy. "'Their gold coverings and their polished surfaces so plainly reflected my own excited visage that it seemed I was looking into the faces of my own ancestors,'" he said.

"But surely," said Marion, "once something is buried, it should stay buried?"

"Then how would we learn about other lives?" said Jack. And he pointed out the hair still visible on the head of Rameses II, and the shadow of a beard that had grown after death.

Marion knew he was only trying to entertain her, and she pretended to be interested in order to please him.

She knew what he would have said about her intention of going to a séance. Such gatherings were for those whose faith was not strong enough—they wanted proof of miracles. Jack's faith was the one thing that he had never questioned, that he had not needed to debate. During Sunday church services she had sometimes stolen a glance at him, but he had been so lost in the readings and the hymns that he had never noticed. At certain times of year, sun had penetrated the stained-glass window above their pew, casting red across Jack's features. Marion had felt that she was looking beneath his skin then, and she had been glad when the days were overcast.

⌒

Rafael knew he was lucky to be living with the Estradas and their two children, Miguel and Serafina. His bedroom was next to the kitchen, at the back of the casita. Like the other rooms, it was lined with buttery pine, and beneath the window was an altar to Oyá, goddess of wind, fire, and the thunderbolt, guardian of the gates of death, invoked whenever transformation was necessary. Rafael had thought that the old Cuban saints would have been discarded in this

new place—after all, it seemed that the saints had discarded Cuba—
but most families still had shrines in their homes, and few had taken
to Methodism or Baptism. Those who did attend church were from
wealthy and prominent families eager to establish contact with
wealthy and prominent Americans, and they had some degree of
success, inviting the right people to their fiestas and picnics, balls
and concerts, the most lavish of which appeared on the society
pages of the *Tampa Tribune*. There were even a few mixed mar-
riages.

From time to time, however, Rafael read of other events in Ybor
City: ceremonies at which animals were sacrificed, at which drums
beat out an agitated rhythm all through the night, and at which par-
ticipants died from frantic dancing. *To the onlooker, one journalist*
wrote, *the dancers appear possessed, but whether by the devil or by cheap
gin and marijuana cigarettes is a matter for some skepticism. Although
such voodoo is confined chiefly to the black Cubans, large numbers of immigrants from that troubled island, both white and colored, practice witchcraft.
This too has its origins on the Dark Continent, but has been grafted to a
debased form of Catholicism to produce a particularly profane hybrid.*

Rafael paused to look up the meaning of *debased* and *hybrid*.

*When Negro slaves came to Cuba in the 1500s, their new masters tried
to instill in them a Christian sensibility. And so the Negro bowed his head
and crossed himself, and knelt on sharp rocks or grains of corn before the
likeness of a Christian saint, sometimes for hours at a time. "How pious he
is!" his master observed, without realizing that, in his own savage mind,
the slave had fused the saint with a pagan deity. As the deception continued
unchecked, it spread to the white community, corrupting those very folk who
had been the black man's master. Everything about the cult is a falsehood,
for Saint Barbara is simply a disguise for Changó, god of lightning and
war; the Virgin Mary, Our Lady of Charity, is really Ochún, goddess of lust
and beauty, teacher of pleasure; Saint Francis is none other than Orunmila,
predictor of the future, cheater of death. Today in Ybor City homes, where
the drinking of alcohol is widespread even on a Sunday and where there is
always a loaded firearm at hand, it is common to find shrines to these false
gods, just as it is common for a Cuban to visit his local witch when he needs*

to attract a wife or place a curse. These sorceresses, known as brujas, *supply their customers with such outlandish instructions as placing a bird's nest on one's head and blowing into a bottle in order to alleviate pain; they also encourage gambling. One has only to think of the numerous "bolita shootings" in Ybor City of late to realize just how dangerous the encouragement of this loathsome pastime is, yet on the day of the lottery draws there are more customers waiting at the* bruja's *door than there are at the house where the Snake—that shameless Negress—plies her trade.*

The Snake was often mentioned in the press. Rafael had never seen her, but he had heard the cigar-makers talking, and once had watched them queuing at her door. The line curled across the wooden sidewalk and onto the street, leaving ripples in the sand as it advanced, hissing with impatience. The men rattled their coins in pockets and palms, and when they saw Rafael staring they called to him to come and take his turn, but he turned and ran home to the Estradas. As for the *bruja*—sorceress, seller of curses—he knew her as Señora Chiquita, a short, plump woman who lived on Sixth Avenue and did not mind children flying kites or jumping rope in the lot behind her house. Señor Estrada visited her when he needed relief from his back pain, or when he could not decide which *bolita* numbers to choose.

It was true that most Ybor City households possessed firearms; Señor Estrada kept a pistol, and there was a rifle standing at the back door like an umbrella.

"Is that why they're called shotgun houses?" said Rafael on his first day there, and the Estrada children giggled.

"No," said Señor Estrada, and he explained that when both doors were open it was possible to fire a bullet in the front and watch it shoot straight down the hall and out the back without touching anything inside.

"But you might hit someone out in the yard, or in the lane," said Rafael, and again the children giggled, and Señora Estrada smiled and said, "It's just an expression, Rafael." He blushed and felt quite ignorant of this new town, and at the same time a little disappointed.

"You should take some kind of weapon, though, even just a cane, if you're going very far at night," said Señora Estrada. "Not because of the people, but the dogs. And you might still meet an alligator or a snake. All this land was swamp once, and sometimes the creatures who lived here come back."

When she and her family arrived in the late 1880s, she told him, she carried a shotgun every night on her way to work. She began at the cigar factory at two A.M., preparing the tobacco for the men to roll, and so saw her husband only for a few hours each evening. All through the dark morning she stripped the tobacco, tearing the damp, papery leaves open at the tip, then taking hold of the stem and winding it around her hand like thread as the leaf split in two.

"Have you ever had to use it?" said Rafael, running his fingers over the mother-of-pearl inlay in the rifle. It was so smooth that he could not detect where the lustrous shell finished and the beech-wood began.

"Never," said Señora Estrada.

"Father fired at a tree root once," said Miguel. "You know the paradise tree, on Seventh Avenue?"

Rafael nodded, although he could not picture the spot.

"He thought it was an alligator."

"It was nighttime," said Señor Estrada.

Rafael said he would rather meet an alligator than a Spanish soldier, and everyone fell silent at that.

"Your family, they're in one of the camps?" Señora Estrada asked in a quiet voice.

Rafael nodded, and told them how his sisters and their husbands planned to re-establish themselves in Havana once the fighting was over. They had all invited their father to come and live with them, but he had refused: he had no desire to stay in the city any longer than was necessary. Perhaps, they had suggested, he would like to join Rafael in America? But he had refused that too, insisting that soon he would be able to leave the reconcentration zone, leave his job at the factory, and return to his little house with its thick, white-washed walls and its shrine to the saints and the Virgin Ochún. He would not accept that all the cane fields and many of the tobacco plantations were burned, and that Spanish soldiers and bandits infested the countryside, slaughtering the livestock and setting fire to crops and food stores, felling the banana trees, razing entire villages. Some places simply did not exist anymore.

The children had stopped giggling. "What about the police?" said Miguel.

Rafael gave a brief smile. "The police are as bad as the soldiers."

"I think it's time to go to bed," said Señora Estrada, and she led her children into the hallway, making sure she kissed them on the forehead.

"The Americans will help us," said Señor Estrada. "Soon, they'll send their soldiers. The lector said so."

Señor Estrada believed in the Americans as fervently as Rafael's mother had believed in Ochún, but then, he did not read the papers. Although he was an intelligent man, capable of spirited oratories at the Liceo Cubano, whenever Rafael offered him a section of newspaper he declined, saying he had no time to waste on reading. They had the *afilador* to bring them information, and of course there was the lector, which meant they could get on with their work, which meant they could donate more money to the cause.

"Then I'll tell you what the Americans think of us," Rafael said, and read to him from the *Tampa Tribune*, translating as he went: "The Latin group of humanity inclines toward excessive emotionalism, romantic violence, and un-American values. It has a volcanic tendency that is well-nigh universal. The Cubans and Spaniards are alike mercurial in temperament and quick to act. When subjected to the devilish influences of even one unprincipled socialist, communist, or anarchist, they are transformed into madmen."

Señor Estrada stroked his mustache. "That is one journalist's opinion—but there are plenty of decent Americans. They've been supplying Cuba with arms and munitions, and Mr. Plant saved the cigar factories from ruin two years ago." He told Rafael of the Spanish plan to stifle the cigar industry by stopping the export of Cuban tobacco. News of the embargo was delivered by the lector, and by the time he had finished reading, every man had stopped rolling, as if the supply of leaves had vanished already. The *torcedores* knew that if they had no leaves then they could make no cigars, and if they made no cigars then they earned no money, and if they earned no money then they could not keep providing the Revolutionary Party with funds for the war. "But then, Mr. Plant was persuaded to send his two steamships to Havana," said Señor Estrada. "The S.S. *Olivette* and the S.S. *Mascotte* left Cuba the day before the embargo took effect, their ballrooms and galleys and bedrooms and hallways bursting with tobacco leaves. The crew could hardly move. And when they arrived here, everyone went down to the port to celebrate, and to cheer Mr. Plant, who had saved us."

"Of course he agreed to send his ships!" said Rafael. "He needed to keep the cigar factories in business so his guests would keep coming and he would keep making money! Do you think they would visit a ghost town? Do you know how much two nights at his Hotel cost?"

Señor Estrada was silent.

"More than we earn in a week," said Rafael. "His guests flock to the pretty picnic spots around Tampa, but have you seen the signs there? At Sulphur Springs, and at Ballast Point? 'No Dogs or Latins Allowed.' 'No Dagos.' 'No Cuban Niggers.'"

"Mr. Plant is a good man," said Señor Estrada, closing his eyes and shaking his head as if willing Rafael to disappear. "He brought us the tobacco. He's a good man."

In the evenings Rafael sat in the parlor, reading the newspaper and books or writing letters to his family. Señora Estrada had screened the opening to the hallway with a beaded curtain, and even at night the tinkling lengths shimmered and moved with the currents of the house. Every few days she placed a vase of fresh flowers on the sideboard: roses, carnations, bougainvillea, jasmine, even the blooms of the passion vine—but never marigolds, which were the flower of death.

If the Estradas went out to a concert or a dance, Rafael stayed home with Miguel and Serafina, who were eight and eleven years old. Having no younger siblings himself, at first he did not know what he should do to pass the time with his charges, but it soon became clear that they had an array of activities in which they were determined to involve their boarder. Miguel liked to go to Seventh Avenue and watch the *bolita* dealers selling chances, the buyers becoming more frantic as the day of the draw approached. Some men spent all they earned on trying to guess the right number, he told Rafael, buying chances rather than buying food for their families: just ask the baker how little bread he sold on *bolita* day. Those tiny ivory balls made you crazy; every so often there was a stabbing or a shooting.

Serafina made kites from sheets of Chinese paper and cigar-box sticks. She was restless on calm days, standing in the yard and frowning at the motionless corn stalks, and as soon as they began to move in a breeze she was off to the vacant lot behind the *bruja*'s house, kite tails dancing as she ran. She challenged other children to mid-air fights, attaching razor blades to her kites and maneuvering the strings so as to sever those of an opponent. Even though he pretended he was too old for such games, Rafael was as delighted as any of the children when a vanquished kite drifted away from its owner, away over the black oaks to the sea, the colored paper shining like a church window, the string falling in coils and tangles to earth.

When Señor Estrada visited the *bolita* house, the cockfights, or the saloon with its back-room gambling tables and its portraits of coy shepherdesses and milkmaids, his wife stayed at home. Rafael liked those evenings best, when Señora Estrada sat with him and the children, sewing on lost buttons and mending tears, making everything right again. On winter nights she warmed a brick in the stove, and at first Rafael had not dared ask the purpose of this curious dish, deciding it must be something mothers did in Ybor City. Now, however, he considered the procedure quite normal, and it struck him that the strangest of actions can come to seem acceptable if they are repeated often enough. Tonight, as he sat in the kitchen, he watched Señora Estrada open the stove door and drag out the heated brick, testing it with a quick tap of her finger as if it were a loaf of bread. Satisfied, she wrapped it in an old blanket and gave it to Rafael.

"Take this out to Pedro, would you?"

In the yard the hens were shaking their metallic feathers and the mourning doves were calling in the mango trees. Somewhere close by a frog chirped, looking for its old home. Rafael opened the door to the spider monkey's cage and the creature ran to him, jumping onto his knee, then his back and his shoulder, winding its little spider hands through his hair. Rafael placed the brick inside the cage and the monkey scurried to it, chattering and cooing, hugging the bundle to itself. The blanket was the same color as the monkey's fur, and Rafael wondered if it mistook the hard, heavy block for its baby, or perhaps its parent.

At the end of February 1898, when Rafael turned fifteen, the Estradas gave him a set of dominoes.

"Your poor mother," said Señora Estrada, and she squeezed his hand.

Rafael did not know what to say, so he admired the cake baked by Serafina, and the little box of bone tablets that were as smooth as the finest soap. Miguel gave him a slingshot that he had made from a rubber band and the tongue of an old shoe. It was a powerful weapon, he told Rafael, not like the Y-shaped ones American boys used; loaded with a glass marble, it would kill a bird. When the season was right, he promised, he would take Rafael to the wild berry bushes where the mockingbirds fed. He lisped as the spoke; he had just lost a tooth. This he had placed beneath his pillow for Señor Rat, who would exchange it for a penny in order to build his house of teeth. That evening, while Miguel was outside breaking in the slingshot and the spider monkey was cowering in its cage, Rafael and Serafina played dominoes. Their games crept across the parlor's pine floors and rugs, snaked down the hall, made bone patterns in the bedrooms.

On Sundays, Rafael went for walks. He put on his fine flannel suit and strolled along the better streets of Tampa like a gentleman, his pocket watch keeping time against his ribs. He wore soft gray gloves, through which it was almost impossible to detect the scent of tobacco leaves, but he wished there was some way of removing the stains from his fingers.

One mild day as he was walking down Fortune Street, the spreading oaks shielding him from all but coin-sized spots of sun, a flash of silver caught his eye. There it was again, flickering like a fish leaping into the air. He looked up and saw a woman at an upper window of a handsome frame house. Next to the window was a citrus tree just beginning to flower, and the petals were the same shade as the woman's long, loose hair: palest ivory. Her silver brush flashed in the sun, her hand moving down and up, down and up over the white-blond lengths. She did not see Rafael, but gazed at the open window as if it were a mirror.

PART II

The Wig-Maker's Craft

April 1898

One of my little sidelines—it is true, I have many tricks up my sleeve—is the manufacture of hair jewelry. These days it is fashionable to wear, say, a brooch or a pair of earrings woven from the hair of a sweetheart or a deceased loved one. A number of disastrously home-crafted examples may be seen on the earlobes, wrists, cuffs, and bosoms of the citizens of Tampa, but thankfully there are some wise souls who choose to employ a professional, an Artist in Hair, to do the job.

Often these customers come to me with very stubborn ideas about the piece they want—both grief and love, in my observation, bring out obstinacy in a person—but I am happy to advise them on a better choice. I have a range of mounts and settings from which, with my discreet guidance, they may select. I have bracelet clasps and earring mounts, empty brooches and watch guards and cuff links—for although it is mainly women who order such pieces, occasionally a grief-stricken father presents himself, or a new widower, or a lovesick youth. My hair jewelry customers are all mad with sorrow or lust, and sometimes I find it hard to tell the difference between the two.

They want miracles, of course. They bring me their oily little wads of hair and expect me to transform them into works of art. The lock is usually unevenly clipped, and it is a constant vexation that they never, but almost *never*, take it from the nape of the neck, where it is softest and finest. Perhaps it is more difficult to get at the nape of a cadaver than it is to snip a tuft from the brow, and perhaps the lovesick wish to look into the cherished one's eyes as they take their mementos; how would I know what occurs in such intimate scenes? But the coarser the raw material, the more difficult it is to work, and they do not realize that Grandpa's wiry forelock simply will not lend itself to the contours of a weeping willow or a fleur-de-lis. I am always gladdened when they say that it is a child who has died, for the hair of children is the easiest to manipulate.

By now, I am sure you are beginning to see what an inventive type I am—and this quality is of especial use in the manufacture of hair jewelry. At the moment, for instance, I am at work on an order for the widow of a naval captain lost at sea. She clipped a lock of his hair some years ago (before he left on a more successful voyage), and when first she visited my premises she withdrew this mousy material from a handkerchief saying, "I'd like a pair of earrings, but I'm not sure I have enough." Of course, the meager tuft would not have covered the private parts of an aphid, but I assured her that if she chose a suitable design there would be no difficulties.

"When the hair is limited, Madame, the item is all the more precious. In these cases I recommend an open weave, so that the finished piece is hollow." I paused, lowered my voice. "I personally find this most pleasing to the eye—one may more readily observe the delicate workmanship." And I showed her the appropriate pages in my catalogue, pointing with my little finger to the illustrations. "These, for instance: three dainty globes of hair, hanging smallest to largest from a little hook." She was nodding, and I played her a little longer. "Think of three very tiny fish-nets, Madame, in which you may capture memories of your dear husband," I said, although the weave always made me think of the stockings of a whore.

In the end, the late captain's contribution accounted for just one of the tiniest baubles; the other five were fashioned from miscellaneous left-overs of a corresponding shade. In my workshop, nothing is discarded.

Any kind of epidemic is excellent for the business of commemorative jewelry, but Tampa has been free of serious outbreaks for some years. (They are still common in Ybor City, of course, where the drains are full of mosquitoes and the standards of hygiene are questionable, but few of my customers hail from that part of town.) In the absence of disease, the other condition for which one hopes is war, and I am delighted to report that I have received a number of orders from the fiancées or mothers of American soldiers keen for adventures in Cuba. This began in the middle of February when a battleship, the U.S.S. *Maine*, was blown up in the harbor of Havana, devastating the waterfront buildings and shattering thousands of windows in the city. The Spanish were blamed for the explosion, but I hear whispers that spontaneous combustion in the coal bins may have caused it. Could the bungling Spaniards in their foppish uniforms have master-minded such an attack? Unlikely, but the press has ignored the possibility of accident, and so outrage against Spain is running high, with sons keen to spill their blood, and mothers hungry for a family hero. It seems we may have a war on our hands, which could be an even greater boon than an outbreak of yellow fever; according to the papers it will not be long before America pokes her virtuous nose into the affairs of the Latins. I am not a political man, and it matters not a jot to me whether the Spanish or the Cubans or a tribe of naked savages govern that sultry southern isle. Where such affairs impinge on my own comfort, however, I care a great deal, and as the winter season is again drawing to a close, the guests departing the Hotel and leaving me in peace, I cannot help but hear rumors that Mr. Plant will allow the military to stay here. It is enough to make one applaud the ravings of Mr. Trueblood's American Peace Society.

Perhaps you wonder why I have seen fit to diversify to such a degree. The answer is that mine is a profession on the wane. I dream of the days when the Perruquier was called upon to produce elaborate constructions: wigs supported by padding and springs, built on frames, ornamented with ribbons and fruit and feathers, garnets and diamonds and pearls. My master told me of such creations, which his own master had seen as a child in the 1770s: wigs topped with frigates in full sail, garlanded wigs with water bottles concealed in their folds so that the flowers might remain fresh, wigs so high that door openings had to be raised. Coiffures were dressed *au bandeau d'amour* or *au désir de plaire*, *à la sylphide*, or *à la Dauphine*, which featured a chignon in the form of a *croix de chevalier* with a curl *à la Sultane* falling onto the neck, two side curls, and two shoulder curls, the whole being adorned with ribbon and a rose of diamonds crossed by a row of pearls. In such a wig, many a lady of society riding in her sedan chair dispensed with the seat entirely and squatted on the floor. The Perruquiers were the darlings of the Court and of the aristocracy, and ours was the privilege of touching royal hair, ours the right to kiss the brides whose fantastical head-dresses we had conceived.

My creations are not elaborate. They are intricately constructed, it is true, but they are small in scale, plain, discreet. These days the chignon is ordered mainly by older customers wishing to maintain a pretense started in their youth; the younger women rely on their own locks at the back of the head, choosing a curled fringe or a transformation to soften the brow if they do not wish to sacrifice hair in front. Whether I am called upon to produce an ornate chignon or a simple fringe, however, it is my job to make the people of Tampa appear ordinary. Many are secretive about their visits to my studio; they are reluctant to admit that they require my services. In some cases even the spouse is deceived, and the illusion of a full head of hair is maintained until death—and even then, occasionally, the truth is not revealed. Once in the Paris Morgue, I recall, I was about to cut a blond mane, only to find that it came away all of a piece as soon as I took hold of it, and that the woman was as bald as the moon. I turned to see Monsieur Bourgeon holding his stomach and shaking with silent laughter, bowing slowly back and forth as if accepting applause for his little joke. He made me reposition the hair-piece, however; the owner had stipulated in her will that she was to be buried in it, and that her body was not to be viewed without it.

From time to time I attend a funeral and see my own handiwork displayed in the coffin. Naturally, on this point I am as silent as the guest of honor, but I enjoy the reward of observing a relative drawn to one of my creations, stroking and kissing it as if it were genuine, sometimes even clipping a lock to treasure as a keepsake. And now and then I am treated to a delightful postscript: the bereaved person brings the lock to me to have made into a piece of memorial jewelry, a piece of wearable grief, and I supplement it with hair from yet another source, so that by the time the brooch is pinned to the client's bosom or the earrings hooked through her lobes there is no telling who is being commemorated. Without effort I can call to mind half a dozen pieces of mourning jewelry worn by Tampa widows— charming little brooches and bracelets and pendants fashioned from the hair of donkeys, or from the locks of hale peasant girls who are presumably still alive and well and milking cows in Sweden.

I have scant fondness for children, and it is a profound irritation when they accompany their mothers to my studio. However, in order to run a successful business one must sometimes feign interest in that which repels, and so I listen to Miss Susie describing her new kitten, or to Master Douglas explaining his favorite fishing spot, or to Miss Katie reciting some piece of doggerel about *fairies blithe*, and the *gauzy nebula which films the pensive sky*.

"Delightful," I murmur. "Such an enchanting child."

If one maintains an open mind where offensive tasks are concerned, one is sometimes rewarded. Let me outline the origins of what is now another profitable source of revenue.

One day, when a Mrs. Crouch (large Combativeness; negligible Agreeableness) called to collect her new chignon, there was a child attached to her hand.

"And whom have we here?" I said, smiling my Goulet smile.

"This is Miss Crouch," said Mrs. Crouch. "She's a little upset today," she added in a loud whisper. "Her brother has cut off Janie's hair."

"Families!" I smiled. "I hope the mischievous scamp has apologized to Janie."

"No he hasn't," bawled the child.

"But he has been properly disciplined, Mr. Gilty, have no concerns about that," said Mrs. Crouch.

"Discipline is so important," I agreed, eyeing the dirty fingers smearing the front of my counter. "I hope you will not think me forward, Madame, but may I ask whether Janie's hair was very long?"

Mrs. Crouch frowned.

"It was down to her waist," sniffed the child. "It was all in ringlets."

"You see, Madame," I continued, "I may be able to make you an offer for the clippings." Seeing her frown deepen, I added, "I'm sure that it is of the most glorious color and quality, if your own tresses and those of Miss Crouch here are any indication."

"This is Janie," said Mrs. Crouch, taking a doll from the child's arms and holding it under my nose. Its dress was stained, and it smelled of bedding that has not been changed in a month. She removed its hat, and indeed the hair was all but shorn, and the bisque skull quite visible.

"Give her back!" screeched the child. "Don't let him touch her!"

"Now now, my dear, I would not consider it," I said in my most soothing voice. "But you know, I might be able to repair your dolly for you. I might be able to make her some new ringlets, in any color you like."

Mrs. Crouch bent down to the sulking child. "What do you think, Amanda?" she said. "Shall we let nice Mr. Gilty fix Janie?"

There was a pouty silence, then: "Will it hurt?"

"Oh no, not a bit," I said. "Does your hair hurt when it grows?"

The child thought for a moment, then shook her head.

"Well then, that is how it will be for Joanie."

"Janie."

"Yes. Janie will be the prettiest doll in Tampa. Shall we say two dollars?"

And so another lucrative industry was born.

There is a belief that the hair of cadavers is of inferior quality. In my opinion this rumor springs from the unease the vain feel when confronted with death: they do not wish to entertain the thought that their postiche has been fashioned from the tresses of a corpse. Between you and me, I am happy to confirm that the dead of hospitals and prisons provide a reliable supply, although I suspect some wardens make a quick job of it, for often the quality of the cutting is not all it might be; the hair is jumbled, and must be turned so that roots are level with roots and points with points. The mortician's clippings are tidier, but even there I suspect a certain amount of wastage. I have attempted to remedy this by offering to clip the hair myself, but Mr. J. M. Tucker, Jr., Funeral Director and Embalmer, has never allowed me access to his Madison Street premises. Since morticians have become Funeral Directors and Embalmers, I find, they have become convinced of their status as artists, and more possessive of their cadavers. It was of no use to tell Mr. Tucker of my many years' experience in the Paris Morgue.

"It's not my concern, Mr. Giblet, how they do things over there," he said, his nostrils quivering with distaste at the word *morgue*. "I cannot allow all and sundry to handle my clients."

And so, every month, I receive a parcel of hair from Tucker, along with a bill.

It was my master who first made me witness death. There were the Sisters at the Home for Foundlings, of course, who were always directing my attention to that skinny man they kept nailed to their walls, but it was my master who made me a spectator to the startling colors and smells of death, its leakages, its coarse noises. I was eleven when he sent me to the mortician. Monsieur Bourgeon was in the middle of a job—and, I soon saw, in the middle of an elderly gentleman—and he had his back to me, his elbows extended as if he were knitting a tricky stitch.

"You can have those," he said, motioning with his head to three sheeted forms. Two were female: one aged around twenty with dark blond hair, and one elderly and pure white—the rarest shade, and the most expensive. The third was a boy about my own age. His brown hair was just long enough to be of use, and I snipped as closely to the scalp as possible. He had dirt under his nails, I noticed, and a grazed elbow, which had almost healed. As I lifted the head to get at the nape, he let out a long, low groan, his mouth falling open. I jumped back at once, and the half-shorn skull thudded against its porcelain bed. Without turning from his work Monsieur Bourgeon said, "Gases in the stomach cavity." For some reason I said, "Thank you," but neither Monsieur Bourgeon nor the boy replied, and so I took up my shears once more. When I had finished I looked at the three heads protruding from their sheets, as bald as my master's wig-blocks, and it struck me that they now looked so alike they could have been a family.

From then on I was sent to Monsieur Bourgeon on a regular basis, and as he became accustomed to my presence he began to show me certain points of interest: arms so bloated that bangles had to be cut away, curious tattoos, enlarged hearts. It was in his morgue, he told me, that Dr. Andrew Combe, one of the most important authors on the noble science of Phrenology, had conducted much of his study. "He was a suicide man," said Monsieur Bourgeon, and indeed, when I consulted the writings of Dr. Combe, I unearthed his Paris observations: that in the suicides he had found Hope generally small, with Cautiousness and Destructiveness large. As my interest in Cerebral Physiology grew, Monsieur Bourgeon allowed me to examine the skulls of murderers and madmen, noblemen and thieves, prostitutes and priests. In his cool rooms I learned to identify the contours and boundaries of all the important organs: Cautiousness, Ideality, Destructiveness, Parental Love, Imitation, Secretiveness. Sometimes he would save an especially engaging case for me, even if it meant delaying a funeral by a day or two. I was sorry when he died; his successor was far less thoughtful.

But to return to the question of my sources: in addition to Mr. Tucker's morgue hair—I always refer to it as such, especially in our correspondence, for I know how he despises the expression—I am sometimes able to purchase stock directly from the bereaved. I visit their homes dressed in my fine morning suit, as lustrous as a blue-bottle. A funeral is an expensive event, I sigh, and at an appropriate moment I present them with my card.

"He was a good husband, a good provider," I say. (Or, as the occasion demands, *She was a loyal daughter*, or *a devoted mother*, or *a delightful child*—you see the pattern.)

"Yes," sniffs the widow, her nose dripping like an Ybor City water pump. "I don't know what we'll do now."

"Perhaps there is one way he could still assist you, Madame," I say. "One last time he could provide for you, in your darkest hour."

She stops blubbering for a moment and regards me with her puffed, piggy eyes. "Oh yes?" she says.

And so I explain, as gently as possible, that God blesses us with different talents, and that some of us—I gesture at the corpse—are blessed with a fine, thick head of hair. And there are other of God's children who are not so fortunate. I have a client, I say, whose son has lost his hair due to severe illness. In addition to the ongoing rigors of his malady, Master Tommy must also endure staring in the street and the taunts of other children. I have offered to make the little mite a wig, yet I have not found the color to match his. I look at the corpse. A piece of your loved one would be kept alive, I murmur.

Master Tommy is something of a chameleon; he has been ash-blond, chestnut, black-haired, a redhead, and mouse brown. He has even been a girl.

In addition to the hair of the dead, I also buy that of novitiates entering the convent, and here again the lengths are often jagged, indicating a great deal of waste. I would prefer to cut this hair myself—as well as ensuring better-quality stock, I think it would benefit the novitiates to have contact with a man before they take their final vows, and I would find it great sport to whisper in the ear of the prettiest, "Are you sure?"—but as yet no convent has come around to my way of thinking.

The bulk of my stock I purchase from the peddlers. These men travel from country to country every spring and summer, buying the hair of peasants who have no use for it—Germany and Sweden for blond; Italy, Spain, and France for brown and red. It was a job I myself performed for some years, when I was a young man and still went where my master told me—but I shall come to that story in due course. The recent and lingering popularity of enormous chignons and waterfalls attached to the top of the head led to the harvesting of a great deal of hair on the Dark Continent, for the peasant follicles of Europe could not keep pace with demand. This filthy material, clipped from the heads of one of the world's most squalid populations, was shipped to London for purification, after which it was perfectly serviceable. Unfortunately, the practice of cleansing the Hottentot hair in London was disallowed because of the stench produced—as if that city does not create a multitude of odors!—and it is this ridiculous piece of legislation, I believe, that has prompted the virtual disappearance of the chignon, and the return of the waterfall to stingy proportions.

I have an arrangement with several local barbers and hairdressers, including Zefirelli, the Italian at the Tampa Bay Hotel, who is adept at persuading the guests to have just a *little* more off. Let me tell you a story that still brings a chuckle to my throat, even though it took place some years ago now. A female Hotel guest had her hair cut, removing a substantial length. Zefirelli saved it for me, and after a good deal of haggling I laid the length of chestnut in Bluebeard's Chamber. Two weeks later this same woman came to my studio, explaining that she had been invited to a grand ball, and wished to have a hair-piece made. I have just the right material, Madame, I said, and showed her the skein of chestnut. What luck! said she. And so I made a quick return on my investment, and she wore her own hair to the ball, and was much admired.

Do not imagine that I am the only man in history to behave in this manner. There is a limited amount of hair in the world, and someone in my position must be canny and resourceful; it is a matter of survival. I often think of Mausolus, King of ancient Caria, who one day discovered that his treasury was almost empty. Did he hold his head in despair? Did he retreat to his private chambers and drink away the remaining funds? Did he flee into exile, leaving his people without a ruler? No. Inventive man that he was, he decreed a universal shaving of the heads of his subjects and had the hair made into an array of wigs. These he sold back to his people, thus replenishing the treasury and saving Caria from ruin.

I have one final source of raw material, more covert than the others: I collect hair combings from the refuse of Tampa. This method is not of my own invention, for it has been used by wig-makers since wig-makers have existed, and it can yield a surprising amount of hair, provided one knows where to look. When it is dark, I slip from my glittering minaret and, dressed from head to toe in black, proceed to a residential part of town. In the sleeping streets I make myself indistinguishable from the bricks and the clapboards; I am invisible in the shadows. I thread my way along the narrow lanes behind the houses, along the sandy tracks that stink of tomcats and garbage, stopping at each yard and locating the trash pit or rubbish heap. I cannot help but pick up secrets; they are tangled in the combings. I know which husbands visit brothels and which content themselves with the whores who wander the scrubland at night. I know which debutantes bleach their fuzzy upper lips and which gentlemen sleep in mustache nets. There is a woman who writes shameless letters to her brother-in-law, and a butcher who writes poetry to the son of a stockbroker. I can tell you which pastor uses rouge and which husband clips advertisements for ladies' foundation garments from his wife's journals. I know who takes valerian in unnatural quantities, and who takes potency powders. Once I found a still-born child, but the little hair I could recover was too downy for my purposes.

Sometimes, when I return from an evening's sorting and sit sipping brandy in the bar, or replying to my correspondence in the Ebony Writing and Reading Room for Gentlemen, or preparing to visit my actresses, I feel I am still knee-deep in refuse. I can smell it rising from my pores, and I wish myself back in Paris, or back harvesting the hair of the Continent's pretty peasant girls. And then I think of all the combings I have gathered that night, and I imagine the beautiful switches and torsades I will construct from them, the *plicaturas*, the Spanish coils, the cache-peignes, all the elegant deceptions, and I also imagine how they will transform my drab and lardy clientèle, and how some of them might end up on the heads of their original owners, and I smile.

I am a well-traveled man. Unlike the plump citizens of Tampa, with their vulgar upholsteries and their sticky children, their poundcakes and their pink teas and their lapdogs, I have seen the world. Sometimes, when I am in a melancholy frame of mind, I recall the happy months I spent free from the pressures of Paris, tied to nobody. I was a young man then, and each spring my master sent me to harvest hair in the rural areas of Italy or Germany, Scandinavia or France. I moved from village to village, setting myself up at fairs or in marketplaces, and the local women and their daughters queued to have their turn in my hands. I always found lodgings in their homes, or at least in their barns, and someone was always willing to feed me.

And yet other times, if my mood is particularly dark, I think I was not welcome at all, and I remind myself that one should not romanticize certain periods of one's life. I was given food and a bed, perhaps, but was I not as hated as disease? And the prettiest girls, who allowed me to touch their glorious hair, did they not shrink from the blades at their necks as if I might clip away their souls? And I force myself to remember properly. In truth, I could not abide their whimpering and sniveling, their shaking shoulders, which made me cut crooked. The sullen creatures were paid: unlike some unscrupulous buyers who bought their hair with beads or gaudy scarves, I gave them coins for their trouble—and what is more, I left them a fringe. Once they donned a headscarf, none but a lover would know of their deception.

With younger girls, in order to negotiate a fair price, it was always best to conduct business without the mother present. "May I have a little water?" I would ask. "I believe I have a hair caught in my throat." And while the shrewd woman was away I would bargain with the daughter.

"I should think we have enough for more than one peruke here," I would say, cupping the hair in one hand and wielding my scissors. "That will bring a tidy sum for you, Mademoiselle." Sometimes the brainless creature would squirm and protest that I should not begin cutting as we had not agreed on a price, but I would assure her that I was a professional and would not dream of cheating her or her charming mother. And then I would cut, taking the hair away in a single hank so that it would not have to be turned. "A little scantier than I had estimated," I would murmur, holding the severed tresses at arm's length. "And look, here is a gray hair, and here another"—I always traveled with a store of these in my cuff. "Mademoiselle, such a crop is of little interest to my master, who is a man of the most exacting standards." Then, just as the creature began to weep, I would drop my hands to my sides and say, "All right, Mademoiselle, now calm yourself. We'll not mention this to your mamma, have no fear. I'll pay you ten sous, although it's more than my master will pay me. There now."

It astonished me how easily these girls could lie. The mother would return, a tumbler of water in her red hands, and the daughter would smile and say, "Look, Mamma, I have earned eight sous." And she would bind her shorn head with a scarf and walk around the fair as if she were the May Queen.

I tied the hanks with cotton, then placed them in my sack. As I went from village to village it became heavier and heavier, and when I was alone I would think of all the girls whose best feature I carried with me. And what about a pretty mouth, you say, or a clear eye? But a woman's hair is truly her best feature, for it does not nag and it does not refuse. I could recall the owner of each skein, and sometimes I would unbind them from their lengths of cotton and inhale their scent, and it would be as if Rosa or Birgit or Blanche were standing before me. I had favorites, of course, and these I kept in the deep lid of my traveling case, for ease of access. One smelled of grass and of freshly turned soil; another of fallen leaves; a third of clean straw; a fourth of walnuts. I enjoyed myself with these souvenirs as often as possible while traveling; I knew that when I returned to Paris my first job would be to wash every hank I had harvested, and my obliging girls would be rinsed into the gutters.

This is my favorite time of year, despite the approaching heat, for it is the official end of the winter season—the Hotel is closing for summer, and all the guests are departing. The rooms are being dismantled, the silk rugs rolled up, the furniture sheeted, and the mirrors covered as if there has been a death. The orchestra is folding away its music, including the "Tampa Bay Hotel Galop" by Mrs. J. M. Murphy—and not a moment too soon, for I have awoken humming this fatuous piece on several recent mornings. The Ballroom chandeliers are swathed in white cambric and will hang from the ceiling all summer like clouds. The thirty thousand yards of carpet once intended for the English Royal Family are being swept; the throne chair of Marie Antoinette and the Queen Victoria sofa are indistinguishable from any other pieces of furniture. And yet, while I am looking forward to my solitude, I do not relish the thought of sorting through the steaming refuse of Tampa. Already I have spent four summers trying to ignore the stench, and I do not intend to pass a fifth in this manner. My business in all its little facets is becoming so successful that I cannot keep pace with demand, and I need more and more raw material in order to keep Bluebeard's Chamber stocked—yet I do not wish to keep digging through garbage for combings. Apart from anything else, I find I have less and less time in which to pursue hobbies such as my actresses. Therefore, I have decided to hire an assistant, and have today placed an elegant announcement in the *Tampa Tribune:*

> *Assistant Sought.*
> *Must be nimble-fingered, discreet, and available*
> *during evening hours. Apply in person to*
> *Monsieur Lucien Goulet III, Wig-Maker,*
> *No. 618, Franklin Street, Tampa.*

The word *wig* appears, that is true. It was a difficult decision to reach, for I know that a good number of my regular customers scrutinize the newspaper announcements, looking for the latest faith healer or fortune-teller, checking the venues of the meetings of spirit-rappers or the price of vanishing creams. They are used to my cosseting them with words like *imperceptible*, *Perruquier*, *invisible*, *waterfall*, *chignon*, and I am at pains to avoid blunt truths in their presence. However, as I do not anticipate a surplus of intellect amongst my prospective assistants, I decided that *Perruquier* would simply confuse—and so *Wig-Maker* I am.

The men who replied to my announcement were an overwhelming disappointment. Dolts, drunkards, greedy rogues, and not a clean collar amongst them. Some, I am certain, were refugees who have fled here from Cuba—and not cigar-makers, who at least attempt to support themselves, but jobless wretches who are beginning to clog this town like scum in a drain. In my observation, that sorry race would be incapable of governing their island even if the Spanish were ousted. One has only to visit Ybor City to see how they drink themselves blind at the saloons and bawdy-houses, and stroll into work at whatever hour suits them, and bet all their earnings on little ivory balls, and shoot each other because of them. A number of Negroes applied for the position, which puzzled me, as I did not think they could read. After I had interviewed eleven men, all impossible, I even considered employing the twelfth despite the fact he was Negro. His skin was very black but he was well spoken, and I decided I should not be prejudiced but should keep an open mind. After all, I reasoned, he would be less visible at night. And then, as he spoke, I realized that the wily Negro can commit so many crimes because he is difficult to see in the dark; he uses his skin to his sly advantage. And I concluded that the twelfth candidate, no matter how well spoken, was not to be trusted.

I saw over twenty men on Tuesday morning alone. Just as one left and I settled back to work, greasing my fingers with the pig fat that lets me manipulate the hair with ease, the bell jangled and another man entered. I do not know how many times I had to wash my hands. Eventually my small front room was overrun with candidates. The smell of hair oil and perspiration assaulted me long after they had left, but I did not dare throw open the windows and the doors for fear of a draft—a catastrophe, as you can imagine, for my stocks of hair and feathers. As if that weren't distressing enough, late in the day a woman had the audacity to apply for the position. She was in her early forties, and may well have been pretty in the first flush of youth, but time is not fair to the fair sex. Her hair was scraped into a knot, and beneath the thin strands the scalp was clearly visible, flaking and unclean. She wore a pair of ill-fitting dentures that caused her to squash every sibilant, and more than once during our interview I was obliged to blot my face with my handkerchief. The selfish creature appeared unaware of this, neither directing her spittle away from me nor attempting to modify her speech. She had produced a dozen children, she told me, eleven of whom had survived, ranging

in age from four to four-and-twenty. From the sour, milky odor that
arose from her I concluded she was still nursing the four-year-old—
and yet, despite these failings, I did consider employing her, so
dejected was I. Perhaps a woman would be suited to such a position,
I reflected. Women are lighter on their feet and quieter than men;
their hands are small and quick, their natures devious.

"I am a forward-thinking man," I said, "and if I am convinced of
your suitability I am prepared to overlook the fact that you are a
female. I must tell you, the work can be very dirty—"

"I don't mind dirt, sir."

"That I can see," I continued, "but one must also be quiet and
deft, with a solid constitution."

"Do you have children, Mr. Gully?" she asked.

Somewhat taken aback, I replied that I had not been so blessed.

"No one who has raised eleven children can afford to be squeam-
ish," she said. "And I can be as quiet as a mouse, for fear of waking
the little ones, and as for deftness, well, these hands have sewn more
tiny garments than I can count."

I observed her outspread hands, which were indeed small and
able-looking. "You would be working at night," I said. "And out of
doors."

The smile faded from her lined face. "I'm afraid I don't quite follow, sir."

"You would be collecting waste hair for me, from trash pits."

"Oh," she said, and I am certain she wrinkled her nose. The poor
do not really want to work, you see. There is no shortage of jobs;
they are simply too choosy. "So I wouldn't be assisting you in the
workroom, then? There's no sewing or handwork involved?"

"As I said, you would be required to collect raw material for me."

She nodded, her small, mean eyes roaming my studio. "You make
such pretty things," she said. "Such lovely disguises. They look so
real." Her gaze returned to me. "I'm sorry, sir. I'm not sure such
work would be safe for a lady."

And so another half hour of my time was squandered.

I made my way to the mineral baths at the Hotel, intending to isolate myself in that cool chamber from all the intrusions of the summer, but a gardener stopped me at the door.

"They're being cleaned today, sir," he said, and I could not enter.

I wandered along the pathways in the garden, seeking shelter beneath the guavas and the oleanders, but the sun was in the wrong place, everything was wrong. Wherever a tiny patch of shade was to be had, there I found a gaggle of soldiers whose crude conversations—I am certain I was not imagining this—faltered and died as I approached. The kennels—*the most complete dog accommodations of any hotel in existence*—were empty of their wintertime assortment of poodles and pugs. Even the screeching peacocks were silent, contenting themselves with crossing my path as if to trip me, and rattling their plumage to ward me off, each feather a dark eye. I kicked my toes into the crushed shells as I went, spraying the bony fragments to the left and the right, leaving marks that suggested the disposal of something heavy. By and by I came to the Casino building, and I saw that one of the doors was open. Inside, the floor had been rolled back to reveal the swimming pool. It was drained of all water, and I listened for a moment, then descended the ladder and walked across the inclined floor, the china tiles and gutters and the slab seats surrounding me like a vast embalming room, and I thought of the Paris Morgue, and Monsieur Bourgeon, who was so kind to me, and I was soothed.

The soldiers were streaming into Tampa, more every day, and Miss Harrow insisted that she and Marion do their duty as Americans and invite some of them home for a meal.

"I don't know," said Marion. "They took a horse into a restaurant over in Ybor City—and they invaded the beer factory there and offered drinks to anybody passing."

"They're just boys," said Miss Harrow. "You'd be a little high-spirited too if you were going off to war."

"I don't think I'd take a horse into a restaurant. They got the waiters to feed it carrots. And they've been taking over the streetcars and making a mess of the traffic."

"If they were our sons," said Miss Harrow, "we'd want them shown a little hospitality, wouldn't we?"

Marion nodded, but part of her was wistful for the shy Miss Harrow, the timid companion who would not even take the knives out to the sharpener. The spinster and the widow: society—that is, men—demanded little of such figures.

For the dinner, Marion sat at one end of the table and Miss Harrow at the other. It was a long time since there had been guests in the house, and the companions had spent the day polishing the silver and pressing the creases out of the damask tablecloth. Now, as Miss Harrow asked the soldiers about their home towns and conditions in the camps, Marion sat erect, with no part of her back touching the chair. She recalled a deportment exercise she had been taught as a girl: to discourage slouching, she was to imagine a thread running up her spine and neck, exiting her body through the top of her skull. It was as taut and strong as piano wire, pulling her straight if ever she felt the temptation to bend. She remembered asking what the thread was connected to, or whether someone was holding it. God, she was told, was at the other end.

"Mrs. Unger and I have heard some terrible things about the camps," Miss Harrow was saying. "Flooded tents . . . swarms of flies . . . centipedes . . . tarantulas . . ." She shivered.

"Yes, ma'am," said a dark-haired boy. "And one night last week, Private Baker here was woken by an eight-foot 'gator that had burrowed into the sand and come up through the floor of his tent."

"My goodness," said Miss Harrow.

"It wasn't so bad," said Private Baker. "There was a soldier from New York who, on his first day at the camp, was bitten by mosquitoes, stung by a tarantula, had a touch of malaria, ran his bayonet into his hand, sat on a giant ant nest, trod on an alligator, and found a snake in his boot. He said he felt like a dirty deuce in a new deck."

The soldiers looked uncomfortable in their woollen uniforms, and Marion wondered how they would stand the heat in Cuba. One red-haired boy kept scratching at his wrists, which were not protected from the heavy fabric, and she wanted to lift his jacket from his thin shoulders and soothe his skin with calamine lotion. He noticed she was watching him then, and he stopped scratching and folded his hands in his lap, blushing.

"You must miss your mothers and your sweethearts," Miss Harrow was saying. "Have you no indication of when you might be sailing?"

"No, ma'am," said the red-haired soldier. "They keep telling us it will be soon, but we've been waiting weeks now."

"I wouldn't mind if we stayed in Tampa a little longer," said the dark-haired boy. "They know how to treat you here." He told them about the picnics and balls organized by the local Cubans, and the young ladies who distributed home-baked cakes and thousands of cigars to the camps each week. There were bazaars and fairs, too, where pretty girls dressed in white insurgent jackets and carrying machetes mingled with the soldiers, serving punch and coffee, and entertaining them with songs, recitations, and dancing. The delay was a great thing for the merchants of Tampa, he said: newsboys were earning thirty dollars a week, butchers were selling thousands of pounds of meat within a few hours, the lemonade and frankfurter stands on the edges of the camps were making twenty-five dollars a day, and a single soda fountain had cleared one thousand dollars in a week.

"I understand some of the young men have been a little high-spirited," Miss Harrow said, and their dinner guests laughed. "There's no harm in having a little fun," she continued, "but you must be careful, particularly in the Latin part of town." Things were often not what they appeared to be there, she said; only recently the

Tribune had cautioned readers not to be surprised if, upon entering a boarding-house or the premises of a seamstress, they discovered a young girl with rouge on her cheeks and slang on her lips.

Their guests laughed again, more politely this time, and Miss Harrow frowned; Marion knew that her warning had been in earnest. But these boys could not have been involved in the disturbances in Ybor City—Marion considered herself a good judge of character, and one could tell just by looking at them that they were honest, courteous young men. Still, she could not help recalling the other reports in the *Tribune:* stories of the Ybor City brothels where the women were raped at gunpoint by a mob of soldiers, and of a Cuban mother whose baby was taken from her to be used for target practice, the soldiers firing five shots at the child before returning him. Marion excused herself and went to the kitchen to check on the lemon parfait, even though Miss Harrow had finished making it some hours earlier.

The Liceo Cubano was just a few blocks from the Estradas' house. It had been Vicente Martínez Ybor's original factory, and when he moved to Eighth Avenue he donated the building to the residents. There was a fine opera house on the second story, and a number of rooms used for evening classes. The women's clubs held social functions there, too, donating the money to the Revolutionary Party, and on these occasions the building filled with young and old, and there were raffles and music, dancing and food, games of cards and dominoes, glasses of wine, long discussions about the fight for independence, and cigar smoke that hung in the air like dust in the sun. Sometimes the *lector de tabaquería* arrived with a special announcement, and the hall fell silent as he spoke his news, and Rafael saw that his powers extended well beyond the factory walls.

It was the speeches that Rafael went to the Liceo Cubano to hear. As the orators pounded the lectern, pleaded, and proclaimed, bellowed questions to which there were no answers, Rafael felt himself pulled into the whirl of words and thrown high above the fug of smoke and the heat, a leaf on a jet of water. All around him were the flag-draped portraits of Cuban patriots, teachers, poets, and scientists, and he stared back at them, searching their faces for similarities to his own. And then the orator listed the numbers of dead, or described the burned plantations, or quoted the writings of a Spanish army officer, the words nails in his mouth: "Not a single Cuban will remain on this island, because we shoot all that we find in the fields, on the farms, and in every hovel. We do not leave a creature alive where we pass, be it man or animal. If we find cows, we kill them, if horses, we kill them, if hogs, we kill them, men, women, or children—we kill them all. As to the houses, we burn them. So everyone receives his due, the men in buckshot, the animals in bayonet thrusts. The island will remain a desert." And Rafael descended to his seat.

He had been at the Liceo Cubano in February, the night the lector had brought word of the U.S.S. *Maine*'s destruction in Havana Bay. Two hundred and sixty men had died when the battleship exploded, but there were parties all over Ybor City: finally it looked as if the United States would intervene in the war.

"I'll buy you a chance, to celebrate," Señor Estrada had said, clapping him on the back. "Then you'll come with me to the *bolita* house for the draw."

Rafael thanked him for his invitation, but said he did not believe in buying chances; he needed to save his money for the Revolutionary Party.

Señor Estrada stared at him for a second or two, then laughed and said, "You won't be spending any money; *I'm* buying you a chance. And who knows? The Party might be in for a windfall." He put his arm around Rafael's shoulders and scooped him toward the door.

In truth, Rafael was a little afraid of the numbers game and the hold it had over its players.

"Don't ever start," Señora Estrada had warned him. "Umberto plays every week, and it makes him crazy whether he wins or loses."

Rafael had seen his landlord in this state; Señor Estrada was a dedicated *bolita* player, always buying three chances for the weekly draw and keeping the little slips of paper in his pocket. He had a chart that he had bought from the *bruja* Chiquita, and it told him how to choose numbers based on his dreams of the previous night, each number corresponding to a picture. With its grinning cat and its butterfly, its untied shoe and its kite, it looked as simple as a child's game, a chart of the alphabet, but Señor Estrada spent hours studying the symbols, running his finger along the rows, his lips moving silently. If he dreamt of a horse, he bet on number 1; if he dreamt of a cat, number 4; a corpse, number 8; a lady of the night, 12; a wildcat, 14; a witch, 37, and so on up to 100.

"What's your lucky number?" he said as he steered Rafael along the wooden sidewalk. "What did you dream about last night?"

"I don't remember," said Rafael.

"But you must have dreamt about something," said Señor Estrada. "Boys your age—their sleep isn't peaceful."

"I don't remember my dreams," said Rafael, and he chose a number at random: 12.

"The lady of the night," said Señor Estrada. "Well, you never know."

The *bolita* house was full of men, some clutching their flimsy paper tickets, some buying last-minute chances from the dealer. There were one or two women in the crowd, their hair adorned with carved combs that jutted like peacocks' tails, their fringed shawls tickling Rafael's forearm and the back of his hand as they passed him without a glance. When the draw began, a man in a top hat and tails climbed the steps to the stage and held aloft a red velvet pouch. From a small table he began taking the ivory balls, each one polished and shining like a moon. He dropped them into the bag and the crowd became quieter, and in a matter of seconds the only sound was the chinking of the balls as he mixed them. He pulled the drawstring tight and passed the bag to one of the men in the front row, who shook it and passed it on. Some gamblers closed their eyes as they took their turn; some kissed the velvet; one man made the sign of the cross. When seven or eight men had shaken the bag, the man in the top hat motioned for it to be returned to him. He walked to the left of the stage, scanning the crowd; then to the right, searching every face. "You," he said finally, and pointed, and for a moment Rafael thought he had been chosen, but the man was saying, "Yes, you, Señorita," and a woman who smelled of artificial jasmine stepped past Rafael and walked to the stage, her heels clicking.

The man gave her a ribbon and held out the velvet bag. Smiling, as if selecting an expensive piece of candy, she caught one of the ivory balls through the fabric and tied it, separating it from the others.

"*Gracias, Señorita,*" said the man, and he kissed her hand and waited until she had descended the steps. Then, taking a pair of long scissors from his pocket, he cut through the bag at the ribbon's knot and read the number on the released ball: "Fifty-two! The bicycle! Fifty-two is a winner tonight!" And there was murmuring in the hall as chances were checked and discarded.

"Who won?" said Rafael, looking around. But nobody had.

By April the mornings were clear and humid when Rafael awoke, the sky as blue as a sheet of kite paper. When he went to the yard to fetch water, the spider monkey was always still sleeping, curled up to its blanketed brick. Rafael felt happy as he made his way to the factory, and as he climbed the steps of the big brick building one morning it seemed the other *torcedores* shared his mood, for he heard cheers and whoops and bellows of delight. The United States had declared war on the Spanish in Cuba.

"You see?" shouted Señor Estrada. "I told you they would help us. And Mr. Plant is the most generous of all!"

Henry Plant, Rafael learned, had agreed to open the Tampa Bay Hotel to the American officers as well as to the large numbers of journalists and foreign correspondents who were coming to cover the war.

Rafael studied his face in the mirror. Whichever way he turned, however he angled the lamp, his upper lip was as smooth as a girl's. He flexed his thin arms, examined his ribby chest. Every speech he heard at the Liceo Cubano, every article the lector read about the deeds of the Spanish in Cuba reminded him of his own feebleness. There were plenty of men not much older than he who were fighting for their island, who were the kind of heroes of whom a mother could be proud. Rafael worked the Día de la Patria, of course, but it was not enough. How many horses would his single day buy? How many bayonets, how many bullets?

Rafael knew he was no soldier. The trick, he decided, was to make an advantage of an impediment, and so at the factory, whenever he was certain nobody was looking, he slipped a cigar into the folds of his clothing. Some days he could conceal as many as ten in his sleeves, his pockets, the cuffs of his trousers. When he added to these the three he was permitted to take home each day, he soon had the equivalent of a box of the finest Havana Robustos, or Romeo y Julietas, or Monte Cristos. It was a simple matter to shut himself in the cloakroom and transfer his takings to his bag, and once home and in his bedroom he tied the cigars into bundles ready for sale. It was not stealing, he reasoned, since all his profits went to the Revolutionary Party—and he would give up his little sideline business when the war was won or when he was old enough to volunteer, whichever came first.

As soon as he had amassed sufficient bundles, he left Ybor City for the wealthy parts of town where the white Americans lived, and he began knocking on doors. He smoothed his hair each time he passed a store window, for he found that his customers responded to neatness, often looking him up and down for flaws as closely as they examined his merchandise. It did not take him long to empty his bag—usually less than an hour. The rich liked a bargain, and in the wide new streets around the river, where the verandas were trimmed with wooden lace and the windows with silk and velvet, Rafael found a ready market for his cut-price cigars.

Late one afternoon, as soon as he had finished at the factory, he decided to try some of the businesses along Franklin Street.

Mr. B. B. Newman, Manufacturer of the Only Reed Organ that is Absolutely Insect Proof, told him that Mrs. Newman did not care for the smell.

The Davis Brothers, Everything for Gentlemen's Dress including Fancy Hosiery and Underwear, Neckwear, and Suspenders, and the Celebrated Monarch Shirt, said they bought theirs at the cigar store.

Dr. Hiram J. Hampton, Tapeworm a Specialty, said no.

After a dozen rejections Rafael was ready to try elsewhere, but when he glanced at the next door he did not recognize it, although he knew the area well by now. There was no sign outside and no display window, only a name picked out in gold on the fanlight. The letters were shadowed with black paint to make them look three-dimensional, like the carving on a tombstone. Rafael raised his hand and knocked.

"How may I help?" said the man, answering immediately, as if he had been waiting. He was small but broad-chested, and dressed so immaculately that Rafael thought he must have interrupted him on his way to an important engagement. His dark brown hair was smoothed straight back from his forehead, a neat widow's peak drawing attention to a long, fine nose.

"I hope I'm not interrupting you, Señor," said Rafael.

"Not at all," said the man, fixing Rafael with his greenish eyes. "I have just finished my work for the day."

"I wonder if you would be interested in purchasing some of the best cigars to be found in Tampa? They're rolled from the finest tobacco leaves imported from the Vuelta Abajo. Are you familiar with this area of Cuba?"

"I am not," said the man.

"It's a beautiful place," said Rafael, and he described the green slopes that lay between the mountains and the Caribbean, and the soil that was the color of roses. Mile after mile was covered with the lush tobacco plant, and the silky wrapper leaves, used to make the finest Clear Havana cigars, were shielded with cheesecloth. The white sheeting stretched into the distance, as if all the plants had been put to sleep, and when there was a breeze it waved like one vast butterfly net.

This was a speech Rafael liked to use on potential customers. Although it was a little flowery, perhaps, it was also true—or at least Rafael hoped it still was. As he spoke, he opened his bag and displayed a bundle of cigars.

The man took one. "I thought Cuba was a smoldering ruin these days."

Rafael swallowed. "Some areas have been affected," he said. "And of course, with all the fighting, these may be the last Cuban cigars available for some time."

The man rolled the Monte Cristo between his finger and thumb, listening for any crackling sounds, then scrutinized it from head to foot, checking for holes or ripples in the wrapper, feeling for gaps that would burn unevenly and produce a hot, unpleasant draw.

"These cigars have no band," he said.

"Nobody smokes the band," said Rafael.

"My tobacconist"—the man gestured across the street—"he told me that it was added as a protection for the fingers of high-born Spanish ladies."

"That's a nice story," said Rafael. He knew of the tobacconist on Franklin Street: a former cigar-maker who had invested his money in several Ybor City real-estate projects. Within six months, so the rumor went, he had doubled his capital and moved his wife and children away from Ybor, opening his store in the American part of Tampa. They jostled with other affluent Latin families to invite the Americans to their parties, often hosting an event on the flimsiest of pretexts—a child's birthday, a name day, some fictitious Cuban festival—and when they were invited back to an American function they shouted the news as if it were a military victory. Their children spoke perfect English. Rafael glanced across the paved road—no sandy streets here—to the store, its door guarded by a carved and painted Indian. The wooden figure held in his hand a platter upon which, each morning, the tobacconist placed cigars.

The small, green-eyed man was examining a second Monte Cristo.

"I can see you appreciate a fine smoke, and need no labels to identify one," said Rafael. "These are well priced," he added.

The man smiled briefly. "There's a good living to be made if one is enterprising," he said. "You show potential in this area. What do you do for a living?"

Rafael shrugged. "I do this and that."

The man smiled. "Come now, you can tell me. It will be our secret." He sniffed the cigar, drawing it under his narrow nostrils and closing his eyes for a moment. Rafael could see the fine blue veins threading beneath his lids. "I could have a business proposition for such an enterprising man as yourself."

Rafael glanced over his shoulder. "I work in a cigar factory," he said. "I roll cigars."

The man opened his eyes. "*You* roll them?" He jabbed the cigar like a finger. Rafael nodded. "Again I have been misinformed. My tobacconist told me that beautiful Gypsy girls roll them on their thighs."

"Many smokers believe that," said Rafael.

"Hmm," said the man, and he handed the cigar back. "The world is full of lies. I tend to think people want them. Do you know what I do for a living?"

"No, Señor," said Rafael.

"You might say I weave lies. Beautiful, custom-made, indistinguishable from the real thing. Tell me, how much do you earn at this factory?"

"Around fourteen dollars per week."

"Such work requires a deft hand, I imagine."

"The apprenticeship is usually four years. I began little more than a year ago."

"I see," said the man, his green eyes glittering. He reached into a pocket and handed Rafael a trade card printed in small black script, and then he outlined what he called *a proposal*. The word made Rafael think of a marriage.

"You would be working at night," said the man, taking Rafael's hands and turning them over, scrutinizing the fingers. "You would be answerable solely to me, but the work itself would be done alone. If you produce no material you receive no compensation, no matter how many hours you may tell me you have worked. Supplying any of my rivals is out of the question, of course; the slightest hint of this would mean immediate dismissal."

Rafael nodded as the man continued, answering his occasional and sometimes strange questions as confidently as he could. Yes, his health was excellent; no, he had never been prone to infection from refuse and the like; yes, his eyesight was perfect; no, he would not mention this conversation to anyone; yes, he understood that if he did so, the man would be obliged to mention Rafael's cigar sales to the factory owner. When he had finished the man said, "We'll be seeing each other soon, I trust," and although Rafael did not answer, in his heart he knew that this was true.

⁓

May 1898

For my most delicate work I draw the strands through one at a time, knotting and weaving and knotting again. Each thread, finer than the finest embroidery silk, must be caught with the barb of my hook. If it is true that the great Creator knows the number of hairs on our heads I pity Him, for I too am weighted with such information. A Goulet hair-piece comprises between twenty thousand to one hundred and fifty thousand hairs. Mr. Newman, a reed-organ manufacturer who possesses the head of a horse, needed close to ninety thousand for his scalpette, whereas Mrs. Rim required only twenty-five thousand for her frisette.

"You are transforming me into a *princess*, Mr. Gauntlet!" she exclaimed at the final fitting, pressing me to her bosom.

No matter how irritating or tasteless a customer may be, however, it does not pay to become ill-mannered. I maintain a balanced temperament: I rarely raise my voice, and find that a calm demeanor can check even the shrillest harpy. Woman is an easy creature to command if one knows the right tricks—a fact that was proven to me time and again on my hair-harvesting trips.

At many of the fairs I frequented, I was fortunate enough to witness protégés of the distinguished Dr. Mesmer at work. It was fashionable in those days to put on such shows, and I first saw the phenomenon demonstrated in his native Austria. A man trained by the great doctor himself had cleared a small space between the two-headed calf and the singing midget, and was describing his master's early experiments, which involved up to two dozen female patients occupying a vast oak tub. At this point, an audience began to gather about him; even the midget stopped singing "I Lost My Stocking at the Babbling Brook" and listened. Dr. Mesmer, said the man, connected magnetized jars of water to the tub via a series of metal rods, and while wearing a lilac cape he would stimulate the invisible energy in his patients by waving a metal wand and playing the glass harmonica.

"And now," said the Mesmerist, "may I have a volunteer from the audience?"

He scanned the burgeoning crowd, then selected a comely girl of around sixteen years of age. He stared into her eyes and fixed her thumbs with his own, and in a moment she fell into a trance so deep that she did not stir when he passed a vial of ammonia under her lovely nose, nor when he pricked her finger with a pin. However, when he withdrew a red handkerchief and announced it was a snake the girl drew back in terror, and when he remarked that she was covered with rats she began clawing at her bodice. It was most entertaining to watch, and it was a valuable lesson: say the right words and any female is biddable. I imagine my mother was the same.

Sometimes it troubles me when I think that I may not see the place of my birth again. Perhaps, if I had family, I would have reason to visit, but there is not a soul in France with whom I maintain contact. I do not even know my real name; indeed, I cannot be sure I have one. Perhaps the creature who bore me and put me to bed among the refuse, all bundled up with the empty wine bottles and the vegetable peelings and the eggshells, perhaps she did not think to give me a name. When she looked at me for the first time, it is possible that she saw no name in my face, that she saw nothing but her own ruin.

Despite my mother's absence of imagination, however, I have been given many names in my life—so many, in fact, that I no longer know to which I should answer. First there was the man who found me in the alleyway: he called me Chouchou, I was told, because I was lying on a bed of moldering cabbage leaves. He took me to the Home for Foundlings and deposited me in the Tour d'Abandon— the Desertion Tower—where the Sisters found me along with a note. They called me Michel after their beloved archangel, although there were already ten Michels under their roof, and seven Michelles (like my mother, the Sisters lacked creativity, except where punishment was concerned). After a few years I was given to a husband and his wife, who agreed to take me home because my eyes were the same color as theirs. They named me Pierre for their son who had died, but within a week they returned me to the Home for Foundlings and chose a baby instead.

"He's a demon," they said. "Such a malevolent creature we've never encountered."

"Boys are naturally energetic," said the Sisters.

"He hanged our cat and then skinned it," said the husband. "It was a pure-bred Turkish Angora."

The wife jiggled their replacement baby, saying, "Hello, Pierre. What a good new Pierre you are!" And she sniffed its silky head, and gave it her little finger to suck.

I had meant no harm. I had simply wanted to see what was beneath the animal's hair; what made it work. I did not mean to kill it, but it would not co-operate when I tugged at its coat, and so I made a deft little cat-sized noose.

After that, the Sisters rebaptized me. "You will have to earn back the name of the holy archangel," they said. "Until then, you shall be Judas."

My behavior, however, did not improve, for they had not counted on the fact that I preferred being Judas: it set me apart from all the Michels. Try as they might, the Sisters could find no family who would take me, and as I grew taller I moved back and back in the group of scrubbed foundlings assembled for viewing until I found myself at the very rear. I did not mind: from here I could refine my acts of sabotage. At critical moments, for example, I could pinch the legs of the children I especially disliked, making them squeal and be passed over for selection, or I could sing off-key in the hymns, or make up my own words. Judas they wanted, Judas I was. Each January, on the feast of the Three Kings, the Sisters hid a clay charm inside a cake and gave us all a slice; whichever foundling discovered the charm was then crowned King or Queen for the day. The little figure varied from year to year—sometimes it was a fish or a hare, sometimes a pair of clasped hands or a tiny chalice. I once found the most coveted charm—the Christ-child—in my piece of cake; when I bit into the sweet pastry and the almond filling the thing cracked against my teeth. I spat it onto the floor, and for that I was denied my crown and banned from all games for the rest of the week.

I did not mind. I spent as much time alone as possible, preferring my own company to that of the other children, who never wanted to play according to my rules. One evening when I should have been at chapel I slipped outside and crept to the front gates, and as I approached I heard a clamoring and a wailing much like the noise the pure-bred Turkish Angora had produced in my hands. I was drawn to the little door in the wall at the base of the Tour d'Abandon, but when I opened it I found nothing but an empty space. When I turned the revolving enclosure, however, the other side— the street side—came into view, and like a magician's trick there appeared a child. Sister Marie-Bernadette came running toward me then, her starched head-dress flapping like a gull's wings, and she screeched at me to get away, and that I had no business there. I strode back to chapel and pretended to join in, saying the right words and kneeling and standing at the right times, but all the while I was thinking of the little necklace of colored beads the baby wore, and the little medallion that hung from it. I knew it was an identification mark, which would be kept safe by the Sisters, and if the mother wanted the child back when times were easier she could claim it. The Sisters had a large collection of these labeling devices: glass beads and bracelets, iron medals and ribbons, even pieces of string with scraps of paper hanging from them like papillotes. They kept them in a locked box; a strange collection of treasures. I, however, had come naked of such adornments.

It was an icy November day when the Perruquier Dubois called at the Home.

"I had wanted an older one," he said, casting his eyes over the range of Michels. "One who could serve as an apprentice."

"But look at his long fingers," the Sisters said. "His eyesight is keen, and he's a very tidy child."

The Perruquier Dubois looked me up and down, then took my hands in his. At first I thought we were going to play a game, and I waited to be told the rules, but he merely scrutinized my fingers.

"He's very good at tying knots," added one of the Sisters, and she began to elaborate on my cat-noose.

"Yes, he's an exceptional child," the other Sisters said quickly, pushing me toward the Perruquier. "He'll make a good companion. We'll be sorry to see him go."

My master called me Gustave, for he did not like the connotations suggested by Judas. He gave me his last name, too; in time, he said, he would have a sign painted saying *Dubois and Son*. And so I, Gustave Dubois, learned the delicate trade of the Perruquier.

In the early days of my apprenticeship I wasted many hours and a good deal of hair in trying to perfect my handiwork. My knots were loose and uneven, my cutting crooked. I had only myself to blame, of course, for no matter how expert a teacher my master was, nobody can impart ability to another. Through many hours of practice, often well into the evening, when my master had retired to bed and the light was so poor I could no longer see my own fingers, let alone the fine strands of hair, I forced myself to improve. Sometimes I would awake to find myself still seated at my worktable, the incomplete wig before me, as mangy as a victim of slow poisoning. Little by little, however, I learned to make my knots tight, my stitches invisible. I learned to hide all evidence of workmanship so that each peruke seemed formed by the hand of Nature or God, whichever you prefer. And, to my ever-increasing ranks of customers, who would wait months for an appointment if I told them they must, I felt all-powerful.

It was my master, the only person to whom I felt any attachment, who put a stop to this in the end. As the years passed and I grew more and more skilled, he grew slower and blinder, until there were so many complaints from his customers that we were losing more business than we attracted through my now celebrated creations.

"Perhaps it's time for you to retire," I suggested.

"My hand is as steady as ever," he replied, his fingers quivering, his brown eyes milky.

Jealous of the reputation I had gained in Paris, he conspired to ruin my career of some forty years by circulating all sorts of foul rumors about me, and I was forced to take action that some may condemn as rash. It is one thing to produce poor-quality work when still an apprentice—those inadequacies are one's own, and may be overcome. It is quite a different matter, however, for one's projects to be ruined because of the malicious actions of another, and the more I learned about the world's design, the more I saw that such events are all too commonplace. That is why I think it best not to form strong attachments: they are sure to lead to disappointment.

When I came to America I gave myself a new name, unconnected with anybody from my past. And I added the "III," for everybody has ancestors, after all, even if we cannot say who they are.

I find I am being led astray. I have been struggling to compose a letter, and although I write every day to strangers—plume merchants seeking to ensnare buyers, for example, or suppliers of silk thread and galloon ribbon, or the New York importer from whom I order my stock of French soaps—the words for this particular piece of correspondence elude me. As I sat at my bureau this afternoon and tried to write to a woman I had never met, my pen froze even as I addressed the envelope to her: Mrs. Marion Unger.

And again I must double back in time, for I have not yet explained our first encounter. Usually I am a methodical man, but since that moment my mind has been in disarray; it is as if there were a door in the back of my skull that has been left ajar by mistake, and in she has slipped to move things all about.

I had finished the box of Monte Cristos that I had purchased from the enterprising Cuban, and that had turned out to be very fine. I had an engagement with my actresses that afternoon, and on my way there, when I was just about to enter the cigar store, I noticed her. I was so struck by the sight of her hair that I almost forgot my manners. It shone beneath her black hat—she was in mourning dress, some distant part of me noted, although the jet jewelry and the gray bodice and the almost festive black fringing suggested that the death was not recent—and I longed to remove my glove, place my fingers to her neck as if checking her pulse, and stroke that smooth, snowy mass. I did no such thing, of course; I simply raised my hat and wished her a good day, and she gave a sad little smile as she passed. Such an expression is rarely seen on the faces of the women of Tampa; they titter and grin, and show both rows of teeth, and display their moist little tongues in a manner they think charming. I continued on my way, and the white-blond woman paused in front of the Maas Brothers' window, examined the tawdry display of hats trimmed with chiffon, gauze, and net—these days everything is veiled—and then, I am sorry to relate, she entered the premises.

You see, I said to myself, she is as shallow as the rest of her sex. Perhaps the mourning dress made her seem otherwise for a moment, or perhaps it was the way the light was falling, or her wan little smile, but in truth she is an unexceptional creature and as distracted by fripperies as any other.

I went on to the residence of my actresses, but stayed only an hour, and since then I have been unable to concentrate on my work. This morning I had to unpick several rows of a scalpette; I did not notice that I had reached the point at which the edges were to give way to the longer hair, and I continued threading through the shorter lengths and knotting them in place until I had almost covered the foundation.

When I saw what I had done I threw the thing aside like a spoilt child who has tired of its toys. I paced my studio, unwilling to give in to the images of the woman that projected themselves like magic-lantern pictures on the inside of my skull. I thought of all manner of things instead. I thought, for example, of the slattern who had applied for the job of my assistant as if it were the most natural thing in the world for a woman to work. And I mused on the hypocrisy that characterizes the New Woman, who makes a great show of speaking her mind at meetings of the Temperance Society, the Christian Endeavor Society, and the Society for the Suppression of Vice (who, I am informed, last year seized 134,000 pounds of obscene books, 194,000 lewd pictures, 5,500 indecent playing cards, and 60,300 rubber articles). While the New Woman declaims the evils of men, her every action betrays her desire to be one: she sports mannishly cut costumes, she rides bicycles astride, she plays at smoking cigars. And yet, once she has transformed herself into a grotesque imitation of Adam, she finds that the trappings of masculinity do not bring her contentment and she must admit that, deep in her heart, she still seeks to ensnare a good husband, and so she returns to me. For a moment I wondered whether the white-blond woman might not be of this dangerous breed, but again I pushed her from my thoughts.

I picked up the scalpette from my studio floor, where it cowered like a cur, and made myself sit at my table. I began to unpick the surplus rows, and the simple nature of the task calmed me, and I reflected how, in some instances at least, it is possible to undo one's mistakes. I began to consider the amount of hair that has passed through my hands: the tresses I have harvested myself, or purchased from peddlers, or cut from the cool scalps of the dead. I thought of the clippings sold me by barbers, and of the knotty little tufts I have recovered from trash pits and washed and untangled and matched root to point. I imagined all this hair in its true state—not primped and curled, scented and pinned, but natural, as if it had just been cut. One could bury a man in it; one could fill a room floor to ceiling. I pictured it jamming the doors shut, suffocating the inhabitants, pressing against the windows like mementos in some great locket. Laid end to end, it would stretch all the way to France.

And when I thought of France I thought again of my master, who had taken me in and fed me and clothed me and filled my head with his own knowledge, his trade secrets. And when my seven-year apprenticeship was up, and by rights I should have been dismissed from his service and free to begin a business of my own, he came to me with a gift. It was wrapped in blue paper, and the ribbon was tied with his own special knot that could not be undone unless one knew its secret. He had taught me that knot, just as he had taught me everything else I knew, and so it took but a moment to unwrap the present, and inside were one hundred trade cards, each with the words *Dubois and Son, Perruquiers* embossed in gold. And so I stayed with him and pretended to be his son, and visited Europe each spring and summer in order to keep his shelves stocked. Gradually I did more and more of the wig-making itself, while he grew older and I grew more proficient, until, one day, my skills surpassed his, and although he knew that his work was becoming slipshod he would not admit that it was time to retire.

That much I have said already. I have not related, however, how he began to deceive our customers; how, in the end, he passed my work off as his own, this man who had named me, as if I did not exist. And I remembered the way he had inspected my hands at the Home for Foundlings, so many years earlier, and I began to understand that he had wanted a worker, not a companion, not a son. As each day passed I felt his resentment more and more keenly. He no longer praised my work, although it was the finest in Paris. Should skill be punished? Should I be blamed for becoming exactly what he wanted? I knew that, for my own safety, I had to take action.

After the initial blow he did not struggle, but looked at me as meekly as a child who knows he has done wrong. He said, "Master," but I do not know which of us he meant. And then he was lying across his workbench all broken and staring, and I knew that I should have to leave France, leave my homeland for good—and I also knew that I had to put the studio to rights in great haste, for our three o'clock engagement was due to arrive.

I finished unpicking the scalpette and began to add strands of the correct length. The hair felt alive as I worked it with my greased fingers, and I pondered the fact that although expert hands can create a semblance of health and vitality, and although it is a simple matter to undo certain mistakes, there are other actions that can be neither mended nor undone.

Precious things can be discarded by accident. The attention drifts, or haste makes one careless, or a second party, not recognizing an item's true value, disposes of it. Over the past five years, since I have been sifting the refuse of this town, I have collected an assortment of lost treasures. I have engagement rings and wedding rings, mourning rings and collar studs. I have pieces of memorial jewelry, some my own design. I have bracelets of diamonds and of braided hair; I have single earrings; pearls that have worked free from brooches and necklaces; gem stones fallen from loosened claws. I have two glass eyes. I do not store these baubles in a jewelry box, the earrings in neat rows, the necklaces and bracelets in plush hollows and secret drawers, the rings slipped into velvet clefts; rather, I keep them in an old cigar box. The label features La Camporita—a buxom, rosy maiden in a scarlet gown who exists, I now realize, only in the mind of the lithographer.

I open it from time to time and reach inside, random tangles dripping through my fingers like tufts of weeds and glistening pebbles pulled from the sea. Today the glass eyes watched me, one blue, one brown. They had rolled into a corner and sat side by side, a mismatched pair, looking in different directions like a maiden aunt, regarding my jewels and chains without a word. The owners have ceased searching for their treasures, have stopped hoping that they might turn up in a child's toy-box or the lining of a cushion. They are all lost—except that nothing is ever lost, not properly. It is only misplaced.

And finally, like a shell that keeps bobbing to the surface no matter how long one holds it beneath the water, the white-blond woman filled my head, and I knew there was nothing else for it but to engineer a meeting.

A Maas brother—there are two but I cannot tell them apart, since both are bald and fat—was pushing hatpins into a velvet cushion when I entered his premises.

"Mr. Gruelly," he said, glancing up and then continuing with his work as if it were no surprise that I should enter his shabby little store. "What can I do for you today?" He jabbed the pins into the shape of a heart. "I have some new bowlers—"

"Monsieur Maas, I simply wish to pass on some information," I said.

He looked up at that, his mean eyes narrowing still further.

"As one businessman to another," I added.

"What sort of information?" he asked, giving me his full attention. He held a long pin between his fingers, the sharp end pointing at his chubby thigh, the paste jewel catching the light and sparkling like a ruby.

"I suspect I've been duped by a customer," I said. "A female confidence trickster. I've seen her frequenting your store, and thought I should warn you."

"Oh?" said Maas.

"She's a white-blond woman, not yet thirty, I would say; an attractive creature. She told me her name was Michelle Dubois."

Maas raised his eyes to his sticky ceiling and, slowly shaking his head, said, "No. No, she's not one of mine."

"I believe Michelle Dubois is a pseudonym, Monsieur Maas," I said.

The fat milliner drew the pin from between his fingers and placed it on the counter. "Just how has she duped you, this woman?"

"She ordered a hair-piece from me," I said. "When she collected the finished article she gave me an address to which I should send the account, but my letter was returned. There is no such address and no such woman."

"I see," said Maas. "And the authorities have had no success in tracing her?"

I spread my hands in a gesture of hopelessness. "That's why I've come to you—to see whether you know anybody matching her description." He was nodding his head. "And to warn you, as one businessman to another, to accept only cash from her."

"Is she taller than average, with green eyes?" he said.

"Yes," I said, my voice calm as I toyed with the hatpins, stroked the velvet cushion. I am not a violent man, but at that moment I imagined jabbing the fat milliner with one of his pins, then standing back and watching him deflate until all that was left was a puddle of poorly cut clothes.

"Is she in half mourning?"

"That is she."

"But that sounds like Mrs. Unger," Maas said, smiling and frowning at the same time so that his piggy eyes practically disappeared. "You must be mistaken, Mr. Gruelly."

"Unger?" I said.

"Mrs. Marion Unger. Her husband was an orange grower who died right after the '95 frost."

The man said this with as much discretion as a schoolgirl. I have found that his type is always free with information, which is one reason his business will never flourish as mine does. There are many other reasons, of course—one need only look at his garish window displays—but that is a separate matter.

"She deserved better," he said, and I was not sure whether he meant the frost or the husband. "But Mrs. Unger wouldn't deceive anyone. She's always settled her accounts promptly with me."

"I see," I said. "Thank you, Monsieur Maas."

A group of soldiers entered the store, no doubt looking to purchase cheap trinkets for their sweethearts.

"War is excellent for business, don't you agree?" said Maas, but I was already leaving.

When I returned to the Hotel I consulted the Tampa City Directory. Although many local businesses advertise in it, I choose not to do so—it would profit me little to place an announcement alongside those of the Tampa Horseshoeing Co., All Interfering and Faulty Gaited Horses a Specialty; or Wah Sing & Co., Novelties and Laundry. The beauty of this volume is that it not only lists the residence of every citizen but also indicates profession, whether someone is a boarder, and whether a woman is unmarried, married, or widowed. The directory has been a great source of intelligence to me professionally; the little asterisk denoting colored skin, for instance, has been an invaluable guide to the location of black combings.

Having found Unger, Marion, widow, of 613 Fortune Street, I took a crisp piece of paper from my bureau, dipped my pen in the inkwell, and began to write. As related above, however, my hand seized at the end of her name, and I must have sat there a good half hour before I could think how to continue. In the end I simply emptied my mind of all trifling thoughts; I discarded every irrelevant notion and began to write before I could think better of it. My hand moved so quickly then that it was almost as if someone else were dictating the words, and when I had finished I thought of Mrs. Rim and her spirit-rappers, who in this way transcribe messages and prophesies from the Otherworld every Wednesday afternoon at two o'clock. I am a man of logic, of course, and the only predictions I make are based on such concrete evidence as the measurements of a person's skull. This information is gathered in broad daylight, with no need to resort to the trickery that takes place in candle-lit parlors, where tables tap and glasses move of their own accord and nothing is as it seems. The meetings attended by Mrs. Rim are led by Adelina

Flood, a quadroon hussy married to an American, and one of the most empty-headed of my customers. Perhaps this quality is what allows the spirits to communicate through her with such ease—no brain obstructs their passage.

I knew that the force moving my hand across the page was of my own making, that no specter but my own desire told me the words with which I might ensnare the pale-haired woman—why, then, did I shiver? As soon as I posted the letter I regretted it, and wished I could reach in and retrieve it, and undo what I had done. I made my way back to my premises feeling most vexed, and it was not until I was almost at my door that I saw Marion Unger standing there, and I wondered how she could have received my note so soon. For a moment I believed that a full day and night had passed without my realizing it. Then I gathered myself together and took my keys from my pocket.

"Good day, Madame," I said, and turned my attention to the lock. Why is it, when a thing is truly desired, it is the last thing one can look in the eye?

"Good day," she said, and followed me inside. And I had the strangest feeling, for although I knew she could not yet have received my letter, it was as if the act of writing it had drawn her to me.

It was to Marion's lasting sorrow that she had kept so little of Jack's hair. She had seen other women wearing beautiful pieces of mourning jewelry fashioned from the hair of the dead—buttons and lockets and rings, braided bracelets and watch guards caught with heart clasps, brooches of willow trees weeping over graves. When Jack had died she had taken the pair of small, sharp scissors she used for embroidery and cut a small section of hair from the back of his head. She had not thought of taking enough for a memorial piece until he was buried, and it was too late. Perhaps it was for the best, she told herself. She was not good with her hands—she tangled even the most basic needle-point designs into knots—and she did not think she could have borne it had she made a bad job, for once the hair was ruined there was no more. She could have taken it to a professional, of course, but she had heard stories about the hair being all mixed up in common boxes—gray here, black there, white in another, and so on. She kept the small amount she had saved in the little drawer of her escritoire intended for stamps or coins.

The Splendor of Eve had been a present from her mother, as if to make up for all the things she had never told Marion. Marion consulted it now for information on hair jewelry, turning over pages depicting the insides of women, the lithographs so detailed they seemed drawn with a needle. There was a cross-section of the womb; a ten-week-old fetus with bulbous head and blank eyes; an embryo growing in the wrong place, lodged in the fallopian tubes like a tumor. The illustrations were never shown in isolation, but always in the context of the female form: the trunk was outlined, the small waist and full hips those of the ideal bride. She flicked through the chapters: "Development of Female Charms," "Animal Love and Moral Excellence," "How to Expand the Joys of Wedded Life," and "How to Make Child-Bearing Healthful and Desirable." Further on came "Splendor of the Wife and Mother," "How to Prevent Self-Abuse Among the Young," and "How to Recognize the Signs of Self-Abuse and Cure It." There were hints on How to Restore and Perpetuate Female Beauty, and How to Promote the Growth of the Female Bust, but the only advice on memorial jewelry was to engage an Artist in Hair.

Marion wondered whether she had enough. She looked at the little tuft in her hand and tried to imagine it shaped into a spray of roses or a weeping willow, or woven into a ring or bracelet. Then she placed it back in its envelope, a letter without words, tucked it in her purse, and went to the house of Mrs. Adelina Flood.

It had been some weeks since she had clipped the notice from the newspaper, but she had finally summoned the courage to write to the Harmonious Companions. Their reply had been brief:

Dear Mrs. Unger,

Thank you for your letter. I am delighted that you are interested in joining our little group—we are small in number, but blessed with enthusiasm in abundance. I look forward to making your acquaintance at our next meeting, which will take place at my home on Wednesday the 18th. We shall begin at two o'clock P.M. and finish at five, or perhaps a little later, depending upon the mood of our Invisible Friends.

Warmly yours,
Mrs. Adelina Flood

The house was a two-story frame structure painted pale yellow. There was a stone chimney from which little smoke signals were escaping, and on the tip of each of the four gables, as if watching for visitors, sat a carved owl. The ceiling of the front porch was painted blue to create the illusion of coolness in summer and to make the walls appear whiter, and at one end, pouring its shade through the white columns, was a vast strangler fig.

Mrs. Flood greeted Marion, hooking her with a slim arm into the parlor. They stood just inside the door as if they were old friends, the two of them, Adelina Flood's palm at the small of Marion's back. Marion had always been envious of that type of woman—the type who thinks nothing of touching another on the arm when telling a story, of stroking the hair of a downhearted friend, of greeting mere acquaintances with a kiss. Such actions put people at their ease, and Marion wished they came naturally to her.

Adelina Flood was small-boned and pretty, with glossy black hair and dark brown eyes that kept resting on Marion for slightly longer than usual, as if she were trying to remember where they had met before.

"Ladies, I am pleased to introduce our newest friend, Mrs. Unger," she announced, the traces of a Spanish accent all but smoothed away. "Mrs. Unger, if you would like to sit here by the hearth, we can all get acquainted."

It was late spring and there was no fire lit, but Marion imagined she felt heat on the side of her face. She would have preferred to sit somewhere else, on the edge of the group rather than in the center, but the way Mrs. Flood had motioned her to the armchair, as if it were a treat, stopped her from shifting. In one corner of the room an oval table was covered with a white cloth, and in the middle, surrounded by three white candles, lay a small object, also draped in white. All along the walls were cabinets of shells, and Marion wondered who might have assembled such a vast collection.

"They belong to Mr. Flood," said Adelina. "They're tree-snails, from the Everglades. It is his little obsession. They're hermaphrodites, you know."

For a moment Marion imagined that they were alive, and that if she looked closely she might see a pair of long thin horns reaching to her and shrinking away again at the touch of a finger, but then she realized that it was only the shells which interested a collector, and the snails would have been long since removed.

"—a little about yourself," Mrs. Flood was saying.

Marion did not know which of the six women she should address, so she focused on a tapestry hassock depicting an English hunting scene. "I live over on Fortune Street," she told the footstool. "I read your notice in the *Tampa Tribune* and I wanted to come along and see what you do." There was a pause. She noticed that one of the tapestry hounds appeared to have five legs. "I have no experience with Spiritualism."

There was another pause, and Marion glanced into the unlit hearth. When she had moved here with Jack she had thought they would never need to light a fire, but she had not reckoned with the frosts. She remembered how she used to watch the flames in their hearth at night, strands of sparks quivering on the black bricks at the mouth of the chimney: soldiers marching up the wall, Jack used to say.

"Well. Very good. Thank you, Mrs. Unger," said Mrs. Flood.

One by one the members of the group introduced themselves.

There was Mrs. Friskin, a woman of around fifty who spoke with a Scotch accent. Her hair was a rusty gray, her pale skin and colorless eyelashes suggesting she had once been a redhead, her dress of blue silk tailored to disguise a thick waist.

There were the Misses Rathbone, two unmarried sisters who lived next door to the Floods. The elder Miss Rathbone wore a lorgnette on a long silver chain, and now and then she unfolded it and held it before her watery eyes, goggling like a fish in a bowl. The younger Miss Rathbone barely spoke, but when she did her hand fluttered to her mouth, her fingers playing around a misshapen upper lip.

Mrs. Rim must have been in her late fifties. "Mr. Rim would love to meet you, I'm sure," she said, and added, "He is a *good man*," as if Marion had suggested otherwise. "He is of the finest English stock—one of the Hartlepool Rims. Hartlepool, England," she said, diamond drops flapping on her creased earlobes.

"Mrs. Rim is a widow, but the late Mr. Rim sometimes visits us," said Adelina Flood.

Miss Needham, at around twenty years old, was the youngest of the group. She had a heart-shaped face that seemed always on the brink of smiling, and very pale blue eyes; in certain lights the irises were as transparent as water. Her parents were strict Calvinists who forbade her and her sisters to dance, read novels, or play games of chance. "They think I'm attending prayer meetings," she said. "Mrs. Flood has been good enough to corroborate this little deception. I'd be grateful, Mrs. Unger, if you'd not mention my name in connection with the Companions."

"Of course," said Marion.

"We often meet with opposition in religious quarters," said Mrs. Friskin. "Are you a church-going woman, Mrs. Unger?"

"No," said Marion. "Not anymore."

"I couldn't help noticing you're in mourning," said Miss Needham, turning her heart-shaped face directly toward Marion. "I hope I'm not intruding, but have you a special reason for joining our group?"

"I'm in half mourning now. I'm a widow," said Marion. The statement sounded strange to her, and she realized she had probably never spoken it before, not those exact, bald words. She thought of the lock of hair in her bag and wished she could take it from its envelope and hold it in her palm like a cupped moth.

Mrs. Rim was patting her on the arm. "We all come for a reason," she said, her diamonds quivering. "But the dead don't want us to mourn them, my dear. Mr. Rim doesn't want me to drag myself around in weeds."

There was a small yelp from the area of Mrs. Rim's lap, and Marion saw that she held a little dog. It stood and turned two full circles, its paws swishing against her green shot taffeta, then sat down again and grunted.

"You've never worn mourning?" said Marion.

Mrs. Rim shook her head. "Why should we, when our departed ones are as alive as you or me? I wore white at Mr. Rim's funeral. I walked up the aisle like a bride. And Raisin wore a white ribbon around his neck, didn't you, my darling? Didn't you, my treasure?"

The dog grunted once more.

"And now I shall tell you the history of our little group," said Adelina Flood. Her slender arms opened and curled like a ballerina's and she paused, as if waiting for music. "One quiet night last year," she said, "something happened in this room." She was smiling, her eyes fixed on a point above the fireplace, and she told how her husband had been cleaning a snail shell and she had been working at a tapestry—a cushion of Westminster Abbey, to complement the hassock cover given her by Mrs. Rim—when she fell into a deep trance. "Not even Mr. Flood could arouse me," she said. "As I gazed at my work, an image materialized between the half-stitched spires: the face of a beautiful young man. 'I have come to guide you, Adelina,' he said. 'I bring messages from the spirit world. Take this relic and use it to summon me when you will.'"

"It was Abayomi," said Mrs. Rim, mauve with excitement. "He's three thousand years old and a Nubian prince!"

There was another yelp from her lap.

"Adelina is telling the story, Harriet," the Misses Rathbone said.

"He's *her* Nubian," the elder added.

"Where was I?" said Mrs. Flood.

"The relic," said Miss Needham.

Mrs. Flood nodded. "When I came to, I found a beautiful white bone at my feet. I asked Mr. Flood if it belonged to him, thinking it perhaps part of his collection, but he took one look at it and shook his head and returned to his shell. The next day I told my neighbors— the Misses Rathbone—about Abayomi, since I knew they shared my interest in the occult, and that night we succeeded in summoning him using the holy relic. He told the younger Miss Rathbone the name of a childhood beau she had all but forgotten."

"It's true," said the younger Miss Rathbone, her hand darting to her lip.

"Our little group has been growing ever since," said Mrs. Flood, rising from her chair, the other women following. "Abayomi some-times communicates with my voice, and sometimes through auto-matic writing. You're familiar with the planchette?"

Marion nodded. "That is to say, I've read about it."

Mrs. Flood placed her fingers on Marion's shoulder and steered her to the table so gently it was hardly noticeable. She indicated a heart-shaped board supported on china castors. A pencil, standing vertically, passed through the board and rested on a sheet of paper. "We may see it working today," she said.

Mrs. Friskin drew the shades and the crimson draperies, and the women moved to the table. Miss Needham lit the candles, and after a pause Mrs. Flood uncovered the relic. Marion regarded the clean, straight bone. In the candlelight, against the damask, it glowed like the petal of a flower. Miss Needham took Marion's left hand and Mrs. Friskin her right, and there was a moment of silence until the voice of Mrs. Flood said, "He is here." Her fingers, resting against the planchette, began to move, the china castors gliding beneath the board, the pencil whispering against the paper. When her hand stopped she opened her eyes and held up the message. It was only one word but it covered the entire page, *jackjackjackjackjack*, as if a girl had written a sweetheart's name over and over in the hope of summoning him. The women read it aloud, laughing, wondering, and Marion thought of the insistent call of the jackdaw: one spring, when she was a girl, a pair had tried to nest in her parents' chimney. "Jackdaws in Detroit!" her mother had said. Such birds did not belong in America, and must have come on a ship from Europe. They were noted for their thievery. Marion's father had smoked them out.

"Jack was my husband's name," she said now.

"Oh!" said the women. "Your husband! Good, very good!"

Mrs. Rim kissed her dog. "That was quite a response for someone so new, wasn't it, Raisin? And nothing from your papa again."

"Pay no attention to her," whispered the younger Miss Rathbone, her lisp even more pronounced. "Mr. Rim's not as obedient now as he was in life."

Mrs. Rim turned to Marion and smiled. "One would think you had used up all the energy in the room, my dear."

On her way home from the meeting, Marion called at the wig-maker's and was disappointed to find it closed. She was just about to leave when he came up behind her, greeted her in a curt way she supposed was French, and opened the door of his studio.

When she explained what she wanted, he took the envelope from her and slit it open. She wanted to grab it back and tuck it away somewhere safe, somewhere close to her skin, but she did not move.

"There is enough, yes," he said, peering inside and shaking it a little, a gardener with a packet of seeds. He did not touch the hair itself, but motioned Marion to a chair and said, "What I suggest is that we take a little of your own, Madame Unger. A combination of colors is always attractive, as well as being a reminder of the insepa-rable bonds of man and wife. *N'est-ce pas?*"

His voice was gentle, like that of a physician one has known since infancy.

"All right," said Marion. She unpinned her hat and leaned forward for him as he held the scissors to the nape of her neck, and in a moment it was done.

"There now," he said and showed her the little tuft he had taken, holding it in his palm like a baby bird fallen from the nest, and suddenly it felt neither strange nor dangerous to be leaving Jack's hair in his charge.

"You have an apartment at the Tampa Bay Hotel, I understand," she said, and blushed. "I mean, I've always wanted to stay there."

"You would adore it, Madame Unger," said the wig-maker. "There are so many diversions for the female guest. You can sit on the verandas and listen to concerts by Mr. Stubbeline's Sixteen-Chair Hotel Orchestra, and there are a number of parlors in which you can read or write or indulge in some quiet needle-point. In the evenings the Casino is transformed into a ballroom or sometimes a theater, and by day the floor is rolled back, and there at your feet is a fully heated swimming pool where ladies' maids and a swimming instructor are always present."

"I do enjoy bathing," said Marion. But the wig-maker was already tying her hair and Jack's with thread, and she was not sure he had heard her.

"I'm afraid I'm terribly busy right now, Madame. Is a month acceptable?"

The next day she went to Franklin Street and examined bolts of fabric, fingering the silky plaids and stripes, the jewel-colored velvets. At the Maas Brothers' Shoe and Millinery House she looked at pearl buttons like mounds of baby teeth; she admired the stiff new boots, the cards of ribbon and lace. It was late in the afternoon before she returned home.

"This came for you," said Miss Harrow, handing her an envelope the color and texture of lemon pith. On the back a blister of wax had been stamped with a serpentine letter G.

"Esteemed ladies of Tampa; dear Mrs. Unger," began the note.

Although ball season is still some months away, it is never too early to turn one's attentions to that matter so close to the female heart: personal adornment. While it is true that the selection of gowns, slippers, fans, and reticules is of the utmost importance, there is one accessory which no woman can afford to overlook: her coiffure.

It may please you to learn that my Ladies' Imperceptible Hair-Pieces and my Gentlemen's Invisible Coverings are in demand the length and breadth of our nation, with a number of my customers traveling from New York, Chicago, and even abroad to avail themselves of my services. My many years of experience in Paris, France, and my present location on Franklin Street mean that I am in a unique position to offer you access to a postiche of the highest quality. Whether you require a traditional yet elegant chignon, a curled fringe, or a partial or full transformation, particular care will be taken to match the shade exactly to your own. I am aware that a number of ladies make a point of saving their combings, and if you so desire I would be happy to fashion these into a piece of your choosing.

I should be delighted to receive you at my premises on Franklin Street. Any lady contacting me before the end of August is entitled to a special discount of twenty-five per cent.

I look forward to making your acquaintance in the near future. In the meanwhile I remain,

Your humble servant,
Monsieur Lucien Goulet III
Perruquier

Marion smiled, remembering the wig-maker's nimble hands at her neck. "I was there only yesterday," she said, passing the letter to Miss Harrow.

Her companion scanned the page. "He has a very good reputation," she said. "Nobody's knotting is as skilled as Lucien Goulet's."

"I'd never met the man before," Marion murmured, "but only yesterday I was there, and today this. He's everywhere at once."

Miss Harrow's hand skimmed her own curly hair as she read the letter again. "That can happen sometimes," she said.

~

When Rafael emerged from the cloakroom the *lector de tabaquería* was standing in the doorway.

"You're always one of the last to leave," said the lector, his voice quiet now that he was not up on his tribune. "You're never in a hurry to go home, it seems to me."

"Home?" said Rafael.

"Don't you like the Estradas? They like you. Señor Estrada was just telling me how diligent you are in the evenings, reading all the time, teaching yourself English."

Rafael shrugged. "I'm just trying to better myself."

"You're an ambitious young man. Perhaps you're after my job," he said, smiling.

Rafael hitched his bag farther up on his shoulder. "If you'll excuse me, I need to be on my way."

The lector did not move from the doorway. "Shall I tell you a secret?" he said, not waiting for an answer. "I left Havana ten years ago so I could make a new life. I'm like you in that respect, like all the men in the factory. I, too, left family behind, but the difference for me is that they don't know where I am. They don't care." He stopped. "Have you ever wanted something you couldn't have, Rafael?" Again he did not wait for a reply. "When I was your age, I wanted to be rich. I had a good start, working on a tobacco planta-tion in Sancti Spíritus, earning enough to save a little each week. My employer was a wealthy man, but I saw how he treated his wife and children after he had drunk too much, and there I saw my opportu-nity to—what was your expression?—to better myself. There was nothing wrong in taking a little here and there from such a man. He wouldn't notice, and a tiny amount for him meant a big difference for me. Just a little more, I told myself. Just a pinch more, and then I would leave for the city." He paused, sighed. "The thing about stealing is that it never stops. It's like love. You do it a little and you want to do it some more. I did make it to the city, to Havana, but not in the way I'd planned. I arrived there a prisoner, and spent seven years in the Arsenal. That's where I learned how to read aloud."

"I don't know what this has to do with me," said Rafael. His bag felt heavier, the strap cutting into his shoulder.

"You'd be amazed at what I could tell you," the lector went on. "I sit high above the *torcedores* so that my voice will carry, but I see much more than the page in front of me. For instance, I've never observed you smoking, either while you're working or during a break. Not even at the Liceo Cubano. But you always take your three free cigars at the end of the day."

"Only a fool would refuse them," said Rafael.

"You take more than three, though," said the lector, and this time he waited for a reply.

"Are you going to turn me in?" Rafael said finally.

"No," said the lector.

In a way, Rafael was relieved he had been found out. He did not like himself for stealing from the Ybors, who had been so good to him, and every time he wrote his home address on a letter to his father he was reminded of his dishonesty. Fifth Avenue, Ybor City: he was stealing from the ones who had given him a job, the ones who had created a whole city for their workers. It was like stealing from family.

Rafael believed that the lector would not turn him in; the older man seemed satisfied with the small drama he had created in the cloakroom, and content to leave the bigger scenes to the masters from whose books he read. There remained, however, the problem of money: now that war had been declared, the Party needed more funds than ever. Besides, Rafael had seen all the wonderful things for sale on Franklin Street and Harrison Street, and once he knew they were there, just across the river, he could not pretend they were not. If he was to stay in America, he needed to live like an American. That evening he took the bone-colored card from his drawer, and the next day he went to the wig-maker's premises.

I am full of excitement today, and the fact that I had engagements with two of my most irritating customers hardly bothered me. I was balking at the prospect of another summer spent digging up the stinking trash pits of Tampa, but just when I believed I would never find an assistant, the nondescript Cuban who sold me his excellent Monte Cristos called and agreed to work for me. There is another reason for my light-heartedness, however: I have been hard at work on Marion Unger's bracelet. Once I had supplemented her husband's hair with her own it was obvious that there would be quite enough for the design she had in mind, but something made me add a little extra from a third source—and one readily to hand. Perhaps it was when I noticed that the late Mr. Unger's hair was close to my shade of brown; anyhow, I arranged my mirrors so I could see the back of my head, and then, from the nape, I cut a few strands. These I have woven into the spine of the bracelet, placing myself dead between Jack Unger and his widow so that all three of us are bound together and it is impossible to tell which is the husband and which the Artist in Hair. With a piece of memorial jewelry there is always a moment of stupor when the customer beholds what I have made of his or her loved one. I could imagine just this state settling on the lovely brow of Marion Unger, and I decided I would use it to its best advantage, reaching across the counter to touch her luminous skin.

I had to suspend my work when Mrs. Friskin called, and I covered the bracelet with a cloth so that her sharp eyes would not alight on it. No doubt owing to her underdeveloped Secretiveness and large Acquisitiveness, Mrs. Friskin has a quenchless thirst for gossip and is always interrogating me about my other customers. She is a Scotch emigrant who has retained a most disagreeable accent, despite living in Tampa for ten years, and it is only of recent times that I have been able to decipher her every mutilated vowel.

"Something a wee bit ostentatious," she was saying as she settled herself on my red silk divan. "Mr. Friskin suggests a piece that reflects—I believe his word was *affluence*."

Hamish Friskin, inventor of Friskin's Magnetic Life Tonic, is a particular man. He admires a well-proportioned mustache cup, possessed as he is of a large waxed specimen; on the other hand, he spurns fruit cutlery, umbrellas, and the diagonal arrangement of furniture, and will not allow an aspidistra in the house. He is partial to a dish of Muscat raisins, but never after seven o'clock in the evening—as Mrs. Friskin puts it, they tend some hours later to cause *untimely evacuations*. Legend has it that he mixed his first batch of Magnetic Life Tonic in his wife's laundry copper—presumably on a day when the maid was not boiling his undergarments therein—and fed the potion to their ailing infant son, who was quite crazed with what the locals call breakbone fever. That infant is now a chubby child with arms as thick as logs, if his likeness on the Tonic label is to be trusted.

"—an ornamental birdbath," Mrs. Friskin was saying. "Hardly de rigueur at an afternoon musicale, but she couldn't have known that, of course."

"Of course," I said.

"I should have waited for instruction from the spirits. They were such a comfort when I lost poor Gertie."

I was aware that Mrs. Friskin, like Mrs. Rim, was a member of Hyde Park's band of spook-raisers, but for a moment I did not know who this lost Gertie might be—an unusually thorough housemaid who had been offered a better position, perhaps? And then I recalled that the Friskin daughter had died of consumption a year before, just when the Tonic was starting to sell, and that Mrs. Friskin had discovered Spiritualism soon afterward. I also recalled that I had purchased the girl's magnificent yellow curls and, following meticulous decontamination, had stored them in my cabinet for future use. I do not know why, but on that occasion my usual delicacy failed me, and when I called at their house I said not, "Where is the deceased?" but "Where is the diseased?" A slip of the tongue—but strangely enough nobody noticed, and I began to talk about little orphaned Tommy, who had lost his hair in a house-fire that killed his parents and his baby sister. As I was led to the late Gertie's chamber, I noticed that the hallway was lined with cases of Friskin's Magnetic Life Tonic, and in some places I had to walk sideways, like a crab. There was an empty bottle of it on the girl's bedside table, too, which Mrs. Friskin glanced at and tidied away.

"Poor Miss Friskin," I said now. Poor, bald Gertie. "Has she contacted you recently?"

Unfortunately, this encouraged Mrs. Friskin to list all the achievements of her party of spirit-rappers, from correct predictions of the weather to stock-market advice. She described each one in detail, and when I remarked on her extraordinary powers of recall she explained that Spiritualists, at a certain level of advancement, can remember every event of their lives, even those many years distant. I could think of nothing worse, although I did not say so.

"Mrs. Flood is Cuban, is she not?" I said, attempting to change the subject.

"I believe she has some sort of Latin lineage," said Mrs. Friskin.

"Latin?" I said. "Not African?"

Mrs. Friskin gave a little sigh and smiled. "Isn't it just too confusing? In Ybor City they don't seem to know who they are themselves. They have white men who call themselves Cubans, and they have men as black as pitch working right alongside them who also call themselves Cubans, and they have Cubans of every color in between."

"It is a place of slack principles," I agreed, and I was just about to ask her Marion Unger's views on the morals of Ybor City when she started up with her spiritual achievements again, spurting as much waste as Mr. Friskin after a nocturnal dish of raisins.

Go to a fairground in a town of any importance, I wanted to

remark, and there amongst the whipped animals and the stale straw you will find the Spiritualists. Some of them guess birth dates, some tell fortunes, some paint flowers while blindfolded. Are these your gurus? Have you not heard? Ten years ago Miss Margaret Fox, who started the whole business, confessed that her rappings were produced *by her deformed big toe*, which she could tap like a hammer.

I remained silent, of course. The news that Spiritualism is nothing more than a side show, a carnival amusement, did not appear to have penetrated the parlors of Tampa, and I was not about to offend a customer by telling the truth.

Mrs. Rim, that armchair of a woman, was my next customer. As she swept through my door her first words were "We can perform arithmetic," and she bent and cupped the Pomeranian's pinched little face in her hands. "Shall we show Mr. Gauntlet how clever we are?" She placed the animal square in front of her on the floor. "What's one plus one?" she said very slowly, her lips working like a pair of worms.

"Arf! Arf!" said Raisin.

"Astonishing," I said.

The dog began to lick itself.

"Now, Raisin, Mamma will ask you another question. Raisin, what's two plus two?"

"Arf! Arf! Arf! Arf!" said Raisin, and it resumed its licking.

"Why, Madame Rim, this is an astounding creature!" said I. "You must notify the *Tampa Tribune*!"

Mrs. Rim beamed. "We knew a man of your finesse would appreciate our achievements."

Lick, lick, went the dog.

"You know," I said, smiling down at the hairy object, "the taxidermist at the Tampa Bay Hotel does an excellent job, very lifelike. Something to bear in mind, perhaps?"

I am a man not often surprised, but I admit I marveled that the woman batted not an eyelash.

"He is an artist," she said. "He prepared the last three of my dogs, and his work was so fine one would think they might blink their little eyes and snuffle at one's skirts. Poor Sultana was done such a disservice," she said, shaking her broad head.

"Sultana?"

"Three Pomeranians ago. I had her prepared by a charlatan of a man, a butcher—I can hardly bear to look at her."

Mrs. Rim tried to frown and smile at the same time. She succeeded only in turning an unflattering shade of pink, resembling, I noted briefly, those organs with which Raisin seemed most intrigued.

"Monsieur Raisin," I said, "if x equals twenty-four and y equals six, what is the square root of xy?"

As they both stood staring at me and breathing heavily I thought how little time it would take to shear the animal, and how entertaining it would be to weave its clippings into its mistress's costly wig.

"Raisin is a little fatigued, I expect," I said.

And then Mrs. Rim, like Mrs. Friskin, began to drone on about her phantom-chasers, and to wonder aloud whether they might not try to contact Raisin's mother, since he had felt so despondent lately.

"Perhaps the Master Abayomi could intervene," I suggested, for I find the ramblings of this antique Nubian fine amusement. Mrs. Rim pronounced this an excellent idea, and began to elaborate on the last meeting at which the Prince had made an appearance. Adelina Flood claims to be in possession of his finger-bone, but I have it on good authority that the relic is, in fact, the femur of a chicken.

"Tell me, Madame Rim," I said when the matter of the bone arose, "exactly how did Madame Flood come to own this holy artifact?"

"Perhaps you have heard of the process of precipitation," said Mrs. Rim, brightening.

"It came down with the rain?" I said.

"Oh, no, Mr. Gauntlet!" She laughed; the dog yapped. "Precipitation occurs when objects or letters appear from the ether. A famous Spiritualist in New York, for example, was instructed by her spirit guide to look in her sister's rose bed, and there she found a beautiful brooch of rubies and pearls."

"And this bone, it was given to Madame Flood in the same way?"

"It materialized in her parlor while she was in a trance, yes," said Mrs. Rim.

"You are certain it did not materialize in the kitchen?" I said.

"The kitchen? No, no, it appeared before the hearth as she communed with her Invisible Companion."

"It is just I have heard that the relic in question resembles, well—"

"Yes, Mr. Gauntlet?"

"It does not matter. I have spoken out of turn."

"What does it resemble, Mr. Gauntlet?" Mrs. Rim was again coloring.

"The thigh bone of a pullet," I said.

For a moment she and the dog looked at me without speaking, without blinking. Then, in a low, controlled voice I had not before heard from her lips, she said, "The Master Abayomi has taken many forms. It is possible that this sacred memento with which he has honored us is the relic of a nonhuman incarnation."

"The Master was once a chicken?" I said.

I have not been so mischievous for a long time, but I was feeling in such an agreeable mood that I could not help myself. When she left, that dreadful poultry-worshipper, I was quite spent from devilishness, and I canceled an engagement with my actresses. I returned to the Hotel, ignoring the soldiers and the cocksure officers who grow in number by the day, and I made for the Solarium, where I could rest awhile in the sun, admiring from my briarwood bench the groups of bronzes selected by Mrs. Plant.

Returning to this haven is always a relief for me. It is an oasis of good taste; the vases and statuary and fine furniture calm me, and the antique tapestries and the rugs from Eastern looms remind me that there is beauty in the world. The moment I step into the Reception Hall and see the Spinning Girl from the South of France in her filmy bronze robe, one thumb and middle finger raised as if drawing an invisible thread, I feel at ease. Whenever I pass her, if nobody is looking, I stroke her life-size thigh—the type of thigh upon which I still like to imagine my Monte Cristos are rolled.

During my stroll along the Grand Hall to the Solarium, I mused on how different this setting is from the landscape that greeted me when first I arrived in Florida. As I observed the glittering mirrors in their gilt frames, I was reminded of the myriad pools that had glinted through the grass at me, the water stained and brackish from the mangrove roots. I do not care to recall that unsettled time, but now and then it comes to me unbidden. Like the swamps that lurk just beyond this town, it is always prowling at the edge of my obedient thoughts.

I had left the country of my birth not knowing where I would go, only that I could not stay in Paris. I needed a disguise of some sort, I realized, and at first was at a loss as to how I could make myself unlike myself. Perhaps you may not believe me, but in all my years of fashioning perukes I had never tried one on my own head. I examined the range of postiches in our studio and finally settled on a dark blond Gregorian made for a pâtissier who had refused to pay, pronouncing the item unflattering. Knotted as it was by my master, the workmanship was inferior, and I had to agree with the pâtissier that the style was unfavorable, but I could find no other to fit and there was scant time for vanity. I adjusted the tension springs, tweaked here and there—and the pâtissier's wig could have been intended for my own skull; it hugged me like an animal's pelt.

I draped a sheet over my unfortunate mess and proceeded with my packing, placing into a trunk my postiche oven and my scissors, my wig-blocks, pinching irons, twisting machine, my hackle, my needle combs, my hooks, wrapping them in clothing so they would not rattle. Around them I stowed lengths of hair, coiling each into a bundle so as to fill every space. When I forced the trunk shut I saw that the lid still bore my master's name, and I scratched it away with a knotting hook until no trace of it remained. As I left the workroom for the last time, I passed a mirror and caught sight of myself wearing the pâtissier's peruke. I started at my own reflection, as if a stranger had entered undetected.

I traveled by train to Le Havre and bought a passage on the first available ship, which was bound for New York. From there, I decided, I would go by rail to Florida: the Land of Flowers. I would have preferred a more sophisticated destination, but distance was important, and as I boarded I sensed a little thrill pass through me; it had been many years since I had traveled. When I had turned twenty, some thirty years earlier, my master had decided to make better use of my skills. He kept me in the workroom, where I could turn out pieces for his most discerning customers, who would pay well for a Dubois and Son original. He hired another young man to visit the hair harvests—cow-eyed thing that he was, the youth had no trouble convincing the beauties of Regensburg and Flanders, Avignon and Ravenna to part with their tresses. I devoted myself to my master's business and, eventually, to his care, for which he repaid me with increasing fussiness. His coffee was too bitter, his bed too cold, the bath water too shallow.

I deserved some new adventures far from France, and America seemed as good a place as any to visit. My English was almost perfect, thanks to my master's tireless instruction: many foreigners had featured on our books, and with a matter as personal as a postiche one must take care to express oneself exactly. I had quite forgotten our customer from New York, a Mrs. Henry Plant whose husband was building a luxurious resort hostelry in Tampa—four years had passed since I had constructed a waterfall chignon for her, and as far as I was aware I knew nobody with any connection to Florida, and nobody knew me. All I could think was that it was *warm* in that part of America, and I was eager to escape the frigid Parisian winters; on some days it was noon before my fingers were able to execute the simplest knot, and I was tired of sprinkling red pepper in the feet of my stockings just to make my blood circulate. I have always loathed the cold. My master used to remark that this surely was due to the hours I spent as a newborn in that rancid, icy alley, but I place little faith in the importance of one's early experiences. If I remember nothing of that first cold day, then the day is of no significance.

During my two weeks at sea I frequented the ship's small library, partly because it was always deserted—the passengers, by and large

American, passed the time playing shuffle-board and quoits—and partly because I could research my destination there. I plotted a course from Miami south through the saw-grass prairies, where I would leave no tracks; from there I would select a small town and establish myself. I would have to be on my guard for slinking dangers, I discovered, such as the coral snake, the diamondback, and the pygmy rattlesnake. There was the alligator, too, and there were spiny-edged pinnacle rocks, and holes that would suck at my feet. I learned to recognize poison ivy, the black wounds of the poison-wood, and the leaf of the manchineel, the sap of which could cause temporary blindness.

I had planned to avoid all company on board, but this proved difficult when not in the library, and I could not spend the entire journey there. The American women took an interest in me that was unlike anything I had experienced in Europe, even from our most devoted female customers. Perhaps, to them, I was more exotic than their drawling, bewhiskered husbands, or perhaps it was due to the casual intimacy afforded by travel, or perhaps they wished to prolong their memories of their time in France; for whatever reason, they would not leave me alone. They sought me out wherever I tried to hide, scurrying across the decks like vermin. They found my accent quaint, they said, and after a little too much sherry one crepe-throated matriarch announced that she would pack me in Spanish moss and take me home as a souvenir. Some even tried to speak French with me, and I replied in the crudest and most offensive terms, knowing there was not a chance the women would understand. In fact, they deemed my obscene murmurings romantic—and I resolved that if such sentiments passed for romance in America, I should remain a single man. They told me how refined I was, and how they wished that their daughters could spend some time in Paris gleaning the manners of the well-to-do, in response to which I spoke a few filthy lines concerning sheepdogs and Belgian peasant girls.

"Such a pretty language! So musical!" they jabbered, shaking their heads and smiling.

When they inquired after my profession, I was evasive. "Oh, but you are too mysterious, Monsieur!" they exclaimed, mangling this last word, my title, so that it seemed to rhyme with *cancer*. They cocked their heads to one side and smiled their open-mouthed smiles. "Let me see," said one, her eyes sliding from my collar to the gleaming tips of my boots and back up again. "I think you are a banker!"

"*Je suis désolé, Madame*," I said. "I am not a banker."

"A solicitor!" yelped another. "Something to do with the law, anyhow."

"Alas, no," I said.

"I've seen him heading for the library more than once," said a third, addressing her gaggle of companions as if I were not there. "And reading on the deck. He is always hiding behind a book. I think he's an author."

They all turned to look at me again, and after a moment's pause I said, "You have guessed correctly, Madame. I am an author. And now, if you will excuse me, I must see to some notes—"

"But how romantic!" they said, their smiles growing wider still. And they redoubled their questions, aiming them at me from all sides as if I were a fairground duck. Where did I get my ideas? Did I write in pencil or ink? Did I use a nom de plume? Would they be in one of my books?

Toward the end of the fortnight the captain announced that there was a hurricane passing through Florida, and sure enough we encountered strong winds as its tail moved north. I observed one of the sailors casting a hair-charm into the water to try to appease the storm, and I had to stop myself from reprimanding him for throwing good material overboard. I mentioned the ritual to no one, for I expected the American women to be frightened by the weather conditions, and I did not want to provoke panic by suggesting we were in the hands of witch doctors and voodoo artists. In the dining room that night, however, the women chattered like starlings, their eyes glinting, their voices more cacophonous than ever. And was it my imagination, or were their husbands more subdued?

"Isn't it thrilling, Mr. Ghoulies?" the women said. "Isn't it such a treat?" They beamed at me as if the storm were of my making, and although I am not superstitious I admit I was excited that this upset in Nature coincided with my arrival in the New World.

The hurricane killed nineteen thousand in south-eastern America, and upon disembarking from the train in Miami I was advised to be on my guard, as there were many vagabonds made homeless by the storm who were waiting to pick pockets. I feigned concern at the news, and furrowed my brow and clicked my tongue as the other passengers did, but for me the hurricane could not have come at a better time had I arranged it myself. I was glad when I thought of the people hurled from their houses, for it meant that nobody would take the slightest notice of a man drifting through the region alone—a little dishevelment, and I would appear most convincing. And there was something else which added to my sense of relief: since the forces of Nature had moved the world for my benefit, to assist me in my passage to a new life, therefore that life was one I deserved. I thought of the warm air that had risen, spun by the turning of the earth, and suddenly I felt at once powerful and light, as if lifted by that same current and enfolded in its hot core.

In Miami I purchased a few essentials: a map, a length of mosquito netting, matches, and a hunting knife. After tugging my trunk a little way and finding it as heavy as a tombstone, I had to admit that I could not take it with me, and so I packed as many of my tools as I could into my pockets and tied my wig-blocks and my coiled switches into a bundle. The trunk with its scratched-out name I abandoned.

For the first day I traveled south, following the flow of the sawgrass prairie as it made its way to Florida Bay. This was not grass as I knew it—soft, fragrant, manicured—but sharp-toothed and wild, a river of knives. So this was the Land of Flowers. For many hours I was ankle-deep in water, and when I removed my boots that night my feet were white and wrinkled like exposed grubs, and they looked so strange I thought they did not belong to me at all, and I did not know where they might lead me. I was moving downhill, I knew, for the Everglades are on a slope, although one cannot discern it with the naked eye: to me they appeared flat and even, as level as the workbench at which I had learned my trade. But that is sometimes the case—things happen so slowly that we cannot tell they are changing until we are at the bottom of the slope and there is the ocean, and one must stop or drown.

That night, against the mosquitoes, I swathed myself in netting like a bride, and as I lay in my watery world I felt that indeed I had entered into a marriage of sorts—a pact between myself and this topsy-turvy place, where the hurricane had left great licks in the grass like the whorls in an infant's hair, and where roots lay above the ground, and where the mangroves, their limbs stained with the salty high tide, stalked the shore. I was fascinated by these walking trees, with their arching roots and their garlands of moss trailing into the water like hair. A new plant is formed when the parent sheds its progeny; and when the currents are favorable, the discarded pod sails away like rubbish, gathering debris to itself and making its own new island.

Although there was much wreckage scattered by the hurricane— broken china, scraps of clothing, a brocade curtain with brass rings still attached—during that first day I saw no one. On the second day, however, I came across a young woman lying in a stand of bald-cypress trees. At first I thought she was sleeping, but as I approached I saw that there were flies on her lips and cheeks, and that the area around her left eye was a dusky purple. She made no sound when I prodded her with my boot, nor when I pinched her slack skin between my nails, an action that left two tiny red cuts like a coral snake's bite. They did not bleed. I hauled her upright and steadied the lolling neck between my knees, and unlike the squirming peasant girls guarded by their bossy mothers—*Be sure to leave a fringe; mind her pretty ear*; as if I had never shorn a head in my life—she sat quite still while I located my scissors and clipped the tumble of muddy curls. When I had finished I saw that the dark stain extended well past the temple and into the hairline, and indeed there was blood dried in the strands I had gathered and bound with thread. This was of little importance, of course, as all my stock is cleansed by boiling, whether it comes from a convent or a corpse, but it gave me a lucky idea that was to prove the key to my fortune.

When I observed the dead creature's apparel I saw that it was torn and stained about the waist, and upon cutting it away with my serrated hunting knife, as if I were skinning a fish, I discovered that her insides were partially exposed. Now, here is a curious thing: as I regarded this scene, flicking away the flies and the mosquitoes with the chestnut switch of hair, do you know what came back to me? The plump little cat belonging to the man and woman who had taken me, temporarily, from the Home for Foundlings. I remembered my fascination with the animal's insides, the way they all fitted, and I could not believe there was so much contained in such a small creature. Everything was so closely packed that, try as I might, I could find no room for a soul, and I wondered what was inside me. And then my mind skipped the years, and I thought of my visits to Monsieur Bourgeon, the mortician, who was so generous with his cadavers, and under whose twinkling eye I was to learn the fundamentals of Phrenology.

After this brief reverie I laid the girl's body down amongst the swamp lilies and began to explore it with my knife, and it was then that the idea occurred to me. Retrieving a pencil and a notebook from my bundle of possessions, I made a few sketches of the exposed vital parts—nothing elegant, you understand, just some modest little outlines which I could use as an aide-memoire once I had established myself in better-equipped surroundings. I had a reasonable idea of the location of the organs that interested me, thanks to the thoughtfulness of Monsieur Bourgeon, and bit by bit I exposed them, pausing every now and then to wipe my knife on tufts of Spanish moss and to make my rudimentary drawings. The principal obstacle was the bloated bowel—if you have ever dismembered a cadaver, you will know what I mean—but happily my hunting knife again proved a fitting tool. The art of dissection came naturally to me, and I reminded myself that it was not so long ago that wig-makers and barbers were surgeons, removing tumors and pulling teeth and lancing boils as deftly as they dressed the hair.

When I had finished with the hurricane victim I rolled her back into position beneath the cypresses, and I swear that anybody happening upon her would notice nothing out of order: her injuries might as well have resulted from the force of the gale as from my knife. On the tree trunks the resurrection ferns were a bright, new green, and there, in the middle of the stinking swamp, I had such a feeling of anticipation that for a moment I hardly noticed the heat or the mosquitoes or the squelching ground. I felt sure that my drawings would be the key to my new life, and I tucked them away inside my shirt as if they were promissory notes or valuable deeds.

I continued on my way, passing by hammocks of wild tamarind, Jamaica dogwood, pigeon plum and poisonwood, their trunks glistening with tree-snails. They clung like Christmas ornaments, these hermaphroditic creatures, the patterned shells at their most vibrant around the base, where new growth takes place, each season marked by a scar. Already composing the captions that would accompany my final illustrations, I smiled as I remembered the American women on the steamer who so despaired of their daughters making their way in society, and I recalled how I had posed as an author. And, as can happen with a lie if it is spoken with conviction, it became truth, for although it would be some months before I decided upon even the title of my book, let alone completed the text and the illustrations, the scraps of paper I now carried next to my skin would be the germ of the best-selling volume *The Splendor of Eve*. Most amusing of all, the shorn creature I had found beneath the cypresses, the laundress or seamstress or scullery maid, was to be the star of the show—and I thought how gratified her family would be if they knew the immortality afforded their plain young nobody.

As I took my drifting course through the Land of Flowers I came across more evidence of the hurricane's might: I would spy a hand protruding from a tangle of mangroves, or a foot caught in low-hanging branches, or a disheveled head nestled in the saw-grass blades. Curious flowers, these. I found no more complete specimens, however, and I realized how fortunate I had been to stumble across my life-drawing model (a little joke: she was already turning green) before the alligators and the vultures found her, and indeed before the heat and the peaty juices of the swamp did their worst work. Resourceful man that I am, when I did happen upon a relatively unmolested specimen with hair of the appropriate length—it must be over three inches to be of any value—I slipped my scissors from my pocket and harvested what otherwise would have gone to waste. I stored my clippings in a buttoned shirt: at night it made a comfortable pillow, and the fatter its chest grew the more comfortable I was. If I met with any persons looking for missing family members, I simply pretended I was searching for someone too. I called my old name, Gustave Dubois, into the swamp as if I were the lost one, and the brown waters and the rustling grasses took it without question. Despite the hurricane, Nature was regenerating the place—the hardy mangroves had survived, and the stilts and egrets were probing the mud with their bills, and the golden orb spiders had rebuilt their webs, some of which were so large and strong that they caught small birds.

It was becoming more and more difficult to carry all my belongings as well as my growing stock of hair, and I feared I would have to abandon even more of my old life, dropping it into the swamp for the alligators to gnaw. I imagined my prized scissors sinking into the muck, my hackle catching in the mangrove roots, my wig-blocks floating on the surface of the water like marker buoys. I veered away from the Keys, that perilous coral hook that catches big fish in a storm, and at Cape Sable I purchased a canoe and began to make my way up the west coast toward the jumble of the Ten Thousand Islands. All the world was fluid, and with my belongings packed around me I allowed myself simply to float. Cocooned in my birchbark vessel, I drifted from island to island like the strange pod of the red mangrove, traversing the currents in search of a place to take root. I do not pretend that this was an untroubled time, but one tends to forget unpleasantness. Or rather, one does not forget that it happened, but the sensation fades; memory removes the sting. So, I recall having scratches and bites, and I recall being hot, but I no longer know how that felt; I recall the crude repasts I killed and consumed, but not their taste; I recall the mud between my toes, but not its stench. Man is constructed this way; it is a survival device. If he remembered every pain, he would perish.

After I had passed through Naples I boarded a north-bound train and watched the dull scenery slip by. I had visited the real Naples many times during the hair harvest, and to my eye it had nothing in common with this steaming, swampy area. It is folly to name one thing after another; the original will only be missed all the more, and the pretender always found wanting.

I was shaken from my musing when, reaching a little place called Tampa, I saw silver minarets and domes and cupolas glinting in the middle of nowhere, seeming to rise up from the river. Although I am loath to embark upon conversation with other passengers when traveling—it can so easily lead to misery, and I had not forgotten the clawing American women on the steamer—so enchanted was I by this vision, this palace in the middle of dreary Tampa, with its sandy streets and its wooden sidewalks, that I turned to the man next to me and asked him what it was.

He looked at me as if I had just emerged from the jungle—he could not have known how close to the truth that was—and said, "That's the world-famous Tampa Bay Hotel, of course. Hot and cold running water in every room, telephones, electric lighting. It has its own barbershop and orchestra, and you can take a ride through the grounds on a rickshaw, which is a kind of Oriental buggy, only they put niggers where the horses should be."

I let him talk on and made the occasional interested remark, while through the window of the train car I watched the magnificent palace, my silhouette a phantom against it. I remembered Henry B.

Plant then, and the waterfall chignon I had made for his wife in Paris, which my master had pretended was his own work. I remembered lurking in the shadows of the studio, sweeping up hair and cleaning the hackle while Mrs. Plant told my master of the fabulous pieces of furniture and objets d'art she had purchased. The Plants would not recognize me, I was sure: four years had passed, and besides, the wealthy have little recall of the faces of those who serve them, especially if those faces are confined to the background, the unimportant edges. For once I was glad of my master's deceit. On this savage peninsula, in this state shaped like a pistol, here was a place I could settle.

So proud was my traveling companion of his home town's celebrated landmark, however, that he neglected to tell me it was a winter resort only: when I made my way to its fine portals I found it closed for the steaming Florida summer. As it was early September, I would have to wait three months for it to open, and therefore my first lodgings in Tampa amounted to a single room in a dank boarding-house. Electric lights—none. Hot running water—none. Obliging Negro porters to draw one's rickshaw—none. Rickshaws—none. Still, I reasoned, it was probably wiser to place myself somewhere unobtrusive at first, and any boarding-house was an improvement on the swamp. The Hotel attracted a great many international guests, and who knew whether amongst them there might not be nosy Parisians who kept abreast of the news? Considering the mess I had left behind me, I knew I could not have failed to feature in the papers—a thought that aroused in me a mixture of anxiety and pleasure.

For more than a year I did not dare practice my art. I locked my last remaining wig-block in my new valise, keeping the key always on my person. I devoted myself to my book, observing closely all the graceless American women I encountered and taking my inspiration from them. My landlady provided many an insight: *It is not uncommon for women to become slatternly after marriage. They say they have other matters to attend to, and grooming is habitually ignored—except, perhaps, on great occasions, when there is a display of finery and bad taste in public, to be followed by greater negligence at home. When a woman says to herself, "It is only my husband," she must prepare herself for consequences which she may regret to the last day of her life.*

The dispirited girl who served me a cup of tepid coffee: *As far as is possible, we should never show gloom or melancholy to those around us. If we conceal what is unpleasant in our bodies, we should do no less with our humors or temperaments.*

My landlady again: *In dressing the hair there is room for the display of a good deal of taste and judgment; but every lady will be able, after a few experiments and a visit to a reputable Perruquier, to decide what mode renders her face most attractive.*

Practically any woman in Ybor City: *No one has the right to appear in public in a dirty, disorderly, or unbecoming costume. In this matter there is a world of difference in different countries. You may go every day to the most frequented public resorts in Paris without ever seeing a man, much less a woman, in offensive attire. Can the same be said of all places of public resort in America? What belongs to the toilet should never be done in public. One may repair an accident, put up a stray ringlet, arrange a shawl, tie a ribbon; but one may not comb the hair, clean the nails, or touch the nose or ears. It is not delicate to scratch one's self.*

A fawning young woman I observed making a spectacle of herself on the arm of an older gentleman: *The lack of sensible and useful employments drives women into unladylike and immoral practices. A young lady, full of health and animal spirits, cannot spend all her time in reading novels. She is driven to dissipation and flirtation. What she reads so much about she wishes to experience. She preserves her reputation, no doubt, but what becomes of her character? And, in the absence of other interests, there comes to many young women the feverish desire for marriage—a thing which should never repose in her thoughts. Match-making mammas are bad enough—spouse-hunting girls are intolerable.*

My own thoughts: *Be what you would appear, certainly; but also appear what you wish to be. Assume the air and manner of calmness, and it will help you to be calm. Thus we refine and purify the character. The carriage of the body, and habits of dexterity, grace, and elegance are of great importance. Children, it is said, are always graceful—they are simple, unrestrained, unaffected. But we fall into bad habits; stoop until we grow round-shouldered; get into awkward, lounging ways; carry our hands uneasily as if they did not belong to us. A woman must train herself in good conduct as well as in good posture. It wants but a resolute will to secure either bodily or spiritual uprightness.*

The Hotel guests, of course, provided me with many opportunities to observe the American woman at close range, which only confirmed my opinion of her. The following passage, composed in the sanctuary of the Ebony Writing and Reading Room for Gentlemen, always makes me wistful, for it was inspired by a guest I saw on my very first day there. She, the indulged daughter of a New Orleans banker, was strolling the grounds with a governess who was attempting to tutor her in the various species of tropical plants so lavishly set out. I was walking just ahead of them, listening to the harassed descriptions of the papaya and the pineapple and the lewd banana flower, when I heard the governess utter a cry. I turned to see that she was grimacing and rubbing her shin, while her sulky young charge had settled herself so firmly on a mushroom-shaped jardinière that it was hard to tell where the fungus ended and her dove-gray gown began: *A young girl, and especially one of a light and airy style of beauty, should never wear heavy jewels. A simple flower in her hair or on her bosom is all that good taste will permit. When gems or other ornaments are worn, they should be placed where you desire the eye of the spectator to rest, leaving the parts to which you do not want attention called as plain and negative as possible. There is no surer sign of vulgarity than a profusion of jewelry carried about upon the person, suggestive of a Mexican mule loaded down with gold.*

When in December, after almost three months of hard work, I submitted six chapters and an outline of the remainder of the book to a New York publisher, along with a covering letter written in a feminine hand of my own devising, I was rewarded with an immediate and enthusiastic response. The editor who read my manuscript was impressed by my mixture of prudence and good taste, adding that it was refreshing to peruse a text aimed at women that neither harped on about the vote, nor recommended the smoking of cigarillos and the wearing of trousers. With a great deal of interest he had read "How to Prevent Self-Abuse Among the Young" and "How to Recognize the Signs of Self-Abuse and Cure It"; he applauded "Sluggish Brains," "Perverted Passions," "Wives and Money," and "Perfecting the Race"; he had positively devoured the special chapters on "How Young Husbands Should Treat Their Brides" and "How to Increase Their Love and Avoid Shocking Them." My advice was sound yet entertaining to read; my drawings were frank without being vulgar. He not only made me a lucrative offer for the completed text, he was eager to meet me next time I came to New York. (I politely declined his invitation—my postiches can disguise a multitude of unfortunate characteristics, it is true, but I doubted they could accomplish that particular metamorphosis.) When I forwarded my next chapters to him—"Important Truths for the Newly Married," "Morbid Longings," "Hotbeds of Disease," and "Unpleasant Odors"—he replied with a marvelous suggestion. In addition to my own drawings, he arranged for a series of captioned photographs to be inserted, accompanying the chapter on "Healthful Physical Exercise." These instructive pictures would feature young women performing a range of movements to enhance the shoulders, the arms, the lower limbs, and the bust, and would include examples of fencing maneuvers in a girls' gymnasium and graceful acts of balance on the parallel bars, as well as two portraits entitled *The Feminine Form Divine* and *Superb Womanhood*. The photographer made a fine job of it, and I suspected that this section, tucked away on silky pages at the book's center, would prove educational not only for the lady of the house, but also for her husband or curious son.

Finally, in December of 1893, I was able to leave the boardinghouse and settle into my apartments at the Tampa Bay Hotel. While I could not afford one of the parlor suites, each with its own private entrance hall, I was delighted to secure a minaret room. Within its rounded walls I felt a security with which I was unfamiliar, and I mused that its curving dimensions recalled the Tour d'Abandon at the Home for Foundlings. I had not yet made contact with Mr. Plant, for I wanted to be sure that the circumstances under which I had fled Paris had not reached American ears. (By now, of course, I realize that little outside America reaches American ears, except when there is a chance of sending some of their men to war.) I had my trunk stowed in one of the luggage cupboards—little half-height compartments up on the fourth floor. It is hot there—the higher one climbs in the Hotel, the hotter it becomes—and there is a corresponding drop in the price of the apartments. The ceilings are lower, the keyhole windows smaller, and one encounters a lesser class of guest; in addition to mill owners and life-insurance men and department-store proprietors, the nannies and servants of the more well-to-do guests are accommodated there. I made certain my cupboard was locked, for I have found that the less wealthy tend to be more inquisitive.

As the end of the winter season approached and the guests left the Hotel, I was aware that I too would soon have to vacate my gracious minaret room. After six months my book was developing so well that I felt uneasy about changing my habits in any way, and certainly I had no wish to return to the boarding-house. I gazed at the bronze African Girls, the bronze Esmeralda tending her bronze goat, the Spinning Girl from the South of France, and I decided that Mr. Plant was a man of sound judgment. And so I visited him in his rail-car office, and reached the special arrangement with him that continues to this day: I am what you might call a tenant, a permanent guest.

During that first year, when the book so occupied my days, by no means did I neglect my true profession. I began collecting hair combings at night, building up my stock in readiness for the time when I would establish myself as Florida's leading Perruquier: Monsieur Lucien Goulet III. In the shabbier parts of town I came across many an unpleasant episode—pistols and knives, beaten men and reeking whores, youths half-dead from drink, and foul disputes over the little ivory balls with which the poor are obsessed. Then in the morning, as if the night had been a bad dream, I continued writing, plucking my ideas from the scenes taking place around me. More than once it occurred to me that the construction of my book was not so different from that of a wig: I gleaned much of my raw material from my surroundings; I wove a basic foundation to which I added strands of varying shades, some lighter, some darker, to create the illusion of authenticity; and little by little my knots became a harmonious whole.

When I completed the book, in September of 1895, I set about building my wig-making business. Many months had passed since I had opened my valise, during which time I had almost forgotten its contents, and when I unlocked it I started: I was face to face with a shrunken head, such as explorers collect on trips to the Dark Continent. Then, of course, I realized that the case must have been moved many times—perhaps when a departing guest needed to retrieve his luggage, certainly when the porter brought it to my rooms that morning—and that the wig-block had simply escaped its wrappings and rolled upright. And I rubbed my palm across its smooth oak scalp and was comforted.

The Splendor of Eve; or, Love and Marriage, by Dr. Evangeline Montpellier, M.D., Containing Full Information on All the Marvelous and Complex Matters Pertaining to Women, Including Hints on Courtship and Etiquette, Promoting Health and Beauty, and Vigor of Mind and Body; Embellished with Many Superb Colored Plates, Phototypes, and Wood Engravings; Bound in Extra-Fine Satin Finish Cloth ($2.00) or in Rich Full Morocco with Gilt Edges ($2.75), was published in March of 1896—in the late winter, timed to catch the flurry of nervous spring brides. It seemed the elements once again had co-operated with me, for the weather was poor that season, obliging lovers to stay indoors, and a few months later, aligned with the publication of my book, there was a rash of weddings.

It was an instant success (in all probability you have a copy in your own residence—look on top of the closet, or behind the washstand, or wherever the lady of the house keeps her secrets) and allowed me to establish my business in the summer of that same year. Dr. Evangeline Montpellier—Angèle to her many friends and to the dashing Colonel Montpellier—receives a number of intimate letters from worried brides-to-be, expectant mothers, and the like, all of which she answers personally. Invitations to address various worthy groups are declined with regret, however, for the lady doctor's busy medical practice leaves her barely enough time for her charity work and her malaria research (the Colonel almost died from it while stationed in Tunisia). Her relationship with her publisher is maintained solely through correspondence.

PART III

A Woman Is a Pretty Disguise; She Is Hooks and Eyes

It was *bolita* night, and Señor Estrada told Rafael that he felt luck fluttering in his stomach. He had dreamt of a cat—not just a nameless stray, but the Persian he had owned as a boy. It was pure white with blue eyes, and when it was not sleeping on his bed it had hunted mice or lizards or birds in the garden, moving through the grass as slowly as a summer cloud, until it pounced. Señor Estrada left the house humming to himself.

Rafael was playing dominoes at the kitchen table with Miguel while Señora Estrada ironed clothes. The windows were open to the May evening, and everyone heard it at once—a faint, sad sound threading down the hall like smoke. There it was again, closer now: the arpeggio call of the *alfilador*.

"Do we need anything sharpened?" said Serafina, appearing at the kitchen door. She had been shut in her bedroom for the last hour, and Rafael noticed that her long thick hair was looped about her head in plaits and curls, a mess of different styles.

Señora Estrada was already opening drawers, selecting carving knives and paring knives, cheese knives and cleavers, scissors and bread knives, and passing them to her daughter, handle first. Soon Serafina and her mother each held a sheaf of blades, the edges splayed like the sharp fronds of the palmetto.

"Rafael, do you have anything?"

"He came to the factory today."

Down the hall the ladies of the house went, and in a moment Rafael and Miguel heard the sting of the metal against the *afilador*'s wheel.

When Señora Estrada returned, she took the hot iron from the fireside, exchanging it for the cold one. "Make Señor Rivera some bread and cheese," she told Serafina. "Rafael, he'll be sleeping in your room tonight."

"But he's Spanish," said Miguel, glancing down the hall at the *afilador*, who had taken off his black cap and was smoothing his hair in the mirror.

"Ssh!" hissed Señora Estrada. "Do you want him to hear?"

"Papá said the Spanish are a disease. What if we catch something?" Miguel was turning a domino—a double blank, the most treasured—over and over in his fingers.

"Listen," said his mother, running the iron across the narrow shoulder of her husband's shirt, "it's not the Spanish in Ybor City who are the problem, and it's certainly not Antonio Rivera, who has no house of his own, and no possessions except his whistle and his wheel." She held up the shirt and inspected it, shaking it before her like a cape.

"Why can't he stay with the Delgados, like he always does?" said Miguel, still peering down the hall.

"They have the twins now," said his mother.

"Papá won't like it," said Miguel.

But when Señor Estrada returned from the *bolita* house he kissed his wife on the lips and shook the hands of Rafael and the *afilador*.

"Number four!" he said to his wife, as if it were an endearment they shared. He poured four glasses of wine, and everyone drank to the *bolita* dealer who had sold him the winning chance, to the woman who had made the draw (the beautiful black-eyed sister of the factory foreman, but even if she had been a crone he would have kissed her), to the number 4, to cats, to the man who had invented the game, whoever he was, and to the little ivory ball itself.

I was wondering, Mrs. Unger, why you don't remarry. Surely you'd like to have a family? Stop me if I'm prying," said Miss Needham, her blue eyes glittering.

Marion gave a brief smile. "We did have a child, but it was a stillbirth."

The other women murmured and nodded. The younger Miss Rathbone patted Marion's hand.

"There's still time, my dear," said Mrs. Rim. "How old are you—twenty-five, twenty-six? Plenty of men would love to have a pretty wife like you. We just need to brighten you up a bit."

"And there are lots of handsome officers in town, and more arriving every day," said Mrs. Flood. "There are so many, the trains can't hold them all!"

"I'm thirty," said Marion. "And there's plenty of wear left in my mourning clothes." She did not mention the two new dresses she had ordered, one green and one yellow. Those she would keep to herself for now.

"I couldn't help seeing you going into the wig-maker's a few weeks ago," Miss Needham went on. "I don't mean to be inquisitive—"

"I've ordered a piece of memorial jewelry," said Marion.

"Ah," said Miss Needham. "I was thinking, perhaps a pretty curled fringe."

"Mr. Gauntlet does a marvelous job," said Mrs. Rim. "There's none better if you want a new look." She patted the tendrils of hair coiled at her temples.

"Well," said Marion, and hesitated. "Well, I'm thinking about ordering a transformation. Just thinking about it, at the moment."

"But that's a wonderful idea!" the other women said. Even the Misses Rathbone were enthusiastic. "It's time for you to move on," they said.

And then Miss Needham began talking about the seven famous Sutherland sisters, who each had hair many feet long, and who performed songs in Barnum and Bailey's traveling circus. She had seen them in New York, unbeknownst to her Calvinist parents, and then and there had decided to grow her hair as long as possible; the tresses of the eldest sister, Victoria Sutherland, measured seven feet.

That evening, Marion took the combings from her crystal hair-receiver and began to untangle them. She drew each hair between her finger and thumb, feeling for resistance, distinguishing root from tip. The pale strands sparked in the lamplight and she thought: soldiers marching up the wall. Useless soldiers, these, as useless as smoke.

She knew there was a quicker way of sorting the hairs. A professional like Monsieur Goulet, she recalled, would pass them through a solution to see which way they turned. Soap and water? Water and vinegar? Some simple potion, but she could remember neither the ingredients nor the exact method. She wondered when her bracelet would be ready. If it was a success, she would order a hair-piece from him: that was the pact she made with herself.

The room was growing dark by the time she had amassed the shimmering hank. She took the other combings from her drawer and smoothed them across her coverlet, watching them shine in the half-light. They felt soft to the touch, almost alive. She twisted them into a rope, turning the ends in opposite directions until the hair looped and curled in upon itself like some strange flower, and she held it to the nape of her neck, peering into the dark mirror to see herself. She smiled: the small, tight knot she wore every day was transformed into an elaborate chignon, something fit for a ball. And then she thought of the other strand of hers, the clipping that the Frenchman had taken to weave together with Jack's. She ran her finger over the tiny patch where the hair was growing back. Monsieur

Goulet had been so gentle with his scissors she had hardly felt him cutting: it was as quick as a slip with a paring knife.

"Mrs. Unger?" said a voice at her door. "Don't you want any supper? Oh, what's this?" Miss Harrow's short pink fingers scooped up the combings.

"I want to order a transformation," said Marion.

"How nice!" Miss Harrow began to wind the skein of hair about her forearm. "Monsieur Goulet is the best you can find."

"Do you know him well?" said Marion.

"Only by sight," said Miss Harrow, "but one hears things. He did the braided marteau for Mabel Slater's wedding—with the garnets and seed pearls, you remember."

"I wonder why he lives here," said Marion. "You'd think someone like him would have a studio in Paris, wouldn't you?"

"Perhaps there are too many there already," said Miss Harrow, waving the combings to indicate rows of studios filled with knotting and weaving men.

"London, then," said Marion. "Or New York. Why would a man like him choose to live in Tampa?"

"I should love to visit Paris someday," said Miss Harrow. "I remember when I was a girl—seven or eight, perhaps—my father took me to see the French circus."

She was still playing with the combings and Marion wanted to take them back, to wrap them in their silk cover and put them away, but she said nothing.

"I suppose there were acrobats and animals and contortionists," said Miss Harrow, knotting and unknotting the rope of hair, a silky cat's cradle, "but the automatons were my favorite. They were all in a circle, and at the center stood their ringmaster. He was real." She flicked the combings like a whip. "One by one he wound up his dolls and they performed their little acts." She told Marion about the monkey doll dressed in top hat and tails, his long toes protruding from his trousers like fingers, and one hairy hand raising a cigar to his lips. He exhaled real smoke, and his eyebrows moved up and down. There was a poet, whose words changed into a painting as if by magic, and an acrobat who raised himself on spindly arms to a bar and spun and spun. Miss Harrow's father had liked the snake-charmer automaton, a curvy female Indian with a scrap of satin caught about her hips, her thighs gleaming behind a fringe of glass beads. Across her breast was gold brocade—shaped like wings, Miss Harrow said, as if a rare butterfly had landed there—and she wore armlets and anklets studded with gem stones, and a head-piece that covered her ears with filigree flowers. In one hand she held a brass bugle aloft, and in the other was the snake, its long body coiled around her arm and hanging down to her feet, and its head aimed, like the bugle, at her lips. "And I said in a loud voice, so that every-one laughed, 'Which is she going to play, Papa?,' as if she might bring the serpent to her mouth." Miss Harrow smiled, and twisted the glossy combings, winding them around and around her arm. "And when the doll began to play, I decided that the filigree flowers served to block her ears, so that she would not charm herself. Funny, the ideas children have."

Marion watched the combings glide across her companion's silky forearm and wished she had her yellow curls, her pink com-plexion. Miss Harrow was like a doll herself, with her subtle shad-ings of rose and cream, and her plump, sloping shoulders, and her little straight teeth.

"And there was a conjurer doll!" said Miss Harrow, closing her eyes for a moment, as if she were absorbing these images and mem-ories from the combings. Marion recalled the look of bliss on the face of Adelina Flood when she spoke with the voices of the spirits. "He was made up like a clown, with a white face and a red nose and a little heart painted on his forehead. In his hand he held an open fan, and beside him was a stack of boxes decorated like dice. He moved the fan in front of his face and opened the top box, and there was his smiling head, and when he moved the fan back again his body stood headless. I cried, and said that France must be a terrible place, and I never wanted to go there."

"What did your father do?" said Marion.

"I think he was still looking at the snake-charmer doll," said Miss Harrow. "But the ring-master was very concerned, and he fussed over me and made the conjurer's head come back. 'Not real, look, not real,' he kept saying, and he wound the monkey up again, but I wouldn't stop crying. He tried to give me a piece of French candy, but I said I hated him and I hated everything from France, and could I please go home."

When her companion had left the room, Marion prepared herself for sleep, putting her things back in their proper place. She hung clothes, shut cupboards and drawers, replaced lids, straightened rows of bottles and jars. She liked to wake up to orderliness; it made the day seem easier. The one thing she did not tidy away was her length of hair. She left it on the dressing table, where it slowly untwisted itself, and as she lay in bed she could hear it moving as softly as a secret.

⁓

On May 28th, 1898, his first night in the service of Monsieur Goulet, Rafael chose the suburb of Hyde Park—a wealthy area, where nobody would recognize him. He would avoid his own territory for now, until he had learned all the tricks of the job; apart from anything else, there were too many soldiers on the streets of Ybor City at night, visiting the saloons and the restaurants, riding their horses up and down the sandy avenues, raising their hats to mothers and daughters, spinsters and children. Hyde Park was quieter, the silver minarets of the Tampa Bay Hotel appearing like sharpened knives in the spaces between the houses. As Rafael moved from one property to the next he heard snatches of conversation, arguments, tunes. Some windows were illuminated as if by footlights and he could observe the occupants quite clearly, and although he knew that from a bright stage no actor can see his audience, instinct made him shrink from these scenes. He had to keep reminding himself of the wig-maker's advice: that dark windows were the most dangerous.

It was well after midnight by the time he made his way home. He was a little disappointed with the small amount of hair he had recovered, for he had left no trash heap or pit unexplored, plunging his arms into even the ripest, ignoring the decomposing fish, rotten vegetables, flyblown bones. It was nothing, after all, compared with the camps in Havana. He tucked the soft fist of browns and blonds into his pocket.

As he crept into the Estradas' casita he bumped the mahogany table that guarded the front door, and a figurine fell to the floor: an image of Eleggúa, gluttonous messenger of the gods. It did not shatter but broke cleanly in two, the head skittering away from the body and coming to rest at the edge of a rug. Rafael listened for a moment but there was no sound from the rest of the house, and the only movement was the gentle swaying of the beaded curtain, as if someone had passed through a moment ago. He lit a lamp and picked up the figurine, surprised to find that it was hollow, and he ran his finger around the inside of the break to inspect the damage, the unglazed interior as cool as bone against his skin.

In the kitchen he sprinkled a little flour into a dish and mixed it with water from the kettle the way Miguel and Serafina did when they were making kites. Then he took Eleggúa's head, a curious thimble under the low light of the kerosene lamp, and he thought of Monsieur Goulet, who wore a steel thimble when he stitched his costly wigs. Rafael applied the paste to the break and pressed the head back onto the body, holding the pieces together for a minute or two, his breathing the only sound in the silent house. When he had replaced Eleggúa behind the front door and climbed into bed he found he could not fall asleep; he kept wondering whether he should remove the head again before the paste hardened, and confess to Señora Estrada in the morning. He could buy her another statue with the money he earned from the wig-maker, perhaps—and then he caught himself. A fine revolutionary he made. Every cent of his hair money was intended for the war. For a moment he considered returning to the kitchen, putting some food in a dish, and lay-ing it before the damaged figurine, an offering to atone for his sins. Soon, however, he was falling asleep, and dreaming of his mother's altars with their morsels of coconut meat and honey, and their little pools of wine, and their candles wreathed with pepper cress and nightshade.

At the factory over the following days Rafael imagined he could feel the eyes of the lector upon him, but he did not look up to meet his gaze. He concentrated instead on familiar objects: his wrapper leaves, his barky filler, his half-moon knife. His fingers were long and tapered, slightly stained with tobacco juice—a typical *torcedore*'s fingers; honest fingers. Surely the lector, who saw everything, had seen that Rafael was not stealing anymore? That he was not even taking the three cigars per day to which he was entitled? Why, then, was the man watching him so closely? Rafael knew it was unlikely he had been observed doing the wig-maker's work at night—not even the lector could see down black streets and behind houses—but still he waited for some kind of confrontation. It never came, however, and as the lector read each day from newspapers and books, Rafael worked swiftly and quietly, settling into the rhythm of rolling, losing himself in the stories. Words could change many things: Rafael thought of the reports about the destruction of the *Maine*, and how they had forced America to intervene, and he also recalled the lector quoting Mr. Hearst, a newspaper magnate, when one of his illustrators told him there was no sign of fighting in Cuba: "You furnish the pictures, and I'll furnish the war."

Outside the factory, the day was unusually hot. The streets were filling and filling with American soldiers, and the Cubans of Ybor City invited them into their homes for drinks and meals and, of course, cigars. Many houses in the neighborhood flew the American flag as a sign that they would welcome men preparing to fight for Cuba. Every week there was some kind of social event to raise more money for the cause: a fiesta at Sulphur Springs or at Ballast Point, a ball or a minstrel show, a play or a concert. Men rode through the streets announcing these occasions, followed by beautiful girls in decorated wagons. Everything was going to be all right.

One morning in the middle of June the lector began to read a news story. His voice grew more sonorous, and the men around Rafael slowed in their work and then, one by one, stopped altogether. An Italian photographer by the name of Secondo Pia, it seemed, had taken photographs of the Shroud of Turin, and in his darkroom the face of Christ had emerged as never seen before. A negative of a negative, the lector explained; a secret hidden in the linen for centuries, now revealed by the camera's true eye. Like a priest holding a jeweled monstrance he lifted the newspaper high, moving it slowly to the left, then to the right, and the men all craned their necks to see it, this photograph of the Son of God, this proof. Rafael looked at the picture of the crucified man. It stared out from the page as if through a window, and a few of the cigar-makers murmured of miracles, and some made the sign of the cross. To Rafael, the face was as sad as that of any of his mother's statues.

The *torcedores* approached the lector and reached their hands up to him, and the newspaper was passed from man to man. They held the pages reverently, careful not to smudge the photograph or mark it with their stained hands, although several kissed it. Only Rafael did not leave his seat. He continued rolling his cigars, his fingers working faster and faster.

"You there," said the lector. "Why are you still working?" He was pointing at Rafael like an evangelist, his white shirt damp beneath the arms.

The other *torcedores* parted to let Rafael through.

"Let him see," said the lector.

As Rafael held the photograph he began to feel dizzy. The dead man had long hair; it reached to his shoulders at least. Hair worth taking. The eyes of the reversed figure stared at him from their winding sheet, the dark sockets blank, waiting for an answer. To make sense of a thing, Rafael thought, perhaps you had to turn it around; look at its mirror image; examine it from a new perspective.

In the afternoon the lector began reading from a new book, *The Count of Monte Cristo*, and Rafael became so enmeshed in the story he quite forgot he had felt unwell. Serafina was waiting on the porch when he came home. She was folding and unfolding a fan, a newly hatched moth drying its wings, and Rafael thought of the splayed knives she had carried so casually. Inside, Señora Estrada was arranging some yams and corn before the statue of Eleggúa, and he held his breath for a moment, expecting the head to come away and roll across the floor like an unlucky *bolita* ball. But it never did, not that day nor any other, and eventually he forgot about the fracture, forgot that he had done anything deceitful at all, and he came and went at night as freely as he pleased.

⌒

As if it were not enough that I am forced to share my home with bustling strangers for five months out of every twelve, this year, just when the winter season was reaching its end, in swarmed the military. It has been two months since war was declared, and still the city is clogged with soldiers and sailors awaiting the order to head for Cuba, and still the Hotel is overrun with journalists and officers. A more poorly organized event there surely never has been: the rail tracks are so busy with trains bringing in provisions and men that there are carriages backed up for miles and perishable goods are putrefying in the hot boxcars. I suppose the publicity has been advantageous to Mr. Plant, but to tell the truth, I am surprised he allowed the use of his Hotel. The war correspondents, who still have no war about which to correspond, have instead written numerous articles about the beauty of their accommodations, and I imagine reservations will be brisk next season. They spend the rest of their time recounting tales of their adventures in more interesting parts of the world—I heard one reporter telling a large audience about his time in Russia disguised as a Russian, and his time in China disguised as a Chinaman, and his explorations in Africa, where he spent a year without meeting a white man.

The officers themselves, with their ridiculous mustaches and their center partings, clutter the verandas and talk about strategies while the maids bring them trays of iced tea and Cuba Libres. This cocktail is made by diluting perfectly good rum with a faddish new sugar-water called Coca-Cola, and is so dark it might have been dredged from the tannin-laced mangrove swamp. The military men fill the Gentlemen's Bar—my subterranean bolthole—with smoke from their inferior cigars; they rumble and roar in the Ebony Writing and Reading Room, their pomade dulling the glossy swans' heads carved into the chairs. When the chronically unwell General Shafter squeezed himself into one of these delicate seats, I feared it would splinter beneath him—he is known as the fattest man in the Army, and has spent most of the campaign lying in a hammock. In the evenings the officers enjoy the society of the more attractive female members of the Red Cross and the Salvation Army, as well as that of various Tampa beauties brought in for the endless balls and parties and arranged about the place like Mrs. Plant's china jardinières. Everywhere there is morale-raising music, with the Army and Navy bands competing night and day with the Orchestrion. The daily horse sales in front of the main building are ruining the lawns and the crushed-shell pathways, and even on the outskirts of town, where a man might reasonably go for a relaxing, solitary stroll, the soldiers are inescapable. They have turned the bay into a camp, pitching their musty tents all about the city, and one sees them lolling on their stretchers in their woollen uniforms, swatting mosquitoes and playing cards as they await the war. There are more than thirty thousand of them crowding the sidewalks, and more than twenty thousand Army mules and horses filling the streets with muck. The place has been made unsanitary by this invasion—indeed, sickness rather than the battlefields of Cuba has killed hundreds of the men right here. I hope it will not be too much longer before they depart. As it is, simply making my way to my studio exposes me to infection.

I do not know why the Cubans are so eager for independence; so many of them are living here it is a wonder there are any left on that sorry island. They have become quite carried away with excitement, as is their wont, and are holding celebrations and parading about the town as if the war were already won. Only yesterday they held a picnic right opposite the Hotel, on the banks of the Hillsborough, with military drills and rifle practice constituting the entertainment, along with mock battles and noisy re-enactments of insurgent victories and successively louder cries of "Viva!" For lunch the women set out a typically vulgar spread, only this time, in a patriotic vein, they replaced the usual dishes with foods such as they imagined the soldiers might eat in the open field: yuccas and yams, cassavas, sweet potatoes and cabbages, all cooked over open fires and served on plantain leaves.

In order to distract myself from this nonsense, I have been visiting my actresses more often. Theatrical women are the only kind for whom I have patience; they make no secret of their artifice. My two ladies of the stage are skilled mimics and can reproduce any voice I request of them, and after the hours I spend bowing and fawning in my studio, it entertains me no end to see this wicked pair impersonate my most disagreeable customers.

"Mrs. Rim and her counting dog called on me this week," I will say, and immediately one of them will take the part of Mrs. Rim and one the part of the dog, and they will enact *The Naughty Puppy*. Other productions of our own devising include *The Inquisitive Schoolgirl*, *The Naïve Governess*, and *The Bride to-Be*, each representing a customer (or, in the case of the schoolgirl, an unpleasant child who accompanies her mother to my studio and meddles with my materials and pulls all the hair from the shelves in Bluebeard's Chamber). My actresses have a range of props and costumes on hand for these impromptu performances, and are able to reproduce each mannerism so precisely one would think them possessed. Sometimes I am drawn into particular scenes and am permitted to do with my actresses as I please. When they are playing especially loathsome customers, I find this an effective means of relaxation, and I reward them as I see fit. They are truly most enthusiastic and inventive creatures, and fully deserve the coins I tuck into their costumes.

I met them in 1895, when they were taking part in a local production entitled *The Redemption of Lady Beverley*, for which a number of wigs were ordered. I constructed a vast head-dress for the actress Clare, which required numerous fittings at my studio, and she and the actress Lilian, who came to be my favorite, visited me regularly over a period of eight weeks. If other customers needed an emergency repair or, more usually, if they decided they wanted their item *today, Mr. Gibbet*, rather than on the date arranged, the actresses did not mind waiting. They draped themselves across my red silk divan and fanned each other with bunches of egret feathers, and while I was occupied with my other customers they watched through half-closed eyes, taking in every detail and blowing cigarillo smoke through their nostrils. A comelier pair of dragons I have never seen.

I could tell from the moment I took the first measurements for their hair-pieces that they were different from the average female. Both exhibited small Veneration, indicating an absence of respect for authority—an unusual finding, since this faculty tends to be larger in women, who are naturally more devotional and obedient than men. Unsurprisingly, I found Imitation generous on both heads. A fascinating organ, this is also found large in many of the lower forms of life, such as the mockingbird, which takes pleasure in mimicking the call of other avian species in its vicinity and then, when these approach, uttering the screams of the appropriate bird of prey. Imitation is also possessed to a high degree by lizards, giving them the ability to simulate motionless objects as a means of survival. When I came to know the actresses on a more personal level I revealed to them this intelligence, but I do not think they understood, for one of them asked if she was moving too much and whether I wished her to be more lizard-like, and the other said she once had a gentleman friend who liked her to dress as a lizard and she was sure she could still find the costume.

For my sins, I attended the opening night of *The Redemption of*

Lady Beverley. While the actresses Clare and Lilian were a credit to the hair-pieces they wore, the play itself was intolerably sentimental—the story of an orphan girl who becomes an aristocrat thanks to the assistance of an elf, or some such slop. Need I mention that in Tampa it received a rapturous ovation, played to full houses every night, and went on to complete a sell-out tour of the whole of Florida? The most entertaining aspect of the evening for me was the knowledge that, in addition to the cast, more than half the audience wore Goulet hair-pieces. Few of my clientèle greeted me in public, of course.

I took marigolds to the actresses' dressing room afterward and congratulated them on their fine performances.

"That's sweet of you to say, Monsieur," said the actress Lilian, "but you know the show stinks worse than horseshit."

I was startled at such candor, particularly as the elf was present, and my expression for once must have betrayed my feelings, for the actress Clare said, "Nobody minds themselves back here, Monsieur. We're not on stage now, and neither are you." She poured me a large brandy and we spent a pleasant hour or so in the dressing room, her monstrous head-dress watching from the corner like some hairy beast.

She and the actress Lilian had been famous for their Languorous Dances, performed at the Cherokee Club in Ybor City, I learned, and were familiar with many of Tampa's most well-to-do gentlemen—cigar manufacturers who met and entertained clients there, along with local bankers, lawyers, and industrialists, and high-ranking members of the military. They furnished me with many an amusing detail about these pillars of the community—but I could have told them more. I could have spoken of the gentlemen's society that ran for a time at the Cherokee and showed magic-lantern slides of a particular bent. When first I arrived here and did not know anybody, I attended one of the monthly meetings, but soon realized there was nobody in Tampa I wished to know.

The Society for the Appreciation of the Photographic and

Related Arts convened in an upper apartment at the Club, from which the busy port could be seen, but nobody was there for the view. The men made a pretense of conversing when they arrived, and sipped their drinks and smoked their cigars and asked after businesses and hunting and wives. By way of breaking into the discussion, I inquired whether they were aware that the magic lantern had first caught on in Paris. "The city of lights," I said, feeling like a stranger. "The city of illusion." I thought they might have been interested to hear of the early shows, held in an abandoned crypt, where phantasms were made to appear like visions before the excited crowd, and specters flitted across the dark air as if sprung from a nightmare. Sometimes, I continued, the phantascope was hidden inside a coffin and the terrible images were projected onto smoke, and sometimes, to the amazement of the bereaved, likenesses of the deceased appeared—but the men had little to say in response to my descriptions, and the lights were turned down, I felt, to silence me. The sauciest new pictures were then shown, some imported from Paris and Berlin, some featuring American girls; I believe my actresses were friendly with a number of the stars, and the Snake of Ybor City was said to appear in a forthcoming set.

One or two of the men had their own projectors, and over the following days were giving game and champagne suppers at their homes, where certain choice slides would be enjoyed—but I was not invited to these. I left before the dancing girls came on. Months later, when I had established my business, I was able to identify many of the faces present that night: the fat milliner and his brother, for example, and my tobacconist, and a number of my future customers.

Although I did not share this memory with my actresses, I so relished their company that I took up their invitation to visit them at their apartments. And so I found myself, at first every month, then every week, knocking at their door and waiting for my private performance. And it was to them I made my way last evening, shortly after the tireless regimental band stationed at the Hotel had begun to belch and fart its way through another set of tunes, and the officers had begun to maneuver their partners about the floor. I was reminded of the words of the elegant Shah of Persia on observing a ballroom full of whirling American figures: *We do this much better in our country; we hire others to dance for us.*

"Any engagements with Raisin and Mrs. Rim this week?" the actress Lilian asked as she ushered me inside.

"Alas, yes," I said, and they took their cue.

The actress Clare, who plays Mrs. Rim, donned a colossal hat festooned with cherries, flowers, and a stuffed mockingbird. She clipped a pince-nez to her nose and called, "Raisin! Raisin! Come here at once!" and she jiggled a leash. I settled into an armchair, and soon enough the actress Lilian appeared, sniffing the rug and yelping with excitement, and not a stitch on her. She is enormously talented in her own right, of course, but I do take credit for this aspect of her performance. "No animal covers itself with clothing," I had pointed out after *The Naughty Puppy* premièred some months ago. "A dog needs no costume." Dedicated thespian that she is, she had agreed wholeheartedly.

"Oh, you are a naughty doggy," the actress Clare said now, attaching the leash to her pet's neck. "I hope you won't steal any more sausages. I don't want to have to spank you again."

The actress Lilian whimpered and rubbed her shapely flanks against her mistress's leg.

"Well, somebody is a friendly boy today," said the actress Clare. "Perhaps I shall reward you with a treat."

And so they continued, improvising a little here and there to hold my interest. Raisin was especially disobedient this time, refusing to respond to any of Mrs. Rim's sums, and gnawing and scratching at her skirts, and placing his snout in all kinds of impolite places.

And then, a new twist in our favorite tale: he crouched beside the piano stool and made a little pool on today's edition of the *Tampa Tribune*, all over a story about America's Finest Sons defending Cuba! I could scarcely contain my delight, and leapt to my feet to assist the actress Clare in administering the punishment. She mimicked Mrs. Rim's screeches so exactly one would think the dreadful woman really was there, albeit without her clothes on. (Perhaps I neglected to mention: in our little production Raisin is such a playful, untrained dog that when he tugs at Mrs. Rim's skirts he often tears the fabric, and she is obliged to remove her entire outfit save the pince-nez.) I suspect that the actress Lilian will incorporate this new scene into all future performances of *The Naughty Puppy*. She is a true professional.

In addition to my hair-pieces and memorial jewelry, my accessories and cosmetics are in demand by the fashion-conscious lady. I have curling-irons and crimping-irons, perfumery, pomades and creams, soap leaves, brushes, puffs, hair oils, rouges, face powders, and French enamel. For the lady who wishes to shimmer at the theater as if she were playing the lead, I have hair powders of diamond, silver, and gold—although I regret to say that this fashion is on the wane. I have decorative combs of tortoise-shell and of silver, beads which may be looped and woven through the tresses in any number of elaborate designs, diadems and tiaras which will enhance the plainest wallflower, bejeweled pins which glitter like stars in the hair. The one item I do not stock is coral, although the reefs around the Keys provide an inexpensive and unlimited supply for other merchants. Its popularity stems from the belief that it repels the evil eye, and I refuse to feed such silly superstitions; in fact, I will not have coral under my roof.

I do a robust trade in feathers, and if a lady wishes to pin a single plume in her hair I am prepared to sell her the item just as it appeared on the bird. I find I have a skill for improving on Nature, however, and each season I bring out a range of feathered combs set with garnets and marcasite, seed pearls and jade, onyx and turquoise. The women of Tampa, zealous followers of trends set in more attractive locations, festoon themselves so liberally with these aigrettes that one half-expects them to warble and twitter and coo rather than speak. I wonder if they realize that feathers were once the sign of a cheap wig? Sporting gentlemen donned the feather-top for outdoor activities, as it was practical in wet weather, and it was also favored by parsons too vain to do without a peruke but too mean to purchase a good one; perhaps they believed that, from the pulpit, the tail feathers of drakes and mallards could pass for human hair. Nowadays, of course, the plume is a costly fashion accessory not to be disguised, and the women here pin them to their heads and their hats and stalk up and down, preening and displaying themselves, fluttering their fans like stunted wings. One wonders that there is sufficient bird-life to support this fashion, but the wet-lands of Florida appear inexhaustible, and it is a simple matter for me to procure my stock from one of the local plume-hunters. They are wily individuals, these men who live in the swamps, and one must be on one's guard with them at all times, for they are accustomed to thriving on shifting ground. It is wise to deal with the same fellow each time, despite promises of a better deal from a rival supplier.

I stock heron feathers and ibis feathers, feathers from the tern, from the bird of paradise and from the roseate spoonbill, but the most popular by far are the mating plumes plucked from the egret's back. Pure white and as delicate as skeletonized ferns, they are in demand in all the fashion centers of the world. During the nesting season, when egrets are plentiful, Florida is overrun with feather merchants from New York and Paris, London and Milan. They buy enormous quantities of bird scalps—my plume-hunter Swope told me of an Italian who purchased one hundred and thirty thousand—and are the focus of much attention from ambitious Tampa debutantes. With each scalp yielding up to forty mating plumes, and with the price of a single plume reaching seventy-five cents, feathers are as costly as gold here.

The beautiful Adelina Flood has purchased a number of my ornamented combs, and I am hoping my new designs will attract her back to my studio. Do not misunderstand me—I do not enjoy the company of beauty; rather, my interest lies in the fact that she plays hostess to the group of spirit-rappers attended by Marion Unger.

Mrs. Flood (full Vivativeness; puny Benevolence) is the type of society lady who hosts a dinner party, a *soirée dansante*, or an evening of dramatic readings not because she desires the friendship of certain guests but because she craves their admiration. She selects them with care, the first and most important requirement being that they are American. A light-skinned quadroon, she was born and raised in Spain, and had a Negro grandmother who was brought from Africa as a slave (there is nothing I do not know, or cannot discover with a little digging). Adelina Flood, however, has all but erased her Spanish accent, and since marrying Mr. George Flood, a fruit exporter from a highly regarded family, she has been welcomed into fashionable American circles as if she too were of pure blood.

I have never attended one of her dinners; in her eyes that would be akin to asking the cook to sit at the table, or the butler to join the gentlemen for a cigar. I know enough about her to know exactly what these occasions are like, however: the men must be a little in love with her so that they hang on her every word, admire her new dresses, and laugh at her witticisms, and the women must be less attractive than she and not nearly as droll. Traditional white napery is eschewed in favor of the new silk- and gold-embroidered affairs, and the table bows under the weight of silver trays lined with mirrors to simulate miniature lakes upon whose surface float artificial swans and ships of flowers. The dinner cards marking each place display merry ink drawings, executed by Adelina herself and identifying the hobbies or occupations of the guests: for an artist, a small easel draped with a scarf; for a keen hunter, a gun and game-bag; for a lady fond of domestic animals, her pet poodle or pug presented in his most engaging attitude. While the husbands cast furtive glances at their hostess's bust—which has been artfully shaded with rouge to accentuate its swell—the wives sit twining their hands in their laps and resolving to order a gown in the style of Mrs. Flood's, and to decorate their hair with a spray of lacy white feathers just as she does. They feel coarse beside her, and they study her and try to glean her secrets, making note of how she dabs her lips with her napkin, how she crooks her little finger when she takes wine, how delicacy compels her to refer not to the turkey breast but to its *bosom* and not to a cock but to a *gentleman bird*. The pottery trifles containing sugared fruits, caramels, and chocolates, and the favors given to each lady as a souvenir of the occasion, must be both attractive and costly. The *bonbonnières* might, at the Flood household, take the form of a small donkey carrying chocolate-filled panniers, a gaily decked peasant with a large fish-basket brimming with sweetmeats, or the head of a Turk whose fez can be removed to display the sugar plums within. Upon departing, the lady guests might be presented with a hand-painted fan, a lace handkerchief, or an artistically chased silver box, and they will express their thanks to their hostess for her hospitality and her generosity, and they will call on her, as etiquette demands, within a week of the occasion to reiterate their gratitude. And they will know that no matter how they copy her dress, her mannerisms, her ascending laugh, they will never arouse the same interest in their husbands as does she.

I also know how Adelina behaves when she is not in society. She speaks to me as frankly as one of my actresses might, explaining why she must have this type of fringe, that ornamented comb.

"The blunter fringes make my face appear too square," she said on her last visit. "They detract from my cheekbones, which are very fine, don't you think?"

"Very fine, Madame," I said.

"And this transformation makes me as squat as a pepper-pot, whereas this one lengthens the neck and enhances the bust."

"Yes, Madame," I said.

I believe it troubles her that I do not respond in the way the dinner-party husbands do. The distance I maintain with her—as I do with all my beautiful customers—drives Mrs. Flood to ever more flagrant displays.

"Do you think this comb suits my new gown?" she asked me

yesterday, twisting in front of my mirrors, the stripes on her dress rippling and curling. "It's of French glacé silk, Monsieur Goulet, and was made for me in Paris on a mannequin that is adjusted exactly to my measurements." She ran her hands over her comely hips. Her sleeves were in the latest style: so full at the shoulder that she had to turn sideways when passing through my door. It seems that women are determined always to draw attention to some part of themselves—the bustle may have disappeared, but the excessive puffery has merely shifted to the upper arm. By contrast, the fashionable gown is now so tight from elbow to wrist that one must employ sleeve-tongs when dressing.

"Ah yes?" I said, placing another selection of combs on an occasional table for her perusal.

She nodded, still gazing in the mirror. "If I grow a little fuller here, for example"—the back of her hand caressed her bosom—"I must advise my couturier immediately."

"But of course," I said.

"Can you imagine what anyone intercepting such a telegraph might think?" she giggled.

I did not reply.

She took a feathered comb and held it to her face, fluttering it like the fan of a saucy Spanish lady. "Perhaps the silver would be more in keeping with my satin slippers, rather than the tortoise-shell?" And she lifted her hem and wriggled her foot from side to side, pointing her little toes at me. "Did you know, Monsieur Goulet, what a wily bird the snowy egret is? It attracts fish and other aquatic life with a flash of its yellow feet," she said, still twitching her toes in my direction. "Then, once the prey is lured near, the egret strikes, snatching it up and eating it in flight."

"An efficient means of consumption," I said, ignoring the wanton yellow slipper beneath my nose.

"Mr. Flood is always taking trips to the Everglades. Do you know them at all, Monsieur Goulet?"

"Not at all, I'm afraid," I said.

"I can think of nothing worse than visiting a swamp for my amusement," she said. "He is away a great deal, Monsieur Goulet, almost every weekend. I have a lot of time to myself."

According to his lonely wife, Mr. George Flood collects the shells of the tree-snails found in the Everglades and displays them in custom-built cabinets that line every wall. "The collection has become something of an obsession with him," she went on. "He places each new shell just so, ensuring it is pointing in the same direction as all the others. Mind you, he used to arrange them so that their colors could be best admired. He would turn each one over and around for hours, Monsieur Goulet, sometimes returning the following day or week to adjust it, or to observe it in different lights at different times of day. For a period of time he was moving them as the day progressed so that they caught the sun, but as the collection expanded he needed more and more time to do this, and eventually he was doing nothing in his leisure time but moving the shells. He did this so gradually that at first, before I knew he was responsible, I thought they still housed the snails! Isn't that silly?"

"Not at all, Madame," I murmured. "The mind is easily deceived by the eye."

"Of course I soon found out what was happening," she continued. "But the house is so full of them that sometimes, Monsieur Goulet, at night, when I hear the fig tree rustling outside, or the movement of the waves, I think all the tree-snails are coming back to reclaim their shells."

As I pushed a silver comb into her hair and felt the metal teeth piercing her sleek black topknot, I amused myself by imagining the naked mollusks crawling through the house, leaving their wet trails behind them, perhaps crossing the sleeping cheek of Mrs. Flood as they searched for their homes, and beside her Mr. Flood, free of his wife for a few hours, retreating to sleep's thin shell.

"No, no," she said, yanking the silver comb out. "I must have *feathers*, Monsieur Goulet. Then I can creep through the ballroom like a Seminole warrior!"

~~~~~

Marion Unger had a fair complexion. Jack said it reminded him of the moonflowers that grew in profusion in the swamps around Tampa, opening their great white trumpets at dusk. In some places they covered the custard-apple trees, twining from branch to branch, their fragrance so thick it settled like oil on the skin. Marion sighed at her reflection in the mirror. She had been attending meetings at Adelina Flood's house for one month now, but nothing more had happened. She wondered whether she should take some sort of memento with her the next day: a piece of Jack's clothing, perhaps, such as a tracker dog might use when searching for a lost person. Miss Needham had done so the previous week, when she wanted to contact her drowned sister; she had produced three hairs from a brooch pinned to her breast, placed them in a brass ashtray, and burned them with a taper. And then, as bitter smoke hung in the air, Eleanor Needham, drowned in Lake Magdalene some ten years earlier, wrote her name. Marion had seen the planchette moving beneath Adelina's fingers and had studied her pink nails for signs of pressure. She found nothing.

Eleanor, the heart-shaped piece of wood had spelled. *Cold. Cold.* And that had been all.

That night Marion heard a noise outside, a crashing sound as if something had fallen, and then a cry. She went to the back window and peered out, and there on the path was a young man—a soldier, perhaps. He crouched low, clutching his hand.

"Are you hurt?" she called, and his eyes darted open and up, the whites glowing like half-moons.

"No," he said, his voice breaking. "I'm not hurt." He stared up at her, his breaths short and quick as if he were frightened.

"Your hand is injured," said Marion. "You've cut yourself." As she shone a lamp on him she could see blood running between his fingers, tracing the lines of bones toward his wrist. He lowered his eyes.

In a moment Marion had wrapped her silk kimono about herself and rushed downstairs. She was hurrying because she knew the young man was wounded, but there was another reason for her haste, and she felt it like a tightness in the chest, a lack of oxygen: *If I am too slow, he will disappear.* She threw open the back door and ran along the side of the house, her slippers thudding on the flagstones, her robe billowing behind her. When she saw him bent in the shadows, relief rushed into her, as heady as a gulp of air after one has been underwater too long.

He was leaning against the clapboards, his eyes closed. He was really just a boy; sixteen years old at the most. Dotting the path were jars and bottles, balls of paper, ashes, scraps of wool, the peel of an orange in one careful spiral—things Marion recognized, things she had discarded. The way they were arranged made her think of a museum display, as if experts wished to represent the life of a people long dead. And there was nothing of interest there, nothing.

"You're all right now, it's all right," she said, touching the young man's elbow, and he allowed her to lead him inside and clean and dress the cut. She performed the operation in the kitchen, which was a place she enjoyed in the daytime, when sunlight bleached the pine table as white as bone and made the copper pans and molds glow. Now, by the light of the spirit lamp, they gleamed like Moorish gongs, and she thought how strange a familiar place could look in unfamiliar circumstances. There was a shard of glass in the cut, and she removed it with tweezers, her hand steady. She could feel the young man's breath fanning the back of her wrist.

"Now then," she said when she had finished, "I will pour you some brandy, and you will tell me why you were sorting through my trash."

When she handed him the glass balloon the boy cupped it in his left hand and studied the bright liquid, swirling it up the sides of the glass so that it left little tidemarks. Then he raised it, a little clumsily, to his lips.

"Are you hungry?" she said.

He shook his head. "I'm sorry for waking you, Señora."

"I'm a light sleeper," she said, and lit a cigarillo.

The young man glanced at the label on the box. "You shouldn't smoke this brand."

Marion exhaled in surprise. "My doctor himself recommended them."

"They're poorly rolled, and made from the cheapest tobacco. You should smoke Ybor-Manraras."

"Well," said Marion, taking in his clean-cut features, "thank you for your advice. But why would a young man with such refined tastes be searching through a stranger's trash, I wonder?"

The boy took another tiny sip of brandy. "I didn't mean to pry. And I'm not a thief, I've taken nothing from you." He glanced at her, then away again. "You have very lovely hair, Señora."

Marion laughed, a plume of cigarillo smoke escaping her lips. "Please don't change the subject. I'd like to know what you were doing out there with my rosewater bottles and my cold-cream jars and my—*orange* rinds. Do I have such an interesting life?" She remembered peeling the orange three days earlier; how the zest had stained her thumbnail, how she had concentrated so hard on not breaking the spiral of skin, as if like a girl she might cast it over her shoulder to form an admirer's initial, how pleased she had been when she had succeeded. And she also remembered how fleeting that pleasure was, and how empty she had felt even as she ate the sweet segments.

"I wasn't changing the subject. Your hair—" he began. "I was searching for combings."

The explanation seemed to make everything quieter, stiller; it hung in the air about this softly spoken boy who sat in her kitchen and sipped from Jack's brandy balloon. Marion closed her eyes as if to decipher it. She could smell the smoke rising from her cigarillo, and beneath that the roast pork Miss Harrow had made for dinner, and the traces of lavender water on her fingers. She thought of Miss Needham, burning hair to summon her dead sister. Hair could be used against a person, thought Marion. Spells could be cast, curses invoked. English country people never discarded their combings, for if a magpie lined its nest with them the owner would die within a year. As a safeguard, some cast their waste hair into the fire—if it burned brightly, the owner would live long, but if it smoldered, death was approaching. Irish people, on the other hand, buried hair cuttings; if they were burned, a person's spirit would return after death to find the destroyed locks. Marion flicked her long braid over her shoulder and stared at the stranger. He had a Spanish accent, and she had read in the newspapers about the voodoo rituals that went on in Ybor City. Jack had warned her not to visit that part of town alone, and never after dark.

"Who are you?" she said finally, her voice a whisper. "Have you come to cast a spell on me?"

The young man gave a little smile. "I'm no magician, Señora. My name is Rafael Méndez. I wasn't gathering the hair for myself."

"But for someone who knows about spells?" If she had a name, a contact, she thought suddenly—perhaps an Ybor City witch could achieve what Adelina Flood had not.

"No," he said, smiling again. "It's not for the *bruja*. I work for Señor Goulet."

Marion frowned. "The wig-maker?"

The young man nodded. "I collect hair combings, and he pays me for them."

"You're not serious," said Marion, laughing. "You creep around at night, going through people's garbage, looking for *hair*?"

"I've only been doing it two weeks," said Rafael, as if this made it less strange.

"But how do you know where to look? How do you know which houses have women living in them?"

"Señor Goulet has compiled a lot of information over the years," said Rafael. "He's provided me with maps."

"Hair maps?"

"Yes."

There was a noise at the kitchen door, and Miss Harrow's sleep-creased face appeared. "I thought I heard voices," she said, her eyes shifting from Marion to the boy to the brandy and back again. "Is something the matter?"

"No, no," said Marion, and she introduced them to each other. "Mr. Méndez cut his hand, and he's just recovering."

"You friend has been very kind," said Rafael.

"Yes," said Miss Harrow. "Well. I just thought I'd check—I'll see you in the morning, then." She glanced at Rafael again. "Good night."

The next day Marion was very tired, and she sent Miss Harrow away when she came in with the newspaper. She began to wash and dress with a heaviness in her limbs, as if she had not slept at all. She considered missing her meeting with the Harmonious Companions; although she enjoyed the quiet company of the Rathbone sisters and the charm of Adelina, the others could be draining. She knew they meant well, and usually she could deflect or ignore the bluntest of their remarks, but today, when she was at a low ebb, she was not sure she wished to hear suggestions that some new dresses might be in order, and that blue would suit her, and perhaps a little tuck of lace might brighten things up, and she had such a lovely complexion it was a crime not to enhance it.

Miss Harrow knocked on her door. "Mr. Rafael Méndez is here to see you," she said, coming in.

Marion's fingers fluttered to her hair. "Rafael?"

"Our visitor from last night." Miss Harrow smiled. "Perhaps you thought he was a dream?"

Marion splashed her face with water again and was suddenly awake. "I'll be down in a moment."

She smoothed and buttoned, brushed and pinned, cringing as she recalled how the young man had seen her: her hair hanging in a messy braid over her shoulder, and her nightgown covered only by a thin kimono. It had been part of her trousseau, selected with a bride's vanity—she liked the way the silk made her eyes shine, and she had thought Jack would too. The day before her wedding she had wrapped the blue cloth about her shoulders and stood with her back to her mother's cheval mirror, whirling around again and again, trying to catch sight of whatever it was that had made Jack want her. She could not deceive herself, however; all she saw was a girl dressing up in her mamma's mirror.

Marion fingered the slippery robe now. It hung across the back of a chair, the walnut struts making points in the shoulders, thin wooden bones. With her toe she nudged the blue length spilling across the floorboards, and it rippled and was still again. The silk was beginning to fray a little, she realized as she inspected it in daylight, the neat French seams pulling apart, exposing the construction. Miss Harrow was right; the previous night did seem unreal, and what had felt perfectly acceptable in the warm, dark kitchen now struck her as absurd. She wished that nobody else knew of her behavior, that she could keep it to herself the way one stows away an immoral dream. She could not imagine why she had acted as she had. Downstairs, she thought, in my parlor, sits a young man I entertained in my nightgown and robe.

She secured her hair with a decorative comb, pushing it so firmly into her bun that she could feel her scalp tug whenever she turned her head. Then, as stiff as a doll, she descended the stairs.

"Good morning, Señora," said the young man. "I've brought you a small gift, to thank you for your kindness."

He gave her a box of cigarillos, keeping his bandaged hand drawn in close to his chest.

You look a little peaky today, my dear," said Mrs. Rim, her diamonds quivering as she spoke. "Are you feeling all right?"

"I had a wakeful night, that's all," said Marion.

Miss Needham peered at her, blue eyes flicking from side to side. "You do look unwell," she said. "I don't mean to intrude, but perhaps you should see a doctor."

Marion shook her head. "I shall be quite recovered after a good night's sleep."

"Friskin's Magnetic Life Tonic," said Mrs. Friskin. "I've taken it twice a day for one year and I've never felt better. That'll put the roses in your cheeks." She lowered her voice. "It's very effective in the area of feminine complaints."

"What a pretty comb," said Mrs. Flood. She ran a finger along the scalloped edge, and although Marion saw she meant to touch it only lightly, she could feel the teeth digging into her scalp, the skin on her brow pulling.

The seven women took their places around the table. Marion held the dry little hand of Miss Needham and the broad one of Mrs. Rim, hard with rings and stones. Today, she told herself, she would be silent; she would not even think about Jack. Every time she had asked him to speak to her, willed him to come, willed it so hard that she saw patterns of blood rushing and exploding behind her eyes, nothing had happened. Perhaps it was a mistake to want something too badly. When she was married, she had wished for certain things, prayed for them each night, and they had not come. Perhaps she should stop asking.

"Master Abayomi, Guide to the Otherworld, we ask you to open the door to us. We ask you to act once more as our messenger, O Great Prince, he who has given us of his very bones," began Mrs. Flood.

When she had finished her speech there was silence for several minutes, the only sound an occasional snort from Mrs. Rim's lapdog.

"Most gracious Master, hear us," said Mrs. Flood. "We your servants beg you to open the gate."

Again there was a period of silence, and then Mrs. Flood said in a deep, clear voice, "My little bee. My honeybee."

Marion felt her fingers turn cold, as if Mrs. Rim and Miss Needham were holding them too tightly. "What did you say?" she whispered.

The elder Miss Rathbone repeated the words for her, also in a whisper.

"My honeybee," said Mrs. Flood again, then opened her eyes. Following her cue, the other women withdrew their hands, resting them neatly on their laps as polite guests waiting for a meal might. "Perhaps we should try the planchette instead," said Mrs. Flood, smoothing her hair as if something had slipped out of place. She looked around the table. "What's the matter?"

"You spoke," said Miss Needham. "You mentioned bees."

"I'm sure I don't know what you mean," she said, still fussing with her hair.

"You said 'My little bee,'" said Mrs. Friskin. "In a voice that was not your own."

"You did," said the others.

"My little bee?" said Mrs. Flood. "But how silly! I don't know what I meant by that. Perhaps I was just clearing my throat. Would anybody like some tea before we try the planchette?"

And she rose from the table, and Marion watched the movement of her throat as she swallowed and swallowed again as if to dislodge the strange voice.

"I think it was Jack," said Marion. "I think it was my husband." She could hear Mr. Flood walking around upstairs, and she listened to his footsteps, the sure, unhurried steps of a man at home.

Marion did not tell Miss Harrow what had happened at the meeting, how the women had clustered around her, kissing her cheek, rubbing her hand, pleased that Jack had spoken at last. Adelina Flood still denied she had said anything significant, but then, as the younger Miss Rathbone pointed out, the workings of the spirits are mysterious, and there was no reason why even the most gifted medium should have knowledge of them. As Marion lay in her bedroom she tried to remember the voice that had come from Mrs. Flood's lips. She wanted to remember the sound alone, to screen out the face of Adelina, for the two did not belong together. She tried to recall Jack's voice, its exact patterns and contours, but it reached her only as a muffled call, like sounds heard through a locked door. Perhaps the Harmonious Companions were right; perhaps she should stop dressing in mourning. True Spiritualists did not mourn their dead, for if the departed were enjoying the rewards of the afterlife, was not grief a selfish emotion? She had taken extra care with her toilet today, because of the visit from the Cuban boy, and had worn a pretty comb in her hair when ordinarily she wore only pins. And today Jack had come, when she had allowed herself a little bit of beauty.

Her thoughts turned to a newspaper article she had read some days earlier, about an exhibition of sacred art in Turin. A local city councilor, Secondo Pia, had obtained permission to photograph the famous Shroud, and when the first negative image began to develop in his darkroom he all but dropped the plate: it showed in startling positive the face of a tortured and crucified man. The faint markings on the cloth, the hints of features, were rendered with such clarity and detail that Mr. Pia felt certain he was looking on the face of Jesus. The other plates, showing the flagellated chest and back, the pierced hands and feet, the lanced side, were just as vivid. The cloth, he realized, was itself a photographic negative, and had kept its secret for centuries until science had reversed the evidence, uncovered the truth. The relic could not be a medieval painting, as some skeptics argued, for no forger working before the advent of photography could have painted a negative.

"What does that prove, though?" Miss Harrow had asked when Marion had finished reading the article aloud. "That the resurrection really happened? That there is an afterlife? That God exists?" Miss Harrow could be very bitter when it came to spiritual matters.

"They want to conduct tests on the fabric," said Marion. "They want to perform experiments with blood and myrrh smeared on clay models. Maybe even on real cadavers."

"And what will that tell them?" said Miss Harrow.

"That the image was formed when the body of a crucified man was wrapped in the cloth."

"And what will that tell them?"

"Well, that it's not a forgery."

"And what will that tell them?"

Marion saw what she meant.

She imagined Secondo Pia now, developing the plates in the dark, watching for proof to appear as if by magic.

⌒

I see that the Maas brothers—the fat milliners—have begun attaching entire birds to their hats: cardinals, warblers of many varieties, mockingbirds, even a juvenile gull. My plume-hunter Swope carries examples of all of these, but I do not purchase such articles in commercial quantities, for naturally they are impractical on the bare head. I enjoy inspecting the sample birds, however, and have built up a small collection that I have placed at jaunty angles around my studio. They regard me with their glass eyes as I work, and are a pleasant diversion when I am tired from hours of close weaving, knotting, and stitching. So lifelike are they that I can imagine them reanimated, plucking strands of hair from my workbench for their nests, and when first I positioned them I found myself starting each morning when I unlocked the door, and raising my hands to shield my face from their outstretched wings and their claws. Eventually, of course, one becomes accustomed to even the most unnatural sights.

Sometimes, as I am weaving my little nets to cover the empty heads of Tampa, I envy the plume-hunters and knife-sharpeners of the world. They wander where they will, earning just enough to survive. They remind me of the summers of my youth, when I followed the hair harvest through Europe and lived by my wits, and sometimes I think I should like to live that way again. I imagine myself leaving Tampa behind, leaving all the soldiers in the streets and the officers in my home. I would head for the Everglades, where a man can make a living from Nature, and everything I required would be packed into a skiff. There is such a supply of valuable plumage in the great southern rookeries that I could drift from swamp to swamp as the mood took me, a shotgun slung across my back, resting when I pleased and working when I pleased. If I felt weary I would lie back in my boat and sleep. If I felt hungry I would pluck custard apples and eat them with a spoon, or I would spear fish, or steal egret eggs from the nests. I would boil the claws of the stone-crab, and pick wild oysters fresh from the mangrove roots, and lobster would be as familiar to me as bread. I would clip the fangs from a coral snake and keep it as my pet. I would line my skiff with trophies to deter the swamp rogues from robbing me: the tooth of a crocodile, the claw of an alligator.

There is Nature at my very doorstep, of course—on any winter's day at the Hotel one sees gentleman guests heading for the river, where they can shoot at game from comfortable pleasure boats. They dress up in boots and tweeds, these wealthy men, and off they march behind Mr. Arthur Schleman, the Hotel's hunting and fishing guide, to board the electric launch. (A long-haired Briton of German extraction, Schleman revels in his work, swaggering about in high boots and making the ladies gasp with his stories of alligator-wrangling and snake-charming. The only way to silence the man is to ask him about his 1895 deer-hunting expedition, sadly terminated when he shot himself in the foot. He also recites poetry.) When the gardeners beat the brush along the riverbanks and the birds rise like spray, even the worst shot is unlikely to shame himself. The more adventurous trek farther into the wilderness with Schleman, hunting on horseback to avoid rattlesnakes. And now, of course, the officers are practicing their aim on the wildlife, although how closely the magnificent frigatebird or the lesser golden plover resembles a Spanish soldier I cannot say. All over the Hotel they boast of their tallies: this week a general from New York has been the most vocal, bellowing about the two hundred and eighty-three snipe and plover he has bagged during his stay.

Such excess is not the reason I am attracted to the life of a plume-hunter, however: it is his freedom I covet. I have enjoyed my swampy daydream for some time now, imagining myself rid of customers knocking at my door and forever interrupting me, expecting me to listen to their babbling, to flatter them no matter now plain they are, to debase myself for the sake of their children's amusement. Lately, though, a new fantasy has begun to usurp it. I have found myself thinking, Perhaps I do not wish to leave Tampa after all. Nature is full of barbs and poisons, and I am not the fit young man I was when I traveled the Continent. Besides, in Tampa there is the widow Unger.

I had just seen Mrs. Friskin to the door after a most protracted fitting, during which she talked at length about her newest grandchild. I do not know why even the most level-headed adults lose all sense when confronted with infants; I cannot see the attraction of the creatures, with their froggish limbs and their sea-bird cries.

"Wee Martha is the sweetest child," said Mrs. Friskin in her Scotch voice. "I believe she will have blue eyes, like her mamma, but of course they could just as easily turn brown. I was wrong about Master Freddie's eyes, which are the loveliest shade of brown you ever saw. Still, blue eyes are pretty for a girl. It's curious, is it not, how the eyes change? How so often the eyes we are born with are not the eyes we die with? Now that sounds a little strange, and not quite what I meant. They are the same set of eyes, of course."

I swear I do not know when the woman drew breath.

"Are you fond of infants, Mr. Gullet?" she asked. "You seem like a man who would have a great deal of affection for infants. Mr. Friskin has this in common with you; he is a very proud grandfather, and the wee ones swarm to him with such excitement that he does not know which one to place on his lap first, bless him. Little Miss Martha is the favorite at the moment, which is only right, although one must try not to have favorites. Children can sense these things."

Even as I saw her to the door she did not stop talking.

"We were hoping that the new baby might arrive on her mamma's birthday, but she came a day late in the end. Still, one can't tell Nature what to do, can one? When is your own birthday, Mr. Gullet, if it's not too impertinent a question?"

"The twenty-first of June," I said, although that may not be true.

It may be that I had lain in the rubbish for quite some time before I was found, or that my mother kept me awhile before disposing of me. Still, I cannot say that I have no birthday, can I?

"But that's very soon!" said Mrs. Friskin. "I hope you've something special planned. You bring so much happiness to the lives of others, you deserve a treat for yourself." She skipped one or two steps toward the door. "Oh," she said, giggling and simpering, "I can't wait to see what magic you will weave with my Imperceptible Hair-Piece."

There is nothing more repulsive than a woman of a certain age behaving like a coquette, but I smiled and said, "I am confident it will do justice to Madame's striking features. Perhaps dear Miss Martha will take you for her mother."

"Mr. Gullet," she said, "you are a naughty man!"

And I opened the door, and the jangling of the bell was all but drowned by her kittenish squeals.

I returned to my studio and began working at the newest bag of combings procured by my Cuban, sorting them into piles of different colors, teasing out the tangles. The task is time-consuming but undemanding, and it is a useful foil to the more trying aspects of my art. Indeed, I have begun to await the deliveries of my Cuban with something like excitement, as if he were bringing gifts. Delving into each new bag reminds me of my quiet nights on the Continent when, after many hours of haggling, I would settle into my bed for the night and stroke and smell the cut locks of the prettiest girls, bringing their faces to mind as I amused myself.

When I heard the front door open and the bell jangle again, I confess I was a little slow to answer. I finished unknotting a section of very long black hair, winding it about my fingers as I drew it through the hackle so that when I placed it on the table it coiled and writhed, a glossy garter snake. I imagined the woman from whom it might have come: a smooth-limbed Spaniard, perhaps, with a flower behind her ear and a head full of lust. The sort of woman I had imagined rolling my cigars on her thighs, until my Cuban told me the truth. There are times when I find myself wishing he had withheld it, for the disclosure has quite ruined one of my favorite mental tableaux. His careless divulgence has also had unfortunate ramifications for one of my little theatrical productions—shortly before he came to my door selling his stolen Monte Cristos, I had conceived of a new piece for my actresses in which they were to play cigar-rolling Spanish maidens.

"Hello?" called a voice from my front room, and I looked at the coil of long black hair and sighed. As I walked down the corridor I thought of the Spanish-speaking ladies who live east of the river, in Ybor City. When I used to visit that part of Tampa at night I sometimes saw them dancing, stamping their heels and clapping their bare hands in time to a guitar, their castanets snapping like crabs. They did not dance for me, however; they fell silent if I approached, and drew their black mantillas about themselves, the fringes trembling. Ah, but they did not know that I possessed parts of them which they had thought discarded, and which were mine to do with as I pleased—and that was almost as satisfactory as the real thing.

Of course, no lusty señorita stood at my counter; the figure I saw there could not have been more different. It was the white-haired, pale-skinned Marion Unger, holding my letter in her small gloved hand.

~~~

When she entered the wig-maker's premises a little bell jangled above her head, and she stood for a moment and waited for Monsieur Goulet to appear. She slid the letter from its envelope and unfolded it, scanning its contents once more to be sure of their meaning; a month had passed since she had received it.

"Hello!" she called. There was a vase of feathers on the counter, and she could not resist removing her glove and running her fingers through them.

"They're very pretty, are they not?" said the wig-maker, arranging them with his small, neat hands. "The mating plume of the male egret. Quite useless for flight, but of paramount importance when it comes to attracting the right companion."

Marion could feel herself blushing, the sides of her neck mottling with crimson. The wig-maker's eyes were fixed on her, as if he were trying to commit her expression to memory, and as she backed away from the feathers she felt her locket moving against her chest, the links as fine as stitches of hair.

"I hope I haven't interrupted you, Monsieur Goulet," she said. "I've come to collect my bracelet."

"Of course," he said, withdrawing a red leather box from beneath his counter. Inside sat the bracelet, the ropes of hair shining against the ivory velvet.

"It's lovely," said Marion.

The craftsmanship was so fine she hardly dared touch it, but the wig-maker lifted it from the box and fastened it about her wrist.

"Your work is beautiful," she said. She pressed one of the hollow ropes of hair, a long, winding net, and as soon as she let go it resumed its shape. Through the open weave she could see her skin.

"It's always best when there is a contrast in shades," said the wig-maker.

Marion felt her throat tightening with tears. "Poor Jack," she said, surprised to hear herself speaking his name. She never mentioned him to strangers, but she felt suddenly grateful to the wig-maker who had woven this beautiful memento for her; it was as if she owed him something. She found herself telling him about the frost, when the fruit had hung frozen on the trees and the eggs had cracked in their shells. She told him about the splintering of the branches in the night, and the acres of budded oranges that had only just shown their flush after the first freeze, and about the old grove of grapefruits, also destroyed. She gave him segments of information that, until then, she had kept stored inside herself, as untouched as the contents of an attic, and he listened to her every word, his eyes glittering, she thought, with tears. And she wondered what sufferings, what losses, her own story summoned for him.

For a moment or two neither spoke. Then, as if the wind changed, Marion said, "I received your letter some weeks ago, just after I ordered the bracelet. Your special offer? I do have some combings I've been saving—" She withdrew the envelope from her bag.

"Ah yes," he said, his hands again worrying at the vase of feathers. "Yes, I've had an overwhelming response to that little piece of advertising. And since I've been commissioned to produce the head-dresses for *Carmen*, I'm quite snowed under with work."

"Oh," said Marion, the letter drooping in her fingers. She placed it on the counter, where it seemed to cover the space between them, a bone-white expanse as wide as one of Tampa's streets of sand.

"If you were to come back in, let us say, six weeks? At the end of August? Then I would have more time for you."

"Yes, I see," said Marion.

He stopped arranging the feathers then and smiled. "Had Madame something particular in mind?" he said, inclining his head to the left and right like a bird. "If you'll permit me to say so, Madame Unger, it appears you do not need my assistance."

Marion blushed again.

"There are plenty of designs for you to consider," said the wig-maker, whisking some catalogues from beneath the counter and opening them for her.

"Oh, I don't think I'm quite settled on the idea yet," Marion said quickly. "Besides, with a war on—it seems a little selfish. But I'll certainly come to you if I decide I'd like something."

"It would be my pleasure," said the wig-maker, although a sadness had crept into his voice. "You can contact me here, or at the Tampa Bay Hotel after business hours."

"The Hotel?"

"I have apartments there."

"You *live* there?" She was aware of how rude she sounded even as she spoke. "I mean to say, Monsieur Goulet, wouldn't you prefer your own home?"

"The arrangement suits me very well, Madame."

"Mr. Unger always said we would stay there, for a special occasion. I haven't been inside for some years, but I imagine it's very lovely, now that the Casino and the Exposition Hall have been added."

"I'm a poor substitute for your husband," said the wig-maker, "but if you will permit a somewhat irregular invitation, I would be honored to show you the Hotel. It's normally closed at this time of year, of course, but with the officers and the correspondents staying, all the facilities are open. We could listen to one of the military bands in the Rotunda, or attend a dance in the Oriental Annex, or observe the pleasure boats from the Japanese Teahouse—or perhaps take part in a moonlight riding party. There is a fine Orchestrion renowned for the beauty of its selections. There may even be a show in the Casino—it is not unusual to see the likes of Mr. and Mrs. Oliver Bryon and their Comedians on the bill, or Edward Weckel, the Great Impersonator, or the ever-popular Minstrels and Bell Ringers. It's really rather festive."

Marion knew she should decline his invitation, but she found herself saying, "That's very kind of you, Monsieur Goulet, thank you. I'd love to come."

On the day of her visit I took a long, long bath, then shaved closely and carefully, applied a little cologne, and dressed. When she arrived in the early evening I was somewhat disappointed to see she was still wearing half-mourning; although the black grenadine set off her pearly complexion and her hair, in my thoughts I had always pictured her in white. They make a feast of grief here; it is three years since the death of her husband, and still she is in funeral weeds. The English Queen is to blame for this and other ridiculous fashions.

We took tea on the western veranda, as far away from the rowdy officers as possible.

"May I compliment you on your gown, Madame?" I said. "A fine grenadine, if I am not mistaken."

"You have a keen eye, Monsieur Goulet," she said.

"Papa was a cloth merchant, God rest his soul," I replied. "As a boy I would accompany him to the docks whenever a new shipment arrived. I would watch the bolts of cotton and velvet and silk being loaded onto our wagon, and often Papa would unroll them just a little way and I would glimpse their colors. When I arrived home, my sisters would cluster around me, asking me which shade would suit which of them best, and I would tell them that the rose moiré silk would be perfect for Jeanne, and the royal blue velvet for Michelle, and the chartreuse taffeta for Nicole, and so on until I had outfitted all seven of them in the most fashionable colors of the season."

Marion Unger laughed. "With so many sisters, your services must be in constant demand."

"Yes, we're a close-knit family," I said.

"I wonder," she said suddenly, "your father, being in textiles. I wonder, did he have any thoughts on the Shroud of Turin?" She raised her eyes to mine.

"Thoughts, Madame?"

"Yes. Whether he believed it to be, well, genuine."

In all my rehearsals, I had not foreseen such a twist. "My poor dear father was a man of simple faith," I said. "He did not require evidence."

"Oh," she said, and looked away again.

"I have seen the holy relic with my own eyes, of course," I added. "As a young man, I made several trips to Turin."

"Pilgrimages?"

I could hear her breath quickening. "One might call them pilgrimages, yes."

"And what is it like, the Shroud?" she said, her speech quickening too as my information took life in her.

"Ah." I paused, lowering my gaze as if in prayer. "It is kept in a silver casket which is lined with the most exquisite panels of embroidery. Since it is so fragile it is wound on a wooden spool, just like a bolt of cloth, so that no folds form, and it is protected by a swathe of red taffeta sewn by the Princess Clotilde."

"But the Shroud itself? What does it look like?"

"The image grows fainter with each unveiling," I said. "When first one looks, one sees nothing. Or rather, one sees what appears to be a dirty cloth: there are rusty smudges, creases, scorching, and burns; there are repaired holes. Gradually, however, markings begin to emerge from the fibers of the linen—a beautiful herringbone weave, Madame—like the camouflage design on a moth's wings. And then a human form becomes clear. It looks as if it has been singed on the cloth. One sees a bearded man, unclothed, hands crossed before him. One can discern the finger bones, the eye sockets, the brow, the lips. One can make out the shape of the legs and the nose."

"Extraordinary," said Marion.

She was on my arm now, and as we walked through the keyhole arches and the curling corridors and I caught sight of us in the carved mirrors, I thought we could have been any well-to-do couple.

"In the Middle Ages, Madame," I remarked, "so many pilgrims came to venerate the Shroud that some died of suffocation."

Despite what you might think, I was not inventing all this, for I have been to Turin—Italian girls are known for their abundant heads of hair, and I found them only too eager to submit to the shears of a traveling stranger. They were proud of their cathedral and its relic, and pressed upon me the importance of seeing it for myself. They told me about it as they sat before me and waited for the touch of my blades while their black-shawled mothers circled like crows, hissing the rosary or something like it under their breath. And yes, I did once go to view the cloth in question. What sort of a religion, I remember thinking, places a rag at its center? What sort of fool worships a tattered cloth? For Marion Unger, however, I could pretend.

Rafael missed the hills. There were few high places in Tampa, few points of elevation from which a long view was possible. He wished he could work in the glassy lookout above the factory; there was a telescope up there, and the watchman could see all the ships arriving at the port, and all the goods being loaded onto donkey-drawn carts. Rafael felt he had lost the perspective afforded by distance. His days were a series of details that lingered even when he closed his eyes: the texture of wrapper leaves, the cuts and nicks on his workbench, the thickness of a single retrieved hair, the patterns of tobacco juice staining his fingertips like the shapes of unfamiliar countries.

He had been collecting hair for the wig-maker for a few weeks, but although his new employer paid well, Rafael found him a distant man, not given to conversation. Since their first exchange at his studio door the night Rafael had sold him the stolen cigars, he had revealed nothing more about himself. The most he had said at one time had come in the form of a warning.

"You won't look at people in the same way again," the wig-maker had said. "You would do well to avoid the houses of your friends— you might discover secrets you'd prefer not to know."

Rafael had laughed and said, "I have no friends with secrets." He had taken the small cloth sack that the wig-maker had handed to him, folded it as neatly as a handkerchief, and slipped it into his pocket.

When he had made his first delivery of combings, he waited while Monsieur Goulet weighed them on shiny scales. Rafael had tried to chat with him, asking him where he was born, whether he missed his home country, and how long he had been in the business of false hair. The wig-maker had not replied, but continued placing the little brass weights on the scales like coins. He had not even looked up from his work; he'd simply raised his index finger like a teacher demanding silence. And Rafael had asked no more questions.

Using Monsieur Goulet's meticulous notes and charts, Rafael learned which areas of town and which individual houses were the most fruitful. The hair maps were crisscrossed with colored lines, and marked with arrows and stars, and each evening Rafael studied them, choosing streets, plotting a course. There were two kinds of households that were useful, he discovered. The first kind produced large quantities of hair—the boarding-houses and casitas of Ybor City, for instance, were a reliable source of black—while the second kind yielded smaller amounts of rare, more valuable shades—the various reds, or pale blonds as soft to the touch as an infant's locks. Occasionally one struck volume and rarity in the same household. There was a residence in Pierce Street where a German lithographer lived with six flaxen-haired daughters, the eldest of whom, it was said, was the model for his more risqué cigar-box labels. Certain spacious manses in Hyde Park, where mothers, daughters, and servants of Scotch descent were to be found, were useful when red was required. These addresses were marked in bold on the wig-maker's maps, and they stood out in the tangle of lines: black stars caught in a net.

In addition to the maps, Rafael made his own notes. If he collected a large amount of hair from one particular address, he wrote it down along with the date, and returned there only after a fortnight had passed. He kept a record of the location of trash pits, and which houses had particularly vigilant servants or aggressive dogs. If he happened to rouse the occupants, he avoided that area for a few weeks. When he returned home each night, his eyes drooping, his bag was as light and soft as a pillow. Its contents seemed little to show for three or four hours' work, and indeed it was hard to believe that the combings he collected, those little wisps of nothing, were a commodity worth trading. But it was just as well that the lector had discovered him stealing cigars, he told himself, for he was earning almost as much from the wig-maker as he was at the factory.

He could not give all the money to the Party, he reasoned, for questions would be asked about its source, and so he began to save some for himself, placing the notes in a cigar box and hiding it in the spider monkey's cage, and as his fund grew he could not help thinking about what he would do with it. He could buy himself a fine new suit, perhaps—his old one, although smart enough for Ybor City, was not fit to wear to Mrs. Unger's house; he had felt shabby when he had visited her. With some of the money, perhaps, he could buy her a present as a token of his appreciation for her help—a necklace or a bracelet, something precious that she would keep close to her.

One night in an alleyway, as Rafael was out doing the wig-maker's work, an American soldier tripped over him.

"Pardon me," said the man, his voice hot with whiskey. His eyes fell on the litter at his feet. "Say, are you hungry, friend? Do you speak English? English?"

"No," said Rafael.

"Well, soon enough you won't have to pick through the trash for food," said the man. "We're going to liberate Cuba for you. *Lib-er-ate*. Understand?" He sprinkled some coins on the ground and stumbled away. When Rafael returned home he added the money to the hoard in the monkey's cage, and Pedro chattered at him, his thin hands scrabbling at the box until Rafael nailed the lid shut.

As he became more skilled, Rafael learned new kinds of stealth: how to walk without making a sound, how to stifle a sneeze, how to duck beneath lit windows, how to conceal himself in shadows. One month into his employment with the wig-maker, he had progressed far beyond his first fumblings. He was as dexterous with trash as he was with tobacco, and he had never again been detected. Besides, the soldiers were leaving Tampa, finally setting sail for Cuba, and the streets were quiet again. Rafael felt more at ease with each passing night, his long fingers sifting more quickly each time, feeling for the soft touch of hair. He had a gift for the job, he told himself, and you had to take advantage of your gifts, even if that meant rolling cigars all day for other men to enjoy, or sorting knots of hair from trash all night.

At first the widow had invited him back to her home because she had a lamp that needed fixing, some pictures to be hung, some heavy furniture to be shifted. Miss Harrow, her companion, brought him a glass of lemonade, setting it before him with a few brisk words and eyeing him as if he might steal something as soon as she turned her back. He could see her looking over the ornaments in a room, making a mental inventory. She then began fluffing pillows on the divan, straightening rugs, watering plants, sweeping away crumbs with a little silver brush and pan, its handles two silver women with swirling hair. She even locked a bureau drawer and hurried away with the key clutched like a charm in her fist. Rafael tried to chat to her but she would not let him; she did not sit with him and Mrs. Unger but was always close by, listening, busy in the background. He was offended by her behavior, but then he thought: She is right to be suspicious, for although I now take only discarded scraps, it's true that I was once a thief. His mother would have understood the difference, and these days he allowed himself to think of her more often than when he had been stealing, and to talk to her in his thoughts. I am no thief, he told her. I am an entrepreneur.

Mrs. Unger did not seem to notice her companion's manner toward him, and although she asked about the cigar factory, she did not mention his nighttime job. He could not decide whether she was being polite or simply was not interested or, as he feared, pitied him. Perhaps she regarded him in the same way as the American soldier had: an unfortunate who knew no better than to scavenge, a creature that hung around trash like a rat. Rather than coins, however, she gave him books, and said he could borrow as many of hers as he liked. He stood before the glass-fronted cases as if before store windows, watching his reflection in the vitrines, the outline of himself against the glittering spines.

His eldest sister was pleased he was making friends with Americans; it was important, she advised, to try to fit in. *But I worry about you all alone in that big country*, she wrote. *Be careful in whom you place your trust: American women have few scruples.*

One day in June Mrs. Unger mentioned his other job.

"I received a letter from your employer a while ago," she said. "He's offering a special deal for the summer. I'm quite tempted by it."

"Señor Manrara has written to you?" said Rafael.

Mrs. Unger laughed. "I'm not ordering a year's supply of Robustos, no," she said. "I mean your other employer."

"Oh," said Rafael, and he looked at the rug.

"You're not embarrassed, are you? There's no need to be."

Rafael could feel her eyes on him and he wanted to leave all of a sudden, to go to the *bolita* house with Señor Estrada or to take his first turn with the Snake. But the widow was rising from her chair now, picking up the books he had brought back and replacing them in their respective gaps.

"*Uncle Tom's Cabin*," she was saying. "You know, I always found the character of Eva to be an annoyance. I remember *willing* her to die."

Rafael laughed then. "I don't know any six-year-old who talks that way," he said. He took the book and found the death scene: " ' "There isn't one of you that hasn't always been very kind to me," ' " he read, " ' "and I want to give you some-thing that, when you look at, you shall always remember me. I'm going to give all of you a curl of my hair; and, when you look at it, think that I loved you and am gone to heaven, and that I want to see you all there." '

" 'It is impossible to describe the scene, as, with tears and sobs, they gathered round the little creature, and took from her hands what seemed to them a last mark of her love. They fell on their knees; they sobbed, and prayed, and kissed the hem of her garment; and the elder ones poured forth words of endearment, mingled in prayers and blessings, after the manner of their susceptible race.' "

The widow clapped her hands. "You should do that for a living," she said, leaning in close to him to examine the passage, and in a rush Rafael began to tell her about his ambition to become a lector. As he was doing so, Miss Harrow appeared and listened with an amused look on her face. She asked him what he would read, and all words evaporated from his tongue; he felt as mute as the boy the hurricane had hung in the almond tree, his throat pierced. Rafael stared at the hem of Marion Unger's dress, one section of which had turned up, like a cat's ear folded inside out. He noticed that the fabric underneath was an inky, unfaded black, and all of a sudden he wanted to bend before her and gently smooth the little corner of cloth down. He did not explain that the lector did much more than entertain. He did not say that his was a job of great importance, that the stories he read turned and shaped the minds of men.

The widow smiled. "Perhaps you can tell us some more about it when you come back." And she stepped away from him, and the corner of her hem corrected itself.

The *bruja* Chiquita's house was just three blocks from the Estradas'. An old, woody wisteria filled her porch with a mauve light, and the clusters of flowers stirred as Rafael passed. The hallway smelled of coffee and of cooked corn meal, and the kitchen looked out to a yard covered with herbs and fragrant shrubs: white elderberry, witch hazel, nightshade, heliotrope, pepper-grass, rosemary, lantana, and honeysuckle. Hens scratched among the plants, and in a corner, rising like a tree, was a dovecote from which, every now and then, a white feather fell.

The *bruja* cleared a scattering of cowrie shells from the table and invited Rafael to sit down.

"So you want to be sure a sweetheart is faithful, is that it?" she said.

"No," said Rafael, his eyes lowered. "Well, yes. Eventually. I want her to *like* me first, though." He studied the smooth table, the pine bleached from many scourings.

"So a spell to attract her, then," said the *bruja*. She went to her shelves and gathered several stoppered bottles. "Whale oil, almond oil, corojo oil, and balsam," she said, pouring a measure of each into a brass dish. "Now a spoonful of water—and one drop of mercury."

Rafael watched as the silvery bead sank to the bottom of the dish. The oils pulled and twisted it as it moved down and down, and then, as it settled, it resumed its true and perfect shape.

Mr. George Flood, tree-snail fanatic and the husband of Adelina, called this morning to inquire about a partial peruke.

"As you see, Mr. Godley," he said, removing his hat, "I'm thinning. I didn't consider it a problem until I overheard Mrs. Flood objecting to the loss, as if it were in my control."

"I'm familiar with the predicament," I said.

"I wouldn't have minded so much if she'd complained to me, but as it was she announced the problem to her Spiritualist group, and they all sat around the table—*my* table—and gossiped about the virile young soldiers who have been taking over the place. 'Where is the man I married?' Mrs. Flood asked. She knew I was just upstairs."

I clicked my tongue, scolding the absent Adelina. "And the other members of the group?" I said, busy with some papers on my counter, as if the question were of no importance.

"They agreed that balding men are repellent to the female aesthetic—and I have to tell you, Mr. Godley, these ladies are not the fairest to be found in Tampa. In fact, apart from Mrs. Flood and perhaps Mrs. Unger, they are a homely lot."

"Mrs. Unger?" I said, still busy with my papers.

"A grove owner's widow. She'd be quite attractive if she chose to make something of her looks. Mrs. Flood has been channeling the voice of her late husband." He smiled and raised his eyebrows, as if we shared an understanding. "Well?" he said, lowering his head like a bull and almost butting me. "Can you help? Nothing too extravagantly priced, of course."

"Monsieur Flood," I said to his crown, "the question is not *whether* I can help but *how* you wish me to assist."

And I led him through to my studio and showed him a range of sample perukes. He needed no encouragement to try them on—it may surprise you to learn that few of my gentlemen customers do—and soon he was smiling and preening before the mirrors, as giddy as a child playing dress-up.

"This one!" he brayed. "This one makes me look like John D. Rockefeller! Or this one! Don't you think I'm a dead ringer for a young Ulysses S. Grant? 'If you see the President, tell him from me that whatever happens, there will be no turning back.'"

I let him have his fun for a few minutes. It is a stage through which all new customers must pass.

"Perhaps I might suggest something a little less conspicuous," I said eventually. I stood behind him like a shadow and placed a small, sleek toupee on his head. "There now. A little light in tone, but it gives you an idea of what I would propose for Monsieur."

"Hmm," said the chicken-chested George Flood, turning back and forth. I held a hand-glass to the back of his head.

"Hmm," he said again. "Well, it looks fairly natural, I grant you that. How much does one of these cost?"

"It is entirely of human hair," I said. "The net foundation, the stitching—and customized springs will ensure a perfect fit. Come." I guided him to a chair by the window. "Let me show you my best trick." I took a sample caul from my workbench and placed it over the back of his hand. "It's hair lace, Monsieur. It allows the color of the skin—the scalp—to show through, giving the illusion of a natural parting." He nodded. "The parting is always the weak point in a hair covering, for it reveals the foundation, but with this method the net is invisible."

"Finer than a silk stocking," he murmured, and I thought I had him, but again he returned to the cost.

"Being a collector of the fragile *Liguus* shell," I interrupted, as gently as a mother might when waking her child from a bad sleep, "I'm sure you can appreciate the fine workmanship, the hours such a piece demands."

Nodding his wispy pate in excitement—really, it is too easy—he said, "You know, Godley, not many people realize the time one must devote to a collection. Mrs. Flood's friends admire the pretty colors, the porcelain textures of my shells, but they don't see the *labor* involved. Some of my pieces I've bought or traded with other collectors, it's true, but most I have found myself, and extracted the creature—one can't leave it in there, of course."

"Of course," I said.

By now he was warming to his topic, and he cast a slimy eye

around my studio. "I imagine, Godley, you have a range of specialized tools." I bowed my head. "It's the same for any tree-snail enthusiast. Tweezers, needles, the finest crochet hooks, and then of course all the cleaning materials. You can't leave even a scrap of snail inside. An acquaintance of mine, a fellow collector, does a very poor job of cleaning his shells, and when he opens his cabinets to show you a new piece, the odor! He doesn't seem to notice, and naturally one can't mention it." He was stroking the caul net as he spoke. "But I should change the topic—I'll be making you hungry."

I managed a laugh, although it may not have been intended as a joke.

"Well, Godley, you'd better tell me how much my piece will cost," he said.

It is always best to present the more frugal customer with an itemized list so he can see exactly where his money is going. Assuming a blasé demeanor, I made some calculations, noting down the various expenses—labor, galloon ribbon, tension springs, the hair itself, and so on—and the dwarfish Mr. Flood studied the page at length, one finger moving all over it, feeling for errors. I imagined his little white hand picking through his collection of *Liguus* shells as if they were jewels, when in the swamps any fool can pluck them from the clusters of hardwood trees that litter the place.

"Twelve dollars for the hair seems rather extravagant," he said.

"Beware the cheap peruke, Monsieur," I said. "There are some unscrupulous manufacturers who use horse hair and donkey hair and goodness knows what else. My creations, stitched with human hair and featuring the invisible net, do cost a little more, but I guarantee satisfaction." I bent close and whispered, "If you will pardon me, Monsieur, in intimate situations a lady doesn't care to run her fingers through donkey hair."

Now, a less potent specimen than George Flood I have not encountered, and in his congress with the lusty Adelina I imagine he is obliged to take powders to make a man of himself, but he began to nod like an expert and to say, "That's true, very true."

At this point the customer may still be prone to wavering, and it is an unwise Perruquier who pushes too hard—one must not fan the fire before the flame has caught. A method I find most successful is to pretend to change the subject, asking after ugly children or unsightly wives, new gowns or vulgar gardens or, so help me, lap-dogs. The customer is then so flattered by this personal interest that he decides I am a decent man, and the transaction proceeds. With Mr. Flood I outdid myself in this regard, for while we were talking about snails I began to remember a particular area in France, near the Côte d'Azur, where as a youth I harvested a mass of brown hair each June.

"Have you ever visited France, Monsieur Flood?" I asked, although I was well aware that he never travels beyond the swamps.

"France?"

"I am thinking of a region in Provence, where the snail is especially esteemed."

"Go on," he said.

"Four men go into the fields," I said. "The first carries a drum, which he beats to simulate thunder. The second carries a watering can, with which he sprinkles the ground in imitation of rain. The third carries a veiled lamp, which he uncovers for a second or two at a time—"

"The lightning!" said Flood, as overexcited as a backwoods Revivalist.

"The lightning. And the fourth man—he collects the snails, who love wet weather, as you know, and who have been fooled into believing that a storm has broken."

"Intriguing," said Flood.

I paused. "To answer your question, Monsieur, the reason for the cost is that the hair comes from so far away. With such a fine, dark sheen as yours to match, I must look to the Continent, and in fact to this very region of France, for my material."

And I told him of the misty cliffside village of Gorbio, which is indeed in Provence, although shortly before I visited it in the 1860s it was part of Italy. I did not bother to explain this to the thinning Mr. Flood, for history lessons do not sell hair-pieces.

"In Gorbio, on the day of Corpus Christi, the Procession des Limaces is celebrated," I said, and I saw my listener frown at the foreign expression. "The Procession of Slugs," I said, "although in the Provençal dialect it is understood as snails." The magic word; he beamed. "Snail shells are filled with olive oil and wicks, and placed in every window, and when it is dark they are struck with a taper, and the people begin to follow the trail of little flames."

I described for him the White Penitents, an order of flagellants who lead the procession dressed in snowy robes, and I described the girls who lean from the windows, their dark curtains of hair burnished by the flames. And as I spoke, my voice ushering him through the coiling streets, the White Penitents just ahead of us like spirits, the shells shimmering with oil, I felt such a stillness descend on me that I wanted to stay in that misty village, that place of shifting boundaries. Privately I recalled how I had once found myself in Gorbio on the night of the procession without a place to stay. It was my practice to arrange lodgings in the house or barn of one of the women who sold me her hair, but that day it seemed that all the females of Gorbio visited me in the village square, and I was so busy that I had not stopped to organize shelter of any kind. Most chattered about the procession, and it crossed my mind that perhaps they were ridding themselves of their hair as an acknowledgment to the White Penitents, who not only shaved their heads but whipped themselves and willingly performed the deeds despised or feared by others: the visiting of the dying, the burial of victims of infectious disease. I joined the procession, certain I would meet one of my donors, who would oblige me with accommodation. Perhaps it was a trick of the light or the mist, but as we made our way along the close streets every face seemed distorted by the oily flames and I recognized nobody. I was just beginning to consider sleeping on one of the olive terraces—although they make a hard bed, I had done so before—when I was greeted by a pretty girl who watched from her window.

"You are Monsieur Dubois, the hair merchant?" she called.

"I am he."

She bent forward, her dark hair billowing like a cloak, and if I had lifted my hands I might have touched it. "How much?" she said.

"I would have to examine it more closely."

She moved from the window, setting the flames trembling in their shells, and in a moment she was at the door and inviting me inside and pouring me a tumbler of wine.

I lifted her hair in my hands, as I had done with countless other females in village squares and fairgrounds. Here, however, where the ceiling was low and the walls were creeping with roses—surely a fresco, although they looked real—the action acquired an intimacy for which I was not prepared. Her neck glimmered in the light of the oil-filled shells and the candles in their bronze sconces.

"Why didn't you come to the square today, when I was cutting the other girls' hair?" I said.

"I don't know," she said. "Maybe I was frightened." She sipped at her wine, the tendon at the side of her neck flexing and relaxing.

My fingers had crept to her collarbone now, and to the hollow at the base of her throat. I could feel her pulse.

"I can't cut at night," I said. "We'll have to wait until morning."

She nodded, pouring me some more wine. "Do you have any-where to sleep?"

"No," I said.

"Then you'll stay with me." She blew out the candles, but left the snail shells to gutter out one by one.

Under the musty sheets she began to kiss my face and chest, her little tongue leaving trails on my skin. "Do you have to leave tomor-row?" she said. "Can't you stay longer?"

In a voice unlike my own I said that perhaps I could, and I felt I was in neither Italy nor France but some borderless land.

It may have been the wine, to which I was unaccustomed in those days, but I had never slept so soundly, nor have I since. When I awoke the room was just becoming light, and on the walls the painted roses wound about their painted lattice. My young companion lay face down, and as I lifted the covers I saw that she had coiled herself into a knot, her limbs and back and head a tawny whorl against the linen. I hesitated for a moment, then unsheathed my scissors and began to cut. She did not wake, but obligingly stirred her head so that I could reach the other side, and it was then that I saw she was not a girl at all but a woman of forty or more: twice my age. Perhaps it was for this reason that I pulled some coins from my purse and placed them on the pillow, shiny little second thoughts. They amounted to much more than I would have paid had she come to me in the square, but by now I was anxious to leave. And so I slipped outside, to where the streets were cool and silent, and charred shells lined the window ledges, marking my way toward the next village. As I hurried up the mountain to Sainte-Agnès, Gorbio faded below me, and when it had disappeared into the mist I sat and caught my breath. There was not enough air up there. All around me grew patches of mandrake, and clusters of starry cranesbill, and sometimes little moths of the same shade of blue flew up from the leaves, and I had to look very closely to tell the flower from the insect. I held the skein of dark hair in my lap and wondered whether I might not keep it for myself, tucked away in a place where my master would never look. But I could think of no such place.

"A celebration of the snail," George Flood was saying. "An homage to the mollusk."

I could not help but marvel that the home of this drool of a man is each week visited by Marion Unger. Before he could expand any further, I flung open the door to Bluebeard's Chamber and began unhooking lengths of hair. My stock is plentiful since I have taken on my Cuban, who has a nose for the job and sometimes collects more hair in one night than I did in a week.

"Shall we match your color?" I said, and I was back in Tampa.

Today is June 21st, and along with my accounts and some letters for Dr. Evangeline—*Should I marry him when I know he has been intimate with my first cousin? Is dark hair about the nipple a sign of cancer? Would you advise a lady of delicate complexion to bleach or pluck her mustache?—* I received a card. On the front was a picture of a kitten peeping out from a basket of violets, and at the top was printed the following:

This pretty pussy bears a greeting
For your birthday, dear,
May all your days be blissful
And fortune ever near.

It was from Mrs. Friskin, who, in a distasteful move, signed herself as *Fondly, Sally F.* With the arrival in Tampa of the soldiers I had noted the sprouting of a certain lewd abandonment, and when the order had finally come to start for Cuba, the newspapers had showed America's Finest Sons engaged in a Sioux war-dance, leaping about like savages. Now, although their pup tents have been dismantled and their coarse voices no longer spill from every saloon and bordello in town, wantonness still infects the place. I dropped the card into my waste-paper basket, but a moment later retrieved it, tucking it away in readiness for my afternoon engagement with my actresses. I was keen to see what they would make of *Sally F.* I chuckled just thinking about it.

Although it was my birthday—officially, at least—I decided I would be the one to make a present. I took my box of trinkets and sorted through them until I found it: a delicate choker of amethyst and pearls that I had plucked from a pit in Hyde Park Avenue. I polished it with a handkerchief until it gleamed, the thin gold chain squirming in my palm. Then I selected a sheet of my best tissue paper—the perfumed kind, which I reserve for my customers' jeweled combs and aigrettes—and I wrapped it and secured it with lilac ribbon. I placed it beneath the counter, where every so often it brushed against my fingers and released the scent of lavender. When Marion Unger returned to me—for I knew she would—I would give it to her. I locked my studio and went to my weekly engagement.

The actress Clare played my Scotch customer Mrs. Friskin, while the actress Lilian played her daughter-in-law who has recently been delivered of a child—wee Miss Martha, about whose gurgles and giggles and changing eyes I have heard so much. She lay on a couch and pretended to nurse a bundle of rags, holding it to her breast, and the eager grandmother watched and arranged and instructed and tweaked. This was amusing for a time, but I felt the piece was a little lacking in dramatic tension, and so I directed my two adaptable ladies to change their roles. The actress Lilian dropped the bundle of rags, the false child, into the coal scuttle and herself became the infant, and Mrs. Friskin tickled her and said, "Who's a lovely baby? Who's the cleverest baby in the world?" And the grandmother disrobed and took the role of mother, nursing her naked daughter, who made delicious sucking noises, and crowed and smacked her lips. It is curious; no matter how different the characters or the stories, all my little productions end in a similar fashion.

On the way back to my minaret room, one question kept running through my head: what is a woman? All bonnets and ribbons, and scents to cover other scents, and layers of silk, serge, cotton, taffeta, and little wisps of lace designed to trick. A woman is a pretty disguise; she is hooks and eyes. When I weave strands of hair together I create a lovely thing, something pleasing to regard, an object both ornamental and deceptive. I grease my palms with pig fat, and the pretty threads twist and glide in my hands. Is not a woman a similar combination of knots and intricacy? Beauty is most often an illusion, a lie. Clean away the powder and the rouge, wipe off the painted veins, remove the rustling silk, the keyhole crochet. Take away the scaffolding, the hoops and the cages; unlace the bones. What do you have? Perhaps a hag, perhaps a plain girl, perhaps a comely one. It is all the same.

Maybe a woman is like a cigar, I said to my Cuban that evening. Maybe she consists of a tempting outer wrapping carefully chosen to give a favorable impression, delicately scented and embellished with gold, and perhaps, at her core, is filler. And there may be high-quality women and middling women and women of an inferior grade, but in the end they are all the same: a pleasant smell, a distinctive taste. Their charms are fleeting; one is left with nothing more than pretty plumes that dissolve into smoke and ashes.

"What is your opinion?" I asked.

But my Cuban did not reply.

At every meeting of the Harmonious Companions, Adelina Flood spoke a message from Jack. Sometimes it was detailed and coherent, as if a letter were being read aloud, and sometimes it was just a few words, as the first had been—but Marion always knew it was him. He referred to excursions they had taken together, or features of their house, or the plans he had made for the orange groves.

"You've become quite the star of our little circle," said Mrs. Rim. "My poor Philip can hardly get a word in."

Marion looked forward to Wednesdays with the excitement of a child at Christmas, and each of Adelina's speeches was indeed a gift, exactly what Marion wished for.

"What good can it bring?" asked Miss Harrow, but Marion paid no attention. She had always felt that her companion, unmarried and likely to remain so, begrudged her the flirtatious but harmless attentions of the men who crossed their path—the knife-sharpener, or Rafael, or Monsieur Goulet; now it seemed she was jealous of a spirit. At times she wished Miss Harrow had never answered the notice she had placed after Jack's death, and she wondered who had benefited more from the arrangement, and who was supporting whom.

There was something about the young cigar-maker that reminded her of Jack. She had dismissed this thought when first it occurred to her, but each time she saw Rafael, there it was again. He bore no physical resemblance to her husband—the blue eyes were black, the fair skin dark, the deep voice only just broken—but there was a certain elegance in the way he held his slim shoulders, and a certain way he had of looking at her without blinking that was very familiar.

She had wanted to own everything about Jack, including his life before her, and she remembered resenting the twenty years he had lived without her, as if they were something belonging to her that she had lost. Perhaps, she thought, Rafael was the sort of boy Jack had been.

At times she could sense his nervousness in her house. He blushed when he spoke, and could not cross the room without stumbling over a hassock or the edge of a rug; he did not relax into a chair but remained balanced on its edge, and when he shook her hand she felt his fingers trembling. Ascribing this to Miss Harrow's abrupt manner with him, she told him not to mind her companion. "She's reserved with strangers, that's all," she said. And gradually he became more comfortable when he visited, and as the July weather became hotter and hotter and gave way to August, the sadness Marion had felt for so long began to soften and trickle away. She was aware that her friendship with the boy had begun around the time that Jack had first spoken through Adelina, and she could not help thinking he had sent Rafael to her. She started to call him by his first name and invited him to do the same with her, as if they were a family—brother and sister, perhaps.

"Let's begin the next scene," she said. There was to be a local production of *Carmen* at the end of the year, and they were taking turns reading the libretto aloud, translating from the French as they went.

"It's good practice for him," Marion told her companion. "He wants to be a lector."

Miss Harrow's mouth became a thin line and she said, "Does he, indeed?" And as he found the correct page of the libretto she began to dust the pair of luster vases that sat on the mantel, the crystals swinging and tinkling as they touched one another. Marion had inherited them from her Californian grandmother, who called them her earthquake vases; in shaky Los Angeles, the crystals betrayed the movement of the ground long before one could feel it, shimmering and trembling, sending out a warning to those who paid attention to such things.

"'When will I love you? My goodness, I don't know,'" said Rafael. "'Perhaps never, perhaps tomorrow, but not today, that's certain.'"

In the background, Miss Harrow unhooked the crystals from the vases, the sun catching them now and then and throwing colored shapes against the walls.

"'Love is a rebellious bird that nothing can tame,'" continued Rafael, "'and it is in vain to call it if it wants to refuse. Nothing will work, threat or prayer—'"

The tinkling of the earthquake vases became music in Marion's head: threads of *Carmen*. She wondered what she might wear when she and Miss Harrow went to the opera, and whether her transformation would be suitable. She smiled when she thought that she could be sitting in the audience wearing one of Monsieur Goulet's designs, just like the singers on the bright stage.

"'Love is a gypsy child; it has never, never known any law. If you don't love me, I love you; if I love you, beware! If you don't love me, if you don't love me, I love you!'" said Rafael.

When they came to the second act, they puzzled over a complicated line.

"I would translate '*sur ma fois*' as 'upon my word,'" said Marion.

Rafael nodded. "'When it comes to cheating, deception, thievery, it is always good, upon my word, to have women with you,'" he read, smiling.

As Marion bent to study the words once more, a length of chain swung loose from her neckline.

"What's this?" said Rafael, and before Marion could tuck the chain away he was withdrawing it from her bodice. Her breath caught in her throat for a moment, as if he were lifting some living part of her in his mottled fingers. He placed the locket gently on his palm, however, and cupped it like a pretty leaf that might blow away, and so she did not snatch it back from him.

"It's a lucky charm," she said. He was so close to her now that she could smell his skin: a peppery, masculine fragrance mingled with the scent of tobacco leaves. She knew she should move away, invent something to be tended to in the kitchen or remember an engagement—

perhaps a fitting with the wig-maker—but the fine chain held her to him, and she closed her eyes and breathed in his spicy, leafy smell, and then she felt him opening the locket, pausing for a moment and closing it again, then replacing it between her breasts. She opened her eyes and said, "Perhaps we should finish there today."

The next day she was running late for her meeting with the Harmonious Companions, and as she alighted from the streetcar and hurried to the Floods' house she felt the locket beating against her chest. She had not been angry with Rafael, although his gesture had been as intimate as a lover's.

"It's all right, I don't mind, it's all right," she had said over his apologies, as if they were singing a duet.

"You'll be pleased to know, Mrs. Rim, that I am brightening myself up," said Marion as she seated herself at Adelina Flood's white table. "I'm taking advantage of the French wig-maker's special offer, and am ordering a transformation."

"You mean Mr. Gullet?" said Mrs. Friskin. "Which special offer is this?"

"He's offering a summer discount, until the end of August," said Marion. "Did none of you receive a letter? It was some weeks ago that it came."

"No," they said.

"Are you quite sure it's Mr. Lucien Gauntlet the Third?" said Mrs. Rim.

"Perhaps you have him confused with one of the cheaper wig stockists over on the east side," said Miss Needham.

"No, it's Monsieur Goulet," said Marion. "I'm going to his studio on Friday, in fact."

"He is making me an item at present," said Mrs. Rim, "and has mentioned nothing about a special offer."

"You must raise the matter with him, my dear," said Mrs. Friskin. "These tradespeople are too careless sometimes."

Jack did not come that day, and there were no messages from him for the next two weeks. When the fourth meeting passed without him, Marion went to visit Adelina alone.

"Perhaps he has said all he wishes to say," said Adelina.

Marion waited to be invited inside; she knew Mr. Flood was away in the Everglades on a tree-snail expedition, and she thought Adelina might enjoy some company. "We might try to summon him together," she said.

"One can never predict the whims of the spirits," replied Adelina. "One must not force them." There was a hard note in her voice that Marion had not heard before, and she held on to the door as if preparing to shut it as soon as was polite. As Marion walked down the path to the gate, she heard a man's voice coming from the parlor, and the sound of Adelina laughing.

PART IV

Raising the Dead

August 1898

Now that the hostilities are over—a ten-week battle was hardly worth the bother, one would have thought—I have the Hotel to myself again. The long, cool corridors no longer echo with the thud of boots, and mine is the only reflection in the many splendid mirrors. There is a lot to be said for peace—but since the Spaniards have been defeated, the celebrations throughout Tampa are almost as rowdy as the soldiers' revelries, with the Cubans in Ybor City and their countrymen in West Tampa saluting each other with booming cannon-fire every hour from dawn until dusk.

Everybody seems in high spirits, including the usually soporific Mrs. Rim, for whom I have begun manufacturing a new piece of blond froth: so delighted was she with the frisette I produced that she has ordered an entire wig. At my premises this afternoon she wondered aloud why she had not seen me at any of the victory festivities over the last two weeks, then began quoting a lengthy passage virtually word for word from the fine text of Dr. Evangeline

Montpellier, M.D.! "As far as is possible, Mr. Gauntlet, we should never show gloom or melancholy to those around us," she said. "If we conceal what is unpleasant in our bodies, we should do no less with our humors or temperaments."

After such a recital—passed off as her own thoughts, I might add, for the stupid creature has none of her own—what could I do but nod in agreement?

He gestured her toward the red silk divan.

"Please sit down, Madame Unger. May I offer you a cup of tea? A small sherry to celebrate the victory in Cuba, perhaps?"

"Thank you, no," said Marion, glancing at his pale eyes. She had remembered them as blue, yet today they appeared green, and she recalled what the Harmonious Companions had said: that they had received no letters from him, that perhaps she had confused him with someone else. For a moment she doubted her own reason, wondered whether she had come to the right place, and whether this was the same man who had entertained her so kindly at the Hotel.

"Is something the matter, Madame? Perhaps I should open another window?"

"I am finding it a little stuffy, yes, Monsieur Goulet," said Marion, making herself utter his name, half-expecting him to correct her. And then she saw the egret plumes arranged in a vase, and she remembered how she had stood at the counter and stroked them, and how they had slipped through her fingers like fog.

The wig-maker brushed past her and loosened the catch on a window, and she caught the soft scent of his cologne.

"Mamma lauded the properties of fresh air," he said. "Every morning she would take my sisters and me for a walk, no matter what the weather. She herself lived until she was three-and-eighty."

A gentle breeze began to flow about Marion's neck, and on the counter the bouquet of feathers opened and closed like a deep-water anemone. "You grew up by the sea, of course, Monsieur."

"The sea?" he said.

"When you were a boy, you would go down to the docks and watch your father's bolts of cloth being unloaded."

"Ah yes, the cloth," he said, and he paused. "What can I do for you today, Madame Unger?"

"Why, it's August twenty-eighth," said Marion. "Six weeks since I collected my memorial bracelet. You told me to come back and order my transformation, because you would be less busy now."

"Of course," said the wig-maker, and he asked her to remove her hat so that he might make the necessary measurements, and as he slid his tape around her head this way and that Marion felt her thoughts were being surveyed, and she concentrated on the vase of egret feathers with their white, white fronds.

That evening she told Miss Harrow about the amiable wig-maker, and his father the cloth merchant, and his long-lived mother, and his seven pretty sisters.

"Well, everybody has a childhood and everybody a family," said Miss Harrow.

Marion did not know why her companion was peeved, but she decided to ignore it. She went to her room and began tidying her hair. This was a time for celebration in Tampa, and would be for years to come. And then she stopped, and her hands sank to her lap. It was the first year she had forgotten. Other women had told her that, in time, the day would come and go without her realization, but she had refused to believe them. *No,* she had said. *This is a date I shall never forget.*

It's better your wife doesn't see it," the doctor had told Jack. "We mustn't put her under any more strain."

They stood on either side of Marion's bed and spoke across her, their voices echoing off the pressed-steel ceiling. Although her eyes were open, she was silent. She had been washed and her hair had been brushed; her hands were folded neatly above the sheet. At her feet the cast-iron bedstead gleamed like fresh tar, and she traced its loops around and around: two figure eights on their sides; two black symbols of infinity.

"She insists she see it," said Jack, spreading his hands.

"It's really not recommended, Mr. Unger. She would most likely become hysterical, and the exertion would be too much for her."

"All the same, she would like to see it." Jack's fingertips pressed into the turned-down sheet, binding Marion to the bed.

The doctor sighed then, the stream of impatient air reaching her cheek. Marion knew she should not feel hostile toward him, for he had done his best to revive the child, striking it on the back and on the buttocks to make it cry—as a rule, once a baby had cried, it was safe—and applying a smelling-bottle to its nose, holding the burning tips of a rag beneath its nostrils and taking care that the singed cloth did not touch the skin. He had sprinkled icy water on its face and rubbed its limbs, back, and chest, keeping its airways free from clothing. Having detected no pulsation in the navel-string, he had knotted and divided it—so quickly, so deftly, Marion had thought, as if he were cutting the string on a gift—and plunged the child into warm water. When there was still no sign of life, he had placed it on its face, turned the body completely on the side, if not a little beyond, and then on the face alternately, fifteen times each minute. Finally, he had pinched the nostrils together and breathed into the mouth, inflating the chest and then pressing it flat again in imitation of natural breathing, listening for the convulsive sob that marked a return to life. And then there was nothing more to be done.

"Please, Dr. Hampton, just let me see it," Marion said, unable to think of any other argument.

He sighed again.

The child was white and cold and very soft. She touched its neck, and the sensation was that of touching one's fingers to a still body of water, and she imagined her hand passing right through the silky skin, the little head dissolving into ripples. The blanket was rough, and she unwound it so the child lay bare on her lap. And then she saw it, the shred of membrane clinging to the skull: the caul. They were believed lucky; the baby born with a caul would never drown. And yet this child had never breathed air, she thought; this child had drowned inside her. She lifted the little piece of skin away and placed it in her bedside drawer, and it was not until much later, when she woke to find that night had come and that the child and the blanket had been taken, that she opened the drawer and felt for the silky memento. She climbed from her bed and laid it on the window-sill, where it would catch the morning sun, and there it stayed for a month, until it was quite cured.

Somebody was knocking, and in the thin strip of light beneath her bedroom door Marion saw a shadow.

"I'm not here," she whispered.

Her companion came in and smiled. "Do you want me to *lie* to your Cuban boy?" She never called him by name, but today Marion made no comment.

"Just tell him I can't see him, I'm not here."

"I'm glad you're coming to your senses," said Miss Harrow, and she turned to leave.

"Wait," said Marion. "No, invite him in. I'll be down in ten minutes."

Marion found Rafael standing before the bookcase.

"There is a fiesta in Ybor City tonight, to celebrate the peace," he said. "The lector announced it."

"Another one?" said Marion.

Rafael smiled. "I didn't feel like going. There has been a fiesta every night lately."

"Do you not feel like celebrating?"

"I wanted to come here."

Marion nodded slowly. After a moment she said, "I hear a lot of Cubans are returning home."

"Every passage is booked," said Rafael. "Mr. Plant's steamers are doing good business."

"He's done well out of the war," said Marion. "His Hotel has featured in all the major papers in the country, and in a few abroad."

"Some people are taking sailboats and tugs to Cuba, they're so eager to go."

"Do you have any plans to leave?" said Marion. "To go home?"

"I don't know. Our house is gone, and all my sisters are staying in Havana—I don't think so." He paused for a moment, and she could feel his gaze on her. "You're sad, when everyone is so happy."

Marion nodded, feeling the tears gather in her eyes.

"Should I go away?"

She shook her head.

"All right." He sat on the couch and was silent then, as if she were a bird who might take fright if she realized he was there.

She forced herself to speak. "Five years ago I had a child," she said. "A still-birth."

He did not run from the room, did not even look away. "The birthday is today?"

"Yesterday. The anniversary was yesterday."

He nodded, his eyes still on her.

"I don't know why it should still upset me. It was such a long time ago, and most women lose children one way or another." She blotted her eyes.

"My mother had seven children, and five of us lived. I'm the youngest, apart from Anna, who died of scarlet fever."

"You must miss them," said Marion.

He shrugged.

"You're never homesick?"

"Not if I never think about home."

Marion smiled and lowered her eyes. The handkerchief lay crumpled in her lap, and tear stains had darkened the front of her dress.

"I need to change," she said.

"All right," said Rafael. "Then come to Ybor City with me and celebrate."

In her bedroom, she searched through her armoire for a suitable dress. Really it did not matter which she chose, she told herself: her visiting toilettes, her evening gowns, her morning dresses, her traveling dresses, and her walking costumes were all of a similar line and all half-mourning colors: black, gray, purple. It was as if she were standing before a closet of shadows. She felt someone touching her head, but when she whirled about she realized that it was just a comb slipping out of place. A fold of hair hung across one cheek, and when she tried to smooth it back the comb fell to the floor. Sighing, she sat before her mirror and removed the comb's mate and the pins. She wished she had wavy hair that stayed in place, like Miss Harrow's curly mass, not this straight, slippery vexation. She began to search through her small jewelry drawers for more hairpins, and she did not hear the bedroom door opening, and she did not hear the footsteps on the floor, but when she felt warm fingers against the side of her neck she did not flinch.

"Your child," said Rafael, taking the silver-backed brush and beginning to run it through her hair. "Was it a boy or a girl?"

She looked at him in the mirror, but he kept brushing her hair, his free hand held beneath each section so the bristles would not scratch her skin. Every now and then she felt his knuckles brush her jaw, her earlobe, the nape of her neck. "A boy," she said. "Nobody ever asks me that."

"He would have been handsome," said Rafael.

As the brush pushed her head with each stroke she felt herself move forward and then relax back, and she did not resist the movement, the gentle swaying feeling it induced in her, and when she watched herself in the mirror it seemed her reflection was nodding a message: Yes, yes, yes. Little silver cherubs glittered and danced as the brush caught the sunlight.

"I envy you your work," she said. "Your colleagues."

He smiled. "I'm sure if you came to the factory you wouldn't. It's the same every single day. You, you do as you please."

"Exactly," she said. "Perhaps we should exchange places. I could go to your factory and roll cigars, and you could sit here and keep house with Miss Harrow." She held up her small white hands. "What do you think, would these do?"

"I think after one hour you would be very bored," he said.

"I'd have the lector to entertain me. My father used to read to me sometimes," said Marion. "I'd feel as if I were a little girl again."

"You make him sound like a story-teller," said Rafael. "A friendly uncle. He is the most powerful man in the factory." In the mirror Marion saw a frown spread across his brow. "Besides, he reads in Spanish."

"I would pick it up, gradually."

"And with such a beautiful *torcedora* among them, the men would get no work done at all."

Marion laughed. "There are women at the factory too, I know there are."

"But they don't roll the cigars," said Rafael. "They strip the leaves, and they attach the bands, and they package them. Oh, and there is the *catadora*, of course."

"And what's her job?"

"She smokes the cigars."

"Now I know you're teasing me."

"It's true," said Rafael. "She sits at a table and smokes the cigars. But I don't think you'd like that job."

"Do you know, I've given up my cigarillos," said Marion. "I find I don't want them these days."

"Some other factories employ *torcedoras*," said Rafael.

"*Torcedora*," said Marion, trying to pronounce it as Rafael did. "It sounds like *toreador*."

"Bull-fighting is a Spanish custom," said Rafael. "They have cruelty in their blood."

"What about Antonio, the knife-sharpener?" said Marion. "He's Spanish. And so was Señor Ybor."

Rafael continued to move the brush through her hair although there were no knots to untangle. "*Torcedor* comes from *torcer*, meaning to twist," he said. "Most cigar-makers spend four years mastering it."

"Four years learning to twist a leaf," said Marion.

"Learning how to *manipulate* the leaves, so that the finished cigar looks perfect." He brushed and brushed. "The wrapper is called the *capa*—the cape—and must be rolled with the smooth side facing out, like a fine cloak showing its lining of silk. It's the most important part of the cigar, but it can also mislead if it disguises cheap filler."

Marion could smell the tobacco on his warm fingers, and it made her feel drowsy, as if someone had left the gas jets on.

"There are left-handed and right-handed cigars," Rafael said. "It depends on which half of the leaf the *torcedor* uses. He can roll equally well with both hands. The *zurdo*, or the left-handed cigar, is said to be quickest on the draw."

"I don't think I could tell one from the other," said Marion. "I'd have to smoke them to see."

"The veins will tell you," said Rafael. "They should run down the cigar, turning gradually to the left or the right. Apprentices' cigars often look like barbers' poles—they're called Venetians."

"Venice," said Marion sleepily. "I'd like to go to Venice, but they say it's sinking. Jack said in a few years it would be gone."

"That could happen to Tampa also," said Rafael. "It's too flat here."

"And all the orange groves and the factories?" said Marion.

"Drowned," said Rafael. "All except the minarets of the Tampa Bay Hotel."

Marion imagined the silvery pinnacles piercing the water, their thirteen crescent moons rising over the flood. "Then I couldn't be a *torcedora*," she said, breathing in the scent of the tobacco. "I don't have four years to spare, anyway. But your other job, that would be exciting. Moving through the streets while all of Tampa is in bed."

Rafael said nothing in response. He simply stopped brushing, pulled the strands of hair from the bristles, and fed them into the hair-receiver. Marion wondered whether his mother had owned a similar item, and whether she had taken it with her when they went to the camp in Havana or left it on her dressing table for her return. She watched Rafael. Some of the strands clung to his fingers, charged with static electricity, and although it seemed they would never detach themselves, the effect did not last.

～

I watched her withdraw a silk-wrapped bundle. We had been making very pleasant conversation, and I had been inventing more details about my family, all the while hoping that she had come to order the transformation she had mentioned in June. I could have made it for her then, of course, but something had compelled me to prolong our acquaintance, to make her wait for my services, to see whether she would return to me. And here she was.

"I've been saving my combings for some time," she said, untying the ribbons that bound the silk at each end. "I thought perhaps I would order a simple transformation, something I could add to my own hair on special occasions—balls, dinners, perhaps the opera—"

"Special occasions," I repeated, willing my fingers to remain still, not to plunge into the luxuriant swathe of white-blond hair that now spilled from the silk and spread itself across my glass counter. I longed to bury my mouth in it, to inhale the delicious scent that rose from the milky switch and seemed to saturate the room. This hair was more beautiful than any I had gathered on the Continent or recovered from the trash pits and rubbish heaps of Tampa; even the glossy black coil I had so recently untangled was as coarse as a donkey's mane in comparison.

"Do you think it's suitable?" she said, holding it by the roots as if unwilling to give it up.

"If Madame will allow me—" I said, and slowly, gently, I slipped my hands beneath the hair and lifted it from the counter, and she relinquished her grip. The scent was stronger now—a scent that recalled fallen leaves, and turned soil, and the rainwater that collects in great puddles on the dusty streets of Tampa and afterward lingers like mirrors. And there was another note beneath all these, one that I had never encountered in a switch of hair: the scent of well-cured leather; animal skin polished to a glossy patina over many years of handling. And I thought of the wig-block that my master had allowed me to play with as a boy; the leather head with the little door in the base of the skull, behind which I had kept my secrets and my treasures.

Marion Unger has a most dangerous type of head. As I took her measurements in my studio I made a discreet Phrenological examination of her skull, and from studying her forehead I observed excessively developed Causality. This organ is what gives man his superiority over beasts; it is what allows him to appreciate that everything in existence is related to every other thing. Those in whom it is immoderately large and active are inclined to draw conclusions from single facts, endeavoring to explain, without the support of any sound information, such mysteries as the nature of the Creator and the fate of the soul after death. This tendency can be boorish in a man: the after-dinner philosopher who trumpets his theories on the origin of humankind or the substance of paradise is certain to possess large Causality. In a woman, it produces an unhealthful curiosity in matters beyond her grasp and a tendency to earnest theorizing.

"I didn't realize such thorough measurements were necessary for a little transformation," she said. "I feel I'm about to be operated upon." And she gave a short, quavering laugh.

"The second-rate Perruquier doesn't bother with these preliminary calculations, it's true," I said. "He twists the hair into shape, he fastens it, he sends his account. With a full hair covering, he draws the strands through in clumps rather than one or two at a time, and the finished product deceives no one. You have perhaps noticed the work of these charlatans, Madame? They're all too common today, I fear."

The widow nodded slowly. "I did read of a case in New York where a lady of high society was holding a soirée. Her wig slipped into the punch bowl during a recital by a prominent counter-tenor."

"*Voilà*, Madame. Obviously the work of a man who cuts corners." I noted down the extension of her occipital bone. "The transformation is not a complex piece," I said, "but it is often in simplicity that shoddy workmanship is most apparent. The proportions must be exactly right, Madame. It must sit naturally on your head. It must blend readily with your existing hair. And in order to accomplish this, I must take comprehensive measurements. I'm sorry if it is tiresome for you, but I am nearly finished."

As I proceeded I made my usual inquiries, for although she had spent over two hours in my company as my guest at the Hotel, I had not been brave enough to ask her about herself, and had gabbled on about the delights of Mr. Plant's building and his wife's tasteful furnishings. Now, in my studio, with my precise rows of scissors and hooks, my hackles and needles, and with her head in my hands, I told myself she was just another customer, and by this small self-deception I managed to put to her my customary questions. In which part of this fair nation was she raised? Was she blessed with children? Did she mind the dreadful heat? And so on. And my heart fluttered with her every reply, and her voice sounded as sweet and soothing as the voice of a mother must.

"I was raised in Detroit," she said. She paused for a moment, then smiled. "Perhaps you've heard of Henry Hamilton, Lieutenant Governor there in the 1770s?"

"I regret I have not, Madame," I said as I watched the little blue vein that beat in her temple and threaded beneath her lovely hair.

"Oh, but he was very famous," she said. "His nickname was the Hair Buyer because he incited the Indians to scalp the settlers. He wouldn't pay for prisoners, but only for scalps."

And before I knew it, I was saying, "Then it's fortunate that you weren't living there at that time, for you would have made some Indian a wealthy man."

Marion Unger, delightful creature, gave a little laugh at my ridiculous flirtation and said, "I trust you're not so ruthless a dealer, Monsieur Goulet?"

⌒

This morning I made a head, cutting the oak according to the measurements taken from Marion Unger, and as I shaped it I thought how useful it might be to construct not just a head but an entire figure. Such a mannequin, I reasoned, would help to assess how the transformation would look on its living counterpart, and whether or not it would be in proportion. Besides, now that I have employed my Cuban, my evenings are long and empty, and as much as I enjoy the company of my actresses I have no desire to visit them every night. And so I made a number of sketches, based on the anatomical drawings of Dr. Evangeline, and I built a wire frame for my woman. She is to be covered with plaster of Paris, and her skin, smoothed by my hand, will be reinforced on the inside with steel, like Mr. Plant's Hotel. It is the hair, however, that will give her an identity, the hair that will make her come alive. It defines us, and without it we are as featureless as any one of the shaven-headed miserables who fill the asylums.

Sometimes, if I cannot locate a particular color, I will dye some of my hair stock to a customer's specifications. Although this is a messy procedure, the Goulet postiche is guaranteed to blend imperceptibly with the wearer's own hair, for I refuse to settle for anything less than a perfect match. I spend hours stirring my potions. I feel like a sorcerer, applying the stain with a glass rod or a rod of bone. Once the lengths of hair have been tinted and rinsed, I place them in the postiche oven and bake them until they are dry and the true color may be seen. I imagine the makers of fine glass and porcelain experience a similar sensation when they open the doors of their kilns to see what has been fired to perfection and what has cracked or shattered. I withdraw the hair from the oven; I compare it with the customer's sample swatch. Then, depending on the results, I proceed with the weaving of the postiche, or I begin to dye all over again.

I cannot, of course, reveal the exact composition of my colors, but let me assure you that the ingredients are innocuous as rainwater:

bruised cloves, rectified spirit, juice from the shells of green walnuts, and the like. I eschew the nitrates of silver and gold, which have acquired a certain reputation for dyeing the hair black—for although they do darken the tresses, direct sunlight also reveals a rather comical iridescence. (I know of a respected cavalry officer whose mustaches are radiant in certain lights with all the shimmering hues one sees on the neck of a pigeon.) Gone are the days when the blistering beetle was used in the preparation of hair restorers, or when bear's grease was applied to the hair to blacken it. Even today, many dyes are composed of sugar of lead, caustic alkalies, litharge and arsenic, all of which burn the hair and, in some cases, cause paralysis of the brain. Fortunately, I take a more enlightened approach to the beautification of the head, and there is nothing in the preparations of Lucien Goulet III to cause offense or harm.

I hoped I should not have to dye any hair to match the widow Unger's, for I did not wish to resort to artificial means—but truly, hers is a most unusual shade, delicate and unlikely, and I was certain I had nothing in Bluebeard's Chamber to match it. My only white-blond stock was the length given me by the widow herself, and it was not enough. I thought and thought on the problem as I worked on my model woman, each evening adding a little more flesh to her, shaping and molding, smoothing every curve by the light of Mr. Edison's carbon filament bulbs.

Mrs. Rim and her dog called today. The hairy little carpet slipper licked my glass display case the way a dying man might lick a sheet of ice.

"Oh, isn't that precious!" said Mrs. Rim, peering through the smeared glass at my rows of feathers and wings. "We think they're real birds, Mr. Gauntlet. We're hunting them!"

I refrained from observing that a single one of my diamond-eyed hummingbirds could have mauled Raisin were it alive. Instead I said, "How can I help you, Madame Rim? Would you like to see how I am progressing with your new postiche?"

"We should like to order a piece of hair jewelry, Mr. Gauntlet," she said.

"But of course," I said. "I do hope it is not a memorial piece?"

"No, no," she said. "There will be nothing sad about this brooch. It will be a very happy brooch, a *joyous* brooch, Mr. Gauntlet."

For a moment I thought she was going to tell me she had fallen in love, but it was worse than that. She deposited the dog on my counter—my Cuban mahogany!—and said, "Where do you think we should clip? There's a pretty patch of a sable on our chin, and we're lovely and red on our tummy."

Correct. She wanted to immortalize the grunting Raisin with a piece of Goulet jewelry—a brooch, to be exact. When I suggested to her that the hair of the noble Pomeranian, while plentiful, might prove too coarse for such a piece, she waved an airy hand and said she was sure I could work my magic. She was giving a pink tea in a few weeks' time and wanted the brooch finished for the occasion; she thought it would provide a merry starting point for conversation with the more awkward guests.

"All the table linen, dishes, and ornaments are to be pink, Mr. Gauntlet, and also the refreshments: ham and tongue and other dainty viands, lobster salad, pink-tinged custards and jellies, pâté de foie gras, salmon, strawberries and raspberries—and I shall be wearing a pink messaline costume of the most delicate tint, and on the tables there will be coral branches and shells and leaping dolphins constructed entirely from pink roses, and I shall even add a dash of grenadine syrup to the tea!" She lowered her voice. "And he does not know this yet," she whispered, "but Raisin is to wear an elegant vest of pink shantung, and a matching silk hat."

And so I clipped a little hair from the dog's quivering belly, and it lay most obediently on my counter with its tongue hanging out and its generative parts bright crimson and upright, and I swear there was a look of bliss on its fiendish little maw.

Mrs. Rim chose a simple wicker-work design—"like the cozy basket we sleep in every night," she said—and paid me in advance, and as soon as she had gone I matched the cuttings to a rather dull red I had in stock. There is no end to the gullibility of woman, I thought, as I disposed of the malodorous sample—and the amusing tale of Mr. Slater occurred to me, and I smiled.

Mr. Slater (significant Marvelousness; pronounced Hope; stunted Acquisitiveness) had purchased an Invisible Covering from me prior to wooing a girl he had admired for some time. Within a month they were courting—I attribute his success to the peruke, as I spent several lengthy fittings in the company of the man and can attest that it was not due to his personality—and she asked for a lock of his hair. Unwilling to expose his deception, he allowed her to snip away a curl from the peruke, which she then enclosed in a locket and kept nestled against her bosom. When Mr. Slater came to me he was in quite a state and his thoughts were far from logical, for his suggestion was that I simply repair the hair-piece by inserting a new tuft.

"But a clipped lock does not grow back in the space of one day," said I. "What will your sweetheart say when she sees the bare patch suddenly restored?"

Mr. Slater's face fell. "You're right, of course, Mr. Glibly. But what am I to do? I can't tell her that I'm—that I lack—that I have no—"

"Never fear, Monsieur Slater," said I, examining the assaulted peruke. "The solution is simple. It will be a little costly, of course, but I can assure you that your ladyfriend need never know of our arrangement."

And so I made for Mr. Slater not one but four new hair-pieces, each displaying a different stage of growth. And not only was the girl taken in, but the secret survived their wedding night, as well as three full years of matrimony thus far.

⁓

On the first day of November, Marion went to collect her transformation.

"Ah! I did not contact you," said the wig-maker, striking his head with his hand. "You must forgive me, Madame, but it's not quite ready."

"I see," said Marion. "Well, no matter. When should I call again?"

"I'm terribly sorry, Madame Unger. Please accept my apologies. I hadn't anticipated the number of new orders my little advertising campaign would generate, and this work is very hard on the eyes. Indeed, I am noticing that some things are becoming less clear to me; that after I have sat for a time knotting, I can no longer see into the distance."

He looked directly at her as he said this, and she noticed that his eyes were blue once again, but perhaps that was because the sun was shining in the open window and the sky was reflected in them. "As I said, no matter," she murmured.

"If you call again in three weeks it will be finished."

"Very well," she said, and she took her leave.

She was surprised how disappointed she felt that the hair-piece was not ready, for she had managed all these years without it. Besides, the only special occasion approaching was the opera *Carmen*; there were no balls or dinners to which she had been invited, and it was ridiculous to think that owning a transformation, a little bit of down to place on her brow, would change that.

When she arrived home she sat in the parlor and stabbed at a piece of embroidery, her stitches small and mean, the clusters of damask roses pinching with each tug of the needle. Three weeks indeed: that would be nearly three months since she had placed her order with Monsieur Goulet. It would be almost December by then. She stared into the heart of the buckled roses, calculating the date as if she suspected a pregnancy.

⌁

December 1898

The weather is cooler and more bearable now, but the guests are back: it seems I must always endure some form of discomfort. It is true that with each intake of guests comes a rash of new customers for me, but bookings at the Hotel are unpleasantly heavy this year, owing to all the publicity from the war. Mr. Plant, canny business-man that he is, has capitalized on the resort's role in the battle; according to his latest brochure, *Its splendid hospitality is known wher-ever the story of our heroes and their brave deeds are on the lips of men.* Furthermore, *In the days of history-making just passed, these walls have echoed to the clank of swords and spurs—for in this beautiful Hotel was the home-life of our brave officers—volunteer and regular alike—and its roof was the last to cover many a head which now has the quiet earth for its pil-low.* Goodness only knows what sort of ghoul such rhetoric will attract. The Americans are very pleased with themselves for winning the war—so pleased, in fact, that they have excluded the Cubans from all peace negotiations. Mr. Plant has purchased an exhibit of life-size paintings of leaders of the battle, which he has placed on show in the Exposition Hall, alongside displays of Florida fruits and vegetables.

The evening is my favorite time of day. When my last customer has gone home, her new hair wrapped in silk and nestled in an ele-gant box, a sleek, obedient lapdog, I return to my minaret room. Having dressed for dinner, I enter the Dining Room through the keyhole archway and enjoy such dishes as Bluepoint Oysters, Con-sommé Celestine, Egyptian Onions in Cream, Quail on Toast with Currant Jelly, and pieces of Chyloong Ginger. Since the tables are set with four places, I must sometimes dine with the guests, but I find that they are usually content to limit their conversation to remarks on the tenderness of the Roast Sirloin of Beef au Jus (the gentlemen) or the wickedness of the Chocolate Soufflé Pudding with Vanilla Sauce (the ladies). Sometimes, just to perplex them, I note the wickedness of the Sirloin and the tenderness of the Pud-ding, and then they ignore me for the rest of the evening, giving all their attention to the peeling and consuming of a banana with a knife and fork, and taking care not to commit the enormity of drying their hands on the finger-bowl doily.

Above the Dining Room is a circular gallery reached through an upstairs door. Sometimes the orchestra perches there and performs for the guests, and often when I have finished my repast—I rarely remain for all eight courses, which can take hours to consume—I like to go there too. Around and around the gallery I walk, just below the dome that is painted to mimic the sky. Now and again I picture its silvery exterior, which can be seen glinting from all over Tampa, and I feel I am within some smooth planet, within the moon, perhaps, or some strange place that wears its sky on the inside. Beneath my feet, stretching right around the base of the dome, is a ring of electric bulbs, dozens of them, to make the room as bright as day. On certain occasions they flash in a festive manner, and they also serve to illuminate the heads of the diners; circling high above, watching through the glassless arches hung with velvet, I can observe the thinning crowns of gentlemen and ladies alike. It is a simple matter to strike up a conversation with these targets when I see them in the gardens, or at the Gentlemen's Bar, or indeed the following evening at dinner.

"And what line of business are you in, Mr. Gourmet?" they will ask without too much prompting.

"Why, I am a Perruquier," I will say.

There is a pause, and then one of them says something like "Ah yes, our gardener has relatives near there, doesn't he, darling? Lovely in spring. And what is your profession?" they ask again, more slowly this time, and most often more loudly.

"I am a *Perr-u-quier*," I say. "A *Posticheur*. I make hair-pieces."

"Ah!" they exclaim, and all around the table hands are raised to heads, and loose strands smoothed, and curls rearranged, and side whiskers patted.

"And what sort of pieces do you make, Mr. Goulash?" they ask.

"Anything at all you can imagine," I reply. "I have made cape marteaux and double loop clusters, Empress bandeaux and scalpettes." They look at me blankly. "I have made numerous merkins," I say, and nobody bats an eyelid. "I have made hair-pieces for some of the most celebrated actresses of our time, for use both professional and private. If you have had the pleasure of attending the better operatic and theatrical productions in Paris, you are certain to have seen my designs. I have had English aristocrats on my books, and members of New York's wealthiest families, and a Russian princess. Here is my card." And abracadabra, another moneyed customer.

Sometimes, to escape the throng, I ascend to the fourth floor in Florida's first hydraulic elevator—with its cage door shut, one finds oneself enclosed in a delightful chamber of polished Cuban mahogany, elaborately carved and with a coffered ceiling. Upstairs, I stroll the curving corridors, catching glimpses now of the river, now of the city, now of the wilderness, now of a looming minaret close enough to touch. I do not allow myself to become caught up in conversation with the nannies and the personal valets, the fruit growers and the shop owners who stay in this stuffy part of the Hotel. I come here for the views, for high places are scarce in Tampa, and this vantage point allows me to see right across the peninsula. On the western side of the building, beyond the manicured grounds filled with tropical plants, stretches the wilderness. This is where Mr. Arthur Schleman, raconteur and reciter of poetry, accompanies guests on hunting expeditions. "The Manly Heart," by Mr. George Wither, is a favorite performance piece of his, and it amuses me to hear him bellowing it out as the men (and more and more women, I am vexed to report) blast away at the wildlife. "Shall I, wasting in despair, / Die because a woman's fair?" he yells. "Or make pale my cheeks with care / 'Cause another's rosy are?" Once Schleman gets started on a recital, there is no shutting him up; it must be the German blood. I am not interested in gazing long at the wilderness, however, for if I narrow my eyes and look to the east, across the river, there is Fortune Street, and sometimes, if the light is right, I imagine I can see Marion Unger dressed in a white lawn gown and Brussels lace, as bright as a cumulus, a bride in search of a groom, and her bright hair glinting amongst the trees.

At intervals along the passageways are curious half-size doors, which at first glance might be mistaken for the cheapest apartments of all, or places to store impudent children. In fact, in watery, low-lying Florida, cellars are rare, and it is only by a unique feat of engineering that the Tampa Bay Hotel has any sort of basement. (One pig-headed customer of mine insisted his architect include a cellar in his new house; now every wet season his children sail their boats there.) These dwarf rooms on the fourth floor are used for storage, concealing the luggage of the Hotel's guests. Late in the day, when the sun reaches through the small arched windows on the opposite walls, it casts tombstone shapes across the little doors.

These days I find myself spending less and less time roaming the Hotel in the evenings, for I have work to do in my room. Under the electric bulbs, their light magnified by a round mirror fixed like a moon in the ceiling, I unsheet my model woman and stand back and look. I circle her, holding a finger to my lips. *I see you*, I say. *I see what you will be.* Then I set to work.

During the first few months after my master took me in, when he was teaching me the lowlier tasks, such as nitting and hackling, turning and washing, he sometimes doubted the wisdom of his choice. "I wonder whether I shouldn't take you back to the Home," he would say when I made a mistake. "I wonder whether I shouldn't exchange you for another more co ordinated boy."

I blamed the Sisters for this. When all the papers had been signed and Monsieur Dubois called to collect me, they told him that there were plenty of bright, able boys available should he require further apprentices.

"It's a shame we can't let you have Michel," they said. "Such a gifted, clever boy! So good with his hands!"

The Sisters always maintained that they had no favorites, and that God's love for each of us, even the worst sinner, was infinite. Despite this, there was one child—the eldest of the Michels—whom they praised and cosseted as if he were a little prince placed secretly in their care. He was a model child, said Sister Thérèse, and I should follow his example of how a boy should behave.

I hated him. I am sure you are familiar with his sort: he leapt from his bed at the first stroke of the morning bell; no sooner had he finished his chores than he was pleading for more; he prayed for such long periods, frozen in piety, that I was tempted to creep up behind him and topple him as if he were an ugly vase that needed breaking. He never forgot the words to the hymns, nor improvised alternative and profane lyrics. His voice was the pride of Sister Camille's motley little choir, and when visitors came he sang so melodiously—*Suffer little children to come unto me, for of such is the kingdom of heaven*—that those who had intended simply to gape at us often left with a child, and those who had wanted one took two. There was, of course, no shortage of willing parents for Michel, but to my irritation he was not taken, for, as he never tired of telling me, he was not a true foundling. His parents had not really abandoned him; they loved him and would return for him when their older children were grown. His mother had fastened around his neck a string of wooden beads carved by his father—see how perfectly round they were, see how fine?—and from it she had hung a little lead medal, so that Michel would always know who he was.

When he was not praying, working, or attending classes, he played with his pieces of straw. He thought it wise to keep himself busy until his parents came back, he said, and so he set himself the task of constructing a scale model of the Home, which he would present to his family once reunited with them. From strips of straw, some yellow, some red, some brown, some bone, some the color of honey, he wove every building within the Home's walls. There were the Sisters' quarters, complete with their jutting, black-framed gables; there were our dormitories overlooking the cobbled courtyard; there was the refectory; there was the chapel. He wove the Salle des Berceaux—the Cradle Room, for the newborns—and the Salle des Poupons, for the older infants. Every detail was true, even the water pump in the courtyard and the row of chestnut trees, even the double-sided door of the Tour d'Abandon. The work was so close, so perfect, that when it was held to the sun not a grain of light showed through. As I watched the model Home taking shape I had to admit to myself that it was a beautiful thing, and yet I knew that the praise he received should have been mine; that I too had designs in me, the intricacy and ingenuity of which would astound; that I too had the potential for beauty.

When the model was complete and mounted on a thin board, Michel made a little honey-colored infant from a single slip of straw and placed it in the Tour d'Abandon.

"What good is that?" I said. "Nobody will see it."

"If they open the door they will," said Michel, tucking the little gold knot into place with a buttonhook.

Sister Thérèse displayed the model in the entrance hall so that the visitors could marvel at it.

"Made entirely of *straw*?" they said, running their gloved fingers along the spire of the chapel, the sharp little eaves. "But it looks so solid, so real!"

The day my future master called to select an apprentice, he stopped and admired the model.

"I'm afraid we cannot let you have the boy who made it," said Sister Ernestine.

"It's out of the question?"

"Alas, yes. His parents say they want him back one day."

On my last night at the Home for Foundlings, when my things were packed and waiting to accompany me to the house of the Perruquier Dubois, I crept to the entrance hall. I picked up a corner of the model, and I heard the straw babe sliding in its straw tower. The entire structure was so light that I felt I could level it with one breath. I opened the little Tour d'Abandon and withdrew the infant. It was very lifelike, but something was missing from the scene: a straw mother, walking away. I replaced the little figure in the tower, an infant Jesus in a Christmas crib, but I did not like the thought of leaving it there, and I recalled the old custom of enclosing a sacrifice in the walls or foundations of a new building in order to keep the occupants safe. A goat, a child. I felt quite breathless.

The courtyard was still, and not a light showed in the windows surrounding me. I crept to the drinking fountain with its open-mouthed lion, listened, then immersed Michel's model in the cool, black water. I drowned the entire complex, crushing the dormitory beneath my open palm, and it was so easy: in a few moments it was wet grass, cattle feed, silage. And the gate to the sodden Tour d'Aban-don opened and the little straw babe rose to the surface and floated there like a piece of refuse, and when I lifted the board from the water everything was collapsed, as if a hurricane had struck.

I was found out by Sister Ernestine, who could prize a secret from the lips of a dead man.

"I forgive you," said Michel, and I wanted to spit in his solemn little face, in his eyes full of sorrow for my sins—or perhaps the emotion was pity; well, you are familiar with his type. It was no surprise to me that his parents had not retrieved him. Given the chance, I would have held him under the drinking fountain too.

That afternoon the Perruquier Dubois came to collect me, and he noted the absence of the straw model.

"There was an accident, and it was destroyed," said the Sisters, and my new master spent a moment agreeing with them that it was a terrible shame, and then he led me to his carriage.

My Cuban, although instructed to gather only white-blond hair, persists in bringing me shades I cannot use. "It's very hard to find," he whines, and it is all I can do not to strike him. I am beginning to think he does not want me to finish the widow's transformation, and in the quiet of my minaret room I sometimes believe he wishes me to fail her so that he can continue to monopolize her time. So many things irritate me lately. The nights are too cool; I almost miss the mosquitoes pricking my face to tell me I am alive, and singing in my ear of the swamp and the heat. My plume-hunter Swope seems to think I am interested in hearing about his literary tastes—and I admit I was surprised to learn he could read at all—but the dime novels he purchases would be better employed in an outhouse. His favorite book at the moment, and one he has not hesitated to recommend to me, is *Nick Carter's Girl Detective; or, What Became of the Crown Jewels*; it features a plucky young heroine called Roxy who displays an ankle on every second page. My food tastes of nothing; wine no longer lifts my spirits; even my actresses grow less interesting by the day. They appear to be tiring of our little tableaux vivants, and their performances are lackluster and unoriginal.

In addition to all this, my model woman is causing me no end of frustration. I cannot execute the lips to my satisfaction: no matter how I work them with my knife, they are wrong, and all I can think of when I see them is the squashed mouth of the younger Miss Rathbone. Let me tell you a little about her and her kind, and about the Phrenological theory I should like someday to explore; I need a break from my work.

The elder Rathbone visited me some two years ago, ordering a curled fringe which made her look like a malnourished poodle, but the deformed younger sister has never crossed my threshold, for she has a luxuriant head of hair upon which, in all honesty, I could not improve. She pays particular attention to her grooming, as disfigured women often do, always wearing the latest and most flattering fashions, the most tasteful jewels. None of this helps her to attract a husband; I have observed the way she hides behind her fan at balls, or sips slowly at little glass cups of punch, or runs her fingers along her lip as if trying to iron out the kink, and I am certain that no man in Tampa can have failed to see through her tricks.

To my tale, however: this week I observed abundant tresses on a second hare-lipped female. I had been summoned by a grieving family whose daughter had just died of yellow fever, and when I saw her laid out on her narrow bed with the hair curling around her face and spreading across the pillow like spilled molasses, I must have let out a small cry, for the mother said, "Indeed, she was a beauty." As

I approached the corpse, having ushered the mother from the chamber—it is poor form to allow the bereaved to witness how one heaves and twists a head in order to cut at the roots—I saw that the glorious stream of chestnut framed a deformed face. Sometimes, it is true, the lips may curl back in death (a discreet and ingenious clip corrects this little problem, although Mr. Tucker, Funeral Director, will never tell you so), but this mouth had been flawed from birth, and after I had removed the hair the deformity was even more obvious. When the mother returned and offered me a glass of cheap sherry (I did not need to taste it to deduce that it was cheap; the lampshades alone told me as much) she moved to the bed, her arms trailing lengths of lace like Spanish moss, and began arranging them about the corpse's neck—whether to draw attention away from the baldness or from the hare lip, I am not certain. The thought occurred to me that in life this girl was probably as artful as the younger Miss Rathbone in attempting to disguise her disfigurement. I wish now that I had taken the opportunity to examine her skull, for it would have made an interesting piece of research—is the deformed woman Phrenologically predisposed to cunning?—but alas, the idea did not occur to me until later.

I know what you are thinking: he is so distracted by the creation of his model woman that he is neglecting the creation of the hair-piece with which to crown her. It is true, the widow Unger's transformation was still not ready when she called, but what she does not know—what I did not tell her—is that I have not *begun* work on it. Do not be mistaken; I am not avoiding the task. On the contrary, I have felt most invigorated about it ever since she visited my premises at the end of summer and left the silky white skein in my care. Many times I have caressed it and thought of her, and I have been pondering her transformation for some weeks now. So occupied have I been that I neglected to attend any of the performances of *Carmen* at which my postiches were the stars. I have sketched various ideas and discarded them all; I have twisted countless lengths of hair—mostly black, of which I have plenty—into rough patterns and undone them again. None of them pleases me. It is not that they are incompetently drafted or difficult to execute, nor are they unbecoming to the female head; indeed, such pieces are an essential component in the armoire of any well-appareled lady. The Goulet transformation is totally believable, totally undetectable, and that is why it is such a success, and that is why it is unsuitable for my newest customer. A woman like Marion Unger is worthy of more than a simple transformation. She deserves something elaborate and unique, a masterpiece of hair construction, something that takes the breath away.

I went for a walk so I could ponder this problem, and my thoughts turned to the magnificent hair-pieces made in the 1770s, those glorious days when the Perruquier was king, when any new design he created was embraced by high society, worn by every woman of consequence, copied by his competitors. He could name his price. Such was his power that he kept his sketches locked away like blueprints. In hair he could express his every urge and fancy; he could transform a woman into a peacock, a sailing ship, a garden festooned with vegetables and fruits. There was no pretense that the hair was the wearer's own; the full-blown artifice signaled one's affluence. And the Perruquier's part in this performance was fully manifest; like a puppet-master dressed in black, he directed the audience's gaze to his dolls, but everyone knew who was pulling the strings.

I was approaching the Tampa Bay Hotel and admiring its majestic silhouette, and it was then that the idea came to me: I shall build for Madame Unger a monument of hair, a construction so intricate, so beautiful and impossible, that she will wonder how human hands could have shaped it.

It will take a little while, and I must not lose her confidence: when I told her that the transformation was still not ready she was perfectly polite, but I saw the look of vexation that passed across her face. And yet, even then, she believed me.

I had an idea that I thought would work, but it has not. It is most discouraging when one's creative vision is thwarted; I am reminded of the latter days in the service of my master. This time the fault lies with my actresses. They are admirable girls, the pair of them, and used to be excellent company, yet like my master they are proving themselves unreliable. Let me tell you about the fine idea I had, the scheme I was sure would be successful.

"What would you like today, Mr. Goulet?" they asked. "*The Naughty Puppy? Hungry Alligators?* How about *The Mating Dance?*" The actress Lilian slid an egret plume between her breasts and shook back and forth.

"I'm tired of the old repertoire," I said. "I'd like you to enact a new story."

The actress Clare clapped her hands and said, "Wonderful! We were just saying, before you arrived, Monsieur, that we want to stretch ourselves professionally."

"To take on new roles," said the actress Lilian. "To meet creative challenges." The egret plume was buffeted by her speech; it swayed and twisted like a palm in a hurricane. "Who are our characters?"

"You are to play a lustful young widow by the name of Unger," I said. "And you, *ma chérie*"—I gestured to the actress Clare—"are her boy companion, who is Cuban. Madame Unger is in her boudoir brushing her hair when the Cuban grabs her from behind and begins to unbutton her dress."

"Unger," said the actress Clare, tapping her full lips and staring at the ceiling. "I don't believe I remember a Madame Unger from your studio. I certainly don't recall any young widows in the company of Cuban boys."

"Nor do I," said the actress Lilian. "We'd remember something like that, I'm sure."

"They did not call at my studio when you were there," I said. "In fact, they're not real customers at all; I've invented them for my own amusement. Think of this new piece as a test of your theatrical abilities."

"Jack Unger!" said the actress Clare all of a sudden.

"Of course," said the actress Lilian, and the two of them were nodding and giggling at each other so hard I thought they would never get on with my new piece.

"We knew Mr. Unger well," they said. "*Very* well. He used to come to the magic-lantern showings at the Cherokee Club."

I thought: Jack Unger was probably there the night I attended. I smiled to think we may have been in the same room, and was more eager than ever to set my new production in motion.

The actress Lilian frowned. "I'm sitting at my dressing table brushing my hair, and I don't hear this Cuban boy approach?"

"That's correct," I said.

"And I don't see him in the mirror?"

"You neither see nor hear him until he grabs you. You are taken quite by surprise, and you resist him for a few moments, but then you succumb."

"Hmm," said the actress Lilian, who is usually my favorite.

"Is there a problem?" I said.

"I'm just trying to understand the motivation behind my surrender to this boy," she said. "Why, if I'm so surprised by his attack, do I not scream? How is it possible that I don't see him in the mirror?"

"Perhaps the reason you're taken by surprise is that you're completely absorbed in brushing your hair," said the actress Clare. "Perhaps you're so delighted with your own reflection, your incomparable beauty"—she glanced at me—"that you notice nothing else."

"Yes." I nodded. "Yes, well done, *ma chérie*." And for a moment the actress Clare was my favorite, and I began to wonder whether I should not have given her the role of the widow.

"When you say *boy*," she said, "just how young do you mean?"

"Ten? Eleven?" said the actress Lilian. "You're very naughty sometimes, Mr. G."

"But that's why we like you."

"Not ten or eleven," I said. "A few years older. I mean a youth, a young man."

"Ah well, that alters things somewhat," said the actress Lilian.

"And how do I gain access to the boudoir?" said the actress Clare.

"That's not important," I said.

"Well, am I breathless and perspiring from having climbed up a drainpipe and in through a window? Have I first seduced the maid, perhaps?"

I gave a deep sigh. "Can you not improvise?" I did not know why they were being so difficult, save that it is in woman's nature to be contrary; and so, with great patience, I added flesh to their characters. "You are a lascivious Cuban boy whose desires override the widow's feeble protests," I said to the actress Clare. "You are strong and forceful, but also wily." I turned to the actress Lilian. "And you have not known a man since your husband's death. Although you play at being the proper, grieving widow in society, in private you are an eager little trollop." They nodded and said *Ah yes* and *Quite so* as if we were producing a Broadway play and they were leading ladies who would be the toast of New York's most influential critics.

While the actress Clare changed into the costume of a lascivious Cuban boy, I settled into an armchair and lit a cigar.

"How can you smoke those?" said the actress Lilian. She unpinned her hair in preparation for her brushing scene.

"I don't expect you to understand all my pleasures, *ma chérie*," I said.

"It's quite the thing for women to smoke cigars these days," said the actress Clare. She spoke from behind her screen, which is painted with lopsided herons and is a most gaudy object. I do not know why she insists on effecting her costume changes behind it, as if she possesses some scrap of modesty. "The tobacco leaf is renowned for its curative properties," she said.

"They do soothe one's mood, and make one far less irritable," I said. "The Indian shamans believed that the smoke was a guiding spirit. Perhaps you should take a puff."

As soon as the production began I saw that the girls are not the professionals I believed them to be. The actress Lilian was wooden in her role as Marion Unger, and I wondered whether I should not have brought her a straight blond wig to wear, for her own hair is curly and dark red and quite wrong for the part—but I doubt whether any prop or costume would have made a difference. The actress Clare affected such a ridiculous accent that both girls were reduced to giggles before even one item of clothing was removed.

"Don't laugh!" I commanded, which made the fatuous creatures laugh even more.

"Is my cigar pleasing to you, Señora?" said the actress Clare, waggling one of my unlit Monte Cristos and struggling to contain herself.

Tears ran down the cheeks of the actress Lilian. "Oh stop, do stop," she said, her face bright crimson, her shoulders twitching.

"You would like to taste it perhaps, Señora?"

And on they went, shrieking and cackling like a pair of fishwives, and thoroughly cheapening the noble vision I had had for this piece. They did not notice that I had risen to my feet and taken hold of a bronze figurine. I weighed the stout milkmaid in my hands, hooked one finger under the handle of her bronze pail. I could have silenced them in a moment, but I placed the figurine back on the mantel with all the other clutter and slipped out the door. They were still cackling as I walked away.

I hurried along with my head down, hoping I would not meet anyone I knew, for I was not in the mood for pleasantries. In Tampa, of course, one can rarely venture beyond one's front door without meeting some acquaintance or other, and although many of my customers ignore me in public, it is often the most irritating who make no secret of our association. Those who have used the Dolls' Hospital are particularly tenacious, as are those who have sold me the hair of their dead. It amuses me when I consider that a person for whom I have made an Invisible Covering, for example, will pretend he does not know me if we pass each other, but if he has sold me the tresses of his deceased wife he will acknowledge me without shame. As I approached my street I spied Mrs. Friskin, my Scotch customer, but I rushed past without meeting her eye, my gaze fixed on the sidewalk.

"Mr. Gullet! Hello, Mr. Gullet!" she called, as persistent as a mosquito.

I stopped, turned. "Why, Madame Friskin," I said, raising my hat, "what a pleasant surprise."

"I am just on my way back from the Maas brothers. They have such an array of hats now, I hardly knew where to start. You are a man who understands etiquette," she said, putting her head on one side. "Tell me, do you think someone in mourning can carry off a mockingbird?"

"A mockingbird is perhaps a little *de trop*," I said, noticing a spot of grease on her bodice.

She nodded, her double chin waggling. "That's what I told Mr. Maas, but he insists they are the latest thing for bereaved Parisiennes! As a Spiritualist I don't hold with such morbid customs, but one must think of the poor young widows who know no better, must one not?" She paused. "You know, Mr. Gullet, it is rare to find a tradesman as genuine as you. I have not forgotten your sensitivity when we lost dear Miss Friskin."

I thought of the cases of Friskin's Magnetic Life Tonic that had lined the hallway, the empty bottle beside the dead girl's bed, and the stink of disease, and I said, "Please do not mention it, Madame Friskin."

"No," she said. "No, I insist. Our sorrow has been eased by the knowledge that, through you, Gertrude was able to help another child. In our household you are an example of Christian virtue, Mr. Gullet. Why, only last evening little Master Hamish was refusing to share his toys with his brother, and we said to him, 'Think of Mr. Gullet and your poor dead sister. Think of how, through her, he showed us how to share even in our darkest hour.'"

"Madame is too kind," I murmured.

"Did you receive my card?" she said with a little giggle.

"It was the highlight of my birthday," I said, and she beamed.

"Tell me, how is Master Tommy?"

"Ah, Master Tommy," I sighed. "Do you know, Madame, I was just thinking about him when you called out to me."

"You did seem preoccupied."

"He is often in my thoughts," I said.

"Is he—" she said, and swallowed. "Is he, has he taken a turn for the worse?"

"On the contrary, Madame, he is much improved. Of course, the doctors put it down to their tinctures and elixirs, but I know the secret of his recovery."

She leaned so close to me that I could smell mothballs on her clothing. "The hair?" she said.

"Just that, Madame. It was beautiful to work with. An honor to use. And since I made the wig for the little mite, he has been a different boy. I hardly know him."

She squeezed my hand and said, "You are a saint. A saint," and I feared I would not be able to prize her away, but suddenly she released her grip and peered at her wrist-watch, peeling back her glove and her tight-buttoned cuff. "Goodness me!" she said. "Mrs. Rim will be thinking I have forgotten her."

"Madame Rim is not the sort of woman one forgets," I said.

Mrs. Friskin smiled. "She is a treasure, is she not? So entertaining."

"Quite," I said.

"In fact, I have not seen her for some time—Mr. Friskin has been so busy with patenting the Magnetic Life Tonic, and my place is at his side."

"Well, let's say that Madame Rim is the picture of health," I said. "Anybody would think she had taken the waters at the Hotel, or indulged in one of their needle baths. She looks years younger."

"It could be the Magnetic Life Tonic. She promised me she would try it," said Mrs. Friskin. "In fact, her letter did mention a surprise, but I thought she meant her dog. He does sums, you know. There was a piece about him in the *Tampa Tribune*."

"Ah," I said. "I have been privileged to witness the arithmetical abilities of Raisin. You must make sure he performs for you."

"She did mention you were making an item for her, but she did not say what it was."

"Madame," I said, dropping my voice to a whisper, "where postiches are concerned, one learns to be discreet."

She frowned for a moment, then nodded. "I see," she said. "Yes, I see."

"It will be our little secret, yes?"

"Yes, of course, Mr. Gullet."

It has been my observation that if people think one has confided in them, one can get away with murder. As I watched Mrs. Friskin scuttle away, I thought how amusing it would be to witness the moment she meets the newly bewigged Mrs. Rim, resplendent in the blond curls of Gertrude. People see what they want to see and screen out the rest; the human brain has a remarkable capacity for self-deception. It is said that when the first sailing ships sighted the continent of Australia, the savages of that great southern land did not see them. It was not that they were uninterested in the arrival of the white man, or that they covered their eyes from fear: the ships were such unthinkable objects to them that they *did not see them*. Mrs. Friskin, I imagine, will greet her friend and will say, "How well you look, my dear," and she will glance at her new curls and she may, if she is a very close friend, even pass comment on them. But she will not recognize them for what they are.

The more I mused on the usefulness of the hair of cadavers, the more I came to realize that there is a wealth of material going to waste. With a little ingenuity, I thought as I entered the Hotel, I might find the solution to that most vexing problem, the head-dress of Marion Unger. I passed the bronze Spinning Girl from the South of France and trailed my fingers across her cool feet. Hair is a curious material, I thought, and can be put to any number of uses—at the Crystal Palace Exposition in 1853, my master saw a complete tea set made entirely of human hair. Although very slender, a single strand is immensely strong; it is not alive, yet it grows, and after death it is said to continue sprouting, as if independent of the life of its host. Would there not be caskets full of it, the threads filling the spaces where flesh once had been, growing through eye sockets and ribs and silent mouths, taking over every territory like fine, blind roots?

I am very taken with my new idea, and cannot imagine why I did not think of it before. I shall direct my Cuban to begin work as soon as possible. He needs more distraction in the evenings; he spends too much time at the Cuban Lyceum listening to incendiary speeches, and far too much in the company of the widow Unger, although I pretend I do not know exactly whom he visits every other day.

"Is she beautiful, this mysterious lady-friend of yours?" I asked him once. But he blushed, and refused to elaborate.

Still, I have spent some time in her company myself over the last weeks: twice more she has called at my studio to collect her transformation, and twice I have apologized and told her that I need a little more time. In truth, I am fearful of the day when it is complete.

Although the war had been over for months, Rafael continued his night work. If he left home at ten o'clock, he could be back by one in the morning, allowing him six hours' sleep—although if the knife-sharpener was sharing his room he sometimes had to wait until midnight before he could creep away, when Antonio was lying on his back and snoring. Rafael had never shaken the feeling that his work for Monsieur Goulet was a crime of sorts. He was embarrassed to discuss it with Señora Unger; he felt she would despise him if she knew he was still doing it, and had not contradicted her when she said she was glad he would not be working so hard now that the war was won. When he attended *Carmen* with Marion and Miss Harrow, he did not feel shabbily dressed or deficient in comparison with the rest of the audience. He needed the extra money, he told himself:

there was so much to buy in this country. Why, had America not made several attempts to buy the entire island of Cuba?

He thought about Marion often, imagining her in the tobacco fields of the Vuelta Abajo, her hair as white as the noon sun. Sometimes he pictured her in the heat of the *casa de tabaco*, lying across a sweltering bale, or beneath rows of leaves strung like garlands, their fine tips brushing her face. He was there too, somewhere, although he was not sure exactly what his role might be. She was thirty years old: twice his age. She was older than his eldest sister; old enough to be his mother. And yet, her hands were soft and graceful, and the nape of her neck as smooth and white as the little slips of bone in his dominoes box. He looked at his own brown skin, felt his beardless cheek. In dominoes, the numbers had to match. Six sat with six, four with four. Those were the rules.

The *bruja* had not told him how long it might take for her spell to work. He had followed her instructions for over six months now, setting beside his bed the dish of oils and mercury she had given him. He had placed a wick in the mixture, and a slip of paper saying *Marion*, and every night he lit the little lamp and prayed for love.

I shall accompany you tonight," the wig-maker said when Rafael delivered another week's combings. "Meet me on the corner of Franklin Street at eleven o'clock, next to the Central Pharmacy."

He did not explain the reason for the meeting, but returned to his work, drawing tufts of white hair through the hackle. It occurred to Rafael that there were certain holy men, mystics from India, who lay on entire beds of hackles. His back pricked as he watched the wig-maker dragging the strands through the rows of spikes, and he wished he were stronger, wished he had the power to resist all the sharpnesses he found here.

As he approached the corner that night there was no sign of Goulet. He leaned against the brick wall of the pharmacy for a few minutes, blinking his eyes in the darkness. He felt something moving in the sand at his feet, and he squatted down and peered at the ground. A thin snake slipped by—harmless, probably, although he still had not learned to distinguish the dangerous ones. The Estradas had told him which markings to watch for, but how did one recognize something one had never seen? Still squatting, he ran his finger along the furrow left by the snake. Perhaps the Frenchman wanted simply to observe him at work, to ensure he was not taking any foolish risks that might lead to his discovery. It was only when Rafael stood up again that he realized the wig-maker was right next to him.

"Take this," said Monsieur Goulet, handing him a steel spade and beginning to walk. As Rafael followed him through the silent street the blade glinted and dulled according to the street lamps.

"There's a block not far from here that should be worth trying tonight," said Rafael, but the wig-maker said, "Shh!" and kept walking.

Rafael did not dare say anything else, and the two figures continued in silence until they reached the Harrison Street cemetery.

"In here," said Monsieur Goulet, and he passed through the gates without slowing his pace, without so much as a glance to check that Rafael was following. And so Rafael followed.

The smell of honeysuckle was powerful, and every now and then the palmetto leaves rattled in the breeze.

"This is where we dig," said Monsieur Goulet, stopping at the head of a fresh plot and scoring a small square in the soil with his cane. "Here only. We're not concerned with the legs or the trunk." He folded his arms and waited for Rafael to begin, his gray eyes steady. Behind him a marble angel glimmered in the darkness, seeming to grow from his head. "Well? Is there something wrong?"

Rafael began to dig, throwing the loosened dirt to his left, and the wig-maker skipped backward whenever a clod came too close to his spotless boots; like an excited child he advanced and retreated from the growing hole. Although the grave was fresh, there had been no rain for days and the earth had hardened quickly, and as Rafael thrust the blade in again and again he felt his bones shudder, absorbing the shock. On his back he could feel the cool stare of the angel, and he thought of his mother's statues clustered in the alcove above the fireplace, and the untouched dishes of honey and coconut meat spread before them, and the glasses of water and wine. He thought of how his mother discarded her offerings each week, unoffended, it seemed, that they had not been consumed; she tipped the drinks on her garden and threw the food into the flower beds, where it was eaten by birds. Then she refilled the dishes.

Rafael remembered one night when, as a little boy, he had stolen from his bed, careful not to wake his two sisters who slept either side of him. He took the food from the motionless statues and ate it, licking some honey between each musty sip of river water, and when he had finished he crept back to his sisters and imagined how glad his mother would be to find that the gods had dined in her house. In the morning, however, she dragged him from the bed and questioned him and his sisters, inspecting their teeth for shreds of coconut meat and their eyes for lies. "Was it you?" she said, checking Rafael's breath with quick little sniffs as if she were about to cry. Her hair hung loose, falling almost to her knees. She had never had it cut. Rafael did not understand why she had to ask about the offerings at all; she was one of the Bamboche, she often told them—a child of the god Changó, born with an image of a cross on her tongue. Such children are blessed with second sight, provided they do not have their hair cut. Trying not to breathe, Rafael had said no.

The hole was level with his neck by the time the spade met with wood. He looked up at the wig-maker, who motioned for him to climb out. In the sky the crescent moon was as sharp as a *chaveta*. Without a word Goulet removed his overcoat and hung it on a headstone, the shoulders hugging the carved marble. He handed Rafael his cane, took the spade from him, and slipped into the hole as smoothly as if he were slipping under water. Rafael heard a series of thuds, then the sound of wood cracking against the grain. There was a snapping and wrenching as the lid of the casket fractured, and the nails moaned. Rafael looked at the marble angel, at Monsieur Goulet's coat hanging like a scarecrow. On a nearby plot belonging to a Captain Frederick Bourne he could see a little bell on a cord that disappeared into the earth. He had heard of such devices: the other end of the cord would be attached to the captain's finger so that an alarm could be sounded in case of premature burial. Everybody had their private terrors, and to Rafael it did not seem strange that a distinguished naval man should express such wishes; it was entirely reasonable for someone who spent much of his life at sea to fear being trapped underground.

After a few minutes the wig-maker reached up his hand. Rafael began to help him from the hole, but the wig-maker waved something at him and said, "Take this." And Rafael reached down, and his fingers closed around a hank of hair.

He crept through the Estradas' kitchen, where everything was just as it always was: there in the corner was the gleaming black stove, its fire dead for the night; and there were the pots and the sharp-nosed irons, and on the wall hung the ice clock, motionless. When he lit the lamp in his room he blinked and frowned in the light, as if he had just awoken. He could not believe what he had witnessed; still less could he understand how he had agreed to play a part in it. Not once had he questioned the wig-maker, he realized; not once had he challenged him. The Frenchman had been so calm, so deliberate in his actions, that there seemed no reason to oppose him. "Next time you'll come alone," the wig-maker had said. "When an appropriate source comes to light." Rafael was to cut close to the skull; he was to minimize waste. Removing the scalp itself was also acceptable, since that way Monsieur Goulet could harvest the maximum yield of hair in the quiet of his studio, where more care could be taken.

Sitting on his soft bed, the quilt stitched by Señora Estrada rippling around him like sand under water, Rafael saw the bank-notes in his fist and he cast them to the floor, shaking his hand as if to rid himself of a sticky piece of refuse. Then, retrieving one of them and smoothing it flat on his thigh, he examined it for signs of forgery. Surely it could not be real. Surely what had happened at the cemetery had not happened at all; it was a counterfeit memory, a bad dream. He turned up the lamp and held the one-dollar bill to the light. There was the picture of History Instructing Youth: a beautiful woman pointing toward an open book, her arm around a young boy, and there in the corner was the Treasury seal. It was genuine.

Rafael rolled only eighty cigars the next day.

"What's the matter with you?" asked his neighbor. "Somebody keeping you up late? What's her name?"

"Just Antonio Rivera," he said. "He stayed with us last night. He snores."

Not even the lector's reading of a new novel, *Germinal,* could keep him alert. As the section detailing Étienne's first descent into the mine was read, he heard the words as if from a great distance. He felt as if he were himself descending into a deep, muffling pit, the daylight disappearing above him. His arms ached.

"She must be something, this girl of yours," said the other *torce-dores.*

Rafael did not answer, and pushed the image of Marion Unger from his mind, but a pale wrapper leaf caught the light and he saw that it was the color of her hair, and it felt smooth and silky beneath his fingers. If the wig-maker asked him to do anything like that again, he would refuse. He rolled a cigar, smoothed the tip with a dab of gum, gathered some filler together, and began again. He tried to concentrate on the story of Étienne and Catherine, but he could not bring himself to picture their work in the mine, their days spent beneath the ground.

~~~

You *would not know our father,* his eldest sister wrote. *We tried to prevent him from visiting the plantation, but if we hadn't taken him he would have gone alone, and thieves and brigands are still about although there is nothing more to steal. We could hardly tell where our house had stood; there were no landmarks left, and even the contours of the earth were changed and strange. Now he does not talk about moving home, but sits in his room and drinks wine, and will not wash, and will not let me change his bedding—and this the man who would not wear the same collar twice. Some of our neighbors are going back to the Vuelta Abajo to plant new crops, and we would take Papá there if only he would agree.*

Rafael did not book a passage to Cuba, as so many had done. The Vuelta Abajo was more foreign to him than Florida now, and besides, had his father not told him to go to America? He would have a better life here. Whatever names the newspapers might give him—*Cuban nigger, Latin dog*—there were no murderous brigands in Tampa. By and large, people were friendly: Señora Unger, for example, made him feel that he was welcome, that he belonged. One day, he would repay her for her kindness. When he had made his fortune he would buy her embroidered dancing slippers, and gloves of supple kid buttoned with pearls, and glossy furs for her white shoulders, and a closet of gowns of silk: peacock green, cerise, fuchsia, butterscotch. In the meantime, he kept lighting the *bruja's* lamp every night, the little slip of paper saying *Marion* becoming so infused with oil that it was almost invisible.

He continued to gather combings for the wig-maker, and now and then, if a white-blond person died, or if it was discovered that the grave of someone already buried contained the correct shade, he received what Monsieur Goulet called Special Instructions. Sometimes word came with the *afilador* that Rafael's *pomade* had arrived, or that the *jeweled comb* he had ordered *for his sister* was ready; other times Monsieur Goulet wrote him to say that the *perfumed soap from Paris* was there. All meant the same thing: that Rafael would be busy that night. He dreaded these messages the way a person living far from home dreads bad news, can smell it on the envelope. As he worked, digging and shoveling, prizing and cutting, he tried to keep the image of Señora Unger uppermost in his mind, welcoming him and liking him. Often other thoughts intruded, however: the Santería rituals of which he had heard rumors, or the face of the man on the Italian shroud. As he dug he could not help but recall his work on the tobacco plantation, when he had made hollows in the red dirt for the seedlings. Sometimes he wondered: What am I planting here? And what will grow? But grave-robbers took jewels and watches and wedding bands from caskets, Rafael told himself, or even prayer books, if the binding was costly. At least he did not do that.

February of 1899 was colder than usual, and when the frosts arrived and the ground became so hard that Rafael could no longer dig for hair, Monsieur Goulet advised him to concentrate instead on the mausoleums popular with the wealthy bereaved. In most cases the locks securing the wrought-iron fences and the heavy doors possessed only the appearance of inviolability, and Rafael soon mastered them. He remembered his mother telling him that the slabs of stone laid on the dead were intended to hold the soul in place, to prevent restless spirits from escaping their coffins and wandering—they were meant to protect the living. Now, he thought, perhaps their function was to keep people like him out. Perhaps the dead were the ones needing protection.

When a young white-blonde by the name of Constance Fowler succumbed to consumption, Monsieur Goulet sent his Special Instructions, and the following night Rafael went to the cemetery. The Fowler family crypt was of veined marble, and after Rafael had released the lock he put his hand to the cool door and pushed. Nothing gave. He pushed again, using his shoulder, but still the door did not move. Finally he turned, placing his back to the mausoleum and bracing his feet against the ground, the many stone monuments spread before him like a miniature town. He pushed with all his weight, and the marble yielded a little, and he pushed again and again until he was breathless.

There was just enough room for him to enter. He squeezed inside, and something brushed at his foot. He lowered his lamp and there, crouched behind the door, was Constance Fowler, her arms and face covered with lacerations, her hair rippling across the floor and lapping at Rafael's boots. He leapt away from her outstretched fingers, which he saw were torn and bloodied, the nails ripped to the quick. Against one wall, the coffins of various members of the Fowler family rested untouched, peaceful in their stone niches. Against the opposite wall, however, the coffin of Constance lay splintered and broken, the lid cracked, the end kicked out. Sprinkled across the floor were little white shreds, which Rafael at first took for scraps of fabric from the girl's satin burial robe. They formed a trail to the door of the mausoleum, the back of which he now saw was covered with frantic scratches—and it was then he realized that the white shreds were not cloth at all, but hanks of wrenched-out hair.

Rafael grabbed his lamp and pushed his way out, back into the sweet-smelling night. He wanted to run all the way to Fortune Street, beat at Señora Unger's door, lay his head on her soft breast and be comforted—but then, what would he tell her? He knew that if he were to continue his association with Marion, he could no longer work for Monsieur Goulet—and so, as he pulled shut the door to the crypt, he resolved that he would cease collecting hair for the wig-maker. He would try to forget all the nights he had devoted to his service, the black hours he had spent digging and cutting. He would spend his time with good, moral people, like the Estradas, and like Marion Unger.

~

On the night of February 12th, 1899, the cold woke Marion. She pressed her hand to her cheek and forehead, the way a mother might, and felt icy skin. As she ran from her bed to the hope chest to fetch another quilt, she heard a distant whistle, and for one sleepy moment she thought, The knife-sharpener is coming. She imagined doors opening into the dark, and women stepping into the street in their nightdresses, their hands full of knives, and the *afilador*'s wheel spinning and sparking in the black air. And then the whistle sounded again, closer this time, four long icy wails, and she knew what it meant: frost. One of Mr. Plant's trains was bringing news of a freeze farther up the line, warning the grove owners to protect their ripening crops. All over Florida men would be rising from their beds, building pyres about their trees. Marion spread the extra quilt on the bed. By dawn, the temperature was below freezing.

I am by nature an innovative man, and I have high hopes for the success of my new source of hair. It must be said that my Cuban seemed quite reluctant to do the job at all, and it has been some days since he has brought me any new stock. I do accept that the particular shade I require is not common, and perhaps he is waiting until he has a good amount to deliver, but I would have thought a certain showy mausoleum to which I recently directed him might have produced a sufficient quantity. I only hope he is not growing lazy, as his race is wont to do (an examination of the Latin skull often reveals deficient Concentrativeness and Firmness, resulting in an inability to apply oneself to a task over time, and a general lack of character). I suspect he will ask me for more money soon.

I do not know why people find such strangeness in that which is entirely natural. The Hotel guests, for instance, marvel at the snakebird, which swallows its prey whole. They gasp as it spears a sunfish that is surely too large for it to digest, then gasp again as the squirming catch slips down its gullet. "Unbelievable!" they cry. "Did you see that? Do you believe that?" There is nothing remarkable about the swallowing of the fish to the snakebird, of course; it is simply following its own nature, and if it did otherwise it would perish. Why is this so difficult for the goggle-eyed guest to understand? I long for the end of April, when I shall be alone in my palace once more, and there will be no more guests until the next century has almost begun.

Mr. Flood called today, demanding immediate repairs on his partial peruke. It seems he snagged it on a mangrove in the Everglades while collecting new *Liguus* specimens—but I made no comment on the vanity of a man who wears a toupee to the swamp. After I had matched the shade and reknotted the damaged strands, he examined himself from all angles in my mirrors and pronounced it a great success.

"You are a miracle-worker, Godley," he said, smiling at his many reflections, stroking the peruke. In the months since it has been in his possession, he has become far more boisterous and has taken to wearing a crease down the front of his trousers (a fashion begun by the Prince of Wales to disguise his bandy legs). I almost expected him to recite "Manly Love" in the style of Arthur Schleman.

I bowed. "And may I inquire after the delightful Madame Flood?" I said.

"I look ten years younger at least in this!" he said. "Hah! I can't get a real view of it in my wife's little mirrors at home. What did you say, Godley?"

"I was asking after the lovely Madame Flood."

"She's just fine. She keeps herself happy with her Spiritualist group, and I have my collection."

"And has she had any success with the spirits?" I asked, sensing a lecture on the edifying pastime of snail ambush.

Flood snorted. "Not unless you count Mrs. Rim, and I don't know why that one bothers coming."

"No?" I obliged.

"No," he said, drawing himself up to his full five and a half feet. "She's so old that she'll be seeing them soon enough!"

I laughed, which seemed to please him greatly, for he slapped me on the back and said, "Good man, Godley!" Then he said, "Don't let on, but sometimes Mrs. Flood pretends she's talking to a certain grove owner. You remember Mr. Jack Unger? Died a few years back, after the frost?"

I ceased brushing away the cuttings and gave him my full attention. "I've heard of him," I said. "I understand he left a beautiful widow."

"Marion Unger." Flood nodded, his curls bouncing. "Well, she's been coming to the group for a few months now, and Mrs. Flood— she loves the attention, my wife—has been pretending to channel poor dead Jack."

I am no longer astonished by the enthusiasm with which my customers will speak ill of family and friends, but it remains one of my great delights.

"But this is a very serious matter, Monsieur Flood," I said. "Madame Unger is unaware of the deception?"

"I do feel bad about that," said Flood, adjusting my mirrors so he could study the back of his head. "I do. But it's no business of mine to go meddling in other people's lives, is it? Besides, it makes her happy."

"Madame Unger is fully taken in, then."

"I think of it this way, Godley," said Flood, suddenly earnest. "Mrs. Flood, for whatever reason, pretends to have some kind of psychic gift. That is a lie, yes. But what harm is she doing bringing a little comfort, a little hope, to poor Mrs. Unger?"

"Hmm," I said. "Jack Unger. A good-looking man, so I heard."

"That he was."

"Probably not the sort of man who would need my services."

"No," said Flood, smoothing his hair, erasing the faint line between the real and the false.

"One or two of my lady customers used to gossip about him. About how handsome he was. I believe he was quite flirtatious with them. In fact, now that I think about it, I believe his behavior after his marriage left something to be desired. Well, you know how women gossip, but I suspect he may have had—" and I stopped.

"Yes?" said Flood.

"I may be mistaken, but I suspect he had extra-marital relations with women of easy virtue, women who worked at the Cherokee Club. And these women"—I noticed as I said the word for the third

time that it forced my lips to move like those of a suckling babe—
"these women introduced him to a beautiful and ambitious young
lady of Spanish extraction. Let me see, what was her name?
Angelina, Alvarita—I had it a moment ago."

"I imagine you hear all kinds of stories," said Flood, removing his
peruke and handing it to me. "If you'd wrap that for me, thank you,
Godley. Time I was getting home. I have some new shells to clean."

"Of course," I said. "Do come back if you have any more problems,
but I don't think you will. A little tweak here, a little tug there"—I
hummed a merry tune—"you'd be amazed what a difference it makes."

Mr. Flood tucked the box under his arm and draped his coat
across it so that it was invisible.

"Don't worry, Monsieur," I said, "I'm well practiced at keeping
secrets. You may use the back exit if you wish." As I opened the door
for him I said, "This little game your wife is conducting. It's time
poor Madame Unger was told the truth, don't you think?"

A little tweak, a little tug. I do enjoy my work.

~

He removed a cigar from a box and placed it in a metal contraption
resting on his table, then with one stroke snipped off the head, which
rolled toward Marion like a dropped button.

"My guillotine," he explained.

He placed the cigar carefully before him, as if he were waiting for
Marion to leave so he could light it.

"I was hoping my transformation might be complete," said Marion.

"If I may be so bold, Madame," said Monsieur Goulet, his eyes
flickering up and down her length, "perhaps a dress of some color
other than black or gray would enhance the transformation."

No man had spoken to her like this before. "Thank you, yes," said
Marion, "but I'm afraid I don't have a lot of time, Monsieur Goulet,
and I'd like to collect my transformation, please."

The wig-maker retrieved the cigar head and disposed of it. "A
dress of moss green, or a rich claret, perhaps. A bewitching woman

should make the most of her charms, especially if planning to emerge from a period of mourning."

Marion made no reply.

"Not that the passing of your dear husband is a matter to be dismissed lightly," he added. "Such a generous man. He had many friends."

"I didn't realize you knew Mr. Unger," said Marion.

"I didn't know him personally," said the wig-maker, "but I knew of him. Why, two of the most beautiful actresses in Florida were his close friends—but you know all that, of course."

Marion raised her head. "I'm afraid I don't understand what you mean."

"Oh yes, Madame," he said. "They're customers of mine, these actresses. I'm closely involved with the theater."

"The theater," echoed Marion.

"The theater, dancing girls—in my profession, Madame, one encounters all manner of people. I do not judge."

"You didn't mention this when I collected my bracelet last year, nor at the Hotel." As she watched his face, she thought, Is he smiling? But she could not tell.

"No," said the wig-maker. "Perhaps I forgot, or did not make the connection."

Marion paused. "May I collect my transformation now, please?"

"Oh dear," said the wig-maker. "I hope I haven't offended you with my talk of dancing girls, Madame Unger. I didn't mean to suggest—"

"My transformation, please," said Marion.

The wig-maker sighed. "I'm afraid I must request Madame's forgiveness. It is still not quite ready. A complex piece such as yours, it takes time."

"Complex?" said Marion, trying not to raise her voice. "I called on you in November, then in December, when I had wanted to wear it to the opera, and again in January. Each time you told me it was not quite ready. It's a simple little knot, surely!"

The wig-maker's face colored. "Madame, things that to the untrained eye appear simple are often the most complex. If you tried to make this *simple little knot* yourself you would see what a detailed operation it is, what reserves of patience and skill it requires—"

"You're right, of course, Monsieur Goulet," said Marion, pressing herself into the back of her chair as he drew nearer to her. "I know nothing of your intricate work. I shall leave it in your expert hands."

He saw her out to the front room and gestured her toward the exit, making a little bow. She unfastened the cord on her parasol as she waited for him to open the door, but when she looked up again he was nowhere to be seen.

"Monsieur Goulet?" she said, her voice too loud for the small space.

"Here it is," said the wig-maker, rising from behind the counter with a tissue-wrapped parcel in his hand. "A small token, Madame, which I hope you'll accept by way of apology."

Marion opened her mouth to refuse the present. She needed to be alone, to think through what this strange man with his darting eyes—they *were* gray today—had told her: *Two of the most beautiful actresses in Florida were his close friends.*

He was watching her now, offering her the pretty parcel as if it were a sweetmeat, a party favor. She knew she should refuse it, as she should have refused the invitation to the Hotel. She had not liked the way the officers watched, their eyes moving from her to the wig-maker and back again, smirking. And she thought, Perhaps these women, these actresses, were simply wives of Jack's business associates. She knew very little of his negotiations with his buyers; perhaps, for instance, when they were haggling over the price of navel oranges, he offered them an incentive. "Something to keep your lady-friend happy," she imagined him saying, slipping them a jar of orange-blossom honey. "Something sweet for you to take home." Businessmen came to such arrangements all the time—little rewards that ensured loyalty. There was nothing immoral about accepting extras, nothing illegitimate about it at all. And so she said, "Thank you," and took the scented parcel, and it was so light that by the time she was home she had quite forgotten she was carrying it. When she paused at the hall table to peel off her gloves she left the wig-maker's little gift there too, curled beneath the empty white fingers. Then she went upstairs.

At the top of the house, hidden under the eaves like memory, was the attic. Marion seldom needed to go there, and had only a vague idea of its contents. One corner, she knew, held Jack's things, but she could not have described them in detail. Miss Harrow had packed them away after his death, under strict instructions to discard nothing. Marion had sat in the parlor while Miss Harrow moved from room to room gathering papers and pipes, cuff links and canes and hats. Every so often she came to Marion with some item she thought was of no value.

"This?" she had said, holding up *Treatise and Hand-Book of Orange Culture in Florida*, by the Reverend T. W. Moore.

"Yes," said Marion.

"This?" A sheaf of old newspaper clippings about pesticide prices.

"Yes," said Marion.

"Not this, surely?" A broken ladder, the upper rungs stained with juice.

"Keep it all. I want everything."

Eventually Miss Harrow stopped asking and continued her packing in silence, filling more than forty orange boxes. Up and down the attic stairs she walked, carrying one box at a time, stacking Jack's clutter under the sloping roof as if depositing riches in a pharaoh's tomb. Marion went and rested in her room, but she could still hear Miss Harrow moving above like a restless spirit.

Marion's unfamiliarity with the contents of the attic was as great a source of comfort to her as the fact they existed at all. It was enough to know that pieces of Jack were stored there, keeping watch over her, and she never unpacked them: if the day came when there was nothing left to discover, Jack would be dead.

Today Miss Harrow had gone to a musicale in St. Petersburg and would not be back until after five. The house was still and empty, and as Marion climbed the narrow stairs she glanced out the window to the glitter of water. All she could hear was the brushing of her skirts, and her short, quick breaths, and her soles patting the polished tread.

The boxes were stamped UNGER, as if the contents had been plucked from the branches of the lost fruit trees and were awaiting a buyer. The first ones contained clothing: empty gloves, collarless shirts, trousers folded in three, a coat with arms resting across its buttoned chest. Each garment lay perfectly flat, relieved of unnecessary bulk, packed for a long vacation, perhaps. After finishing with a box Marion pushed it to one side, gradually building a narrow corridor for herself, a passage into the dim reaches of the attic. She found Jack's shoes, their toes stuffed with paper, their laces tucked beneath their tongues. There were three pairs of work boots, scrubbed clean of dust and polished so they shone like mahogany. And yet, despite Miss Harrow's care, her attempts at preservation, everywhere there were signs that these were items no longer used: there were little indentations in hats, there were impressions of buttons on folded fabrics, and the bottom strata of shoes were deflated like cakes taken too soon from the oven. Marion moved farther under the sloping roof, where it was darker and more cramped. She could feel a cool draft forcing its way through the shingles, licking at her neck, and she began to work more quickly. She opened boxes containing ledgers of figures, lists of long-consumed harvests. The pages were headed according to the variety of orange: "The Bell," "The Egg," "The Navel," "The Blood." Further pages recorded the purchase of ladders, scales, the boxes themselves, the bales of tissue paper that protected the fruit. There were records of wages paid to the Negro pickers—Marion had not realized how little they earned, for Jack was always complaining of their greed—and at the back of each ledger was a page headed "Miscellaneous Expenses" in Jack's steady copperplate. There were loose papers in the boxes, too: notes about

"Enemies and Diseases," recipes for pesticide and fungicide, ratios of water to poison. Marion caught her finger on a splinter, and a bead of blood appeared. She blotted it on a ledger's marbled cover, where it was invisible.

She had to bend almost double to retrieve the last boxes. At first glance it appeared they too contained business records, but when Marion dug a little deeper she realized that many of the books were not ledgers but photograph albums. She inched back through the unsteady passage she had created, pushing a box with her toes, the stacks trembling as she passed, until she was standing directly beneath the small, grimy window.

Women. The albums were full of women. In some pictures they swooped before the camera in transparent veils, backs arched, toes pointed, silky butterflies. In others they lay across chaises longues, strings of glass beads running between their breasts and over their pale bellies. They were caught as they dressed, half-stockinged legs lifted and resting on the rungs of chairs, or as they bathed, their skin slick with soap. They watched from behind lavish fans of feathers, eyebrows raised, or they stood before velvet draperies and, like pensive Madonnas, cupped their breasts in their hands. Marion kept turning the pages, and woman after woman loomed up at her from the black paper and then passed. She has a tinier waist than I, Marion thought, and Her eyes are prettier than mine, and Her breasts are rounder, her ankles finer. Someone had taken a lot of trouble to compile the albums. The photographs were mounted one to a page, each black corner straight, and were organized according to theme: one section was devoted to the butterfly women in their see-through veils, another to bathing, another to the reclining nude. Little family groups.

In the bottom of the last box, beneath the last album, were a wooden case and several small cardboard boxes. Marion thought they were decks of playing cards, but they were too heavy. They were labeled with titles like "A Romp in the Hay," "The Harem," and "Miss Dominique Takes a Bath." She lifted the lid from "The Fan Dance" and found that it contained thick glass slides, and then she read the label on the wooden case: "The Metamorphoser—Lanterna Magica."

When she was a little girl, her neighbors had owned a magic lantern. Sometimes the Brackmans invited her family to showings, and Marion was allowed to attend. In the parlor Mr. Brackman arranged chairs for the adults while Mrs. Brackman drew the shades and the heavy draperies, making sure every crack of light was shut out. The audience fell silent and stared at the far wall, which had been made blank with a double bed sheet, and when the first glowing picture appeared everybody sighed aloud, as if they were happy. Mrs. Brackman always used her best linen for the occasion. "From my trousseau," she would confide to Marion's mother. The story Marion remembered best was one about a girl who would not stop biting her nails. As the lantern flickered the girl appeared to move, her skin the texture of bed linen, her feet hovering just above Mrs. Brackman's keyhole-lace border. The last slide showed the punishment for the girl's persistent bad habit: her little fingers were chopped off. Everybody laughed then, even Marion, although she did not know why.

Marion always tried to sit as close as possible to Mr. Brackman, who operated the magic lantern. She watched him posting the pieces of glass into the slot as keenly as she watched the pictures themselves. "How does it work?" she asked him, but he replied that some things were better left unexplained—and besides, if he told her, it would not be magic anymore. Once, she remembered, a moth had batted the projector, and she had watched its image on the trousseau sheet, as huge as a buzzard above the girl's head. Much later, of course, Marion came to understand the principles of the magic lantern, the secrets of focus and reflection; Jack had explained them to her. What she had never known was that he possessed his own set.

She took the projector from its case and propped it on an orange box, lighting the wick and aiming the lens at a stack of issues of the *Gentleman's Magazine* and *Collier's Once a Week*. She cleared the journals away, dropping them in dusty piles wherever she could find space, exposing the bare white wall that sloped away to the floor.

Dust motes drifted in the lantern's beam, and Marion thought of the scale insect, which could destroy an entire grove if allowed to take hold. The pest was invisible to the naked eye except in the late afternoon, Jack had told her; at that time of day, if an infested tree was jarred, the tiny flies would show up like dust against the rays of the sinking sun. Marion took a glass slide from the first little cardboard box her fingers found—"The Newcomer in the Harem"—and slipped it into the projector.

THE SULTAN ORDERS HIS FAVORITE,

FATIMA,

TO BRING HIM THE NEW DANCER

read the wall, the final line spilling onto the floor. Marion did not stop to raise the projector: she was looking at the picture that the words framed. It showed a woman with kohl-rimmed eyes, and she was cut in two, this glass woman, this trick of the light; the floor bisected her at the hips, so that she performed a contorted bow. Her loose trousers were gathered at the ankles, the outline of her legs clearly visible through the sheer fabric, curvy against the straight lines of the attic floorboards, and in her navel a jewel glittered; her long fingers toyed with it as she regarded a pile of fringed pillows. Above her waist she was quite bare, save for a veil across her nose and mouth. Her dark eyes were familiar to Marion, although she could not place them.

She approached the illuminated wall. She stretched out a finger and touched it, and the woman's hand covered hers like that of a ghost, and she stepped closer, and the woman's bare toes covered her own, and suddenly she was standing square in front of the magic lantern's beam, and she was the bare, ghostly figure cut off at the hips, the newest wife.

She grabbed the little box, the box that looked as if it held playing cards, and she flipped through the rest of the slides, holding them before the magic lantern: "The Arrival of the Harem," "The

Instruction of the Newcomer in the Mysteries of the Flesh," "Two Harem Girls Demonstrate the Mysteries of the Flesh," "The Entrance of the Sultan," "The Selection of the Newcomer as His Companion," "Further Exploration of the Mysteries of the Flesh." The dust motes danced with the movement of her hands. She rushed down the stairs, the river glittering in her peripheral vision, as blue and inquisitive as the eyes of Miss Needham.

Marion shut herself in her room and did not emerge for three days. She lay on her bed, opening and closing the fan Jack had bought for her. The feathers fluttered in the dark and in the daylight as if there were a draft, although Marion felt nothing.

She refused all nourishment, and whenever Miss Harrow knocked at her door she told her she wished to be left alone. She would not even see Rafael, who called twice—for was he not almost a man himself? Was it not likely he would become as secretive and deceitful as Jack? The only thing she requested was a large pair of scissors, and she responded with irritation when her companion insisted there was no such item in the household.

"Don't be ridiculous," she said. "They're in the drawer of the kitchen table. The ones we use for trimming the poultry. Now bring them to me."

On the evening of the third day Marion sat before the mirror and removed the pins from her hair, feeling it uncoil and loosen against her neck. She lifted it in her hands, noted its cool weight. She held the scissors around it, drawing them up as close to her scalp as she could. She paused, then lowered them again, holding them in her lap, where they gleamed against the folds of her black dress as brightly as moonlight. There was an itching, a twitching in her hands, as if she could feel the blood rushing to her fingertips, and she removed her dress and, sitting in her petticoats, began to cut through the hem. She cut up as far as her knee, her thigh, her waist, and she kept cutting, up the line of her spine, past the lungs, the uppermost rib, listening to the blades eating through the cotton lawn, until she reached the neck. The scissors resisted the double thickness of the seam there, twisting a little in her hands, but she set her jaw and made one final cut, the way she did when jointing a chicken. The handle dug into the soft piece of flesh between her thumb and index finger, making a red furrow like that left by a wedding ring, and the cloth gave way, and she went to her armoire and gathered all her mourning clothes in her arms and lifted the bundle— as heavy as a man, surely—into the hallway. She shook out her hair. It was dirty at the roots, and a sharp scent drifted from it, something animal. The locket fluttered against her chest, a full moon on a chain. She was younger now. She put on a white muslin gown and went downstairs.

Miss Harrow did not mention Marion's attire, nor the fact that she had been in hiding for three days. She acted as if nothing unusual had happened, and Marion loved her then.

"Mrs. Flood called," said Miss Harrow, casting about for the note Adelina had written on the back of her visiting card. "Here we are. She said she had a vision of a young man with ice in his hair, and she wanted to know if you're coming to tomorrow's meeting. And Rafael Méndez called again, and was quite anxious when I told him you were still indisposed. He wished you a speedy recovery, and promised to come again soon."

People were kind, Marion thought, and the world was not such a brutal place if one surrounded oneself with kindness. She would invite Rafael to tea that week, and lend him some more books, and she would go to the meeting, where she had friends who cared about her.

⁓

A Mrs. Budge came to see me on Tuesday morning, bringing a daughter with her. As I measured the mother's bony scalp (excessive Approbativeness), she fluttered her scanty lashes and tossed her thin, dun wisps, and told me she should like a rich chestnut.

"But of course, Madame," I said. "It will go very well with your pretty eyes."

And all the while, the snot-nosed child wandered my studio picking up glues and needles and hooks and skeins of my best material and putting them back all wrong. Her one attractive feature—surely inherited from the father's side of the family—was a tight, glossy braid that hung to her waist, and I felt an idea which had hitherto been floating directionless in my head catch and take root.

"Now then, my dear," I called to her—the mother said nothing— "we must be very careful with Mr. Goulet's things. He has needles and hooks and dangerous glues, and we don't want to hurt ourselves, do we?"

The child kept sorting through trays of ribbon and thread, and poking her fat fingers in drawers and cupboards.

"She's a very curious girl, is she not?" I smiled, and noted down the measurement of Mrs. Budge's cranium.

Over lunch I usually read the *Tampa Tribune* (*Le Figaro* it is not, but of the papers available here it is the least inferior) and Tuesday's editorial made me laugh into my coffee. The topic was the local Cubans, who, the writer so wittily observed, "seem to have very little decency in their composition. You can at any time of day if you promenade along the streets of Ybor City or West Tampa see children from all ages one to seven years playing around in the garb which nature gave them with a little additional covering of dirt or cheesecloth, generally the former." After a good chuckle I folded the paper away and returned to work, but the article stayed in my thoughts all afternoon, and when a Mrs. Finkel called, also with a daughter in tow, my idea began to sprout and grow.

"We've come about Dorothy," said Mrs. Finkel, smiling at me as if I were about to make her a present. "We were hoping she might be all better now."

"It's been a month," said a sulky voice behind her, and I saw that the child had sprawled itself across my red silk divan. "Father says it's a disgrace that I should have to wait so long."

Mrs. Finkel gave a fluttery laugh. "I told her that Dr. Gladly would be doing his very best to make Dorothy better. One can't hurry good health, isn't that right, Doctor?"

"Ah, little Dorothy," I said, thinking of the growing pile of dolls in the corner of Bluebeard's Chamber. Since beginning work on the transformation of the widow Unger, and on its companion piece, my model woman, I have put aside other distractions. The dolls are grotesque objects, bald and filthy, fat little bags of sawdust all broken and staring, their china limbs catching at me when I reach for a switch of hair. In dim light, they are nothing more than a stack of bones. "She has been very ill, Madame," I said in a solemn voice. "In fact," I whispered, casting a glance at the heavy-cheeked daughter who was now picking at a bolster, "I suspect we may have to perform radical surgery."

I watched as Mrs. Finkel knelt by the divan and explained to the child that Dorothy was not quite better yet, and I felt my new idea growing, growing. Children, I noted, will believe most anything.

My next visitor was far more welcome: Marion Unger came knocking at my door, and so relaxed in my presence did she seem that I found myself suggesting a tone of gown to complement her transformation. And why should I not instruct a female customer on how to look her best? Is it not my job to allow a woman to capitalize on her physical blessings? The hair-piece itself, of course, was far from ready, thanks to the laziness of my Cuban in finding the correct shade, but she did not seem too indisposed, and I could hardly breathe as I thought that perhaps she enjoyed her visits to my studio as much as I did, and wished for them to continue. I even took the liberty of mentioning her husband, and the fact that he knew my actresses, but she was quick to change the subject, asking for her transformation with more than a little impatience. Before I could think better of it, I gave her the amethyst necklace that had been waiting under my counter for so long.

Her acceptance of my little present so lifted my spirits that I was charm itself to the rest of my customers that day, and I even decided to forgive my actresses their sabotage of my last production. Although they are as coarse as sand is to flour, in times of hardship one must mix a little grit into one's bread—and so I went to visit them that evening. With me I took two costumes: that of a wealthy naval captain and that of a maid, both complete with wigs. These were roles with which my actresses were already familiar, and I looked forward to an enjoyable few hours.

I was approaching their apartments when I noticed that my boot was a little loose. I bent to tie it on the threshold, and as I did so I heard their voices coming from beyond the door.

"Let me help you arrange your new curls," said one in a deep, pompous voice.

"Oh, but they are beautiful!" said the other. "It is a masterpiece!"

"I spent many weeks selecting the right material to frame your pretty face," said the first voice.

"Dear Monsieur!" said the other. "Would you show me how they should fall across my breast? Perhaps if you loosen my bodice a little—"

And then there was laughter, and it was of the same ugly variety provoked by my last production. I pulled my bootlace so tight it would not dare to come undone again, and I strode down the street with no destination in mind—a disquieting activity, and one I usually shun. There were few people about, for the February evening was cool, and as I turned a corner I saw the strangest sight: myself, or rather my own reflection, coming toward me. The gentleman, of my size and build, was dressed in a frock coat and top hat that could have been taken from my own armoire, and was swinging an ebony cane just like mine. As I drew closer, however, I realized he was no reflection, for there was a woman on his arm, and I was alone. And then I recognized him: he was Swope, my plume-hunter, the swamp-dweller who supplies me with feathers. The transformation in his apparel and manner was startling, but even more astonishing was his companion—a glorious, tiny-waisted creature with an elegant chestnut chignon that was most definitely her own hair.

"Good day, Mr. Goulet," he said. "I don't believe you've met Mrs. Swope." And the pretty thing smiled and touched her hand to her hair and said, "I've found your accessories so delightful, Mr. Goulet."

I murmured some greeting or other and continued on my way, swinging my cane as if I had somewhere important to go, my footsteps all the while leading me to the shabbiest part of the neighborhood. I thought, Nothing is as it should be. My actresses mimic me behind my back; my plume-hunter is a gentleman and his wife a great beauty; the widow Unger enjoys the company of a downy-cheeked boy instead of someone sophisticated, someone who would be devoted to her. I grew angry as I thought of my Cuban, who until recently was a most satisfactory employee. Even he has disappointed me now, for despite my instructions regarding the Harrison Street crypt, he has delivered no hair this week at all.

It is two months since I asked him to procure a match for the widow's hair. True, our newest source is perhaps a little unpleasant, but sorting through trash is hardly agreeable and he made no complaints about that. I envisaged that, like the resurrection men who served the early anatomists, he would locate the correct material for me with little trouble so that I could continue my work. I even entrusted him with a lock of the combings given me by the widow, but still he has not obliged. Perhaps the death rate has dropped, for it is true that typhoid and yellow fever are waning. The young die too infrequently here now. Death in childbirth was one of my most promising avenues, but that too has slowed. I even tried to dye some hair (Scandinavian blond, which usually takes the color very well) but could not get it right. My model woman stands bare-headed, as featureless as an egg. I cannot bear to look at her. I leave her covered with a sheet and she lurks in the corner of my minaret room like a phantom.

I found myself in Ybor City, in the area where the Cubans live in their little white crates. It is laughable, the airs these immigrants assume. The cigar workers, for instance, arrive at their factories dressed in white collars, white shirts, and bow ties, if you please, as if they were respectable businessmen! And then they sit like children and listen to stories, and during their breaks they discuss Zola and Hugo, and I doubt there is one in ten who can himself read. My Cuban should be grateful for the steady work I give him, for a man can take no pride in himself if he does not have a sensible job. Musing on these things, I made my way to his dwelling.

"*Sí?*" said the greasy man who answered the door.

"Good evening," I said. "I've came to call on Señor Méndez."

Over his shoulder the man shouted, "Rafael!" and I remembered that this was the boy's Christian name. Then he gestured down the hall. "He's hiding in his room," he said.

The entire house was lined with thin planks of pine, and I felt quite enclosed, as if I were inside a box. There was no response when I knocked on the boy's door, so I let myself in. The shades were drawn, and in the gloom I could just make out the form of the boy. He was cowering on the bed, and when I spoke his name he started and said, "Leave me. Don't come in here, leave me."

"You've delivered nothing this week," I said. "Are you ill? Or have you been spending too many evenings with your friend Madame Unger?"

He turned to face the wall. His body was shaking, although the apartment was too warm for comfort.

"Are you ill?" I repeated. "I have many orders to fill, and my stock is running low. And I still need more of the white-blond."

"You can find someone else to be your thief," he said in a low voice.

I approached him, although the odor of sweat was almost more than I could bear. "Thief?" I said. "Come now, you know we are taking nothing of value. Why, if I collect shells from the beach, is that theft? If I pick wild flowers, am I doing wrong?"

The boy sighed but did not answer, and it took a good deal more coaxing to extract any sense from him. Eventually—with his back still turned to me—he admitted what was troubling him, and although I tried to contain myself, I could not help but laugh. He had made an unlucky discovery in the Fowler crypt, it seems—a simple case of premature burial, and not uncommon, but he gibbered on about how the woman had torn the hair from her head in a fit of despair. "Well, that would have made it easier to collect the material, would it not?" I said, for one must always try to see things in a positive light. But my chicken-hearted Cuban had fled the scene empty-handed. He tried to tell me that he did not wish to work for me anymore, but I knew that he would come to his senses once he considered how such foolishness would affect his earnings.

As I walked back through the filthy streets I recalled the editorial I had read, and the little idea which had germinated in me during the visit of Mrs. Budge, and which had sprouted and grown when the Finkel child was sprawled across my divan, now reached fruition. I slipped into the bathroom of a saloon and took from my case the naval captain's costume, exchanging it for my own clothing. Over my hair I pulled the captain's wig—a little tight, but it would do as long as I kept my facial expressions to a minimum—and I shut Monsieur Lucien Goulet III away and emerged. My own mother would not have known me.

On the streets, children ran wild—Cuban, Spanish, Italian, German, some with hoops and sticks, some with slingshots, some with no playthings save their cunning little minds. There are many urchins in Ybor City, due to the excessive carnal appetites of the poor and their unwillingness to work in order to provide for them, but the naval captain was looking for one kind in particular. It was an easy matter for him to engage them in conversation. They showed him their slingshots and hoops, their spinning tops and their marbles, which recalled glass eyes. He stopped at a confectioner's and bought some boiled candies, and if the urchins were reluctant to approach him, he had only to rattle the bag and they followed him through the streets, little rats, through the grimy alleys and lanes wet with urine. Their parents did not seem to mind that they were wandering farther and farther from home. He had quite a retinue.

Perhaps this all sounds rather merry, like one of the colorful processions the residents of Ybor City enjoy staging, complete with flowers and music and cannon-fire—but if truth be told, I had a vile time and I would never have gone near the place had it not been for Marion Unger. I was the target of continual harassment from beggars and wastrels and other undesirable elements too lazy to earn a living. "Any spare coins, sir? Can you spare a little for a loaf of bread, sir?" and so on and on. It was most tiring. I could not take three paces without having to step over a vagrant. I had to remind myself that sometimes one must endure a little unpleasantness in order to achieve a satisfactory end—consider, for instance, my nights spent combing through the refuse of this crude town, or the ordeal of Saint Lucien's Hospital for Dolls—and in this light it was, I believe, a successful spree.

I did not know if my urchin would be male or female, and I did not know its age, but I recognized her when I saw her, for although she was wandering the streets barefoot and sniveling, and had fashioned a doll from a stick and a filthy piece of rag, she stood out from the dark-haired tangle like a blossom in dark leaves.

"Hello there," I said, giving her an acid drop, and she answered me in Italian by introducing me to her stick, which was called Alessandra. I had no clue from which sorry brood she sprang, for she resembled nobody I could see. She must have been five years old, perhaps six, and I was grateful to my master for ensuring I learned Italian so that I could bargain for hair in Liguria and Umbria and Tuscany. Now, it is true that there are a surprising number of blondes to be found in that country, but they are golden-haired—think of the paintings of Titian—and my little guttersnipe's curls were as white as picked bones. Possibly she was the result of her mamma's hot-blooded romp with a German—the lithographer on Pierce Street springs to mind—or possibly she was a simple abnormality, an accident of Nature. It was of no consequence.

"Do you know the Tampa Bay Hotel?" I said, bending and whispering in her dirty ear. "The big palace on the other side of the river?"

"Yes," she said.

"I'm going to a party there, and if you come with me you can have a whole bag of candies." Her mouth opened, but before she could speak I shoved another acid drop into it. "You can't tell anyone, though," I whispered, "otherwise they'll come too, and there won't be enough candies to go around. All right?"

She nodded.

"Good girl. Come along."

It was *bolita* night and nobody paid us the slightest bit of attention, so intent were they on buying their chances. I could not wait to leave that sweating throng, the oily Latins pressing at me from all sides. Even on the streetcar they shoved against me as we jolted along the tracks, pushing me and touching me as if I were not there at all.

Rafael had not wanted the wig-maker in his room. Ever since his discovery in the Fowler family crypt his sleep had been troubled, and when Monsieur Goulet had appeared he could not shake the notion that his employer, silhouetted against the open door, had risen from a bad dream. Perhaps he should tell him what had happened, he thought. Perhaps, if he made himself speak the words, then the pictures in his head would fade. His voice trembled as he began, and he thought he might cry, but he forced himself to continue, to expel the thing from inside his memory. He imagined the ringing tones of the lector, which reached to every corner of the factory and made the men forget their cares, and he grew a little more confident. It was a story he was telling: something untrue, something calculated to have maximum impact. He was simply the medium. Perhaps, he thought as he described the scratches on the door of the crypt, he would even scare his listener a little—but as he finished his account he heard a sound. Out of the darkness, the wig-maker was laughing. It filled the close little room, and Rafael blinked for a moment before rising from his bed and throwing open the window.

"But that's priceless!" the wig-maker said.

Rafael had never seen him so animated, and he wondered what monster he had allowed into his life, into his home, and he did not know how to make him disappear.

Although it was barely seven o'clock in the morning when he arrived at the *bruja* Chiquita's house, her blinds were raised and her door stood open. A warm stick of bread, just delivered by the baker's boy, hung on a nail on the porch. Rafael took it inside.

"How did the lamp work?" asked the *bruja*. "Don't tell me, you want rid of her now. It happens all the time."

"I see her often," said Rafael. "Just as a friend, though."

The *bruja* nodded. "I can make a more powerful spell, but it will be more expensive—fifteen cents for the dove's heart alone."

"I've come about something else, actually," said Rafael. "I need to get rid of someone—to make someone go away."

"You mean, *away*?" said the *bruja*, drawing a finger across her throat.

"No! No, I just want this person to leave me and my friend alone."

"You want protection."

"Protection, yes."

"And your friend—you still want to influence her feelings toward you?"

"If it is possible," said Rafael, lowering his eyes. "I'd like to try, yes."

The *bruja* sighed and went to her shelves, gathering several items as if she were about to bake a cake. "A peeled guava stick, corojo butter, and colored ribbons for protection," she said. "Seven pins, sesame oil, almond oil, red ocher, honey, and olive oil for love. With the dove's heart . . . that comes to forty cents."

Rafael felt in his pockets. "I can't afford both," he said.

The *bruja* was watching him, her brown eyes clear and still. He could smell the fresh bread, the crust impressed with the palm frond used to hold it straight in the oven.

"I'll take protection," he said finally. Without safety, what use was love?

The *bruja* bent the guava stick into a shepherd's crook, then smeared it with corojo butter and wrapped the colored ribbons around it.

When Rafael arrived home he placed it behind his door, as she had instructed him. He hoped that Señora Estrada would not find it. Soon she would be home from the factory, and he did not want to have to explain why he was not yet there himself. Covering the guava stick with a straw hat, he smoothed down his hair and straightened his collar. Then he caught the streetcar to Franklin Street.

"This is an unexpected pleasure," said the wig-maker. "Am I to understand that you have been working again?" He was already approaching Rafael, his long fingers reaching for combings and cuttings, as bony as the roots of the black mangrove.

Rafael thought, He needs me; without me he cannot continue. The fingers came at him. Smother the roots of a black mangrove, and it dies.

"I don't like the work you do," said Rafael. "I don't like this business, and I don't want to be part of it any longer."

Monsieur Goulet stopped, then smiled. "But you *are* part of it, *mon ami*. You've raided the graves, clipped the hair. Now you're finding a conscience?"

"It's wrong," said Rafael. "It's monstrous. I don't know how I agreed to it in the first place."

The wig-maker laughed. "Such loftiness doesn't suit you, boy. Besides, it's a little difficult to flee to high ground when one is already waist-deep in mud, is it not?"

"I've done the work you asked me to do," said Rafael. "I've fulfilled the terms of our pact. Now I would like my final payment."

"*Pact* is such a solemn expression," said Monsieur Goulet. "I prefer to think we have a special understanding. We are quite alike, you and I."

"Alike?" said Rafael, aware he was beginning to shout. "No. I am no monster, Señor Goulet. I may have done some monstrous things, but I am no monster."

The wig-maker toyed with his cigar guillotine. "I am afraid it won't be possible to release you from your duties. You're a valuable employee, and I found the interview process so trying. I don't wish to endure that again."

Rafael closed his eyes for a second and pictured the *bruja*'s stick bound with ribbons. "Show me Señora Unger's transformation," he said, making his voice softer. "I'd love to see it—and then I won't trouble you again."

"It's not finished," said the wig-maker. "Nobody is to see it before it's complete."

Rafael looked around the studio, and the eyes of the mounted birds seemed to be looking too. In one corner, he noticed, stood a rocking horse, its mane thick but its tail still unrepaired and scrawny, loved too much.

"I'm fixing that," said the wig-maker, although Rafael had made no comment. There was a home-made doll beneath one of the rockers, its stick body crushed in two.

"Don't you think Señora Unger would be interested to know where the material for her hair-piece is coming from?" said Rafael.

"Possibly," said the wig-maker. "Why don't you tell her? You could describe its collection in precise detail. Why, you could even give her names—you have them all in your notes, I expect. Such a meticulous employee. Such a find. It would be madness to let you go."

So much for the *bruja*'s ribbon-wrapped crook, thought Rafael. Whichever way he twisted, he was caught. Would things have been different, he wondered, if instead of protection he had chosen love?

Why don't you tell her?" the wig-maker had said. Rafael knew he should not, and yet he could not rid himself of the thought, of the wig-maker's voice making its smooth suggestions. He sat on Marion Unger's couch and stared at the design in her Oriental rug, trying to follow a thread of blue right around the border until it met its own beginning. He kept getting lost. He wished they were still reading the libretto of *Carmen* together; it was easier when he had the lines in front of him, and did not have to think of something to say. The opera had been a great success in Tampa, and at the factory the lector had promised to read it during the summer months, when enough time had passed to make it seem new again.

"You're quiet today," said Marion.

Rafael looked up at her. Once he spoke the words something would change forever, and yet he felt his mouth opening—*being* opened—and he heard himself beginning to speak, reciting every ghoulish detail of the Fowler crypt, and he felt his arms rising of their own accord, as if he were playing the game he used to play as a boy, when he stood in a doorway and pressed the backs of his hands against the frame for a minute or two, and when he stepped away his arms rose in the air as if on threads and he could not hold them down. And perhaps, he thought in some part of himself as he spoke, it would be better now that it was said, and she might even understand. He felt himself gesticulating, flailing in the air as if to reproduce the desperation of the entombed Fowler girl, and he could not stop himself.

When he had finished, he looked up again at Marion. A frown was on her brow, but on her lips—and he did not believe he misread her—was a faint smile.

"I think you've been listening to too many stories at the factory," she said. "Which text is the lector reading at the moment? Something by Mr. Poe, perhaps?"

"I didn't make this up," said Rafael. "Why would I invent something so horrible?"

"To entertain me, of course," said Marion. "It's a good story. Maybe you should be the lector."

~○

May 1899

"Mr. Flood is here," said Miss Harrow. Marion was sitting by a bright window, a torn stocking pulled tight over her ebony darning egg so that the damage was plain to see. "He says he needs to talk to you."

Marion put aside her mending and smoothed her hair. She had met George Flood a few times before, when the Harmonious Companions' meetings had continued into the early evening. Adelina did not like to be interrupted, however, and told him so whenever he appeared at the parlor door, and more often Marion heard him enter the house and ascend the stairs without greeting his wife and her visitors, corporeal or otherwise. Miss Needham had mistaken his footsteps for a spirit once, until Adelina told her it was nothing. He was usually very quiet upstairs—working on his snail shells, Marion imagined. She thought them rather beautiful, and wished she could see some in the wild.

She heard Miss Harrow ushering him in, and quickly buried the torn stocking in her workbag.

He did not sit down after shaking her hand.

"Mrs. Unger," he began, his face small and pinched. "Mrs. Unger," he said again, and faltered. "I'm afraid I don't know how to begin."

"What's the matter, Mr. Flood?" said Marion, the smile fading from her cheeks. "Is Mrs. Flood ill, is that it?"

"She's not ill," he said.

"Then our meeting is still scheduled for tomorrow? I'd hate to miss it, just when we're making such progress."

Mr. Flood sighed. "I don't pretend to understand the workings of the female mind, Mrs. Unger. It's not for me to say why some women behave the way they do, why some are so weak-willed. They do things without thinking. They order new cushions because they like the color, and do not consider how well the fabric will wear. Or they follow the most ludicrous fashions, buying the latest enormous hat because it is what everybody else is wearing. Or they say things they do not mean, just to fill an awkward silence."

"Mr. Flood, I'm afraid you have lost me," said Marion.

George Flood gave a sad smile. "Yes," he said. "And that is my point. So often the sexes do not understand each other. May I?" He settled himself on the edge of a chair. "Your late husband, Mrs. Unger, was enormously fond of you. He often spoke of you with affection."

"You knew Mr. Unger?" said Marion.

"A little. He ordered some orange boxes from us, and came into the warehouse now and then for advice," said Mr. Flood. "Well, despite these differences, these misunderstandings between the sexes, most men love their wives. Cushion fabric, tapestries, hats—these things are of no consequence. Foolish behavior, by and large, does not matter."

Marion frowned, but was silent.

"And," he said, studying his hands, "sometimes it does matter. Say, for example, a man discovers that his wife, whom he loves in spite of her occasional flightiness, is spending time in the company of an associate of his. Say that this associate visits the man's house during the day, and that this carries on for some eighteen months before the man finds out about it. To make the situation even worse—" He paused, cleared his throat. "Let's say the associate is also married. You must excuse me for speaking so candidly, Mrs. Unger, but this is a little more serious than the wrong cushion fabric, I think you'll agree."

Marion nodded slowly. Although she still had no idea what Mr. Flood meant, she felt a leaping in her gullet, as if she could see that a disaster was approaching—a hurricane, a tidal wave—but was powerless to stop it.

"Well, the man forgives his wife, because he loves her, and the associate's wife is none the wiser, and everybody's lives return to normal. Except that, a year or so later, the associate dies."

Marion caught her breath. Mr. Flood did not look at her.

"And the man's wife is bereft, and the man knows this, but neither discusses it with the other. The wife develops an interest in the occult, in Spiritualism, and still the man says nothing, although privately he believes her new pastime to be nonsense. He allows her to fill her days with this new hobby. He allows her to try to make contact with her dead lover. Gradually, others who have lost someone close find their way to the man's house, and to his wife's meetings, and one day the wife of the associate comes. And although there has been no real contact from the spirit world before, just the occasional movement of the planchette, the man's wife begins to speak with the voice of the dead associate." He glanced at Marion. "And the man—" he said, and stopped. "Mrs. Unger, Adelina is no medium. She has been pretending."

"No," said Marion. "No. You're wrong, Mr. Flood. Mrs. Flood has spoken *with Jack's voice*. She has used certain expressions, a certain pet name, that only he and I knew." She could hear herself becoming shrill.

Mr. Flood sighed. "She knows how his voice sounded, Mrs. Unger. I have no doubt that she also knows certain intimate details about you. Perhaps she has convinced herself she really is channeling Mr. Unger—I have not discussed it with her."

The eyes of the magic-lantern woman appeared to Marion then, and she knew why they were familiar: they were the eyes of Adelina.

Marion stooped beneath the attic's stuffy ceiling. George Flood was everything Jack was not, she thought. She hated the thin little man, the quavering messenger who would not spell out his message. Jack was always to the point—or so she had believed. She thought of Jack's persistent questioning, his need for evidence, and realized that while he was adept at drawing information from others, he also knew how to hide his own nature. A bricklayer, one of the most accomplished in his profession, perhaps, hand-picked by Mr. Plant, perhaps, but still a bricklayer, he knew how to transform himself so as to fit into the most fashionable circles. An image of him collecting the orange-blossom honey came to her: he was breathing cigar smoke into the hives to put the bees to sleep, then taking the slabs of comb with his gloved hands, his face blurry behind the veil; she could not tell if he was pleased or disappointed by the yield. He was always hiding, it appeared.

She looked at the piles of boxes and wanted to be rid of everything that belonged to him, everything he had touched. She would burn the photograph albums; she would smash the magic-lantern women into icy splinters; she would drop his ledgers in the bay and watch the pages drift and swirl like white kelp before disintegrating. She would give away his clothes, donate his books to the library. But then she thought: The crockery? The glass doorknobs? The umbrella stand, the bookcases, their marriage bed? The fruit tree? Her own skin?

Over the next weeks Marion spent a lot of time in Rafael's company, and he seemed as eager as she to continue their five o'clock teas, their book discussions, their outings and excursions. Such a thing could never have happened in Detroit, but here, it seemed, where roses bloomed all winter long, where oranges and lemons grew on the same tree, and where Marion had once seen a gentleman in full evening toilet riding in an alligator-drawn carriage, anything was possible. She delighted in wearing her new dresses; all the color was returning to her life. Although she no longer attended the meetings of the Harmonious Companions, she wished Adelina no ill: perhaps, like Marion herself, Mrs. Flood had simply wanted to believe that Jack was still alive.

Even Miss Harrow had softened, beginning to treat Rafael as a motherless ward or an unrefined cousin who needed instruction in the ways of society. She became most generous with her advice, teaching him the correct etiquette at a ceremonious dinner and at an evening reception *en buffet*, the preferred wording for a young man's visiting card, and the proper form of address when meeting the President. She showed him how to perform the mazurka and the German, and how to shield his palm with a handkerchief when dancing in hot weather so as not to soil his partner's gown.

He, in turn, accompanied his two new friends to the restaurants in Ybor City, explaining the menu to them, coaxing them to try plantain soup, whole snapper with mango sauce, fresh sugar-cane juice, and chicken cooked with guava and lime. Marion suspected that Miss Harrow enjoyed Rafael's companionship as much as she herself did; she was always prompting him to tell stories of his homeland, with its acres of cane fields and lettuce-green tobacco, its red soil and its capricious saints. There was Eleggúa, who saved the mighty Olodumare from a plague of mice by swallowing every last one. There was Orunmila, who instructed a woman whose son was being stalked by Death to strew her floor with okra; when Death entered the house, her bony heels split the fruit and skidded on the sap, and she could not reach the boy. Miss Harrow's favorite tale, however, concerned the warrior god Changó, who was represented by Saint Barbara. He lost his horse during a fierce battle, and could not venture outside for fear of his murderous enemies. His wife, Oyá, to save her husband and king, disguised him in one of her gowns, then cut off her long hair and fastened it to his head in two thick braids. None of his enemies gave a second glance to the woman entering their camp, but once they realized her true identity it was too late: many of their number were slaughtered by the disguised assailant. Oyá, too, took up her axe and slew her husband's enemies, her short hair bristling and shooting out sparks. Whenever Miss Harrow requested this legend, Rafael was only too pleased to oblige, each time adding a little extra detail. There was no deception in his stories, however; they were designed to delight and to entertain, and it was in this respect, Marion realized, that they differed from Jack's discourses. They were not superimposed with a motive, a desire to better himself, to transform himself from one thing into another. Rafael's stories were, in their way, truer than any of Jack's careful facts.

Marion had packed her husband's boxes away and shut the attic up again. She would stay in the home she had made with him, she decided, whatever lies it might hold. Besides, she had grown accustomed to its small movements and breaths, its patterns of light and dark, and she liked the citrus tree shading her window, and each winter the mixture of sweet and bitter fruit, both of which, after all, had their uses.

PART V

The Transformation

There is nothing I despise more than a child who tells tales. In my observation, this quality is especially prevalent in girls, and can easily develop into the gossipy righteousness so common in the woman of today. A Phrenological examination of the skull of a tale-telling child invariably reveals large Approbativeness, which is a sure sign of an anxiety to win admiration, praise, and approval. Such creatures must be given not the slightest amount of attention, as it only encourages the odious behavior.

Take, for example, the child I discovered in the slums of Ybor City in February. After gobbling several pieces of my confectionery on the streetcar, the filthy little savage was all too eager to accompany me wherever I chose to take her. We went first to my studio, and I am sure you can imagine her greedy delight when she laid eyes on a rocking horse I had been repairing. She began stroking its wooden flanks and whining to be lifted onto its back, and I indulged her, although it pained me to see those dirty fingers kneading my handiwork, those grubby little fists tugging at the mane I had so recently completed. I walked around her, observing her from all angles. I was so excited that I almost dared not proceed—perhaps you are familiar with this uncomfortable state—and for some minutes I simply watched her, one finger held to my lips as if to stop myself from ruining it all with an artless word. As she rocked back and forth, her stick doll cast aside, I crept away and retrieved a switch of Marion Unger's hair from my workbench. When I returned the child was still rocking, and singing a one-note song to herself in her own tongue. I held the switch to her head. My eyes had not deceived me: the match was perfect.

"There there," I said in English, stroking her little skull with my free hand. She could have been the widow's own child. "You're a good girl, aren't you, *ma chérie?*"

"Yes," she said. Like most of her kind, she could understand English perfectly well when she wanted to.

I pulled her hair into a single rope so I could estimate the thickness and the length, but the silly creature would not keep still. She kept rocking, and the hair slipped from my fingers, and when I grabbed at it again she screeched as if something had hurt her.

"If you'd just keep still," I said, but she rocked even harder, and for a moment I thought she might upend the horse.

"I'm going to tell my mother on you," she screamed.

I smiled.

She took hold of the reins again, having just wiped her nose with her palm, which I tried to ignore. "I'm telling on you," she said.

"Oh dear," I said. "Tale-telling is a very ugly habit, *ma chérie*. We can't have that. No no."

Something had to be done.

As evening was falling I took her home with me to the deserted Hotel.

"We're taking a little ride," I said, and I ushered her into the elevator with its coffered ceiling. Of course she tried to rub her sticky fingers all over the controls, but I managed to restrain her without allowing her to touch me too comprehensively. On the fourth floor we took the curving passageway until we came to my luggage room, and I unlocked the half-sized door—the child-sized door—and she, behaving now, stood at the dark entrance peering inside so that it was as easy as pushing a cake into an oven. I was glad that the small space was not bursting with trunks and valises as it had been when the officers were resident. I locked the little door and slipped the key into an interior pocket like a secret. There was quite some noise from the chamber to begin with, but when I returned to the elevator it died away, and my nerves were calmed as I descended to my own floor. In my minaret room all was peaceful, and when the rain came, hard against the silvery roof, I fancied it was applauding my cleverness.

I waited, counting off the dates like a prisoner, the daylight growing longer, the air about me thicker. By June 21st, the longest day of all, my urchin had been living off my charity for four months. There were too many hot hours in which to wait, and often I retreated to the empty swimming pool and thought, How slowly human hair grows! Never before had I been obliged to exercise my patience to such a degree. A small part of me, it must be admitted, enjoyed the feeling that I was creating something from nothing, that I was cultivating such precious material simply by allowing time to pass, but my disappointment was keen when I measured my crop and found only an extra half inch to show for my troubles. Perhaps the darkness of the cupboard was to blame, for I was feeding her well enough: milk and cheese to make the strands strong, and glossy fruit to make them shine. I should not be too impatient to cut, I knew; I should wait until I had sufficient hair. Another two weeks, I told myself. Fourteen days and fourteen nights.

Then, on June 23rd, Mr. Plant died at his New York apartment. He could not have chosen a worse time. Very soon, relatives and functionaries would arrive at the Hotel to collect belongings and sort through papers. Tampa being blessed with few celebrities, the reporters and photographers would come too, sniffing out stories about the *Visionary Railroad Magnate* and his *Palace in the Wilderness*.

The child was as limp as a doll when I coaxed her from the cupboard. I had thought she would come running out, and had braced myself for the contact, but she sat there in the dark and blinked at the open door, and I recalled that zoo animals act in a similar fashion if their cages are left ajar. The stench made me shudder—I would have to empty her bucket again, I supposed—but I had put up with worse when searching for combings and when making my sketches in the Everglades. I carried her to the elevator.

I should have known it was a trick, of course, for as soon as I deposited her on the floor of my minaret room she came alive and leapt for the door. She did not get far, but there were a few moments when we were struggling on the rug, all rolled up in fringing and woven flowers, and I recalled a similar struggle with my master in Paris. I hated her for reviving that memory.

The hair was just long enough to harvest. I had to pull it very tightly so as to maximize my yield, and of course she objected as loudly as she could, her high-pitched whining a mixture of peasant Italian and bad English. I felt much more at ease after I had shorn her and put her back in the luggage room, and I set about straightening my apartment, which she had left in quite a state. She was of no use to me now, and I considered various ways of ridding myself of her, but something else was fretting at the back of my head. When I had restored order to my room I went to my studio and washed the new hank of hair, then laid it in the postiche oven. I felt I was cooking a special dish, and I almost smacked my lips. I could hardly wait for the hair to dry; I kept checking it, an anxious baker who fears his bread will fall if he opens the door, but who cannot help himself.

In the end I had to leave it overnight, and I could hardly sleep for excitement. When I arrived at Franklin Street the following morning I left the Closed sign on my door and went straight to my postiche oven, and there, curled like a question-mark, was the new hair, so sleek and warm that it almost felt alive. I took a slab of pig fat and greased my hands, then began to weave the final strands into the widow's transformation. It was then, strangely, that a word came into my thoughts: the word my Cuban had used to describe me, the word that had been fretting at the back of my head since the previous night. *Monster.*

According to the principles of Phrenology, the destructive capacity of man is indicated by the angle of his ear in relation to his eyebrow. The correct angle—that is, the normal one—is twenty-five degrees; as this decreases, so too do energy and will power (I have estimated the angle of the feeble and rather useless Mr. Flood, for example, to be a mere eighteen degrees). A greater angle denotes increased Destructiveness, with a tendency to acts of violence. The angles of murderers range from thirty-five to forty-five degrees.

The science of Cerebral Physiology has its critics, including those who denounce it as nothing more than an elaborate deception. In the light of recent events, I resolved to put it to the test, and that morning, with the help of two mirrors, I calculated my own angle to be twenty-five degrees: that is, the angle of a normal and proper human being. In addition, my Moral region is large and the organ of Benevolence pronounced. My observations demonstrate the reliability of this undervalued science, but they should also dispel any doubts you may have concerning my actions toward the child, whom naturally I would have to discard.

For the first time in my professional life my hands were shaking, but as soon as I fitted the hair-piece to my model woman I knew it was perfect. My nine months of work, my ordeal with the guttersnipe, my trials with the reluctant Cuban—all these, I saw, had been worthwhile. The transformation gleamed like polished ivory, as fine as any of Mrs. Plant's sculptures. I observed it from all angles, enhancing it now with a diamond star, now with a jeweled aigrette. Were my master alive, I thought, he would be tripping over himself to take credit for such a piece. It seemed so precious a thing to me that I did not wish to leave it unguarded, although the Hotel was still empty. However, I forced myself to go to the Ebony Writing and

Reading Room, where I would not be too distracted, and I composed a note to Marion Unger, begging her forgiveness for the lengthy delays with her transformation, and inviting her to come to Franklin Street the following day.

⟋⟍

In the afternoon the lector had begun reading *Carmen*, and it was not long before he reached the final act. Although Rafael had relished the ending before, now he grew more and more uneasy as it approached. Around him he could sense the other *torcedores* listening, their tobacco leaves whispering, their *chavetas* tapping like the feet of a restless crowd. Rafael remembered reading the words with Señora Unger, her laughing and pretending to die, the fine chain about her neck moving with her gasps. He did not want this ending to come. He rolled faster and faster as he listened, his fingers flying, racing to slow time.

"'On the lances the sun gleams,'" read the lector, and Rafael felt himself in the middle of the bull-ring with the crowds around him, and he rolled and smoothed the *capa* of the cigar as if it were a real cape. "'Look at the picadors! Ah, how handsome they are! With the tips of their lances, they will pierce the flanks of the bulls!'"

Rafael heard the rustling of the crowd as they shifted in their seats, and for some reason he thought of the rocking horse in the wig-maker's studio, still only half-repaired.

"'Here is L'Espada,'" said the lector, "'the fine blade, he who comes to end it all, who appears at the end of the drama and who strikes the final blow!'"

Rafael felt perspiration inching down his back, creeping between his bony shoulder-blades, the bumps of his spine. The cuts in his apple-wood board criss-crossed like a net, like a puzzling map.

⟋⟍

Marion stared. The transformation was enormous, far bigger than her own head, a mass of twists and loops, thick ropes of hair, curls and braids and smooth scrolls, all spangled with diamond pins. She had ordered a much smaller piece, barely more than a curled fringe, but the structure she now saw—for there was an aspect of the architectural about it—was a full wig. It would have stood a foot above her brow, and she could not imagine how she could pass through a door or ride in a carriage without disturbing it. There was a smooth area at each side, sweeping upward from the temples, as glossy and as gently curved as a pair of wings. Above these the curls began, small and tight at the brow, growing larger and more elaborate as they ascended, then diminishing again to loose spirals at the very top. Diamond pins glistened at their core, droplets of dew caught in strange flowers, and there were little curls at the nape too, as fine as a baby's. Dividing the back of the head in two was an ample braid composed of at least six strands; Marion kept losing her place when she tried to count them. It parted into four thinner ropes that wound their way up through the curls, now distinct, now invisible. Each layer of the hair-piece provided the foundation for the next, and if she were to unravel just one coil, Marion thought, or loosen just one braid, the whole edifice would come tumbling down. She could not conceive how a person could bear the weight of it, and she imagined her neck bowing like the branch of a tree burdened with fruit. It was beautiful, certainly; it gleamed in the sunlight as if it were made of some rare wood, carved and polished, oiled with a soft cloth. It reminded her of a piece of furniture, an ornate baluster in a ball-room, perhaps, that is touched by each dancer as she descends the grand staircase—something pretty and admired but unnecessarily decorative.

"This cannot be mine," she said.

"I've employed a little artistic license, it's true," said the wig-maker, a modest smile on his lips.

"But there must be some misunderstanding," said Marion. "This is not what I ordered." She looked about the workroom, scanning the tables and the wig-blocks for any sign of her own hair, her simple transformation for special occasions. There were scissors and combs, and an instrument resembling a small loom, a rope of hair growing from its strings. There were hackles pressed together for safety, and a shelf of boxes bearing the black-ink names of birds: Heron, Ibis, Snowy Egret, American Egret, Roseate Spoonbill, Tern.

"I thought it might suit you better," said the wig-maker. "Madame has no idea to what pains I have gone to find enough suitable hair—"

"But this is nothing like what I wanted!" said Marion.

The wig-maker was quiet for a moment. Then, lifting the hairpiece from its block and advancing toward Marion, he said, "If Madame will just allow me to fit it and dress it, she will see—"

"No!" said Marion, stepping away from him. The hair-piece was grotesque to her now as she imagined it on her head, protruding from her skull like a tumor.

The wig-maker stopped, and for a second or two he did not move but simply stood there with his arms outstretched. Then he smiled. "Perhaps it's a little too elaborate for Madame after all," he said, placing it back on its stand. "I was teasing you, I confess. Of course it is not your transformation. The customer for whom it was designed has canceled her order, but she had, by coincidence, your exact coloring. She could have been your sister."

"Alas, I have no sisters," said Marion. She forced a smile, a little ashamed at her rudeness.

"If you like the piece, it's yours. I have no other use for it."

"Oh, but I couldn't accept such an expensive gift, Monsieur Goulet. You've already given me the beautiful necklace—"

"As I said, I have no use for it."

He began packing it into a box and it gleamed in its nest of tissue, a strange bird settling for the night.

"Perhaps you could salvage some of the hair from it," said Marion. "It's very generous of you, but to be honest I would never wear such a piece. My little transformation will be just fine."

"Your transformation," said the wig-maker, without pausing in his packing. "Yes, how silly of me. I took it home with me last night, to add the finishing touches so it would be ready for Madame to collect today—the electric lighting is excellent at the Hotel—and I have left it behind." He continued to pack the rejected hair-piece, covering it with tissue that he smoothed like clay, securing the lid with cord. "But it's just across the bridge," he said, knotting the cord once, twice, then looping it to form a dainty handle. "Would it inconvenience you to cross the river? We could take a carriage and be there in two minutes. Perhaps I can show you some of the sumptuous new artworks collected by Mrs. Henry Plant that we did not see last time?"

Suddenly Marion heard the sound of the knife-sharpener's whistle: a quick arpeggio, like one breath expelled on a harmonica, the prelude to something not yet recognizable.

The wig-maker paused and said, "Will you excuse me for just a moment, Madame?"

Marion watched as he gathered together his tools—knives, scissors, razor blades, scalpels—his hands working quickly, two pale magpies hoarding sharp things. He slipped from the room, and Marion heard the bell chime when he exited to the street.

While he was gone she tested the weight of the knotted box: it felt as heavy as a real head. The waxwings and cardinals mounted on the walls watched her with their glass eyes, and she took her parasol and her gloves and walked outside, where the knife-sharpener's wheel whirled and the blades made little screams against the emery. Sparks shot from the spinning stone, and as Monsieur Goulet watched, motionless, it seemed to Marion that they were reflected in his eyes, whose color she could not determine.

"Señora Unger, the friend of Rafael," said the *afilador* when he saw her, smiling and raising his black cap.

"Good day," said Marion, returning his smile.

Monsieur Goulet handed him a few coins, then gripped Marion's arm and led her to a carriage, and as the knife-sharpener walked away, rolling his wheel along Franklin Street toward Ybor City, Marion could hear his whistle growing fainter and fainter.

Soon they were crossing the sinuous river, climbing the steps to the Hotel's gingerbread veranda, passing through the keyhole door.

"Mrs. Plant has acquired a spectacular new cabinet," said the wigmaker. "It once belonged to the Doge of Venice. You must see it." Already he was leading her to the elevator, the tips of his gloved fingers touching her elbow, suggesting her direction. "Your house is visible from the fourth floor," he said as the door closed and they began to ascend.

Something is wrong, Marion thought. She was nervous of the rising feeling, as if her soul were being left behind.

⌒

Rafael called at Marion's house that evening, but Miss Harrow told him she was not at home.

"She hasn't been in all afternoon," she said. "I think she must be at the Floods'—an extended meeting, perhaps. Would you like to come in and have some lemonade?"

"Thank you," said Rafael, "but I need to be somewhere else."

On Hyde Park Avenue, Adelina Flood looked drawn when she answered the door.

"*Buenas noches, Señora,*" Rafael began, but she cut him off in English. "What is it?"

Behind her he saw Mr. Flood walking down the passageway, a tray of snails balanced on his palms. Next to the specimens was a row of steel tools: fine probes and picks, tiny pincers. "I wondered, is Señora Unger here?"

Mr. Flood glanced up, then continued toward the staircase with his fragile shells, his steps careful, calculated to cause the least disturbance.

"No," said Adelina. "I've no idea where she is." And she shut the door.

Rafael took the streetcar back to Ybor City. Dusk was falling, and in the windows of the restaurants he could see families eating together, talking, smiling. Gentlemen strolled up and down Seventh

Avenue taking their evening promenade, every one of them, it seemed, with a lady on his arm. The trimmings on the women's hats quivered in the breeze, feathers swaying, ribbons flickering, filmy veils lifting and coming to rest again. The *bolita* dealers called to the passers-by, urging them to test their luck, to take a chance.

At the casita, Señora Estrada was making up a bed on the floor of Rafael's room.

"Señor Rivera is sleeping here tonight," she said.

Rafael glanced behind the door and saw that his hat had been hung up and that the guava stick from the *bruja* was gone. Señora Estrada did not mention it. She had probably tidied it away, thinking it one of the children's playthings. When she had left the room, he looked under his bed and on the washstand, in the closet and on the little altar to Oyá, guardian of the gates of death. The stick was nowhere to be found. Rafael unfastened his collar and washed his face and neck.

At dinner the *afilador* was talkative, telling the children stories of the wolves in the Galician mountains, and strange lights seen there at night, and unexplained sounds.

"You never know what might be hiding in the mist," he said.

Miguel was starting to seem frightened, and looked to his mother for confirmation that here in the casita he had nothing to fear, that here he was safe.

Antonio stopped and wiped his plate with a piece of bread. "I met your friend today," he said to Rafael. "Señora Unger."

"Can we play dominoes?" Miguel asked, already pushing his chair from the table.

"Where did you see her?" said Rafael.

"I was sharpening the knives of the French wig-maker and she was there, at his studio, but they were on their way to the Tampa Bay Hotel."

Rafael saw Señora Estrada raise her eyebrows at her husband. "When was this?" he asked.

"Like I said, today." His plate was clean now, and he drank the last of his wine and sat back in his chair.

"But at what time?" said Rafael, his own food forgotten.

The *afilador* yawned a few notes, a sleepy imitation of his whistle. "Three o'clock, perhaps?"

Rafael excused himself from the table and went to put on his hat. Through the beaded curtain he could see the *afilador* carving Serafina a tiny basket from a cherry-pit, the Estradas all watching as he pared away slivers of the stone. The strands of the curtain hung like rosaries. At the front door, before he stepped out into the dark, he touched the cool head of Eleggúa.

The wind began to pick up as he made his way along Seventh Avenue, and by the time he reached Nebraska Avenue, where Ybor City gave way to the American part of town, he was pushing himself through the gusts, bent forward as if poised on the edge of a cliff. The palm trees shook their sharp leaves, and he narrowed his eyes to avoid the sudden blasts of sand from the streets. As he reached the low white walls of the cemetery on Harrison Street he thought how different it looked, and for a moment he did not know why. And then, as he hurried past the rows of graves, he realized he had never seen the care that was taken to maintain them. He had never seen how clean the marble was, how it was scrubbed free of moss and dirt until it shone; he had never noticed how neatly the grass was clipped, or that people brought fresh flowers even to the older plots. And he felt ashamed of the things he had done for the wig-maker. The Spanish moss draping the palm trees tangled and knotted in the wind, long gray snarls of it, and he quickened his stride.

As he approached the main gates of the cemetery he thought he heard something, and he paused, straining his ears. At first he thought it was the whistle of the knife-sharpener, but of course Antonio and his wheel were with the Estradas. The streets had emptied; doors were closed, and windows and shutters fastened against the wind. There it was again, the sound, once more tossed to him in abrupt snatches: the ringing of a bell. The wind was behind him now, pushing him on to the source of the ringing, and when he passed the gates and glanced inside he realized what it was. The bell on Captain

Frederick Bourne's plot was shaking, its tongue loosened by the gale, the cord scraping back and forth through the metal eye. Rafael saw the shells strewn on the sandy grave, like the floor of the sea exposed, and he imagined the bell-cord threading through the earth, piercing the lid of the casket and tugging at the captain's finger-bone. He hurried on, and when he passed Marion Street he began to run, and the bell rang and rang in his ears for a good distance.

Some hours must have passed, for when I opened my eyes again the sun had left my minaret room and the wind was restless. I had been leaning my head on my hands, and they felt dead to me, as if they were not mine. As the blood flowed back into my fingertips, however, the events of the previous hours returned, and I remembered that I now had not one but two problems locked in my luggage room. The wind beat at my windows, and I thought, It is late June, and perhaps a hurricane is coming. The possibility cheered me, for I knew from my time in the Everglades that hurricanes leave behind all kinds of chaos, and it would be a simple matter to dispose of one or two things under such circumstances. I could place both my problems in the street with the other debris, beneath a felled tree perhaps, or a broken wall, their arms and legs arranged at unnatural angles. I could strew leaves on their faces, slide twigs into their hair.

When I thought of the way Marion Unger had looked at my transformation—her transformation—I shook with some kind of emotion I could not name. Sometimes, of course, when a customer calls to collect a finished postiche, inspects it, and pronounces it ideal, there is still a second of hesitation. Over the years I have come to recognize this as an unwillingness to part with the imaginary postiche, the dreamed coiffure which may have been visualized for many months or even years. I liken this moment to the point at which a mother sees her newborn's face for the first time. Perfect it may be, but it exists now in its own right, and no longer inside her, a pliant secret whose features can be molded to fit any dimensions. A little bit of ceremony attached to the occasion is called for, I find, so if I sense this hesitation, I inquire whether Sir or Madame wants the ends of the postiche singed. The process is quite safe, I explain, and is reputed to eliminate splitting (untrue). On hair still growing it is even more miraculous, preventing the catching of a cold (also untrue). It costs an extra fifty cents (true), and I am happy for my customers to observe the procedure if it interests them (polite but untrue). The customer, trusting little lamb, then follows me to my workroom, and I make a great show of arranging the postiche on a block and putting aside my vulcanite combs. "They are flammable," I explain. "For the singeing, I must use combs carved from the shank bones of horses and other large beasts." After I have lit the taper I draw the teeth through sections of hair, bringing the flame to the ends again and again with all the daring of a fire-eater. And the smell of it fills the air like an occult incense, and the customer becomes quite sedate, and often pays me a dollar or two more. However, such tricks would not have worked with Marion Unger. I saw that now.

She was heavier than I expected; a dead weight in my arms. Every few steps I had to stop and rest before carrying her a little farther, and by the time I reached my bed I fairly dropped her onto the comforter. It billowed about her for a moment, a feathery, airy mass, then settled back down. I suppose a little more grace might have been in order—but who, after all, was there to see? With some difficulty I turned her over so that she lay on her back, then I walked around and around the bed. *What shall we do with you?* I asked. *What shall become of you?* And as I heard myself uttering those questions, I knew that they were meant for me also.

I regarded the pale figure who had so occupied my thoughts, consumed so many hours of my life. She was nothing to me now: a lifeless form, a doll. I touched her hand. I ran my fingers over her abdomen, thinking of the sketches executed by the good Dr. Evangeline; I felt the swell of her bosom, the line of her cold throat. Every part of her was cold.

It had not been my intention to disfigure her, but as my hand trailed down her arm in an act of farewell—for believe me, I was going to disappear like a final breath—I could not help tweaking her little finger. I did not expect it to snap, but once I heard the noise, once I felt the cracking the way one feels a wish-bone giving way, I felt such a rush of gratification that I could not stop. By the time I had finished with her, she was no longer recognizable.

I stood back and regarded the mess. I felt no remorse, for although my own hand had created the damage, the blame lay with Marion Unger alone. I could not believe I had been so bewitched by a creature of such obvious ill-breeding. She had sent but a short note to thank me for the tour of the Hotel, and not once had I seen her wearing the amethyst necklace I gave her. Quite how she behaved when alone with the Cuban, let alone with her female companion, I shuddered to imagine.

My thoughts were disturbed by a noise outside my window: footsteps on the crushed-shell paths, then on the main veranda. I stayed quite still and listened. Mr. Plant was to be buried in New York the following day; perhaps his family had sent some of his employees to deal with his affairs, and they were staying in the Hotel. I took a spare blanket from the armoire and covered the disarray, swaddling the broken figure, then crept to the door. I could make out nobody in the darkness of the hall, but if indeed some emissary were inside the building, I was confident he would be in the manager's office or the reception area, and would have no reason to come to my quarters. Still, I felt I should check on the luggage cupboard and ensure that no prying functionaries were exploring that part of the Hotel. I proceeded to the elevator.

Rafael pushed the main door of the Tampa Bay Hotel and it opened soundlessly. Inside the air was cool and still, like somewhere closed for a long time, and he thought of the Fowler crypt and shivered. He had not been in the Hotel before, and did not know where the wig-maker's room might be, but since there were no lights burning on the first floor he ascended the grand staircase, where the bronze African Girls watched him from the balusters. Upstairs was in darkness too, save one band of light beneath a door. He knocked, and when there was no answer he entered the round room. It appeared empty, but had the feeling of a space recently vacated: there was a newspaper open on a table, and a cigar burning in an ashtray, the threads of smoke making fragile question-marks in the air. A hat and coat, which Rafael recognized as the wig-maker's, hung on a stand beside the door. The bed was in a state of disarray—one pillow was crushed against the headboard and the other had fallen to the floor—and the mounded covers suggested that a human form lay beneath them. He wished he had thought to bring Señor Estrada's rifle with him—his mother-of-pearl defense against the creatures that came out at night.

"Señor Goulet?" he said as he approached the bed, his voice low and steady, although his heart shook like the wind. And then he saw it. A hand, a female hand, protruding from a blanket. He touched the white fingers, and they were cold. He thought, He has done it. Gently he pulled back the covers to reveal an unclothed female figure, her arms and legs crooked and broken, her head twisted askew. A pair of scissors lay open on the sheets, the blades poised at her side like the bill of a silver bird. Several of her fingers were snapped, and a tangle of wire like metal veins protruded from a break above the knee. Rafael touched the gouged torso. A fine white dust came away on his hands: plaster dust.

Marion's feet were bound with rope, her hands fastened as if in prayer. She blinked and blinked again, but her eyes could make out nothing in the dark. The cupboard was musty and very warm, and against her arms she could feel the stitched handles of an expensive trunk and the smooth leather flank of a valise. She pressed her fingertips to the ceiling, but could not stand up.

"Help!" she called, banging against the door again and again. "Is anybody there? Please help!"

Behind her, as if within the walls of the Hotel, there was a small movement, and instinctively her eyes shifted toward the sound. Mice, perhaps, or rats? She thought of the old telegraph cables buried in the concrete, holding the building together—the lines that had carried messages under the sea. There was a smell coming from the back of the cupboard, too, something that lay beneath the dusty, stale scent of spaces long shut. Inching forward on her knees, her bound hands outstretched, she advanced. The action reminded her of something she had done as a child, at a picnic. There had been a cave. She had wanted to touch the very back of it but could not see where it ended, and had moved forward one step at a time, completely blind, her index finger a snail's horn trembling at the brush of every web, expecting at any moment to feel cool stone against her palm. She had cast little shells into the darkness, listening for the click as they hit the dead-end wall, and it was as if the shells were leading her on, making a path for her to follow, and she kept throwing them before her and listening, taking another few steps, then throwing and listening and stepping again. But then, when the passage had narrowed so that she could not turn around, and the sounds of the picnic vanished and she no longer sensed daylight behind her, she had grown frightened and wondered whether the cave might not go on tunneling beneath the hillside forever, and she had dropped the last of her shells and, walking backward to undo her foolish actions, withdrew.

Marion paused for a moment. Again she thought she heard faint movements coming from the back of the little space, but the noise was unlike the scrabbling of rats' claws. Rather, it was the movement of cloth, the soft sound of cotton against skin, swishing like a distant ocean. And then, rising in the airless black, a moan.

"Who's there?" said Marion, the words disappearing into nothing, little shells cast into the dark.

There was another low moan, and a shifting of garments. Marion's knee tapped something soft; she lowered her hands and felt the bare arm of a child. It flinched at her touch.

"Are you all right?" said Marion. "Are you hurt?" Her head was bowed by the height of the ceiling, and the smell was stronger here—a damp reek of urine.

"Where is the man?" said the child, with a strong Italian accent. "Is he coming back?"

"He's not here," said Marion. "We're alone."

"Did he put you here too?"

"Yes," said Marion. "But we'll get out, I promise." She sank to the floor, and suddenly the bony little creature was in her lap, and she felt a bristly head against her chin and curious fingers exploring her hair.

"He didn't take yours?" said the child.

"No," said Marion, and she lifted her hands to encircle the little body.

Sometime later—perhaps one hour, perhaps four—Marion awoke. She was still holding the child to her breastbone, and she could feel the silver locket pressed hard against her skin, as if it might merge with her flesh. She pushed herself over to the door and kicked against the wood. "Help!" she called again. "Hello! Please, help!"

No one came.

The child had woken now and was crying softly, its head jolting against Marion every time she kicked.

"Shh, it's all right, we'll be all right. Let's try to sleep a little more, shall we?"

All was well on the fourth floor—the door remained locked, and indeed no sound came from the cupboard. Perhaps I had imagined the noise; it had been a trying day, and the mind can invent all kinds of illusions when it is taxed. There was no cause for concern: I was alone. I would finish my cigar, I decided, and pack my things, and then I would clear away the remains of the model woman and go to sleep.

As I returned to my apartments, however, I heard movements, and when I entered I found the Cuban boy there, looming like an intruder over my bed.

"Where is Marion?" he said.

"Madame Unger? I have no idea where she is. Do you have some combings for me?"

"I don't work for you anymore. What have you done with Marion?"

"Marion," I said. "A pretty Christian name. I didn't realize you were on such intimate terms."

The Cuban's eyes glittered. "My family—the Estradas—know where I am, and I have told them to alert the authorities if they have to. Where is she?"

I stifled a laugh. "Very well," I said, and stepped into the hall, where the Japanese urns made shapes like crouching guards. Past the paintings and the cabinets we walked, our reflections a shifting silhouette over the mirrors. When we reached the elevator, I stopped, opened the doors, and stood aside.

"You first," said the Cuban.

He did not move his gaze from me once, and when we reached the fourth floor, where all the heat of the day had collected, I led him down the curving corridor, the end of which could not be seen.

⌒

Marion had no idea how long she slept, but a thud awoke her, then a slamming door and a voice so loud it seemed someone was shouting right into her ear. For a moment she did not know where she was; she had the strange sensation of opening her eyes but seeing nothing. She felt the child against her, and the wooden floor beneath, and then she realized that the voice belonged to Rafael.

"Open the door!" he was yelling. "Wait! Let me out!"

"Who is that?" whispered the child.

Marion reached forward and her fingers met with skin—the nape of Rafael's neck. He recoiled from her as if she had held a burning taper to his flesh.

"Don't be afraid," she said.

"Marion?" He sighed. "I came to rescue you. He said he would take me to you."

"He did that," said Marion.

"A great hero I make."

"Who is that?" said the child again.

"Who's that?" echoed Rafael, as if they were in a cavernous space.

Marion introduced them to each other, and Rafael said a few words in Spanish.

"Anna is Italian," said Marion, but the child was already answering him in his own tongue. The two of them were giggling, and just for a moment, although she knew it was foolish, Marion felt more alone than ever before.

"She lives in Ybor City," said Rafael. "Her father owns a vegetable stand—I know him a little. They've been searching for her for the last four months."

"Does anybody know where *you* are?" said Marion.

"No. I came alone." Rafael paused. "I didn't want to say—I didn't want to tell them."

Marion smiled to herself in the dark.

"Are you all right?" he said. "Has he hurt you?"

"Can you undo knots?" said Marion.

She guided Rafael to her wrists and he began to work at the cord, picking and worrying at it. She could feel his breath on her hands, and the smoothness of his palms against her skin, as smooth as the wrapper leaf of the best cigarillos. At one point he tried to bite through the rope, and she felt his lips and teeth. He did not apologize and she was not embarrassed by the intimacy of the gesture—in this secret place, she felt, the laws of polite society held no sway.

When the cord finally fell away, Rafael rubbed Marion's wrists as if to bring them back to life.

"He tied my ankles too," she said. "Perhaps I can reach—"

"It will be easier if I do it," Rafael said, and once again she felt his warm hands, this time moving beneath the hem of her skirts. She fingered the undone cord that lay in her lap, and realized for the first time that her bonds were not rope at all, but lengths of finely braided hair.

~⌐

While they made themselves as comfortable as possible, Marion recalled how she and Jack had settled into their house among the wild orange groves. She remembered the way he had walked her from room to room, showing her the staircase and the stove and the rugs, telling her, *This is yours,* and *This is yours,* and *These are yours.* And she remembered the little bedroom at the top of the stairs that she had left empty, reserving it in her mind for a child.

Rafael took off his jacket and folded it into a soft bundle, then placed it beneath Anna's head. She said something to him in Spanish, and he laughed.

"Her front tooth is coming loose," he told Marion. "She's very excited; it's her first one. I have a story for you," he said to the child, and he began to speak in Spanish again. Marion heard the girl's breaths relax and deepen little by little, and by the time Rafael had finished, Anna was asleep.

"What was your story about?" said Marion.

"About teeth," said Rafael. "When you lose a tooth, you leave it under your pillow, and at night, when everyone is sleeping, Señor Rat creeps into your house and comes to your bed. And very, very quietly, so he doesn't wake you, he slips his sharp little paws beneath your pillow and takes the tooth, and in its place he leaves a penny. Then he creeps away again, walking only on the rugs so you do not hear his claws tapping against the floor, and he adds his new prize to the shining white house he is building for himself: his grand house of teeth."

"A house of teeth?" said Marion. "The walls and the roof are made of teeth?"

"Entirely," said Rafael. "They are stacked together like bricks. There is a chimney of teeth, and stairs of teeth, and a porch of teeth. The tables and chairs are made from the big flat teeth at the back of the mouth—"

"The molars," said Marion.

"The molars," said Rafael, "and the picket fence and the gate are made from these." He felt for Marion's mouth and touched an eye tooth.

"The canines," said Marion.

"Yes, the canines."

"And the floors?"

"They are made from all different kinds of teeth, set into patterns."

"And the lamps?"

"Hollowed teeth."

On they talked, making up stories to evade the truth, until a crack of light had appeared beneath the door and another patch at the keyhole. Rafael held his pocket watch to it.

"Six o'clock," he said. "Maybe someone will come soon."

"Yes," said Marion. "One of the staff, perhaps. I'm sure they have a skeleton staff here over the summer." She tried to make her voice sound confident.

"We must be ready to knock on the door and shout as soon as we hear anything," said Rafael.

Marion could just make out his silhouette now, and the familiar lines comforted her. She stroked his hair for a moment, and neither of them said anything. In the faint light from the door she could see her moving hand, and as she watched it seemed to glow, as if it were not real at all but a projection from some concealed lens. Anna had nuzzled up to Rafael in her sleep, one arm thrown across his lap. An odd little family in an odd little house, thought Marion.

They waited the whole day, listening for any sound in the corridor, holding their breath at every creak, but nobody came. Unless they made a point of talking to Anna, asking her questions and repeating her name, the child said nothing—she had become accustomed to solitude, Marion supposed. To pass the time, she and Rafael talked about what they might tell the wig-maker when he returned; neither uttered the thought that he might never come.

"It's you he wants," said Rafael. "He will return for you."

"Well, when he does," said Marion, "I will tell him that I hold him in the highest regard, and then I will begin to sob and say that I do not understand his actions, since over the last months I have come to feel a great affection for him."

"Or," said Rafael, "we will tell him that before I came I *did* report him to the authorities—"

"Or that Miss Harrow must have—"

"Yes, or Miss Harrow—and we will say that unless he sets us free we will expose his hair-stealing."

Marion frowned. "We threaten to reveal that he collects hair that has been discarded anyway?"

"He has . . . other sources too," said Rafael.

He fell silent, and Marion recalled the story he had invented, about his nighttime desecration of a family crypt. She slid her hand across the floor until she found one of Monsieur Goulet's hair ropes; beneath her palm it was cool and smooth, a dead thing.

"These other sources," she said quietly, "if we reveal those, won't he say that you were as involved as he? More involved, even?"

Rafael did not reply—and then Marion heard him begin to sob.

"Listen to me," said Marion. "If questioned about your whereabouts at night, we simply say you were with me."

Rafael sniffed. "With you?"

"You were a guest at my house on certain nights."

"You can't say that."

"Yes, I can." She touched his cheek, wiping away the tears with the hem of her dress, and when she had finished he did not move away but took her hand and kissed it, and then kissed her mouth.

This was just another story, Marion knew. Outside the cupboard, it would fade like a thin plume of smoke, and her life would begin again. She pictured herself dressed in a bright silk costume and boarding a steamer. Her hair would be arranged in the latest style—she imagined Marcel waves rippling across her crown, and a sleek knot at the nape of her neck. Every strand would be her own; she would have no need for artifice. In her cabin she would find all she needed for her journey, and it would not take long to settle into her new surroundings. Perhaps a companion would be at her side; perhaps she would be alone. She would keep a daily journal: a record of the marvels she would see at each exotic port. In it she would describe the sight of the Pyramids as evening fell; the splendid mirrors carved in Venice, that place of many reflections; the song of the parakeet and the nightingale; the colors of the windows in the Sainte-Chappelle in Paris, which were said to resemble a great flurry of butterflies. She would see all the things Jack had described and more.

Another day and night passed and then, on the morning of June 27th, Rafael heard footsteps in the corridor. He and Marion began to shout and knock against the door; and with a little encouragement even Anna, who had not spoken for hours, joined in. The footsteps stopped, then returned. There was a jangling of keys and a rush of fresh air and sun; it hurt Rafael's eyes as it bounced off the silvery roof and in through the window.

The porter picked up the child and carried her, and Rafael followed with Marion. His legs shook and bent a little, as if they were brand-new, as if he were just learning to walk. The porter opened the elevator door but Anna began to cry when she saw the small space, and so they walked down the grand staircase instead.

"Strange sort of trunk, this one," the porter was murmuring to Anna. "Never seen a piece of luggage this shape."

The Hotel was hung with black to mark Mr. Plant's death, the lengths of cloth flapping in the breeze like crows; indeed, the whole town seemed veiled. On Franklin Street, Monsieur Goulet's studio was deserted, the door shrouded in black crepe. Everything was quiet as Rafael, Marion, and Anna made their way north toward Fortune Street and Ybor City, the flagstones giving way to deep sand. It had been rearranged by the wind, licked into drifts, and under the bright daylight it might have been snow, Rafael thought. Had it snowed while they had been in the Hotel? He had kissed Marion and she had not stopped him. Anything was possible.

Still blinking in the sun, he remembered how it had felt when his lips had brushed hers: like sunlight running into his mouth and streaming down his throat, and for that moment everything was true and real and good.

He touched Marion lightly on the arm as they walked, but perhaps she did not notice, for all she said was, "You'll be a great lector one day, when you're older. You're very convincing."

She smiled at him, and although his heart clenched and something locked in his throat, he thanked her.

Señora Estrada was watching from the front window, and had flung open the door before Rafael reached the top step. She hugged him to her.

"I was so worried," she said, and over her shoulder Rafael could see the figurine of Eleggúa considering him, the repaired head slightly tilted. They went inside then, and Serafina ran to him and embraced him too, and he smelled her soapy skin and smiled in spite of himself.

At the next fiesta at the Liceo Cubano, Serafina wore flowers in her hair, and a white muslin dress Rafael had not seen before. She danced with her father, whirling toward Rafael, close enough to touch, her hair spreading out as she turned and turned, the soft tips brushing his arm now as she passed and moved away again, the scent of jasmine lingering behind her. And Rafael moved too, dancing with Señora Estrada but in his own orbit, and each time Serafina passed him she smiled.

Early on June 26th I stood on the Hotel veranda beneath the keyhole arch and the latticework and the silver minarets, which are in the end a falsehood, for they call no one to prayer. I imagined my three captives shut in the luggage room high above: the grimy widow, the bald child, and the Cuban, each growing weaker and less troublesome by the day. It was that moment of the morning when everything is still quiet, and people are just beginning to venture outside, to look from behind doors and windows to see what the day is like. And as I moved across the bridge and down Lafayette Street, doors and windows opened one by one in my wake, as if my foot-steps were a signal that it was safe to come out.

I had hoped to be left alone on that last day in my studio, and to slip away in the afternoon once I had packed my things, but as a sign of respect to Mr. Plant, who was to be buried at three P.M., no trains ran for two hours from that time, and all the businesses along Franklin Street closed at four. So as not to stand out, I sheeted my studio door in black, although to tell the truth I felt little sympathy for the Plants: Mrs. Plant, I learned, was considering donating the entire Hotel to the Jesuits. I pictured it stripped of its fine furnish-ings, transformed, perhaps, into a Home like the one I had been so happy to leave.

In the afternoon Mrs. Friskin called and required me to dress her Imperceptible Hair-Piece, which had become a little untidy.

"You're looking a wee bit peaky today, Mr. Gullet, if you don't mind me saying so," she remarked.

"I expect so," I said, and continued fixing her hair-piece, my movements as involuntary as those of a marionette.

"Well, Mr. Gullet, we can't have you falling ill!"

"No?" I said, twisting and knotting.

"Of course we can't, not with my gala dinner approaching." She reached into her bag and produced a bottle of Magnetic Life Tonic. "Two spoons morning and night," she said. "Now promise me."

"I promise," I said.

She looked around the room, taking in the cleared shelves, the empty cabinets. "Why, Mr. Gullet, where are all your things?" she said.

"I am simply tidying the premises," I said. "Ridding myself of unnecessary clutter. It is very emancipating, Madame."

She rearranged herself on my red silk divan and motioned for me to continue my styling.

"Have you heard from Mrs. Unger lately?" she said.

"No," I said.

"Well, she has stopped coming to our little group. I was just wondering if you might know why."

"And how would I know such a thing?" I asked, empty of politeness now, my fingers working faster and faster.

"Oh, I just thought, a man in your position, Mr. Gullet, you must be party to all sorts of confidences."

"I haven't seen Madame Unger for some time," I said.

"Well, would you like to know what *I* heard?" she said, but did not wait for my reply. "That she and her lady companion have been frequenting the Cuban club in Ybor City. They spend the night dancing with *cigar-makers*." She was watching me in the mirror, but I did not flinch. I continued to twist and to knot, my fingers detecting through the caul net her outsized organ of Self-Esteem. "There are *niggers* living side by side with the rest of them in Ybor City. They're all in shacks, of course, the Cubans, and they dine on the meat of goats. Imagine, Mr. Gullet!"

But I did not care to do so. When she had gone, I packed the Unger woman's transformation away where I could not see it. I did not even take a final look inside the box, but left the hair-piece wrapped in tissue and silk like a treasure. Perhaps I would retrieve it one day, if I returned to Tampa and wished to bring her back to life, or perhaps I would cannibalize it for use in the hair-piece of another; I did not know. Things were reaching an end. Everything was accelerating. Wars lasted a matter of weeks; the century was almost gone; the automobile was coming; Mr. Plant was dead. Nobody wanted a chignon anymore, and one day soon my skills would be obsolete.

It was no doubt as well that I did leave, for ever since the end of the war the Hotel had been changing. The most recent brochure advertised the hydrostatic establishment, with its spout and needle baths, and its ample arrangements for massage and Swedish Movement Cure; it would soon attract a drove of invalids wishing to pummel their sickly flesh. Even with Mrs. Plant's tapestries and vases, cabinets and mirrors, even with the table of Napoleon and the throne chair of Marie Antoinette, I did not think I could bear it.

I traveled south, past Phosphoria and Braidentown, past Sarasota, Punta Gorda, and Naples. When I reached Everglades City I bought a canoe, a tent, and some basic supplies, and rowed into the Ten Thousand Islands; with so many tiny countries at my disposal, I reasoned, surely I would find a home. Some were too small, too new; the mangroves had not yet attracted sufficient debris, and the land slumped beneath my feet. Others were too low, the tree trunks stained with high-water marks, and yet others were home to swarms of mosquitoes that rose like black clouds. Eventually, however, I settled on one that felt stable enough, not because I admired it but because I was weary of searching. As I unpacked my things I could not stop a little refrain from running through my mind, a kind of inventory: Where are the fat milliners now? Gone. Where is the dog of Mrs. Rim? Gone. Where are my actresses? Gone, gone. The white-blond urchin? The nuns in Paris? The dozen Michels? All gone. Where are the fickle widow and her Cuban? Gone. Where is my master? Where is my mother? And as the days passed and I saw no other living soul, I began to believe this refrain. The time of year when hurricanes strike was approaching, and yet I felt safe, protected by the mangroves. They had adapted to withstand the harshest conditions, I reminded myself, and very rarely did the winds skin them of their bark. In a hurricane, one of the safest places to be is amongst the mangroves. I imagined bad weather striking Tampa, catching Mrs. Rim and Raisin while they were taking their promenade. I imagined the wig lifting from her head and the runty animal rising into the air, its leash pulled taut, and Mrs. Rim struggling to hold on: a bald crone with a very strange balloon. I imagined the fat milliners' business destroyed: dry goods scattered across the wooden sidewalks, cheap hatpins glinting in the streets. And perhaps the wind would have driven them deep into the sand, so that it seemed they were growing, a patch of false flowers. My stocks of hair, my Bluebeard's Chamber, would be thrown open to the sky, the switches tangled, the knotted cords undone and all the different shades mixed together, a heaving beast of hair, a creature put in motion by the wind. My feathers would blow from their boxes, returned to the birds, used to line nests. If the gale was strong enough, perhaps the widow and her Cuban would be released from their cupboard. When the storm had passed they would pick their way around the debris, dodge planks that sprouted nails, avoid sharp branches and broken glass, jagged shingles, iron lace. Perhaps, when everything was so disarrayed, as ruined as Michel's model Home for Foundlings, they could be together without anybody taking too much notice, and could even set up house in this topsy-turvy place. In a few weeks, however, when the town had been put to rights, they would come to their senses and realize how ludicrous their union was, how out of place in the real world, and they would part before too much damage was done.

And I resolved that I should not allow myself to dwell on such inconsequential matters, but should set about making my new surroundings as comfortable as possible. I have never shied from solitude, and here on my island made by the mangrove I am as alone as a motherless infant. This is my home now, this mound of sand and roots and shells, and rotting leaves, and the droppings of the most fashionable birds in the world, and all manner of things discarded by Nature. The mangrove does not reject debris; it gathers it in, makes every item welcome. At night I listen to the rustling of the strangler fig, and I breathe in the scent of the moonflowers and the ghost orchids, those curious blooms that have no roots. And, to keep my thoughts orderly, I begin planning my next book, which I shall name *A Gentleman's Companion*. Penned by the esteemed Colonel

Montpellier, it will contain all manner of advice for the man who, while appreciating the need to keep the weaker sex in check, has not yet fathomed how to do so. And perhaps the Colonel need not maintain such a low profile as his wife; perhaps he will consent to meeting with his publisher and being fêted throughout New York, and perhaps he will accept some of the many splendid invitations he will receive, and allow himself to be welcomed into the most desirable circles. It is possible he may even make his home in that glittering, teeming city. He is, after all, the sort of gentleman who can adapt to any situation.

ACKNOWLEDGMENTS

I wish to thank Fergus Barrowman, Jennifer Barth, Sue Brown, Patrick Buteux (perruquier, Paris), Kate Camp, Greg Campbell, Pat Chidgey, Caroline Dawnay, Ursula Doyle, Virginia Fenton, Sandi Fernandez (H.B. Plant Museum, Tampa), Nicola Gilmour, Katy Hope, Nick Hornby, Michael King, Heather McKenzie, Sarah Maxey, Fred and Helen Mayall, Isabel Ollivier, Jane Parkin, Vivienne Plumb, Glenn Schaeffer, and Kim Witherspoon. Special thanks to John Reynolds.

This novel was researched and written with the generous assistance of John and Philip Bougen on behalf of the Doreen Bougen Trust, the French Embassy (Wellington), the Meridian Energy Katherine Mansfield Memorial Fellowship, the Prize in Modern Letters, and the Ursula Bethell Residency in Creative Writing at the University of Canterbury.

Jack's quotes on orange growing are adapted from *Treatise and Hand-Book of Orange Culture in Florida, Louisiana and California*, by Reverend T. W. Moore (New York: E. R. Pelton & Co., 1886).

Some of the passages from Dr. Evangeline Montpellier's *The Splendor of Eve* are adapted from *The Glory of Woman; or, Love, Marriage and Maternity*, by Monfort B. Allen, M.D., and Amelia C. McGregor, M.D. (Chicago: J. S. Ziegler, 1896).

I also acknowledge the use of various texts, brochures, photographs, and ephemera from the Special Collections Department at the Tampa Campus Library, University of South Florida.

The historical events, geographical details, and the Tampa Bay Hotel itself are all described as accurately as possible. In some cases I have used the names of real people, such as Henry B. Plant and the Maas brothers. The personalities of these characters, however, are fictional.

A CHRISTMAS GARLAND

A CHRISTMAS GARLAND

Anne Perry

headline

First published in 2012 by
HEADLINE PUBLISHING GROUP

1

Cataloguing in Publication Data is available from the British Library

Hardback ISBN 978 0 7553 9723 5

Typeset in Times New Roman PS by Palimpsest Book Production Limited,
Falkirk, Stirlingshire

Printed and bound in Great Britain by
CPI Group (UK) Ltd, Croydon CR0 4YY

Headline's policy is to use papers that are natural, renewable and recyclable
products and made from wood grown in sustainable forests.
The logging and manufacturing processes are expected to conform to the
environmental regulations of the country of origin.

HEADLINE PUBLISHING GROUP
An Hachette UK Company
338 Euston Road
London NW1 3BH

www.headline.co.uk
www.hachette.co.uk

GLOUCESTERSHIRE COUNTY COUNCIL	
9934150964	
Bertrams	24/10/2012
AF	£16.99
CR	

For all those who keep hope alive in the darkness

I

Lieutenant Victor Narraway walked across the square in the cool evening air. It was mid-December, a couple of weeks before Christmas. At home in England it might already be snowing, but here in India there would not even be a frost. No one had ever seen snow in Cawnpore. Any other year it would be a wonderful season: one of rejoicing, happy memories of the past, optimism for the future, perhaps a little nostalgia for those one loved who were far away.

But this year of 1857 was different. The fire of mutiny had scorched across the land, touching everything with death.

He came to the outer door of one of the least-damaged parts of the barracks and knocked. Immediately it was opened and he stepped inside. Oil lamps sent a warming yellow light over the battered walls and the few remnants of the once secure occupation, before the siege and then its relief a few months ago. There was little furniture left whole: a bullet-scarred desk, three chairs that had seen better days, a bookcase and several cupboards, one with only half a door.

Colonel Latimer was a tall and spare man well into his forties. A dozen Indian summers had burned his skin brown, but there was little colour beneath it to give life to the weariness and the marks of exhaustion. He regarded the twenty-year-old lieutenant in front of him with something like apology.

'I have an unpleasant duty for you, Narraway,' he said quietly. 'It must be done, and done well. You're new to this regiment, but you have an excellent record. You are the right man for this job.'

Narraway felt a chill, in spite of the mildness of the air. His father had purchased a commission for him and he had served a brief training in England before being sent out to India. He had arrived a year ago, just before the issue of the fateful cartridges at Dum Dum in January, which later in the spring had erupted in mutiny. The rumour had been that they were covered in animal grease in the part required to be bitten in order to open them for use. The Hindus had been told it was beef fat. Cows were sacred and to kill one was blasphemy. To put the fat to the lips was damnation. The Muslims had been told it was pork fat, and the pig was an unclean animal. To put that grease to your lips would damn your soul, although for an entirely different reason. Of course, that was not the cause of the mutiny by hundreds of thousands of Indians against the rule of a few thousand Englishmen employed by the East India Company.

The real reasons were more complex, far more deeply rooted in the social inequities and the cultural offences of a foreign rule. This was merely the spark that had ignited the fire.

Also it was true, as far as Narraway could gather, that the mutiny was far from universal. It was violent and terrible only in small parts of the country. Thousands of miles were untouched by it, lying peaceful, if a little uneasy, under the winter sun.

But the province of Sind on the Hindustan plains had seen much of the very worst of it, Cawnpore and Lucknow in particular.

General Colin Campbell, a hero from the recent war in the Crimea, had fought his way through to relieve the siege at Lucknow. A week ago he had defeated 25,000 rebels here at Cawnpore. Was it the beginning of a turning in the tide? Or just a glimmer of light that would not last?

Narraway stood to attention, breathing deeply to calm himself. Why had he come to Latimer's notice?

'Yes, sir,' he said between his teeth.

Latimer smiled bleakly. There was no light in his face, no warmth of approval. 'You will be aware of the recent escape of the prisoner Dhuleep Singh,' he went on. 'And that in order to achieve it the guard Chuttur Singh was hacked to death.'

Narraway's mouth was dry. Of course he knew it; everyone in the Cawnpore station knew it.

'Yes, sir,' he said obediently, forcing the words out.

'It has been investigated.' Latimer's jaw was tight; a small muscle jumped in his temple. 'Dhuleep Singh had privileged information regarding troop movements, specifically the recent patrol that was massacred. The man could not have escaped without assistance.' His voice was growing quieter, as if he found the words more and more difficult to say. He cleared his throat with an effort. 'Our enquiries have excluded every possibility, except that he was helped by Corporal John Tallis, the medical orderly.' He met Narraway's eyes. 'We will try him the day after tomorrow. I require you to speak in his defence.'

Narraway's mind whirled. There was a chill like ice in the pit of his stomach. A score of reasons leaped to his mind why he could not do what Latimer was asking of him. He was not even remotely equal to the task. It would be so much better to have one of the officers who had been with the regiment during the siege and the relief, and who knew everyone. Above all, they should have an officer who was experienced in military law, who had done this dozens of times, and was known and respected by the men.

Then a cold, sane voice inside assured him that it was precisely because he was none of these things that Latimer had chosen him.

'Yes, sir,' he said faintly.

'Major Strafford will be here any moment,' Latimer continued. 'He will give you any instruction and advice that you may need. I shall be presiding over the court, so it is not appropriate that I should do it.'

'Yes, sir,' Narraway said again, feeling as if another nail

had been driven into the coffin lid of his career. Major Stafford's dislike of him dated from before the time he had joined the regiment. Almost certainly it came from Narraway's brief acquaintance with Stafford's younger brother. They had been in the same final year at Eton, and little about their association had been happy.

Narraway had been academic, a natural scholar and disin-clined towards sports. The younger Stafford was a fine athlete, but no competition for Narraway in the classroom. They existed happily enough in a mutual contempt. It was shattered one summer evening in a magnificent cricket match, nail-bitingly close but Stafford's team having the edge, until Narraway showed a rare flash of brilliance in the only sport he actually enjoyed. The dark, slender scholar, without a word spoken, bowled out the last three men in Stafford's team, including the great sportsman himself. The fact that he did it with apparent ease was appalling, but that he did not overtly take any pleasure in it was unforgivable. Stafford Minor had never been able to exact his revenge in the field, which was the only place where he could redeem his honour. Other quarrels or victories did not count. No practical joke or barbed wit looked anything better than the spite of a bad loser.

But that was boyhood, two years ago and thousands of miles away.

'Captain Busby will prosecute,' Latimer was going on. 'The evidence seems simple enough. You will be free to interview Corporal Tallis at any time you wish, and anyone else you feel could be helpful to your defence. Any legal points that you need clarifying, speak to Major Stafford.'

'Yes, sir.' Narraway was still at attention, his muscles aching with the effort of keeping complete control of himself.

There was a brief knock on the door.

'Come,' Latimer ordered.

The door swung open and Major Stafford came in. He was a tall, handsome man in his early thirties, but the echo of Narraway's schoolfellow, so much his junior, was there in the set of his shoulders, the thick, fair hair, the shape of his jaw.

Stafford glanced at Latimer.

'Sir.' He saluted, then, as he was given permission, relaxed. He regarded Narraway expressionlessly. 'You'd better read up on it tonight and start questioning people tomorrow morning,' he said. 'You need to be sure of the law. We don't want anyone afterwards saying that we cut corners. I presume you appreciate that?'

'Yes, sir.' Narraway heard the edge of condescension in Stafford's voice and would dearly like to have told him that he was as aware as anyone else of how they would all be judged on their conduct in the matter. More than that, the future of British rule in India would be flavoured by report of decisions such as this. The whole structure of Empire hung together on the belief in justice, in doing things by immutable rules and a code of honour that they themselves never broke.

Thousands of men were dead already, as well as women and children. If they ever regained control and there were to be any kind of peace, it must be under the rule of law. It was the only safety for people of any colour or faith. Once they themselves gave in to barbarism there was no hope left for anyone. Right now, there seemed to be little enough in any circumstances. Delhi had fallen, Lucknow, Agra, Jhelum, Sugauli, Dinapoor, Lahore, Kolapore, Ramgarh, Peshawar – and on and on. The list seemed endless. Perhaps there was nothing left but some shred of honour.

'Good,' Strafford said curtly. 'Whatever you think you know, you'd better come and see me and tell me at least the outline of your defence.' He looked at Narraway closely, his blue eyes curiously luminous in the light of the oil lamp. 'You must be sure to mount some defence, you do understand that, don't you? At least put forward a reason why a man like Tallis should betray the men he's served beside all his career. I know he's quarter Indian, or something of the sort, but that's no excuse.'

The tight muscles in his face twitched. 'For God's sake, thousands of soldiers are still loyal to their regiments and to the Crown, and fighting on our side. Tens of thousands more are going about their duties as usual. No one knows what the end of this will be. Find out what the devil got into the man. Threats, bribery, drunk and lost his wits? Give some explanation.'

Narraway felt dismay turn to anger. It was bad enough

8

that he was picked out to defend the indefensible; now Strafford required him to explain it as well.

'If Corporal Tallis has an explanation, sir, I shall offer it,' he replied in a hard, controlled voice. 'I cannot imagine one that will excuse his conduct, so it will be brief.'

'The explanation is not to excuse him, Lieutenant,' Strafford said acidly. 'It is to help the garrison here feel as if there is some sense in the world, some tiny thread of reason to hold on to, when everything they know has turned into chaos and half the people we loved are slaughtered like animals, and the nation on every side is in ruins.' A flush spread up his fair face, visible even in this wavering light. 'You are here to satisfy the law so that we do not appear to history to have betrayed ourselves and all we believe in, not to excuse the damned man! I know you are new here, but you must have at least that much sense!'

'Strafford . . .' Latimer said quietly, interrupting for the first time. 'We have given the lieutenant a thankless task, and he is quite aware of it. If he isn't now, he will be when he has looked at it a trifle more closely.' He turned to Narraway again. 'Lieutenant, we do not know where we shall be by the turn of the year, here or somewhere else, besieged or comparatively free. This matter must be dealt with before then. The women and children need a celebration, however meagre. We need hope, and we cannot have that without a quiet conscience. We cannot celebrate the birth of the Son of God, nor can we ask His help with confidence, if we do so with dishonour weighing us down.